P9-CWE-681

continued . . .

BOOKS BY STUART WOODS

FICTION

Indecent Exposure†
Fast & Loose†
Below the Belt†
Sex, Lies & Serious Money†
Dishonorable Intentions†
Family Jewels†
Scandalous Behavior†
Foreign Affairs†
Naked Greed†
Hot Pursuit†
Insatiable Appetites†
Paris Match†
Cut and Thrust†
Carnal Curiosity†
Standup Guy†
Doing Hard Time†
Unintended Consequences†
Collateral Damage†
Severe Clear†
Unnatural Acts†
D.C. Dead†
Son of Stone†
Bel-Air Dead†
Strategic Moves†
Santa Fe Edge§
Lucid Intervals†
Kisser†
Hothouse Orchid*
Loitering with Intent†
Mounting Fears‡
Hot Mahogany†
Santa Fe Dead§
Beverly Hills Dead
Shoot Him If He Runs†

Fresh Disasters†
Short Straw§
Dark Harbor†
Iron Orchid*
Two-Dollar Bill†
The Prince of Beverly Hills
Reckless Abandon†
Capital Crimes‡
Dirty Work†
Blood Orchid*
The Short Forever†
Orchid Blues*
Cold Paradise†
L.A. Dead†
The Run‡
Worst Fears Realized†
Orchid Beach*
Swimming to Catalina†
Dead in the Water†
Dirt†
Choke
Imperfect Strangers
Heat
Dead Eyes
L.A. Times
Santa Fe Rules§
New York Dead†
Palindrome
Grass Roots‡
White Cargo
Deep Lie‡
Under the Lake
Run Before the Wind‡
Chiefs‡

COAUTHORED BOOKS

Barely Legal††
(with Parnell Hall)

Smooth Operator**
(with Parnell Hall)

TRAVEL

A Romantic's Guide to the Country Inns of Britain and
Ireland (1979)

MEMOIR

Blue Water, Green Skipper

*A Holly Barker Novel
†A Stone Barrington Novel
‡A Will Lee Novel

§An Ed Eagle Novel
**A Teddy Fay Novel
††A Herbie Fisher Novel

STUART WOODS

Run Before the Wind

#2

G. P. Putnam's Sons
New York

PUTNAM

G. P. PUTNAM'S SONS
Publishers Since 1838
An imprint of Penguin Random House LLC
375 Hudson Street
New York, New York 10014

First Signet printing / September 2005
First G. P. Putnam's Sons premium edition / September 2017
G. P. Putnam's Sons premium edition ISBN: 9780451215949

Printed in the United States of America
19   18   17   16   15   14   13   12   11   10

This book is for my friend and editor, Eric Swenson, who seems always to have just the right proportions of faith and skepticism. (Well, *nearly* always.)

Prologue

THE THIRD OFFICER WAS THE FIRST TO SEE THE SAIL. He had been looking for it.

He had seen mention of the race in *Notices to Mariners,* and he had been hearing reports of its progress on the BBC World Service. An Englishman—what was his name?—had been reported leading two days before. The third officer, whose name was Martindale and who, himself, was English, had hoped he might catch sight of some of the competitors, and now he had a moment of excitement in an otherwise uneventful crossing. He walked to the ship's wheel, which was making small movements under the command of the autopilot, sighted across the main compass, and took a bearing on the sail, which was no more than a dot of white on the horizon. He noted the time and the bearing in the ship's log. Six minutes later, with the dot now plainly recognizable as a boat, he took a second bearing. It was unchanged. The 400,000-

ton supertanker *Byzantium* was on a collision course with an unknown yacht in the middle of the North Atlantic Ocean.

It was bizarre, Martindale thought. They might be the only two vessels within an area of some hundreds of square miles, and they were going to strike each other unless one of them changed speed or course. He thought of slowing the ship, but he knew that even with the engines reversed the giant tanker might not slow enough from her thirty-knot speed before running the smaller craft down. He half turned to the seaman standing, daydreaming, a few feet away but did not take his eyes from the yacht. "Switch off autopilot. Hard right rudder."

The man, who had been lost in reverie, looked at him, surprised. "Sir?"

"I said, switch off autopilot, hard right rudder."

"Sir, the captain . . ."

"Do it, *now.*" The seaman stepped to a console, turned a knob, then took the wheel and spun it to the right. "Autopilot switched off, hard right rudder, sir." He looked worried.

Martindale was worried, too. He reckoned they were two, two and a half miles from the yacht. It might take the supertanker two miles to answer the helm. "When she answers come onto course two eight oh." He noted the time carefully and logged the change in course.

"Course two eight oh, sir. When she answers." Now the seaman saw the yacht, too. "Jesus, Mr. Martindale, it's gonna be close."

A few feet down a corridor from the bridge, the captain stirred from his sleep. Something had waked him; it took him a moment to realize what. A bright beam of sunlight was shining on his face; as he squinted into the light, it began slowly moving away from him. God help Martindale; the little Limey bastard was turning his ship! He sat up and reached for a robe, then was propelled to his feet and across the cabin by a long blast on the ship's horn.

The captain burst onto the bridge, his skinny legs projecting from the terrycloth robe. "Let's have it, Mr. Martindale, and it better be good, it better be bloody good."

The third officer half turned again, still not taking his eyes from the yacht. "Sir, I judged us to be on a collision course with a sailing vessel." He pointed and handed the captain his binoculars. "I ordered hard right rudder to go astern of her."

The captain squinted through the binoculars. The yacht was only half a mile away. "Speed?" he asked, taking the binoculars from his eyes. They were not necessary, now.

"Still thirty knots, sir; I judged she would answer faster at speed."

"Oh, you did, did you?"

"Yes, sir."

"Well, you're right, Mr. Martindale, she will. She's answering. Now we'll see if you judged that boat's course correctly. We're going to hit her or miss her in about thirty seconds. Hit the horn again."

Martindale gave another long blast. "He must be asleep or dead, sir."

"He'll be dead, I reckon. Nobody could sleep through that."

The second officer came onto the bridge in his pajamas and quickly assessed the situation. Other men could be seen on deck, now, watching the yacht as the tanker rapidly closed on her. The captain strode quickly out onto the port wing of the bridge. Martindale followed on his heels. The wind, made mostly by the tanker's speed, tore at their clothes. Martindale's cap went overboard.

The two men watched as the *Byzantium* inched into her turn. Suddenly the yacht shot across her bows with less than thirty feet to spare. Then, in the lee of the big ship, she stopped sailing and drifted quickly toward the tanker.

"We're sucking her into us, sir," Martindale shouted over the wind. He watched in horror as the boat came closer and closer, then, suddenly, they were past her. Martindale got a good look down into the boat's cockpit as she went by.

"What the hell is the matter with her crew?" demanded the captain.

"She's a singlehander, sir," Martindale replied, pointing at her stern. "See the wind vane self-steering gear? There's a number on her hull, too, sir. She's part of the singlehanded transatlantic race that started from England last week. Shall I order all stop, sir?"

The captain brushed past him, clutching at his robe in

the wind, heading for the bridge. "What the hell for? We missed her. Log it and report her to Lloyds. I'm going back to bed."

Martindale raced to catch up with him. "Excuse me, sir, but our high frequency radio telephone is still down, so we can't report her until Sparks sorts that out. If the yacht's skipper were able, he'd have responded to our horn. He could be ill, and . . ." He stopped himself short of gratuitously telling his captain that his first duty was to render assistance to another vessel in an emergency at sea.

The captain stopped and scratched his backside angrily. He shot a look at Martindale. "If I stop this ship unnecessarily the Greek gentleman will have my balls for breakfast."

"I'm sure you'd be protected in the circumstances, sir. And anyway, there's the possibility of salvage. I reckon she's close to sixty feet. She'd be worth a lot."

"You know bloody well we don't have a crane that could put her on deck, Mr. Martindale." The captain's eyebrows went up. "Ahh, now I get the picture. You're a *yachtsman*. That's it, isn't it? You're looking for a pleasant sail home in a rich man's yacht. We take aboard her skipper, who's probably got all of a case of the trots, and you sail off into the sunset."

Martindale flushed. "Sir, we don't really have a choice, do we?" He waited anxiously while the captain stared at the deck and worked his jaw.

"Shit," the captain said, finally. "All right. Come onto

a parallel course with her and stop; she'll catch up to us. As soon as I get my pants on I'll take the con, and you take two men and get the motor launch over the side. She's wearing a VHF antenna. Call me on channel 16 when you're aboard her." The captain turned toward his cabin. "Thank God there's not much of a sea running," he could be heard to say from down the corridor.

Martindale's heart leapt. "Hard left rudder!" he shouted at the seaman. "All back!"

Martindale sat at the yacht's chart table, suddenly exhausted, and stared about him. She was beautiful, a dream of oiled teak and polished brass; of able design and perfect proportion; of the finest gear for every task on deck and below. The ship's log lay before him, open to the last completed page. He read for a few minutes, feeling sick and angry, then reached up and switched on the VHF radio, set it to channel 16, and pressed the transmit button.

"*Byzantium, Byzantium, Byzantium*; this is Martindale, Martindale, Martindale. Do you read?" He released the button.

The captain's voice shot back over the crackle of static. "I read you, Martindale. Never mind the fucking procedure. What the hell's going on on that boat?"

Martindale took a deep breath and pressed the transmit button again. "Everything seems to be in perfect order, captain, as far as I can tell." He paused. "Except there's nobody aboard."

One

I AM TWENTY-FOUR YEARS OLD, AND EVERYONE *I* LOVE IS DEAD.

I see the land. The land is green. It invites me, but I must sail past it to my destination. What is my destination? It must be more than a port, a berth, a hot shower. What is my true destination?

I put the unlabeled cassette into the player expecting to hear a lost Count Basie album, and instead my own voice booms from the speakers. It is a profound shock. Those words were the last I spoke into the tape recorder, and now they speak back at me in a curious, mid-Atlantic accent (midway between Savannah and the British Isles), and they are full of self-pity. Granted, I had been through a lot, but I was possessed, at the very least, of parents whom I loved and who loved me, and perhaps even a girl, though I had reason to be uncertain, at that moment and for a little while longer, whether that thing was love on her part.

I see the land. The land is green.

My style has improved since then, I hope. It has been a long time, after all, and I have had a lot of practice. But even through the filter of those words something in that young voice, like a scent that instantly, vividly reconstructs a moment in time, rushes at me, and those two extraordinary years of my extreme and careless youth rise up and demand, at whatever price, to be lived again.

On a Friday morning in May of 1970 I finished the last of my final examinations for my junior year at the University of Georgia Law School. I left the lecture hall and was immediately stopped in the hallway by the woman who was secretary to the dean. "Oh, Will," she said, breathlessly, "I'm glad I caught you. Dean Henry would like to see you in his office right away."

"Thank you, ma'am," I said to her. "I'd just like to get a drink of water, then I'll be right there."

She hurried back toward her desk while I dawdled over the drinking fountain, trying to compose myself. I had spent most of the day trying to forget that the night before had happened, and I had not been able to manage it. I had more than one kind of hangover, too, and my performance on the exam I had just finished had not improved my day. Now, this summons from on high, on top of everything else, had me just about coming unglued. I splashed some cold water on my face, wiped it with my handkerchief, took a few deep breaths, and strode purposefully toward the administrative offices. I would just have to fake it.

Dean Wallace Henry was an aloof, dry, nearly expressionless man in his sixties who had been an assistant attorney general in the Johnson administration and had come to his position in the law school on the election of Richard Nixon to the Presidency. It was said that Johnson, given the opportunity, would have appointed him to fill the next vacancy on the Supreme Court. He was very formal, very southern, and held fixed opinions on what constituted proper behavior and scholarship in a student in his charge. I was afraid of him, as was nearly every other law student, and I had avoided contact with him as much as possible. We had held one or two cramped conversations at teas, when he would arrange his thin mouth in something resembling a smile and try, not very hard, to be avuncular. It never worked.

The door to his office was open (he maintained an "open door" policy, he said, but as far as I knew nobody had ever taken him up on it); he saw me approach his secretary and beckoned me into his paneled and carpeted presence. I approached his desk with my hand outstretched and as much of a smile as I could muster. "How are you, sir?" I began hopefully.

He ignored my hand, pushed back from his desk, and swiveled his chair so that he faced the windows. A shaft of sunlight reflected off his shiny, black head of hair, which hosted no gray. Rumor was he dyed it.

"Close the door," he said, "and sit." So much for the open door policy. I closed it and sat quickly, like a terrier on command. I felt it would be an affront if I should cross my legs. He swiveled back to face me and, to my astonishment, placed a large, Cordovan, wing-tipped shoe against his desktop. Such uncharacteristic informality. I crossed my legs. "You are a very fortunate young man," he said. For a brief moment I thought I had mistaken his reason for summoning me, and a tiny ray of hope pierced my anxious gloom. Dean Henry quickly extinguished it. "Had that been the Athens City Police last night instead of the campus cop, you would have missed your examination today and been out of law school, never to return. I would be bailing you out just about now instead of inviting you in for a chat, and with the subsequent criminal proceedings you would have forfeited a career in the law." I uncrossed my legs.

"Sir——"

"Mr. Lee, in spite of your apparent intelligence and even quite reasonable grades, you are not a shining scholar. And grades notwithstanding, your work—if I may laughingly call it that [he was not laughing]—has been such as to barely keep you in my good graces. Cramming for examinations and getting Bs is not enough to make you a decent lawyer, and that is what I try, given the material disgorged by the undergraduate schools, to produce."

"Sir——"

"You seem to have a minimalist view of the educational process; you apply your intellect to determining the smallest effort necessary to remain in the University of Georgia Law School and out of the United States

Army." The Vietnam War was, you will remember, still raging in 1970.

"Sir——"

"You shine on your feet, Mr. Lee; you perform impressively in Moot Court, if someone has read the relevant law for you; you answer well in class—well, that is, for someone with so little knowledge of your subject. You are a talented politician—you managed, I recall, to be elected president of your freshman law class, in defiance of your peers' usual insistence on accomplishment in their leadership instead of charm. You are a charming young man, Mr. Lee, I will give you that. You are a remarkable tapdancer."

"Sir——"

"Well, you have just stubbed your toe rather badly, Mr. Lee. Those few whiffs of that . . . *controlled substance* . . . last evening have ruined your little tightrope act, and you are falling, falling." He leaned forward, placed his elbows on the leather desktop, and rested his chin in both hands. "Did you wish to say something, Mr. Lee?"

"No, sir."

"I should think not. I have very little more to say, myself." He leaned back in his chair and placed the foot back on the desk. "You will not be rejoining us in the autumn, Mr. Lee. Oh, I'm not going to expel you, nor even make it impossible for you to return. You see, I am an optimist; I still believe that you might possibly make a decent attorney, even a fine one, should you gather your wits about you. I also have a high regard for your father, although I do not know him well. I admired his conduct during his term as governor, and, who knows? He might even serve his state well in the United States Senate one day, should his efforts in that direction not be unreasonably handicapped by the actions of an unthinking son."

I stared at my shoes on that one.

"Take a sabbatical, Mr. Lee. Think. I suspect you've never done much of that. Go forth and serve your country, should it call, and I expect it will, things being what they are on the Asian continent these days. This won't go on your record, and I won't speak to your father. Tell him what you like but don't come back here unless you are willing to exhibit to me a veritable transmogrification." He opened a file on his desk and began to study it. I sat, frozen with relief. "Goodbye, Mr. Lee," he said, without looking up.

I rose and propelled myself toward the door.

"Oh, Mr. Lee," his voice from behind me halted me in my tracks.

I half turned. "Yes, sir?"

"Don't get your ass shot off."

"No, sir." I fled the office, pausing at the building's entrance to press my brow against the cool marble. My relief at not being publicly humiliated was rapidly giving way to anxiety over what I would tell my parents. Shortly, I composed myself and started toward my dormitory. At least I wouldn't get my ass shot off. The old bastard. Apparently, he had not known that I was 4-F in the draft.

The following afternoon I entered my father's study

and confronted him and my mother with my plan, or rather, my lack of one. He was silent for a moment after I had finally stumbled through what I had to say. It was a habit of his to pause a bit before addressing any serious matter. It got him the undivided attention of his listener and, I suppose, gave him time to think. It was a habit that had served him well in the Georgia State Senate, as lieutenant governor and as governor, and might one day, as Dean Henry had noted, serve him well in the United States Senate.

"Two years in law school is a large personal investment to simply set aside," he said, finally.

"I'm not necessarily setting it aside permanently. I may go back and finish, I just don't know yet." I stole a careful glance at my mother, who was, uncharacteristically, holding her peace. She is Irish. "It's just that it doesn't seem real, yet. Law is still just an exercise, something to memorize and discuss, not something to *do*. It was even that way when I interned at Blackburn, Hedger last summer; it was all so technical; I felt removed from it." All of this was true, though it had entered my consciousness only during the time since my meeting with the dean.

"Will," my mother said, "how long have you been thinking about this?"

"All year," I lied. "When I came home for Christmas I didn't want to go back, but it seemed stupid to drop out in the middle of the year."

"It's not sudden then," she said, resignedly.

"No, ma'am." I hated myself a little for deceiving her.

"I take it you don't know exactly what you want to do?" my father asked.

"Well, sir, I'd like to go ahead and visit Grandfather in Ireland, the way I'd planned [that would please them] and then . . . I'd just like to keep going for a while, take a year and travel."

"Travel where?"

"Everywhere, anywhere." I honestly didn't know.

"I see. How were you planning to finance all this travel?"

"Well, I can get about a thousand for my car, and I've got my calf money." We lived on a cattle farm in Meriwether County, near the town of Delano. The land had been in my father's family since the 1850s, but it was my mother who had been the real farmer, building up the place after World War II, when my father was starting his law practice and his political career. "That's a little over three thousand dollars. I can get a student airfare and hitchhike in Europe."

My mother was looking at my father and shaking her head. "Billy, I am *not* going to have him hitchhiking." It was my first inkling that they were not going to try to talk me back into law school—not yet, anyway. I looked back to my father.

He went through his drill of silence again before speaking. "Tell you what," he said. "I'll loan you another three thousand. Buy a good used car—no hitchhiking.

You can sell the car when you come back and pay me back then." It was typical of him to make it a loan. "In September of next year you either go back to law school, or to graduate school if you'd rather, or you're on your own in the cruel world. Fair enough?"

I found that I had been holding my breath, and in my sudden exhaling I found wind to say back to him, "Fair enough."

A few minutes later I passed the study door and heard them talking quietly. "Maybe it's a good thing for him, Billy," my mother said.

"Maybe," my father replied. "I was just thinking about all those unfinished model airplanes when he was a kid. Those just about drove me crazy."

"I know," she said.

"He was never much for finishing things. I hoped he would get over that."

"Maybe he will. He still may go back and finish."

"I hope so. I won't count on it."

Young men who cannot be counted on should not listen at doors; it shames them and stings their eyes. I got out of the house as quickly as possible.

Two

THE TWO-HOUR FLIGHT TO NEW YORK AND THE SIX-hour flight to Shannon gave me an opportunity to think—or rather, forced thought upon me. I was running, I knew that; I had done a lot of running from problems in my short existence. I also knew that, had I wished to summon all the persuasive powers at my disposal, I could have convinced Dean Henry to let me remain in law school. I was good at convincing. Had I remained, though, I would soon have disappointed him again. I would not have been able to back up my persuasion with performance. A long series of childhood and schoolday incidents had brought me to know that as a part of myself. I didn't like it, but I didn't know how to change it. I looked out the jet's window at the floor of rosy cloud beneath us and tried to summon the resolve for an assault on my flawed character, but I was cautious about making promises even to myself. Instead, I began to look forward to my newfound freedom. Maybe in Europe I might find something in myself that I could admire without shame.

I arrived in Ireland with a sense of freedom only partly gained. I had the obligatory family visit ahead of me before finally cutting the bonds. I approached it impatiently. My grandfather didn't know quite what to make of me, but he was kind. I had not visited him in County Cork since I was twelve, but he and my grandmother had stayed with us in Georgia when I was sixteen—and she was still alive. He seemed much, much older and, though in good health, shrunken in his appearance and careful in his movements. He had become accustomed to solitude and was not anxious to change his habits.

I exercised his hunters—he was grateful for that in the off-season—galloping them over long stretches of densely green countryside, down to where his land touched the water at the entrance to Kinsale Harbour. There I would walk, leading the animal of the day, and watch the sailboats cruise in and out, or, on Sundays, watch them race—the tiny dinghies with their red sails, squirting here and there. I had spent six summers at a sailing camp on the North Carolina coast—two as a camper and four as an instructor—sailing dinghies and small cruisers, and I thought I might look for a ride in some neighbor's boat. The neighbors, though, were of my grandfather's generation and were more oriented toward horses than boats.

I drove into Kinsale in Grandfather's Land Rover to

shop for him and passed a squadron of young girls playing field hockey in a meadow beside the road. I stopped and watched for a moment, watched their coach, mainly, a sturdy blond girl of about my own age, with good, if muscular, legs and largish breasts. I experienced a stirring in the loins, I believe the expression is. I have never known exactly where the loins are located, but believe me, they stirred. I must have produced some primitive animal scent that wafted over the field, for she began stealing glances at me, and when the play was over she waved the children back toward their school and ran over to the fence. For a moment I was gripped with a panic that she was angry at my watching, and I nearly bolted, but she was too quick for me.

"You'll be Miles Worth-Newenam's grandson," she said, still panting from her play.

"I am," I said uncertainly. This was before I learned that everybody in Ireland knows everything about everyone else.

She waited for me to say something else, but I couldn't seem to think of anything. "D'you have a name, then?" she asked, impatiently.

"I do," I replied. "My name is Will Lee." I was careful, as always, to enunciate clearly. My name could too easily come out as "Willie," and in my South that was a black's name. I was no racist, but like all southerners, white and black, I made certain distinctions.

"Mine is Concepta Lydon."

"I perceive that you are Catholic." Oh, God, I thought, now I've made fun of her name.

But she laughed. "You are perceptive, indeed. I mention my whole name to get that out of the way. If you ever call me anything but Connie, I'll punch you."

I thought she probably would. "Connie it is." I groped for some way to continue the conversation. The first few minutes with any new female were always awkward for me. "You're a coach, are you?"

"A teacher. At the convent." She motioned toward the group of low, gray, stucco buildings across the field. "But only until four o'clock." She pointed past the Land Rover and up a hill. "D'you see that yellow house up there? It's a pub. If you're there in half an hour you can buy me a pint." Without waiting for a reply she turned and sprinted across the field toward the waiting group of girls, who were clapping and jeering.

I quickly bought my grandfather's nails and paint and found the pub—the Spaniard, it was called. Irish pubs rarely have any of the charm associated with their English counterparts, but Kinsale is on the tourist trail, and the Spaniard was contrived to please a foreign visitor and those locals who liked a bit of atmosphere and a turf fire, even in June.

Concepta Lydon—Connie, lest I get punched—arrived, bustling, speaking to the landlord and a customer or two. She was wearing a loose sweater which could not conceal her breasts and tight, American jeans designed to conceal nothing but skin. Her hair was still wet from her postgame shower, and her ears stuck out. They were nice ears.

"There's no natural turf hereabouts," she said, sipping a pint of lager and nodding at the hearth. "He must go to Galway to get it. The tourists like it, I expect. I like it myself." I liked the smoky, earthy smell, too. "Why aren't you in Vietnam?" she asked without missing a beat. "Your country's at war, you know."

"Bad knee. Sports injury," I replied. "And my country's not at war. Richard Nixon is. I've got nothing against those people." She smiled and nodded, as if I'd made the right response to her baiting, and continued to question me closely. It took her no longer than three minutes to extract a fairly complete life history.

As she asked and I answered a young man came into the pub and sat at the bar behind her. He was in his early twenties, not very tall, a thick, muscular body, long, dirty, sandy hair, a thin beard. As soon as his pint arrived he turned and stared dully, fixedly at me, hardly blinking. I had never seen him before, but I knew him. He was one of the brotherhood of bullies who had haunted me throughout my life—in the schoolyard, on the football field, at summer camp, in the fraternity house. It was as though they were members of some secret fraternal order who had been read my dossier and then sent out to pick at the scabs of my cowardice. I turned my attention to Connie Lydon, but checked on him occasionally. He drank his pint and stared.

"All right, now," I said to Connie, throwing up a hand. "Any more information and you'll have enough for blackmail. Now you. Why are you teaching school? There can't be nearly enough there to satisfy a curiosity like yours."

"I like the sport, and I like teaching it to the young girls. The nuns are all right, if you know how to get along with them. I went to that very convent school myself; I know how. I'm twenty-one, I'm the daughter of a retired bank manager, I've two brothers—one of 'em's a priest—I've an honours degree from the university in Cork, I've traveled on the continent a bit—" She leaned forward. "Will you come to dinner tonight? I'm something of a cook."

I leaned forward myself. "Where are the two brothers?" I asked.

"The priest is in India doing good works, the other is in England," she grinned.

"Do I have to face a bank-manager father?"

"I've my own cottage at Summercove, along the water. Seven o'clock?"

"Seven it is." My stay in Ireland was going better than I could have hoped.

She tossed off the remainder of her lager and got up. I walked with her out of the pub, passing the fellow at the bar. His gaze wavered only to take in Connie Lydon. She nodded curtly to him. Then, as we came out of the pub, I was startled to see him leaning against a car, talking to another young man. It was as though he had vanished from the pub and instantly rematerialized outside. Connie saw me start.

"They're the O'Donnell twins," she said, "Denny and Donal. Was Denny looking at you in the pub?"

"Yes," I said, relieved to know there was not witchcraft afoot. "Does he have an interest in you?"

"Not one that's reciprocated." She got into a shiny, new Mini and started it. "You know Summercove, do you?"

"Sure." Summercove was a fragment of a village on the north shore of Kinsale Harbour. My grandfather's land touched it.

"The cottage stands on its own, just past the village, down by the water. You can't miss it. Seven, then?"

"Seven."

She was off in a spray of gravel. As I got into the Land Rover and drove away, Denny O'Donnell joined his twin outside the pub and sneered me down the hill. God help me, this time there were *two* of them.

My trouble with bullies had started in kindergarten. At the first recess on the first day a boy named Roy Scott had walked over to me and punched me in the stomach, knocking me down and rendering me breathlessly helpless. I somehow attracted more of these types during my school days, but fortunately, with the passing of the years, they hit me less, because that became an increasingly unacceptable form of social behavior. Still, they found other ways to taunt me, and behind this harassment there was always the threat of violence, and I was always afraid of it.

Football was both a blessing and a curse. Our coach was a maniac for physical fitness. I despised the calisthenics and running, but the exercise put some weight and muscle on me, and the physical contact gave me a bit more confidence, showing me that within clearly defined perimeters I could accept and inflict violence without fear. Although fairly athletic, I was not an outstanding player, adding my coach to the long list of adults who were always telling me I was not living up to my potential. In the last game of my sophomore year the cartilage in my left knee went, and I was relieved when after the surgery I was told that I should avoid contact sports. At once, I had my badge of courage and an honorable way out of, then, an unappealing game and, later, the Vietnam War.

Connie Lydon's cottage could nearly be seen across the hills from my room on the third floor of my grandfather's old house but was a five-mile drive on the roads. I was there at the stroke of seven, a bottle of wine in hand.

The cottage was very small—three tiny rooms, with a bath built onto the back—and she had done it up nicely. She cooked wonderfully, too; we had a pasta dish theretofore outside my experience; we drank the burgundy. After dinner she produced brandy, and we curled up on the sofa before a fire of peat briquettes. I had had a rural/small-town upbringing right on the buckle of the Bible Belt and had attended a state university in the same behavioral territory. My sexual experiences, which I could count on the fingers of one hand without using the thumb, had taken place, respectively, on two backseats, a hammock, and a rather gritty beach towel. Now I found myself in circumstances I had experienced only in fantasy: there was a snifter of cognac in my hand, a fire at my feet, a down cushion under my backside, an attractive girl at my elbow, and a double bed in the next room. And there were no parents, housemothers, or roommates to concern myself with.

"How's your brandy?" she asked.

"What?"

She laughed. "You seem a million miles away."

I turned toward her. "I'm exactly where I want to be," I said, then I kissed her lightly on the lips.

She kissed me back. "I'm glad to hear it," she said. We didn't talk much after that. We kissed a lot; I made a pass at a breast, which she skillfully parried; I aimed a knee between hers, but they closed; we kissed a lot more. I left at midnight, and she pressed her body against mine as we kissed at the door. I drove home in a haze of unfulfilled desire, already thinking of the next time.

For three weeks we saw each other constantly. We rode my grandfather's hunters—she rode better than I; we went to the movies in Cork; we sat in on hoolies—drunken songfests—in local pubs; I gained weight on her cooking. But nothing—not physical persuasion, not all the logic I could summon from two years of proximity to the law—could pry her loose from her stainless steel virginity. I came to think of her as two girls: Connie, the fun-loving, funny, athletic, sensual, lovely thing of my days; and Concepta, the convent-educated, maddeningly Irish, immovable object of my nights.

In spite of the wonderful time I was having with her, I began to become irritable. I wanted her so much that it never occurred to me that, perhaps, I didn't want enough of her. Finally, it all came to a head.

We were back on the sofa, in front of the fire. We had progressed to some heavy petting, but I could get no further. I had not counted on the effects of centuries of Irish Catholicism.

"You're not making love to me, Will Lee," she said.

"Okay, whatever you say," I said, trying harder.

"You're a winning boy, but . . ." she gasped and made a little sound.

"You realize where my hand is," I panted.

"Oh, yes, yes, but that's all that's going to be there."

I may have been a winning boy, but I seemed to be losing. I sat up, abruptly. "Connie, do you have any idea what you're doing to me?" I placed my face in my hands for effect.

"The same thing you're doing to me, I expect."

I shook my head. "If that were the case, we'd be in bed right now."

"That's not what's important, don't you understand?"

"It's important to me, believe me it is."

"But that's *all* that's important to you. It's not me you want, it's just sex."

"Now, Connie, that's not true. You know I'm . . . I'm . . ."

"Yes?"

"Well, you know how I feel."

"I'm afraid I do. That's why we're not in bed right now. If I thought you really cared for me, the Pope himself couldn't keep me out of bed with you, but you don't, not really."

"Connie . . ."

"Don't, Will. If you think about it you'll know what I mean. There's something . . . *detached* about you. There's this . . . *distance*; it's the only way I can explain it. I want more than that, and you're clearly not ready to give it."

She was right, of course, and faced again with something that required more than I could give without effort, I did what I had always done; I ran.

I fled to London, with Paris planned for my next stop. I never made it to Paris, for after London my life spun unexpectedly onto a new course, like a Frisbee caught by a gust of wind, and nothing was ever the same again.

Three

I SPENT A WEEK IN LONDON. I FOUND A CHEAP HOTEL IN the Bayswater Road. I did the sights, the museums, and the pubs, but I was depressed about my failure with Connie Lydon. I was on my own, now, but somehow the feeling of freedom I had expected still eluded me.

At the end of my allotted week I set out for Paris, taking a train from Waterloo Station to Southampton, from whence I would take a ferry to France. At the ferry office pandemonium reigned; most of England, it seemed, was on its way to France, and no passenger space was available until the following day. I spotted a ferry to Cowes, on the Isle of Wight, a name I recognized from the yachting magazines I had read during my summers at sailing camp. It seemed worth a look.

The Isle of Wight, I learned from a fellow passenger, used to be part of the English mainland, but the sea came between the two, and they are now separated by a riverlike band of water known as the Solent. We steamed down Southampton Water and entered the Solent. I was astonished at the number of sailboats plying the waters around us. My informant explained that it was the last day of Cowes Week, which I knew was an old and famous regatta. As the ferry approached the terminal he pointed out the sights: the Royal Yacht Squadron, the Royal Corinthian Yacht Club, the Royal London Yacht Club, and, riding regally at her mooring, the enormous white shape of the Royal Yacht, flying her white ensign. Even the Queen came to Cowes Week.

I stepped from the ferry into a maelstrom of foot traffic in Cowes High Street, hundreds of people, nearly all in some vestige of nautical clothing—rubber boots, peaked caps, bright yellow or orange slickers—packed into a tiny village on the water. Every other shop seemed to be a chandlery or a bookstore specializing in the nautical. Over an occasional low building I could see thickets of masts, and when I walked toward them I came upon marinas and boatyards lining the waterfront. I wandered among them, down floating catwalks past boats of every description, from small, family cruisers to bigger, more exotically equipped yachts whose sleek shapes could only have been designed for racing. A parade of other boats, some under sail, others motoring, was coming in from the Solent, each seeking its berth.

Everywhere there were young people on boats, repairing sails, scrubbing decks, sorting through the incomprehensible bits of some piece of nautical machinery, hauled in slings to the tops of sixty-foot masts, in the water examining rudders and bottoms, and here and there, sharing cold beer, or simply sleeping on a sunny deck. I envied them their obvious feeling of community. There was a clear line drawn between them, on the boats, and me, a tourist, shorebound. I was standing at the end of a dock where a lot of dinghies were tied when I saw something very odd. A yacht, of perhaps forty-five feet in length, was drifting slowly backward about a hundred yards out.

I watched, waiting for someone to come on deck and take charge, but no one did. There seemed to be nobody aboard. Then I saw the slack anchor line extending from her bows. The yacht was unmanned, had broken loose, and was drifting downstream in the ebb-tide current. On the dock where I stood, a boy of about ten was climbing into a rubber dinghy with a gasoline tank for its outboard.

"Hey," I called to him. "Can you operate that thing?"

"Of course," he replied, disdainfully. "I run it all the time."

"Well," I said, pointing across the water, "that yacht seems to be adrift. You want to run me out there and see what we can do about it?"

His head jerked around and his face lit up. "Oh, wow! Hop in!"

He quickly connected the gas tank and started the outboard. The yacht had drifted another hundred yards in the meantime and was moving rapidly toward a line of moored boats, all much smaller. "Better open up your throttle," I said to the boy. "If that boat hits any of those others, they might break their moorings, and then there'll be more than one adrift."

"It's already wide open," he shouted back over the little motor's roar. "It's only six horsepower."

We were not overtaking the yacht fast enough. I watched in horror as it drifted down onto the smaller boats, then in fascination as it swung slowly about and slipped through the moorings as if being steered. But beyond were larger yachts at their moorings, and that sort of luck couldn't hold out. We were catching up now.

"Just come alongside her, then stand off while I find another anchor." The boy followed my instructions expertly, and I was able to grab the yacht's stern railing and hoist myself aboard. I ran along the deck to the bows and got hold of the anchor line. It was slack, as I had thought; there was no anchor on the other end. I opened the anchor well in the forepeak, but there was no second anchor. We were drifting down onto the next line of moorings quickly, now; I was running out of time. I ran back to the cockpit and found the engine controls. At least I could motor her out of trouble and get some help. There was no ignition key. I tried the main hatch, thinking a key might be in the chart table; the hatch was padlocked. Shit.

We were now practically on top of the next line of moorings. The yacht had swung about again and was drifting backward. As we came down onto the moored boats I stepped outside the stern railing and tried to fend off the first one, but to no avail. There was a great crashing and scraping as the two hulls met, and I was nearly thrown overboard. The damage done, I tried to hold the two boats together, but we were moving too fast, and the other yacht's lifelines were torn from my grasp. As the two yachts cleared each other a man with shaving soap on his face came charging on deck.

"What the hell is going on?" he shouted.

"I'm sorry," I yelled back, "but this thing is adrift. I couldn't stop her."

"Well, you'd bloody well better get an anchor out before you hit *that*!" He pointed astern. I turned and saw two craft. The first was a small cruising boat of about twenty-five feet, which it seemed we would miss; the second was not a small cruising boat. It was the Royal Yacht, and there was not the slightest hope of missing her.

I stood, frozen, watching this horrible thing happen. Men in white uniforms rushed to the railing, and somebody began shouting at me through a loudhailer. I could only mime a huge shrug. We were nearly upon the smaller yacht, now, and I wished to God we'd hit her, somehow become entangled with her and stop, but it was becoming very clear that we were going to miss her. With one last rush of adrenaline I ran forward and began pulling in the slack anchor line. If there were somebody aboard the other yacht perhaps I could throw it to him. Standing in the bows of the drifting yacht I could see clearly into the cockpit of the other boat, now; what I saw was another padlocked hatch. Nobody aboard; we were going to miss her by some yards. My heart sank. I wondered how I was going to explain all this, or if I would even be allowed to explain before they took me out and shot me.

We were parallel with the small yacht, now, and she was my only hope. The distance between the two boats was one I would never have attempted ordinarily, but even being in the water seemed a better alternative than being aboard the boat that struck the Queen's own yacht. I got both legs outside the bow railing, gathered myself, and, holding the anchor line in one hand, leapt into space. It seemed beyond belief, but I made the stern railing of the smaller yacht, at least, part of me did. My feet didn't make it, but I had an arm around the railing, and I managed to snub the slack anchor line around it before it pulled tight. Still scrambling to get my feet under me I held the line as it tightened. As the light railing took the load of the larger yacht there was a horrible groaning sound, then the bolts fastening the rail to the deck of the yacht popped, and the rail, with me still clinging to it, began to straighten.

Then everything stopped. The larger yacht stopped drifting, and the rail stopped straightening. It wouldn't last long, I knew, before the remaining bolts popped, and I scrambled aboard. By bracing my feet against the cockpit coaming and pulling with all my strength, I began to take the load off the railing and get some slack in the line. I got one foot of slack, then another, then I began to look for something substantial to snub it around. The little boat's cleats did not look made for this sort of load, so I went for one of the main winches. Finally, I got three turns of line around it and cleated it. I looked about. The smaller yacht was at anchor, and, miraculously, the anchor seemed to be holding. A couple of hundred yards away a white motor launch was racing toward me from the shore.

The launch, which bore the initials of the Royal London Yacht Club, came alongside and two men hopped aboard the small yacht. We transferred the anchor line to the launch and she prepared to take the large yacht in tow. I explained briefly to the coxswain what had happened.

"This is our Mr. Thrasher's boat," he said. "I'm sure he'll want to thank you."

"That won't be necessary, but you'd better have him get in touch with this yacht's owner, and that one over there, too. I'm sure they'll want to talk with his insurance company."

"Right. We'll give you a lift in, then."

I beckoned to my young friend in the dinghy, who was still standing by as instructed. "Thanks, I've got a lift." I jumped into the rubber dinghy. "Okay, let's get out of here," I said. I wanted to put as much distance as possible between me and this incident.

"Gosh, that was something!" the boy shouted. "I didn't think you were going to make it when you jumped."

"Neither did I," I replied. "Can you drop me where you picked me up?"

"Sure. Wait'll my father hears about this!"

I didn't want to meet the boy's father. I didn't want to do any more explaining to anybody. All I wanted was to get my gear and disappear into the High Street crowd. When we got back to the dock from which we had departed, my duffel was gone. Terrific. I had my passport and traveler's checks in my pocket, but everything else I owned except the clothes I was wearing had been in the duffel. The boy, too excited to notice, ran off in search of his father. Shaky and pissed off, I went in search of a drink. That was when I saw the girl, and suddenly I forgot how tired and angry I was, forgot about my duffel.

Four

I SAW TAWNY HAIR WITH BRIGHT, SUN-BLEACHED STREAKS falling down to shoulders clad in a yellow sweater, which gave way to perfectly fitting jeans, which ended, quite some distance later, in yellow rubber boots. Before I could see more, a pile of sailbags from a big racing yacht came between us. I forgot the boats and hurried to get a look at the rest of this creature. I caught sight of her again, then she turned a corner and was gone once more, but not before I had glimpsed a high cheekbone and an ample breast. I half ran to the corner. She was gone.

I was looking at an open lot filled with boats ashore for repairs, piles of lumber and parked cars. I chose a direction and jogged through the space, craning my neck here and there. I was approaching another, smaller marina; I could see the masts beyond. Then a flash of yellow through a stack of lumber made me turn toward the water. I was walking quickly beside the long stack, peering through whatever cracks presented themselves. I caught a glimpse of a chin, a snatch of sweater, a flash of hair as she walked quickly along the other side of the lumber stack. I had just gotten a fraction of a second's look at a whole face when my viewpoint changed radically. I pitched forward and fell eight feet, headfirst, into the Medina River.

When I came up, before I could clear my eyes of water, I could hear her laughing. I mopped away water and a clump of weed and looked around. She was standing on a floating dock a few yards downstream; I drifted toward her.

"That was marvelous," she shouted. "Do you do regularly scheduled performances, or was this a one-off?"

"Just this once, and only for you!" I yelled back, coughing and sputtering.

"I shouldn't swallow any of that," she called, as I swam for the dock and continued to spit out water. "I should think half the toilets in the marina are flushing just about now."

"Wonderful," I said, hauling myself from the water. She was English. I had never met an English girl before.

"Come along, we'd better get you dry." She turned and walked down the dock. I followed her like a wet puppy. "You're a Yank, are you?" she asked.

"I'm an American—from Georgia, in the South. We respond poorly to being called Yankees."

She laughed—a wonderful, rich sound. "*Gone with the Wind* and all that?"

"Now you've got it."

"Here we are." She stepped lightly onto an attractive sailboat of some thirty-odd feet. The name, *Toscana,* was painted on her stern. "Shoes off." She pointed to my heavy hiking boots. "Odd footwear for around boats. You'll have to get some deck shoes if you hang about Cowes for very long."

"I had some deck shoes," I said, "but somebody's just lifted them, along with all my other gear." I shucked the boots while she fiddled with a combination lock on the hatch of the boat. I explained to her what had just happened.

"How exciting!" she laughed. "You should have hung about; the Queen might have knighted you for services to the Crown."

"More likely I'd have been mistaken for the owner of the boat and sent straight to the dungeons. Jesus, I'm freezing, can I borrow a blanket or something?"

"I think we can find you something to wear," she said. Momentarily, she tossed a pair of jeans, a sweatshirt, and a towel into the cockpit with me. "You can change in the heads."

A few minutes later I was sipping strong tea and having a close look at my hostess. Broad forehead, longish nose, clear, tanned skin, huge eyes. I reckoned she was a couple of years older than I. Her hands were bare of rings. It had been worth the dive. Whose clothes was I wearing? I worried. It especially worried me that they were too big.

She leaned over from the galley and stuck out a hand. "I'm Anna Pemberton-Robinson. Mouthful, isn't it? Annie will do for the first, Robinson for the second."

I took her hand. It was strong and surprisingly tough for a girl's. "I'm Will Lee."

"Pleased to meet you, Willie."

"No, that's Will . . . Lee."

There was a scuffing of feet on deck and a voice called down, "Hello . . . visitors!" Two men descended through the companionway—two very different men. One was about thirty, handsome, tanned, athletic-looking, wearing jeans and a light slicker over his bare chest. I am six feet one inch tall, and as I rose to meet them I could stand erect in the boat's cabin. He had to stoop.

"Oh, Mark, this is Willie Lee," Annie said. His hand enveloped mine, and I felt that he could have crushed it to pulp had he wished to. Now I knew who the clothes belonged to. "Willie, ah, had a little accident; those are his things drying in the cockpit. Willie, this is Mark, and . . ." She turned toward the other man and offered her hand.

"I'm Derek Thrasher," the man said smoothly. Everything about him was impossibly smooth. He was not handsome, he was beautiful. He seemed in his late thirties and was as tall as the other fellow, Mark, but slimmer, gorgeously barbered, exquisitely dressed in a cashmere blazer and white flannel trousers, a yellow silk shirt, and an ascot tied at the throat. I had never seen a man wearing white flannel trousers and an ascot, except in the movies, and he looked perfectly comfortable and unselfconscious in them. He looked as much at home with the soft, glossy loafers in his hand as another man would with them on his feet. His handshake was firm, personal, but his hand was as soft and buttery as the shoes in his hand.

"He is Derek Thrasher," Mark echoed, "and he thinks he might like to sponsor a large effort in the Singlehanded Transatlantic Race."

Annie's face was lit by the broadest of smiles. "Oh, Mark, that's wonderful! Mr. Thrasher, I can't tell you how delighted I am . . ."

Thrasher held up a perfectly manicured finger. "It's Derek, please."

"Of course." She began rummaging in the galley icebox and produced a bottle of champagne. "I've had this on hand just in case."

Mark opened the bottle, and we settled ourselves about the cabin settees. I had obviously stumbled into the middle of a very happy event for all these people. Thrasher and Annie immediately launched into a discussion about boats. I leaned toward Mark and said, "Excuse me, I didn't get your last name."

He flashed a wide smile at me. "Pemberton-Robinson," he said. "Robinson will do, Willie, if that's a bit of a mouthful for a Yank."

My anxiety at the news of his name was so keen that

I didn't bother to correct him on either my name or regional loyalties. "Ah . . . you and Annie are . . . ?" *Brother and sister,* I said directly to God. *Please let them be brother and sister.*

"Man and wife, old chap." He grinned. There was sympathy in his voice. "Sorry."

Five

"YOU MISSED ALL THE EXCITEMENT," MARK SAID TO Annie. "Derek's boat lost her anchor and bloody nearly went into the Royal Yacht."

I turned to Thrasher. "Was that *your* boat?"

He nodded ruefully. "I'm afraid so."

I felt a rush of anger. "Well, for Christ's sake . . ."

"And this. . . ." Annie interrupted, pointing to me, "is the fellow who rescued it."

"Really?" Thrasher exclaimed. "I certainly want to——"

"What sort of ground tackle did you have out, anyway?" I persisted, hotly. Now I had the bastard at hand whose negligence had caused all this bother, and I fairly flew at him. "Do you have any idea of the damage that could have caused?"

"Of course," he said placatingly. "It certainly could have been much worse, I know. We had out a forty-five-pound Danforth anchor, four fathoms of half-inch chain, and thirty fathoms of two-inch warp in seven fathoms of water."

"That should have held in anything but a hurricane," Mark chimed in, "but you should have seen the anchor line; sawn right through."

"You mean somebody cut it deliberately?" I asked.

"Oh, I think it's more likely that we anchored over some sort of underwater obstruction that chafed through the line," Thrasher said. "Some old piece of iron, I should think." He didn't sound very convincing.

"Looked cut to me," Mark said firmly. "Shitty thing to do to somebody."

"If there'd been a second anchor aboard I could have got that out right away," I persisted, still annoyed.

"The second anchor was in the forepeak, ready for use," Thrasher said reasonably. "But of course, the boat was locked, and you couldn't get to it. I really do apologize for your having to deal with it all, and I really am most grateful to you for what you did. I saw the whole thing from the upper deck at the Royal London. It was a very brave thing to do, jumping like that."

"Well," I said, cooling off a bit with the praise, "there didn't seem to be anything else to do."

"I would have thanked you immediately, but I didn't recognize you. You were some distance out and seemed to be dressed differently."

Annie broke in again. "I'm afraid, Derek, that you owe Willie a bit more than your thanks in this case. While he was out rescuing your yacht, all his belongings were stolen."

"Dear God!" Thrasher came back. "I hope there was nothing I can't replace."

"Oh, no," I said, waving a hand, "just clothes and stuff; I had my money and passport in my pocket."

"Both of which are a bit damp," Annie laughed. "Willie took a spill into the river. That's why he's wearing your clothes, Mark."

"And welcome to them," Mark laughed, clapping me on the back.

We drank the first bottle of champagne, then another, and talked into the early afternoon. Mark and Derek Thrasher talked, at least, while Annie mostly listened and occasionally made a remark. She was very polite to Thrasher but somehow cool. I sat and watched and listened and gazed at Annie Robinson.

Thrasher looked at his watch. "Why don't you all join me for some lunch ashore, and then we'll see about getting Will some clothes of his own."

I began to beg off, not wanting to intrude, but Annie pressed me into the company. As we left the marina and started up the High Street I noticed a man who seemed to be keeping pace with us, stopping when we stopped, watching us closely. I noticed him because he seemed so out of place in Cowes. He was big, built like a linebacker on an American football team, and encased in a tight-fitting, three-piece, blue suit. He was wearing the only necktie in sight. He seemed quite tense.

We found a little restaurant in the High Street, ordered, and Mark and Thrasher were soon into a discussion about boats.

"What's this race you're doing?" I asked Mark.

"It's a singlehanded race across the Atlantic. Held every four years. I did it last time on the boat you were just on."

"And you're sponsoring a new effort?" I asked Thrasher.

"I am indeed, but not out of philanthropy, I assure you. I want the boat when Mark's done with it."

"What would you like to name her, Derek?" Mark asked.

"Oh, name her anything you like. I'll change it when I take her over."

Mark looked surprised. "Don't you want a company name on her? Something you can advertise? Surely, that's a major benefit of sponsorship."

Thrasher shook his head. "As I said, it's the boat I want. The last thing I want is publicity, believe me. That's why I'll change the name when you're through with her." He leaned forward and spoke earnestly. "Mark, you must understand that I do not want my name attached to this project in any way. I prefer doing things quietly, and as far as your boatyard or anyone else is concerned, you are building your own boat, not mine. Can we agree on that?"

"Of course," Mark replied.

"If it's just a boat you want, why not just buy one or build a custom design?" I asked.

He shook his head again. "I want a very special sort of boat," he said emphatically. "I want something that I can take two or three couples on in comfort, but something that can be easily handled by one man, or a couple, and that's just not available in a stock boat. Take the boat you so kindly rescued today: she's only forty-two feet long, but it takes three people to sail her properly with no self-steering and a conventional deck layout. I want a boat of sixty feet, and that would ordinarily mean having a professional crew, which I most definitely do not want. Mark, here, already has a design of that size developed, with every possible innovation for singlehanded sailing included, and with a bit more luxury built in than he'd planned, she's just what I want." He took a sip of his wine. "Oh, I could have something designed and built, of course, but, what with the demands of business, I just don't have the time to work with a designer and supervise a boatyard and keep an eye on costs. Mark, on the other hand, will do nothing else, and when he finishes I believe I'll have the finest cruising yacht of her size afloat."

Mark and Thrasher began a discussion of equipment and Annie turned her attention to me. "Who are you, Willie Lee," she asked. "What brings you to Cowes?"

I told my story, probably with too much detail. She had a faculty of total concentration in a conversation, causing me to feel that what I had to say was not only relevant and important, but fascinating.

I glanced at Mark. He seemed capable of doing anything. His hard hands looked out of place on the white tablecloth.

"Mark's been looking for a sponsor for two years," she said. "It's been difficult, but now he has what he needs to build the best possible boat for the race." She looked at him and smiled. "He's very happy. I'm happy for him." Her face brightened. "Oh, we'll be neighbors of your grandfather in Ireland," she said. "The boat is being built there. You must come and see us."

"I'd planned to buy a car in France and see the continent for a few months."

Thrasher left the table for a moment, and Mark turned to me. "Do you sail?"

"Yes."

"How much experience have you had?"

"Well, there's a sailing camp on the North Carolina coast; I went there every summer as a kid, then, when I was in college, I went back as an instructor."

"What sorts of boats?"

"Everything from dinghies to cruising boats of about thirty-five feet. The camp has quite a fleet. The last couple of years I took the older kids cruising, taught them a little coastal navigation, sail handling, anchoring, seamanship, the usual stuff."

"You must come and sail with us on *Toscana*," Annie said, "and on the new boat, when it's finished."

"You say you're going to France?"

"Yes, tomorrow, on a ferry from Southampton."

"I've got a better idea. We're sailing for Ireland tomorrow, why don't you come and sail down the Channel as far as Plymouth with us? There's a ferry from there to France. Annie's always a bit under the weather the first day out, and we could use an extra hand. You'd get a good look at the English Channel, with a night passage thrown in, and you'll only be a day or two late getting to France."

I did not hesitate even for a moment. "I'd love it," I said.

"It's settled then," said Annie. "We're sailing just before dawn tomorrow, to catch the tide in the Solent."

Thrasher returned to the table. "I'm afraid I must be off. Ferry to catch, and we still have to get Will some new gear."

As we left the restaurant and strolled down Cowes High Street we seemed to be watched from across the street by yet another man, this one tall, skinny, with greasy black hair and bottle-thick glasses. The earlier heavy was nowhere in sight. I would have thought myself imagining it all, except when Thrasher came out of the restaurant, last, the man quickly turned away and pretended to look in a shop window. Thrasher didn't seem to notice; he fell in beside me. "You're from Georgia, you say."

"Yes." I was surprised he'd picked up on that while talking so intently with Mark.

"Would you be related to the Lee who was governor a while back?"

"He's my father. I'm surprised you know about him."

"I try to keep up. There were those murders, too. That got considerable attention in the British press. They're fond of that sort of thing."

At the time my father was running for governor it had been discovered that an old man in Delano had murdered more than forty teenaged boys over as many years. It had made nationwide headlines at the time and had even helped my father's political career, since he had been instrumental in hiring the chief of police who had discovered and solved the crime.

"Folks in Delano are still trying to forget about that."

He nodded. "Do you have any career plans, now?"

"No, I just want to travel for a while. I might go back to law school, I just don't know yet."

"There's a lot of opportunity on this side of the water, you know. My business has reached a size where we're always looking for bright young fellows to join us and be trained for a career."

"What sort of career? What business are you in?" I knew it had to be pretty big if he were giving Mark Robinson the money to build a sixty-foot, state-of-the-art boat.

"Oh, a bit of this and that; property, construction, investments of various sorts. We've just bought a chain of fancy hairdressers, for instance."

"Hairdressers? Beauty parlors? I wouldn't have thought there'd be much money in that."

"You'd be surprised. All the shops are in top hotels and department stores, and they produce a lot of cash flow which we're investing all over Europe in property, holiday condominiums, all sorts of things. We're even dabbling in films." He stopped in front of a shop bearing the legend "Morgan & Sons—Yachting Tailors." "I'll leave you here," he said. "They'll have pretty much anything you need, and I've already instructed them to charge everything to my account." He held up a hand at my protest. "Please, it's the very least I can do after what you've done for me today. I'm glad you're getting a sail with Mark and Annie. When you're next in London come and have some lunch. We'll talk more."

Thrasher handed me a card with nothing on it but his name and a telephone number, then turned, made his goodbyes to Mark and Annie, and walked quickly toward a dark blue Mercedes parked across the street. The heavy who had been following us earlier leapt from the car and opened the door for Thrasher. The contrast between the two men was almost comical—Thrasher, the urbane, mannered, perfectly turned-out gentleman, and his chauffeur, who was a real blunt instrument. I wondered why Derek Thrasher needed a bodyguard. We all watched as the car glided toward the ferry. I noticed that the skinny man watched, too, from the entrance to a news shop opposite us. Mark and Annie accompanied me into Morgan & Sons. We spent half an hour finding jeans, underwear, sweaters and a blazer that fit.

"Don't stint," Annie said, piling another sweater onto the counter. "Believe me, he can afford it."

When we came out, the skinny man was nowhere in

sight. I picked up some shaving gear at a drugstore, and we continued toward the marina.

Mark put his arm around Annie. She did not respond. "Well, what do you think of our sponsor?" he asked her.

She shrugged. "He's very smooth, isn't he?" She made the remark sound like an indictment. "I understand he got his start winkling little old ladies out of their houses in north London, then fixing them up and selling them for five or six times what he paid."

"Now, now, luv, he's the most respectable of businessmen." He turned to me. "You've seen all the signs along the roads?" I nodded; I hadn't made the connection before. The huge signs with the single word "Thrasher" marked construction sites—motorways, industrial parks, all large projects. "I was very impressed with him," I said. "And you're sure lucky to be getting all that money for a boat."

"Oh, it's not a gift, you know. You heard his reasons; he's no fool."

"Certainly not," said Annie. I thought I detected a touch of acid in her tone. I couldn't understand it; I had found Derek Thrasher to be completely charming and even unassuming, apart from his expensive clothes and chauffeured car, both of which seemed perfectly natural accoutrements to a man of his position. He didn't strike me as the captain-of-industry type and certainly not as the sort of man who would build a career on kicking old ladies out of their homes. I wondered if Annie knew something that Mark and I didn't.

Six

MARK SHOOK ME AWAKE. IT WAS HALF PAST FOUR IN THE morning, and I responded slowly. We had dined aboard *Toscana* and had drunk two liters of red wine among the three of us. Mark had had the best of it, I thought, but while he seemed cheerfully awake, I was extremely fuzzy around the edges. I struggled out of the sleeping bag, struggled into my clothes, and struggled from the forepeak, the forwardmost part of the boat, into the head, where a toothbrush and a splash of cold water in the face made me feel more human. In the saloon Annie stuck a mug of steaming tea in my hand and put a plate of bacon and eggs before me. I ate ravenously. Hangovers always make me feel weak, and I always believe I need to eat to build up my strength.

Fortified by breakfast, I joined Mark on deck and helped cast off from our marina berth. The diesel engine chugged quietly as we motored out, past dozens of other sleeping yachts. Another boat or two departed with us, apparently to catch the tide, as well. Annie tossed up my new nylon jacket, trousers, and seaboots, all attributable to the gratitude of Derek Thrasher.

"Better get into these," she called. "It's going to be cold until the sun comes up."

She was right, there was a breeze blowing, and I felt the chill. Clear of the marina Annie switched on lights fixed to the mast, illuminating the deck, then I began to get to know *Toscana*. All yachts, even ones of identical design, have their own idiosyncrasies, like people. I had a look at the engine controls and the deck layout, which was arranged so that all lines came back to the cockpit, making things easier for a singlehander. I noticed that there was a steel bracket fixed to the stern. "Where's the self-steering gear?" I asked Mark.

"Oh, it's stowed. Didn't want to tempt thieves in the marina, and I don't think we'll use it on the passage."

Shortly we were in the Solent. Mark seemed to be watching me closely, as, I suppose, I would have done in his place. I used to watch my campers the same way.

"Okay, luv," he said to Annie, "you'd better get your head down for a while." Annie obediently went below. She was already looking not very well. "She'll sleep for a few hours and then feel a lot better. How are you feeling?" He looked at me closely.

"As well as can be expected after all that wine last night."

He laughed. "Ah, mate, wine is the oil that lubricates

the sailing man. Couldn't go to sea without it; better get used to it." He pointed over the land. "Nice northwest-erly blowing; give us a good close reach down the Chan-nel. Couldn't ask for better."

The stars gave way to a predawn light, now, and I could see both shores of the Solent. The scattered clouds behind us reflected a gorgeous array of colors as the sun struck them from below the horizon. I glanced at the shoreline. "Hey, we're really moving, aren't we? What sort of tide have we got in here?"

Mark laughed. "We've got about four knots under us. That's why we sailed so early. The boat's doing five and six knots through the water, and with the tide to help we're making nine and ten over the ground. That's The Needles coming up to port."

I looked out and saw the rising sun strike the group of white, vertical rocks that marks the eastern tip of the Isle of Wight. We were soon in the Channel, the risen sun feeling warm on our backs. I found that I was sweating and shed my slicker.

"We'll bear away to port a bit, now." He pointed to the chart on the seat next to me. "We'll want to head out a bit to give the Bill of Portland a wide berth. There's a strong tidal race there, and by the time we're that far along, the tide will be against us."

I found the promontory on the chart. As we sailed into the Channel the boat's motion became more pronounced, and I began to feel dull and groggy again, almost as I had felt on rising. Mark glanced at me occasionally.

"Want to get your head down for a while?"

I shook my head. "I think I prefer the fresh air."

He nodded. I began to feel distinctly awful, now. Mark pointed to port. "Right over the rail there, mate."

I lunged across the cockpit and emptied my fine breakfast into the English Channel. My head cleared, and I felt immediately better.

"I expect it's the hangover," Mark said. "Best watch how much you put away the night before a passage."

A lesson well learned.

By early afternoon we were abeam of Portland Bill, some five miles offshore. We had a glorious day for our passage—sunshine, a pleasant breeze and a kind sea. Annie came on deck with sandwiches and beer, looking much better. I felt better myself and ate greedily.

Mark and I stripped off our shirts and enjoyed the sun. Annie went below and came back in a bikini. I could only afford quick glances at her; Concepta Lydon had been relegated to some distant corner of my memory; my mind was all too occupied with the outrageously alluring young woman sleeping in the sun on the deck of that neat little yacht.

Mark gave me the helm and a course to steer and went below for a nap, giving me instructions to call him if needed, and I was left alone with an oscillating compass, my concentration repeatedly shattered by the sight of Annie Robinson, lying on her back, the straps of her bikini loose, dozing, with a little smile on her wide, full mouth. I was relieved when she stirred and came to spell me at the helm.

I gave her the wheel gratefully. My neck and shoulders were aching with the effort of keeping the boat on course with the constant distraction of the supine Annie. It was easier to let her steer while I looked out over the water. "You know all about me," I said, popping another beer. "What about you?"

"Mark and me or just me?"

"You, first."

She smiled. "Oh, I'm a Londoner, born and bred. Daddy was a barrister; good one, too. He died last year. My mother is still there, thriving on her own. We spent our summers on the Isle of Wight—not Cowes, the other side, Bonchurch. Boys used to ask me sailing from Cowes, though, that's where I started."

"School?"

"Grammar school in London. Took my degree at Oxford in literature. Worked in an advertising agency in London afterward. Bored me silly."

"Is that where you met Mark? In London?"

"Nope. Cowes, during Cowes Week, two years ago. Where else? He was a captain in the Royal Marines and was skippering a service yacht in the racing. Very dashing, he was."

There was something sad in her voice. "Still seems to be," I said. "When did you marry?"

"Not long after. Whirlwind courtship and all that. He took leave and we went to Italy together. Incredibly easy to get married in Italy. We did the deed in Florence, that's why the yacht got named *Toscana*."

"Sounds romantic."

"Oh, it was." Still the sadness.

I didn't have to ask why Mark, at thirty, was no longer in the Royal Marines. He came on deck with a bottle of cold wine and three plastic glasses, wearing only a pair of khaki shorts. He had an extraordinary physique, heavily muscled, but well-balanced, except that his left knee was a mass of pits and scar tissue, and the calf was only half the size of the right. Seeing it, I was astonished that he had never shown the slightest sign of a limp, had never favored the leg at all.

Mark poured the wine, and as I was about to sip from my glass, he threw up a hand. "Not yet, mate, not 'til the sea has had his." He tipped his glass over the side and spilled a dollop of the clear, golden liquid into the salt water. "Can't be mean with Poseidon," he grinned. "Give him his sip of your wine, and maybe he won't want *you*."

It seemed a small price to pay for this golden, summer afternoon, sailing down the English Channel into a setting sun with these two attractive people. I could not know then how very much more the sea would demand from me.

"What happened to the leg?" I asked. It was four o'clock in the morning. I had come on deck to relieve Mark at the helm; he stayed on in the cockpit to get me settled with the boat and didn't seem anxious to get below and into a warm bunk. A brilliant night sky burned over us. In the distance, Start Point lighthouse flashed three times every ten seconds.

"A shotgun happened to it," he said lightly. "Sawn-off, twelve gauge, double-naught buckshot."

I was about to ask if it were a hunting accident when what he had said sank in. "Sawn-off?"

"Just a pleasant evening with the lads in a pub. Trouble was, the pub was in Belfast."

It took me a moment to add it all up. "You were stationed there with the marines?"

"Right." He smiled. "Only war we've got, you know. Bit like your Vietnam." From anyone else his tone would have been too like the way the British sound in old movies. From Mark it seemed offhand, natural, even shy.

"I guess if you're a professional that's what you want."

"Not want—need. Careers are made in a war, not least because a number of one's competitors drop out of the competition. I welcomed the opportunity, even enjoyed the work."

"What was the work like?"

"Street patrols, searches for weapons caches, an occasional patrol in the countryside around the border. Very tense, very exciting. Snipers out there all the time. One kept one's flak jacket buttoned to the chin. The old adrenaline was constantly pumping. Except in the pub."

"What happened?" Talking about this didn't seem to

cause him any pain; if anything, he sounded nostalgic. I wanted to know.

"It was early on, after the thing blew, in sixty-nine. We felt safe in some of the Protestant pubs. Dreary places, but one had to get away from it, you know. We'd got outside a few pints, some of the lads were singing; I heard car doors slamming outside—if I'd been sober that would have made me sit up and take notice—it was the singing lulled me, I think." He slouched, propped his feet up on the opposite cockpit seat and gazed at the millions of stars. "They kicked the door in and opened up on us. One of my platoon sergeants was sitting next to me; the first rounds fairly cut him in two. Fortunately, my cowardly streak surfaced through the booze and I dove over the bar. I think I must have been in midair when I was hit."

"Did it hurt a lot?" I had to know *everything*.

"Not a lot, not immediately, anyway. I was spun around sideways by the blast; it was like being hit in the knee with a punch. I landed on top of the landlord, who'd quite smartly hit the deck behind the bar. He had a weapon back there—an American army forty-five, it was, and I grabbed it and got off four or five indiscriminately aimed rounds. Hit one of them." He looked up. "Watch your course."

Held rapt by this horrible story, I was now sailing the yacht directly at the lighthouse. I quickly came back on course. "Did it kill him?"

"Yes. The landlord had loaded the thing with dum-

dums. It blew a very large hole right through him; he practically exploded. I got a look at him as they were getting me out. He was a boy. Thousands marched in his funeral procession; a proper hero, he was. He was fifteen. The bastards sent a fifteen-year-old boy to do *that*. I'd been in Northern Ireland four months, commanding a commando company through all of it, but I don't think I knew until that moment how completely ruthless they were, how little they cared for even their own."

I couldn't think of anything to say.

"Funny thing, I have a lot of sympathy for the Catholics in Northern Ireland; it's their country, after all. We took it from them and kept it for three hundred years. We still have that fragment, the six counties, and we don't know how to let go. I despise the IRA, though, especially the Provisionals, the terrorists, simply because they're willing to indiscriminately kill as many of their own people—men, women or children—as it takes to get the British out. I can understand their wanting to kill us; I can't understand their sending a fifteen-year-old to do it. It's all so stupid."

He was sounding melancholy, now, and we sailed along for a few minutes in silence, with nothing but the sound of the water slipping past the hull. I thought perhaps I knew, now, why Annie had sounded sad.

"Did you like the Royal Marines as a career?" I finally asked.

He smiled broadly. "It was bloody marvelous, it was. Terrific training, you know. I was really fit; five miles every morning, all that. We did the lot—parachuting, diving under the arctic ice cap, exercises off submarines—it was like something out of boys' fiction. Bloody marvelous."

"You got a medical discharge, then?"

"No other choice, I fear."

"Pension?"

"Yes—not much, but I've got the family farm in Cornwall; I rent that. Gives me a reasonable income."

"You ever intend to farm it yourself?"

"Oh, yes, I love it down there, but I've a few things to do before I settle down to that. You've farmed a bit, Annie tells me."

"Oh, sure. Grew up on one. Cattle, mostly."

"Are you good with your hands?"

"How do you mean?"

"Machinery, tools, that sort of thing."

"Fairly good, I guess. I maintained the tractors, learned my way around a car engine. I took all the shop courses in school. Two negro farmhands and I built a small house for one of them; wired and plumbed it, too. It was good experience."

"Interesting," he said, getting to his feet. "I guess I'll turn in for a bit. Call me when you see the Eddystone Light. Flashes twice every ten seconds; it'll be off your port bow. Before that, you'll pick up a buoy, flashing red, pretty much on your nose. That's the only fixed object between you and Plymouth. Don't hit it. There'll be the odd fishing boat or yacht, so keep a sharp eye out. If you see anything you aren't sure about, don't hesitate to call me. Better to turn me out for nothing than to bump into something." He started down the hatch, then stopped and turned. "Pick out a star," he said, "and steer for that. It's a lot easier than watching the compass. The moon moves too fast to sail by, but a star will keep you on course."

Then he was gone, and the yacht was in my hands. Start Point light flashed its signal off the starboard beam, the moon was there off to port, the stars were as thick as clouds; I picked one and sailed for it. Oddly, for the first time since I had left Delano, maybe for the first time ever, I felt truly free.

Seven

I SAW THE EDDYSTONE LIGHT JUST BEFORE DAWN AND called Mark. As we came closer to it in the new light of day, Mark said, "That light sits on a rock out there, but it isn't the first Eddystone. The first one was swept away in the last century by a single, giant wave."

I looked at the three-foot seas around us and wondered what sort of wave it would take to wipe out a lighthouse more than a hundred feet tall.

As we approached Plymouth a huge stone wall seemed to rise out of the sea. This was Plymouth Breakwater, which protected the harbor from the rough seas outside. As we sailed past the eastern end of it I got my first real look at Plymouth. We sailed across the harbor and, under sail with Mark at the helm, picked up a mooring in front of the Royal Western Yacht Club, a low structure built on a shelf of rock just above the sea. As Mark took up on the line and the boat settled with her nose into the wind,

I looked to the right and above the clubhouse and saw a familiar figure. I stuck my head inside the hatch, took the binoculars from their rack, and scanned the railing along the street, but no one was there.

"What are you looking at?" Mark asked as he came back from the foredeck.

"I just thought I saw someone I knew. Must be seeing things." I put the binoculars away, almost certain that I had seen Blunt Instrument, Derek Thrasher's chauffeur, leaning against the railing watching *Toscana* pick up her mooring. Then, as I watched, the skinny man from Cowes appeared on the street above the railing, got into an old car, and drove around a corner. I was bloody well not seeing things, and my curiosity was mounting.

While Annie made breakfast Mark and I busied ourselves with odd jobs. The logbook showed the engine oil ready for changing, so I changed that and the filter and tightened the alternator belt, aware that Mark was watching me closely as I worked.

Mark and I sat in the lounge of the Royal Western Yacht Club, sipping a pint. Annie had gone off in a taxi to do some shopping for the boat. Mark pointed out the open doors past the terrace and flagpole to the harbor. "Looks peaceful, doesn't it? What with the breakwater and all. But in a storm, with the wind from the south, the tides can get ferocious." He nodded at a portrait of Prince Philip hanging on the opposite wall. There was a brown line running across it at about the Prince's knees.

"That's the high-water mark in this room," he said. "I was here when it happened. We shoveled a lot of mud back into the sea."

We laughed about that and sat quietly for a few minutes, sipping our beer. "Well," I said, finally, "I guess I'd better check on the ferry schedule."

Mark held up a hand. "Hang about," he said. "Look here, Willie [I seemed to have got stuck with that name], I have a proposition for you: I could use some help on this project. In fact, I've got that built into the budget in my agreement with Thrasher. We're building the new boat in Ireland, at a little yard in Cork Harbour; there's a lot of work in that, and when we finish, the work really begins. A boat of this size takes a lot of maintaining. You know your way around a diesel engine. . . ."

"Well, the boats I sailed on in the States all had gasoline engines, but your diesel isn't much different from a tractor engine, really."

"Right, and you've had some pretty good experience with woodworking and tools, right?"

"I guess so, right."

"It won't be all work, mind you. It'll be November before we start the actual building—the yard has another boat to finish first—so we'll be doing some cruising in Ireland in *Toscana*. And when the boat's finished we're going to race her out to the Azores; I'll sail her back singlehanded to qualify for the big race. You'd get the best sort of blue-water experience, a bit of everything."

I started to speak, but he held up a hand.

"I know you want to travel, but there's travel in this, too, although we won't get to Paris, and I think you'd have a terrific experience with us, learn a lot, the sorts of things that will stay with you. I could pay you, say, twenty quid a week, cash, and your meals and board, and, of course, any travel expenses involved. Annie and I have taken this marvelous cottage up a little river from Cork Harbour, at a place called Drake's Pool, and there's a spare room. The three of us seem to get on well enough."

I found myself breathing faster. I realized that I had been dreading leaving these two people. Suddenly, instead of a year of wandering there was a plan, a real involvement with something exciting. "You're sure I can hack it?" I asked him. "You don't know me very well, we've only spent a little time together."

"No, but you don't know us all that well, either. If you come aboard you can jump ship anytime you feel it's not working out; just give me a bit of notice. I'll feel free to kick you overboard if you aren't 'hacking it,' as you put it. What do you say?"

If I had needed another reason to accept, it entered the club lounge at that moment. Annie Robinson strode in, carrying a box of groceries, wearing her tight jeans and her bright yellow sweater. She sank into an armchair, grabbed my pint, and took a long draught from it. Oddly, for a woman who had just come off a yacht and gone straight to a supermarket, she seemed freshly groomed and made up. "Sorry to be so long," she said breathlessly.

"There was a long queue at the market. Have I missed lunch?"

"No," said Mark. "You're just in time, too, to hear whether Willie is going to join us."

"Oh, Willie," she cried, reaching over and squeezing my hand, "please do!"

"God, I'd love to," I said. "Where do I sign?"

Mark smiled broadly and stuck out his huge, rough hand. "A handshake will do." I shook, and we all stood up to go in to lunch. "Annie, will you get us a table while I settle the bar bill?" Annie put her arms around me, kissed me firmly on the ear with a loud smack, and hugged me tightly.

"Mark," I said, when Annie had left us, "I don't want to start this whole thing off by making you think I'm crazy, but if this were a movie, I'd say we were being followed."

"Eh?"

"When I got out the binoculars at the mooring, it was Derek Thrasher's chauffeur I thought I saw. He was gone when I looked again, but then I saw another man I had seen in Cowes, who seemed to be paying a lot of attention to us when we came out of the restaurant with Thrasher."

"And you saw him here, too?"

"Yes, I'm sure of it. It was almost as if the chauffeur was following us and the other guy was following the chauffeur."

Mark laughed. "Well, I suppose Derek's chauffeur

could be down here on some sort of errand for him—God knows, he seems to have business interests everywhere—and as for the other fellow, well, we've just gone from one hotbed of sailing to another, and it's not unusual to see a familiar face; you'll probably see a couple more at lunch." He clapped me on the back. "Come on, we're not in the movies. Let's get something to eat."

As we walked toward the dining room, my feet seemed hardly to touch the ground. I was off on a true adventure, something I realized now I had been looking for all along. I was off on something else, too. My elation was pushing a Southern Baptist upbringing into a far corner of my mind; I felt almost no guilt at the realization that, for the first time in my young life, I wanted another man's wife.

I have often wondered how things might have turned out if I had taken the ferry to France that afternoon. Mark might be farming in Cornwall, now, Annie with him. I have a lot to answer for.

Eight

PEARCE WAITED UNTIL HE WAS SATISFIED THE GIRL HAD gone into the club for lunch. He had followed her to the Mayflower Post Hotel, waited for her outside for an hour, then followed the Mercedes to the supermarket and back to the Royal Western Yacht Club. He got out of the car and walked back to the railing where he had stood earlier. The yacht still bobbed at her mooring, in plain view of those inside the club. Below him was a stone enclosure holding a number of dinghies. He walked down the steps toward them; perhaps if he could get one out into the harbor he could circle and come up on the yacht from the other side. He was about to untie one when a man in uniform came out of the club.

"Can I help you, sir?" Pearce knew that tone. The man didn't want to be helpful at all.

"Uh, no, I was just looking at the boats."

"Are you a member, sir?" Same tone. Pearce didn't reply.

"I'm afraid this is club property, and only members are allowed. You can reach the street up the stairs, there."

He retreated up the steps and stood at the railing again. He thought about waiting until dark, but he had to start back to London well before that time. He did not understand Thrasher's relationship with these people, but he knew that the younger of the two men had ruined the effort in Cowes, and that they were at least Thrasher's friends. That was enough for Pearce, but now he was out of time. He had to be at the office.

He got back into the old Wolsley and drove back to the Mayflower Post. The Mercedes was gone. He turned back toward the A30 East, toward London. This was not working out, this following Thrasher; he was not getting the right chances, although he had come close in Cowes. Thrasher was too unpredictable, and Pearce had still not been able to find out where he lived, not even from his coworkers at the office. He would have to find another way.

There was time. And money. With the insurance and the bit his mother had left there was nearly £6,000. He would be patient; he would find another way. He would find it for his mother.

Nine

WE SPENT THE NIGHT MOORED IN PLYMOUTH, AND BY the time we continued west, down the Cornish coast, my relationship with Mark and Annie had changed. Before, I had been a new acquaintance invited for a sail, a passenger; now I had been taken in, made a part of what they were doing. We had become friends.

The weather remained glorious. We got a spinnaker up in a light following breeze, and the brightly colored sail filled and drew us down the green coastline, a mile or so offshore. I had grown up in a place where the coastal region was flat and sandy and, to my mind, rather dull. But here, in the lower left-hand corner of England, rolling green meadows swept down to high cliffs, with the sea crashing at their feet. It was like something out of Daphne du Maurier.

Mark went forward, curled up on a sail on the foredeck and slept soundly. I steered, and Annie kept me company in the cockpit. "Willie . . ." she said hesitantly. There seemed to be something she was having trouble saying to me.

"Yep?"

"I think you ought to know about . . . Mark's . . . injury."

"Oh, he told me about that a couple of nights ago, on the sail down to Plymouth."

She looked at me in surprise. "He told you about that?"

I nodded. "About Belfast and the pub."

"About the boy?"

"Yep, the whole story."

She looked relieved. "I'm glad. Do you know you're the first person he's ever told about it, except for me?"

"Really? He seemed pretty relaxed about it."

She looked toward Mark, sleeping on the foredeck. "Thank God Thrasher came along," she said.

"You said he'd been looking for sponsorship for a long time."

She nodded and sighed. "Oh, yes. He was pretty near the end of his tether . . . and so was I."

"What would he have done if he hadn't got the money? Gone back to the farm?"

"He would have been a caged animal on the farm."

"The way he talks about it, he seems to love the place."

"Oh, he does; but this new boat has loomed large since he had to leave the service. He began drawing it when he was still in . . . hospital. He must have done a hundred drawings—every detail. He read every book available on yacht design . . . he took a mail-order course, bent every professional designer's ear, showed the plans to anybody who could make a suggestion."

"Why didn't he go to a professional for the design?"

"He wouldn't. He couldn't have borne the idea. He had to do it himself. It was sort of . . . therapy, I guess."

"I gather he loved the Royal Marines."

"Loved it? He was *obsessed* with it. He lived and breathed it, and when he found out he couldn't do it anymore . . . well, he withdrew into himself, stayed shut in his room for weeks, barely talked to me. He never once spoke about what had happened—a friend had to tell me about it. I think the boy's death, on top of having to leave the service, was almost more than he could stand. And then one day he came into the kitchen with this drawing of a boat and started to talk. He must have talked for six hours straight, making notes and sketching. It became frightening after a while, and I wanted to call a doctor, but then he seemed to get it all out and went to bed and slept like a baby, with no nightmares."

"He'd been having them a lot?"

"Constantly, when he could sleep at all. I had to sleep on the living room sofa for a long time."

"And he's been okay since?"

"Well, not entirely. The obsession with the boat replaced his obsession with his career, and that was fine until it began to look as if he might never find a sponsor."

She looked out over the water into the distance. "I think that if Thrasher hadn't . . . come into the picture when he did I would have had to leave Mark . . . or go 'round the bend, myself."

"But he's okay, now, isn't he?"

She looked forward at Mark again. "God, I hope so. This project isn't going to be easy, I think you ought to understand that. Things are bound to go wrong, and I just hope Mark can handle them when it happens." She turned back to me. "I'm going to need your help with him, Willie. If he could talk to you about Belfast, that means you have his trust."

"Well, sure, whatever I can do. I'm glad he told me the whole story."

She turned and looked at me. "I'm not sure that he did," she said. "I'm not sure he knows the whole story, himself. The officers he served with told me as little as they could get away with. They were . . . uncomfortable discussing it; there was something there that I never got to the bottom of . . . and to tell you the truth, I'm not sure I want to."

We sailed on in silence.

We had a week's sailing that is still, all these years later, the standard of pleasure by which I judge a successful cruise. We moved west from Plymouth down the coast to Fowey, where we drank at the Royal Fowey Yacht Club and ate lobster in the village; we looked in at Mevagissey and Polperro, timing the tides to be sure we had water under our keel; we drank our pints outdoors at the Rising Sun in St. Mawes, called at the Royal Cornwall Yacht Club in Falmouth for a drink and motored up the lovely Helford River for a spectacular dinner at a tiny restaurant called the Riverside. I slept alone on the yacht that night, while Mark and Annie stayed in a room above the restaurant. I envied him and missed them both.

We had a good day's sail around the Lizard, the last big promontory in the Channel, to Hughtown, in the Isles of Scilly, some thirty miles from Land's End. We had supper ashore and listened to the local fishermen's choir sing in the pub—not in performance, but for the sheer joy of singing. Early the next morning, with their voices still ringing in our heads, we motored through a narrow cut at high water and were in the Atlantic, bound for Ireland. By lunchtime the Scillies had slipped below the horizon, and we were well and truly at sea.

After my conversation with Annie about Mark I watched and listened to him more closely. He went in stops and starts, I noticed. He would be talkative, almost garrulous for a time, then fall silent. I imagined he was thinking ahead about the building of the boat, but I couldn't be sure. Still, he was calm, a reassuring presence on the boat, an aura of utter competence about him.

Annie worked her considerable charm without seeming to humor him, but I could see her concern and her relief. Oddly, she did not seem to me to be in love with him, simply to like him a lot, but I had to admit to myself that that was what I wanted to believe. There was an attraction between us, something palpable. She conveyed affection in small ways—a quick hug, a cool hand on the back of my neck when it was sunburned, an arm draped casually over my shoulder as we sat in the cockpit. She did this even when Mark was present, and he seemed, somehow, to approve. They might have been brother and sister, as I had once hoped they might be. I felt almost like an old beau. I liked it.

Out of sight of land I experienced a curious sense of self-sufficiency that was all out of proportion to the reality. There we were, the three of us, dependent only on the boat and ourselves for comfort and survival. There was a kind of comfort and companionability in that.

Within a few hours we were in a forty-knot gale, with seas running in two directions after a major wind shift. Under short sail we took watches in turn, wet and cold, while those below handed up sandwiches and hot drinks. During that day and night we became more than friends, we became a team, each responsible for the others.

We raised Roberts Head outside Cork Harbour late the following afternoon, delayed some hours by the gale. There was still more than thirty knots of wind blowing, but we had up more sail and kept it until we were abeam of Roches Point Light, where we stopped and put the yacht in order, above and below.

"I like to be shipshape when I enter a port," Mark said. "Makes it all look easy to those ashore."

We started the engine and motored up the Carriga-line River into Crosshaven and tied up at the water dock of the Royal Cork Yacht Club, a neat, white building at the top of a short expanse of very green grass a few yards above the water. Crosshaven stretched along the river in both directions and up the hillside, as well. There were, perhaps, three dozen yachts of varying sizes moored in the river off the club. The tiny settlement of Currabinny lay directly across the water from the club. It was a very pretty place, one I had not visited during my earlier stay in Ireland, even though it was less than fifteen miles from my grandfather's farm. A man in foul-weather gear on the dock looked the length of *Toscana* and said, "She looks very tidy to have come in out of *that*." He nodded toward the harbor entrance.

Mark winked at me. "Oh, she stands up very well, she does," he said, smiling broadly at the man. "She likes a bit of weather."

We trudged up the ramp to the clubhouse in the light rain, dumped our oilskins on a bench outside, and went into the bar. Warmth and the smoky scent of burning turf greeted us. The bar was just opening for the day, and the club was deserted, except for us. Mark ordered Guinness for the three of us. "We'll ring Coolmore from here," he said. "He'll want to know we've arrived."

"Who?"

"It's Lord Coolmore, actually. He owns the castle that our cottage belongs to. I should ring Thrasher, too. He'll want to know we're still alive." He got up and went to look for a phone.

"You'll love the cottage," Annie said. "It was built as

a gamekeeper's house—must be more than four hundred years old."

We chatted idly for a few minutes, the fatigue of the night before beginning to catch up with us. Mark returned. "All set," he said. "Coolmore's meeting us with a key; we'd better be off upriver." We gathered our oilskins and walked back to the water dock in the rain. As we cast off I looked up to the road at the club's gates and saw someone step into a telephone booth. I had only a glimpse before he was obscured by the rain on the booth's glass panes.

I turned to Mark. "Did you reach Derek Thrasher?"

"Yep. He was relieved to hear we'd made port safely. Apparently, there are a couple of yachts missing out there."

"In London?"

"What?"

"Did you reach Thrasher in London, or was he somewhere else?"

"In London."

He revved the engine, and we began the last mile of our passage. I looked back toward the phone booth, now hidden by a wall. I could see only part of a car that might have been a Mercedes. I turned back to coiling lines and found Annie looking at me oddly.

Ten

WE MOTORED UP THE CARRIGALINE RIVER, HEEL-ing slightly in the sharp gusts that came at us across the water and slapped little waves against the hulls of the moored yachts and fishing boats. We came around a bend to the left and another to the right, and it seemed that the river was about to peter out. Still, we continued and rounded yet another sharp bend to come to a placid anchorage, sheltered by heavy brush on one side and an extensive stand of large trees on the other, and by hills on both sides. Carved into the forest on our right was perhaps half an acre of grass surrounding a large stone cottage. A tall, lean man who looked to be in his late fifties or early sixties walked from the cottage to a stone jetty, got into a dinghy, and began to row toward us.

Mark handed me the boathook. "Stand by to pick up that mooring." He pointed to a fluorescent red buoy dead ahead. As we secured to the mooring the man in the boat came alongside and clambered aboard. He greeted Mark and Annie warmly and turned to me with an outstretched hand.

"And you'll be Willie, I expect," he said, grinning at me broadly. "I'm Peter-Patrick Coolmore."

"Will Lee," I replied, taking his hand while inwardly saying goodbye to my preferred name. It was a losing battle. He came below and admired *Toscana*'s interior layout, then we and our gear made it ashore in two trips. We entered the cottage for the first time to a scent mixed from new wood, old furniture, paint and other building materials.

"Oh, it's lovely," Annie exclaimed, walking about. "So much improved since we first saw it."

"You didn't arrive a moment too soon," Coolmore said. "We've just got it together. Joan picked out what furniture she thought you'd need. We've a couple of rooms full of unused things at the castle if you need anything more. Your things arrived yesterday," he said, indicating several large packing crates in an adjacent room. "I'll leave you to it, then." He shook hands all round and departed.

"Let's get at it," Annie commanded.

"Haven't we time for a glass of wine?" Mark complained. "It's the cocktail hour, you know."

"I'm cooking dinner in this cottage tonight," Annie replied firmly, "and I'm not cooking until everything is in its place."

We fell to work and, in an hour and a half, under

Annie's close supervision, we had transformed the cottage into something resembling a home. There was a good-sized living room with a dining table at one end and a large fireplace at the other, two bedrooms, one large and one small, a kitchen, and a newly constructed bathroom. Annie had a talent for nestbuilding. I remembered, now, that *Toscana* had the same look about her, one of lived-in comfort. What had been a bare collection of rooms was now cozy and inviting. By the time another two hours had passed, we had all showered and had a good dinner and some wine and were scattered before a cheerful fire. Shortly after that they shook me awake and sent me to my bed. Before sleep overtook me, I had a moment to reflect on where I was and what I was doing. My father's comment to my mother came back to me, about the model airplanes I had never finished. When reciting my list of manual skills to Mark, full knowing why he was asking me, I had neglected to tell him that I had never finished my shop projects in school, either, or the building of the small house on the farm. There was something in me that, once I learned about something, made me lose interest. I had no staying power, and I knew it. I resolved, with as much resolve as I could muster in my sleepy state, that I would finish this one; that I would make up for my lack of candor with an enthusiasm I would find somewhere. Somewhere.

Next morning, after a huge breakfast that included my favorite Irish foods, smoked bacon and soda bread,

Annie set about doing still more to the cottage, while Mark and I paid a visit to Cork Harbour Boatyard.

We borrowed Lord Coolmore's Land Rover and motored down a bewildering series of country lanes until we came upon a creek running up from Cork Harbour. As we turned and drove up its banks the water receded until there was nothing but steep banks and a bottom left dry by the receding tide. Shortly, a very large tin shed appeared. There was a rudely shingled addition attached to one side and an old, stone quay running along the dried-out creekbed. A little railway ran from the creek's edge into the large shed. Half a dozen yachts and boats, in varying stages of disrepair, perched on cradles scattered about the yard. We parked the Land Rover and entered the shed through a small, hinged door cut into a huge, hangar-type sliding door.

The scents of wood shavings and some sort of glue struck me, and a hammering from a nearly finished fishing boat that nearly filled the shed was temporarily deafening. A short, dumpy man detached himself from the crew of half a dozen working on the boat and shambled toward us.

"Captain Robinson," he said, sticking out the hand not holding a hammer. "Been looking for you to turn up."

Mark took the hand. "Good to see you, Finbar." He turned to me. "This is Willie Lee, who'll be working with us. Willie, this is Finbar O'Leary, the best boatbuilder in Britain and Ireland."

Finbar O'Leary blushed and seemed astonished at the same time. I would learn that he had an astonished expression fixed upon his face at all times, in all moods. "Mr. Lee," he said, "glad to have you aboard. I understand you're handy. We can use the help if we're to give Captain Robinson the boat he wants." He turned back to Mark. "Got some news for you. The little yacht we were to build after this one. . . ." he nodded over his shoulder at the fishing boat, "has been canceled. The owner opted for something in plastic." There was a touch of scorn in his voice at the mention of a glass-fiber boat. "That means you're next; we should be laying your keel in ten days or so."

Mark's face spread in a huge smile. "That's news indeed, Finbar. Will we have materials by then?"

"I came upon a nice load of good Honduras mahogany last week and took the liberty of placing an order. We won't be needing the teak decking for a while, and I've already the oak. I'll put a man to ripping the mahogany as soon as I can free one from this job. We'll make a start on, let's see . . ." He screwed up his face in figuring and managed to look even more astonished. "The first of September; how's that for you?"

Mark clapped him on the back, rocking the smaller man. "That couldn't be better." Mark produced a notebook and they began to compile a list of other materials for the new yacht. I walked a few steps toward the incomplete fishing boat to have a closer look and then stopped in my tracks. A man who had been painting the hull had stopped and was staring at me. We stood for several seconds like that, then with no other sign of recognition, he turned his back and began to paint again. I glanced up to the deck high above the shed's floor and saw an identical man looking at me. He nodded amiably and turned back to his work. Connie Lydon may have told me that the O'Donnell twins, Denny and Donal, were boatbuilders, but, if so, I had forgotten. I felt unaccountably disturbed to see them, like a boy who had unexpectedly come upon the schoolyard bully away from the schoolyard. This time it had been easy to distinguish Denny from his brother, merely by the hostility of his gaze. I rejoined Mark and Finbar.

We went into Finbar's office—the addition to the shed. The plans for Mark's yacht were pinned to a wall, and the two men went over them carefully. They agreed on a list of materials to order and Mark gave the boatbuilder a check to cover the initial order and open an account. We made our goodbyes, and as we turned to leave, I found Denny O'Donnell staring at me again.

"Something between you and that fellow?" Mark asked as we made our way back to the Land Rover.

"Not really," I said. "He had an interest in a girl I used to go out with here."

"You afraid of him?"

I felt my ears go red. "We've never even spoken."

He started the vehicle. "I remember that about the Irish in Belfast, that staring, on the streets when we were patrolling. A fellow looked at you like that, and you knew he was what you were patrolling for, although most times you had no hard evidence to know it." He cocked his head to one side and looked at me again, sharply. "You afraid of him, Willie?"

"He . . . makes me uncomfortable," I said. "I don't know why."

"Well, I've never seen him before today, Willie, but I can tell you this about him: let him know that, and he'll make your life miserable, and he'll enjoy doing it. You know what I'd do in your position?"

"What?"

"I'd pick the right moment, when he was crowding me just a bit, and I'd hit him—hard."

I shrank from even the idea. "That doesn't solve anything."

"Don't you believe it, mate," he snorted. "Don't you believe it. Sooner or later you're going to have to fight him, you mark my words, and the sooner the better."

Eleven

S HE SAT QUIETLY AND WATCHED THE TWINS.

"He's the one, I know he is," Denny said, slapping his hand on the tabletop.

"Ah, come on, Denny," his brother said. "You don't know anything for sure. It's been a couple of years."

"I remember. I remember the name. I think I remember his picture in the paper, in a Dublin paper."

"So what if he is the one?" Donal asked, reasonably. "What are you proposing to do about it?"

"I'd be for doing him, that's what."

"Oh, come on, mate," Donal said, forcing a chuckle. "We're not set up for that. We've not the authorization. You couldn't do that without the authorization. You'd be in it from all sides then."

She smiled to herself. They remained forever in character, these two, the hothead and the peacemaker. Donal was too smart to seem to be backing away from a fight;

he'd invoked procedure instead. She liked that. "Just a minute," she said. It was the first time she'd spoken. "You've both a point. If he's the same one, something would need to be done; we couldn't just let it pass."

"Bloody right, we couldn't," Denny growled.

"But we don't know, do we?" she continued, ignoring him. "We need to know for sure."

"If he is the one," Donal put in, "then do you think we might get the authority?"

"I think we might," she said. "But before we even ask, we have to know for sure."

"So how do we find out?" Denny asked. "Go to Dublin and paw through a great bloody lot of old newspapers?"

She shook her head. "Leave it to me," she said, quietly, gazing out the window across Kinsale Harbour. "I'll find out."

Twelve

THE NEXT DAYS WE LIVED AS IF PREPARING FOR A VOYage, for that was what the building of the yacht seemed to us, busying ourselves doing things we would have no more time for once the yacht's keel was laid. Annie bought paint and wallpaper and set to decorating the cottage. I started—and finished—a large bookcase for the living room and a desk for the small bedroom, which Mark would use as an office when I was not sleeping there. Mark was buried in lists of materials and equipment and paid little attention to us, except at the end of the day, when, surprised, he would come upon our handiwork and offer compliments. We had done a good job, Annie and I, and we were proud of ourselves.

Annie seemed grateful for my company when Mark was so immersed in plans for the yacht. His concentration was such that all else was shut out, including her, and it was not hard to tell she didn't like it much. He ignored even the most cutting remarks from her and ploughed on with his work. She complained wordlessly to me with shrugs and scowls, and, happy for her attention, I lapped it up.

We scoured the classified pages of the *Cork Examiner* for transportation. Mark found a serviceable Ford van, and I, after much searching, came upon a very neat Mini Cooper, a souped-up version of Britain's smallest four-passenger car. It sat right down on the ground and went around corners at a great rate of knots; it was perfect for the Irish back roads, and I loved driving it fast.

We were asked to the castle for dinner by Lord and Lady Coolmore, who insisted on being called Peter-Patrick and Joan. I had expected the place to be run down, as many large, Irish country houses are, but it was kept in perfect condition by a full-time carpenter/painter and a domestic staff of three. We dined on fresh salmon and drank good wines. The Coolmores were comfortable with young people and had a knack for putting them at their ease, but I found myself grateful for my mother's strict adherence to table manners in my upbringing. She, having grown up among people like the Coolmores, had kept a more formal house than those of my contemporaries, so I was at home with good crystal and more than one fork.

Joan Coolmore and Annie disappeared after dinner and left Lord Coolmore, Mark and me to coffee and brandy. I declined the cigars, which Mark, to my surprise, accepted with relish. I had never seen him smoke, but I think the clubbiness of Peter-Patrick Coolmore's study overcame him. The conversation turned to Mark's military career, and Mark discussed it easily, as he had with me and had not with Annie. Perhaps, I thought, now that he had the yacht as a new career, he found it less painful to talk about his lost one.

"Mark," Coolmore said in his lazy, upper-class drawl, then tilted his head back to the leather and blew smoke rings at the frescoed ceiling. "Mark, I'm most interested to know about your experiences in the Royal Marines, but if I were you I should be a bit circumspect in discussing it hereabouts." I looked up in mild surprise. When someone like Coolmore said one should ". . . be a bit circumspect . . ." about discussing something it meant that one should keep one's bloody mouth shut about it.

Mark sipped his brandy idly. "You think my service might be a problem in Cork?"

"Well," Coolmore sighed, "we're a long way from Belfast, it's true, and most people here are against the violence there, but there is an element . . ." He trailed off.

"You mean the IRA is active in County Cork?" I plunged in, ignoring the subtleties.

"Oh, no, no, nothing like that," he came back quickly. "It's just that there are those with . . ." he struggled for the word, ". . . *sympathies,*" he said, finally. "During the troubles of the twenties feeling ran very strong indeed; people were burned out, that sort of thing." He blew another perfect smoke ring. "Still, there are . . . *romantics* about."

"How did your family fare in the revolution?" I asked.

He shot me a glance. "My family are *Irish*," he said. "We came to Cork more than four hundred years ago, before Cromwell went to Ulster. We *bought* our land, paid for it, every acre. Then, during the famine my great-great-grandfather sold off much of it to feed his tenants. During the troubles my father ran in guns in his yacht, like Erskine Childers. Fortunately, unlike Childers, he managed not to get shot."

I knew from our dinner-table conversation that Coolmore was Harrow and Cambridge and the RAF in the Battle of Britain. I had not yet begun to fathom the relationship between the British and the Irish, nor the complex position in the society of people like Coolmore and my grandfather, whose accent and manners and wartime loyalties placed them with the English aristocracy, but who considered themselves Irish. Coolmore changed the subject. Later, I would realize what he had been trying, in his offhand way, to tell us, and I would wonder why he tried.

A few days before building began on the boat, Mark drove the van to Dublin to scout the chandleries there for what might be bought in Ireland, rather than sending to England and bothering with shipping and customs. He telephoned from there in the late afternoon and said he would be staying the night.

I received this news from Annie in a stooped position, as I had been humping large chunks of granite around all day, in a project to repair the stone jetty outside the cottage. "Get yourself into a hot bath for a bit," she said, laughing at my posture. "I'll fix it for you later."

I did as she instructed. By the time I had soaked for an hour it was dark, and she had an inviting dinner on the table. "Don't bother to dress," she called after me as I went into my bedroom. "Your dinner will be cold." I grabbed a terrycloth robe and hurried to the table.

It was the first time I had ever been alone with her. "It's nice not to talk about the boat," she said, sighing. "I was so happy when Mark got the sponsorship, but now I wonder if I can last the distance."

"I suppose I'm guilty of talking of nothing else, too. It's hard not to with Mark around."

She washed down a bit of cheese with her wine and smiled. "I'm glad he's not around," she said.

"Do you like being married?" I asked. "I mean, don't you ever feel confined? Boxed in?"

She looked at me thoughtfully. "Not at first. At first it was a romantic dream. Still, I was old enough, had been about enough not to expect that to last. But I hadn't expected Mark to be quite so absorbed with his career, either."

"I guess a lot of guys are like that, not just the Royal Marines. There are workaholics in business and law and medicine—doctors' wives are always complaining."

She shook her head. "This was something different. It was like a religion to him. He was like a monk in some order that demanded utter devotion."

"Well," I laughed, "at least he didn't have to be celibate."

"No, he didn't have to be." The sadness was there again.

"Do you mean . . . ?"

"Oh, no, we had a sex life of sorts, I suppose, but the commandos got more of his energy than I did."

"Well, that's over, anyway."

"I wonder. He's giving to the boat just about what he gave to the Royal Marines."

I was stuck here; I didn't know whether to offer to fill in for Mark in the bedroom or what. "We'll have to get him out more often; go out to dinner and that sort of thing; get his mind off the boat once in a while."

She suddenly stood. "I'd like a bath, now. Do you mind clearing up?"

"Not at all," I said, beginning to gather dishes.

She passed through the kitchen on her way to the bathroom. "Why don't you get a fire going?" she rubbed her arms. "It's damp down here by the river."

I finished the dishes and lit some kindling in the big fireplace. I added a stick at a time, staring into the flames, until it was hot enough to get the oak logs burning. The kitchen light went out, and I heard the tinkle of glasses. Annie walked to where I sat on the rug in front of the fire and handed me a brandy snifter. I turned to take it from her and found a tanned thigh at eye-level. She was wearing an old shirt of Mark's. I wondered if she were wearing anything else. "Have a large swig of that to relax you, then I'll do your back," she said, sitting down, crosslegged beside me. I barely resisted the temptation to follow the thigh to its source. I took a gulp of the brandy straight down. It worked quickly.

"You aren't going to walk on my spine like a Japanese girl, are you?"

She laughed and gave me a push, toppling me sideways onto the rug. "I weigh a couple of stone more than a Japanese girl—I'd cripple you for life." She tugged at the robe. "Let's have that off; I've got to get at the muscles, you know." I shucked the garment off my shoulders, leaving my lower body covered. She snatched it away and tossed it onto the sofa, leaving me bare on the rug.

"I think there are a couple of baby pictures of me like this somewhere," I said shakily. I could feel the goosebumps come up on the side of me away from the fire.

"Oh, shut up." She slapped me sharply on the buttocks. I heard her unscrewing a bottle cap and her hands rubbing together. A slightly sweet scent reached me, and then I felt her hands rubbing warm oil onto my skin. She worked slowly up and down one side of my back, using more oil now and then, while I groaned with pleasure. Her breathing became faster as she worked. She had been on her knees on one side of me, then she changed to the other side, throwing a leg over and sitting back, straddling my thigh as she rubbed. It was now absolutely clear to me what she was wearing—or rather, not wearing— under the man's shirt. Her hands were warm from the rubbing, but not as warm as the part of her that rested against me. She kept rubbing, moving down until she was massaging the large muscles in my buttocks. Soon, I thought, I would have to turn over, because my changing anatomy would be no longer accommodated by the hard floor beneath the rug.

She began to ease up and went over the whole of my back again lightly. Then she leaned forward and kissed me on the nape of the neck. "There you are, Willie." Her voice was husky through her breathing. "You lie there for a minute." She stood, and my thigh was wet where she had been sitting. Then she tossed the robe over me, and I heard her bare feet padding on the stone floor as she walked toward the large bedroom. She did not close the door. I heard covers rustle and springs squeak as she got into bed.

I'll lie here until my heart stops that thumping, then I'll decide what to do, I thought to myself. I turned on my back to free myself from being pinned to the hard floor. Gradually, my breathing and my heart slowed. I worked at relaxing everything, while my mind spun. The brandy helped.

I jerked awake sometime in the middle of the night. The fire had died, and I was cold. I got up stiffly from the floor and walked to the door of the large bedroom. The moonlight lit Annie's form. She was turned on her side, and her hair spilled over her face, hiding it. I could hear her deep breathing. I crossed the living room and went to my own bed, but light was showing in the sky when I finally fell asleep again.

*   *   *

The sun was high when I awoke, and there was a note from Annie saying she'd gone for a walk. I had some breakfast, then pottered around the cottage until after lunch, all the while still in a state of sexual excitement. I got into the Mini Cooper and began to drive fast down the country lanes. I headed generally west, with no firm idea of a destination, and the concentration demanded by speed helped occupy my mind for a while. I was approaching Kinsale when I realized I had had a destination all the time. Soon I pulled over to the side of the road and stopped. I got out of the car, walked around and sat on a fender, facing the field. The hockey match was in progress, as if it had never stopped since my first visit. The match ended, and Connie Lydon walked toward me across the field. She stopped and beckoned, and a nun joined her.

"Hello, Will," she said. "This is Sister Mary Margaret." I turned and shook hands with a tall, fresh-faced girl in a black habit who seemed too young to be a nun. Connie had not taken her eyes from mine during the introduction. "You're back for a bit, then?"

I nodded, returning her gaze. "For some time, it seems."

There was a silence, then Connie asked, "Will you come to Summercove for a drink? I'm finished here."

"Sure."

"You go ahead; I'll get changed and get my car. The key's in the window box."

"Nice to meet you," I said to the nun.

"Same here," she replied, offering her firm handshake again. They walked away together across the field.

At her cottage I found the key where it had always been kept and moved impatiently about the place, picking up a book, looking at pictures. I heard her car pull up outside. She came into the room and started to mix a drink.

"Jesus, but I've missed you," I said, with a feeling that surprised me. It seemed to surprise her, too.

She came quickly across the room and put her arms around my waist. Her hair was wet and she had not bothered to wear a bra under her sweater. "I missed you, too," she whispered. "I said some things I shouldn't have. I practically accused you of being a heartless bastard."

I didn't say anything. I wasn't sure I could deny it.

"Do you still want me?" she asked.

"Oh, yes," I said, with honesty. I had made no declarations, but I did want her.

"I want you, too," she said.

I pulled her toward the bedroom, as I had tried to do so many times. This time she came with me. We made love quickly, inexpertly, awkwardly, even. We lay in each other's arms for a while, then did it again, this time with more assurance and satisfaction for us both. If we were students of love, we were, at least, learning. One of us was pretending, too.

Later, she brought me a cup of tea and we lay propped

up on pillows, talking. "Maeve thought you were dishy," Connie said.

"Who's Maeve?"

"Sister Mary Margaret, to you. We grew up together and were at university together, in Cork, before she went away. She studied to be a teacher, and after she took her final vows they sent her to our school."

"Can you be friends with a nun?"

"Sure, as long as it doesn't get too worldly, I suppose."

"If she still thinks guys are dishy, you can't be too good an influence. I wonder what the head nun would think of that."

Connie laughed aloud. "She'd wet her pants." We both laughed. "And you've become the great yachtsman."

I was astonished. We'd kept so close to the cottage and the boatyard I didn't think anyone knew I was back. I hadn't even called my grandfather. "How do you know about that?" I asked.

"Helping the intrepid Brit get all ready for his race. Where's he getting all the money?"

I told her about Cowes and Thrasher. I shouldn't have told her about Thrasher.

"What's he like, the great Captain Pemberton-Robinson?"

"He's great; so's his wife, Annie. You'll like them."

"I hear he shoots children in the streets."

"Jesus H. Christ, Connie!" I sat up, spilling my tea.

"In the back."

"Shit! Where the hell have you picked up all this garbage?"

"Ah, you can't keep a thing like that quiet, you know."

"That's not the way it happened." I told her Mark's story. "And if you don't believe that, have a look at his leg sometime."

She was quiet; I wasn't sure whether she was serious or just baiting me. "Did you know that he knew the boy he shot? That he had arrested him for throwing stones at a patrol? *Twice*? Did you know the boy was tortured at the army barracks and that your friend was there?"

I defended Mark as best I could, but I left Summercove filled with dread and guilt—dread that my friend had not told me the truth, and guilt that I had taken Connie Lydon's virginity while pretending she was someone else.

Thirteen

I SPENT THE NEXT TWO NIGHTS WITH CONNIE LYDON, AND it occurred to me that they were almost the only moments I had spent away from Mark and Annie since I had met them. Mark and Annie were delighted that I had found a regular girlfriend (in truth, I would have felt better if Annie had been less delighted) and wanted to meet her at the earliest possible moment. Annie proposed a weekend cruise down the coast of West Cork that would get Mark away, as well.

Connie's reservations about Mark were palpable, even as she accepted, and she was clearly, at least to me, uncomfortable with him as we sailed out of Cork Harbour. I think she had been expecting a stiff, terribly British military type, but not even Mark's informality and easy charm, nor his rugged good looks, had put her at ease. Annie did not exactly fit the stereotype of the military wife, either, moving expertly about the decks and taking no guff from Mark in the sailing of the boat, and Connie was obviously immediately attracted to her. They were soon knocking about the galley together, making sandwiches. By lunchtime we were past Roberts Head and sailing comfortably in a light breeze.

There were fishing boats about, but none very near us, and I was surprised when Mark suddenly tacked the boat. We had a comical minute or two trying to handle the sheets without spilling beer and food. "What was that all about?" I asked, wiping mayonnaise from a cockpit seat.

Mark nodded at the water between two fishing boats. "Drift nets," he said, scowling. I could see a line of small floats. "Illegal salmon fishing. Those fellows all carry shotguns and brook no interference. Bastards."

"Does no one police them?"

"The Irish Navy does, but that consists of two wooden minesweepers, and they're more concerned with catching Russian fishermen violating Irish fishing grounds. They levy big fines and confiscate boats in those cases."

"Fishermen have to make a living like everyone else," Connie said to him sullenly.

A red-bearded man glared at us from the deck of one of the boats as we sailed past. "Watch how you go!" He shouted angrily at us, then seeing our ensign, "Bloody Brits!" I half expected him to produce a shotgun on the spot and start raking our decks.

Mark gave him a cheerful wave. "Morning," he called to the angry fisherman. "Lovely day!" The man turned and went into his wheelhouse without a word.

"Nice countrymen you've got," I said to Connie, who was looking embarrassed.

"I know him," she said. "His name is Red O'Mahoney. He's not such a bad bloke. You can hardly blame him for getting a bit hot about his nets." She went below and started cleaning the galley. She hadn't finished her lunch.

We sailed on past Oysterhaven and Kinsale and near the end of the long afternoon, anchored at Castletownshend. At Mary Ann's Bar we ate lobster, drank wine, and sang and played darts with the locals. Connie joined in but was barely polite to Mark. Back on the boat, Mark and Annie gave us the forward V-berth and retired to the quarterberth aft. The radio did not drown out the noises that came from either end of the small yacht, and someone rowing past noticed the ripples made by the rocking of the boat and called out cheerful encouragement. The four of us laughed uncontrollably for a few minutes, then resumed our previous activity.

We put Connie ashore at Kinsale the next evening. It annoyed me that she seemed relieved to be home. She hadn't given Mark half a chance, I thought. We made Drake's Pool and the cottage in time for a good night's sleep. We needed that, for the boat would begin building the next morning.

We were at Cork Harbour Boatyard at 7:30 A.M., half an hour before the workers were due. Mark carefully went over what was to be done the first day with Finbar

O'Leary, a conversation that, at that stage of my experience with boatbuilding, had little meaning for me.

Mark picked up a thin, narrow strip of solid mahogany and handed it to me. "This is what we work with," he said. "We glue three layers of these over a framework mold, fixing them with staples while the glue dries. When we finish, we have a light, strong hull—a sort of plywood of our own manufacture."

"I thought boats were built of lumber nailed to permanent frames," I said.

"That's an older technique. It produces a strong, but very heavy boat. What we're after is something light and fast, but still stiff enough to take a bashing. We'll build the hull upside-down, then turn it when it's finished."

My contribution to the morning's work was mostly to hand tools to other men while the yacht's construction began. We worked in teams of "a man and a boy," an experienced craftsman and an apprentice. I served as "boy" to Mark; the O'Donnell twins were supported by two young fellows barely out of school, and Finbar was helped by his nineteen-year-old son, Harry. By the time we stopped for lunch, everyone seemed to be working smoothly together with some occasional good-natured banter, into which only the sullen Denny O'Donnell did not enter. His twin, Donal, was much more pleasant and seemed to accept me as one of the crew before any of the others did so.

At noon, I walked outside into the pale sunshine and sat down on a huge mahogany log that rested near the big, old-fashioned ripsaw, and dug into a paper bag for the lunch Annie had made for me. A moment later Donal O'Donnell strolled out and sat down near me on the log.

"Got any salt?" he asked. He grinned at me in a friendly manner.

I looked into my bag. "Sorry, I guess Annie salted my sandwiches."

"Annie? I thought your girl's name was Connie."

I laughed. "Annie is Mark's wife. I share the cottage at Drake's Pool with them."

He nodded. "Ah, yes, Mrs. Pemberton-Robinson. I forgot. How'd you get hooked up with them?"

I told him the story. "Mmmm. You've not known them long, then."

"No, but I've spent so much time with them I feel as though I'd known them always."

"I hear you've been disrupting the salmon-fishing fleet, too."

"Jesus, nobody misses much around here, do they? Well, anyway, I hear they were fishing illegally."

"Ah, well, the law gets winked at now and again."

"Say, your brother's a bit quiet, isn't he?" I asked. "I mean, he never seems to talk much to anybody but you."

"He's like that," Donal agreed. "He's a good lad. Not much for the chat, though. Denny says I chat enough for the two of us."

"It's the only way I can tell the two of you apart."

Donal laughed and unbuttoned the top button of his shirt, exposing a hairless chest. "Here's a surer way." There was a crudely tattooed heart on his chest, containing the initials M. M.

"Who's M. M.?"

He sighed. "Ah, just an old girlfriend. Long gone, now. I should have left the space open until the time I've nailed down one properly."

"Win some, lose some."

He laughed. "Too right. What do you think of the boatbuilding trade?"

"Not like building anything else."

"You'll get the hang of it. You seem to know your way with the tools."

I was a little uncomfortable with my next question. "Ah, Donal, what's going on with Denny? I've never so much as spoken with him, and he seems to hate my guts."

Donal seemed embarrassed, and I was sorry my American bluntness had got the best of me. "Ah, you mustn't pay too much attention to Denny. I think it's mostly that he never got anywhere with Concepta Lydon, and it seems that you have." I wondered if he knew exactly how far I had got. "And he's not much on Brits, either," he said, nodding toward Mark, who was standing at the door to the shed, talking with Harry O'Leary.

"Is it Brits in general, or Mark in particular?"

"Ah, nothing to worry about," Donal replied, stretching out and resting his head on the log. He closed his eyes. "Catch a few winks before we go back." And he was almost immediately asleep. I looked across the yard at Denny O'Donnell, who was sullenly eating his lunch. This time he was staring at Mark instead of at me. I should have been relieved to have his attention focused elsewhere, but I wasn't.

We arrived at the cottage at dusk, tired and dirty from our first day's boatbuilding. Mark had lingered over the plans with Finbar while I swept up and put away tools, and it was nearly eight by the time we got home. Annie was sitting by an unlit fire, flipping impatiently through a magazine.

"Home at last," she said. Mark seemed too tired to notice the edge in her voice. He headed straight for the sideboard where the liquor was kept.

"Where's the gin?" he asked, rummaging through half a dozen bottles.

"We're out of gin," Annie replied, tossing aside her magazine. "Do you think you might clean yourself up before you sprawl about?"

Foiled in his search for gin, Mark was pouring two drinks from a bottle of whisky. He handed one to me. "In a minute, luv." He tossed off half his drink. "Ah, that hits the right places. We've had a helluva long day." He looked up at Annie, who had stood up. "You want one?"

Annie stood, glaring at him, saying nothing. I held the scotch in my grimy hand and looked dumbly back and forth between them. Mark did not seem to understand that she was very annoyed. I had thought our sail down the coast might have put her in a better mood of late, but that didn't seem to be the case. Without another word she walked into the bedroom and slammed the door. I looked at Mark. He shrugged. "What I need is a hot bath," he said, striding toward the bathroom. I heard the water running. He came back, stripping off his shirt. Annie came out of the bedroom carrying a canvas duffel and a garment bag; she must have had it already packed.

"So where are you off to?" Mark inquired mildly.

"I haven't decided," she said, scooping up the keys to the van from the dining table. "And don't be bothering Mother with phone calls. I'll leave the van at the airport and the keys under the seat." She walked out the front door, leaving it open. A moment later we heard the van start up and drive away. I stared at Mark, speechless. The whole scene had taken place with no acknowledgment of my presence.

Mark walked to the door and closed it, then saw my face. He shook his head. "Christ, I don't know. She'll go along for weeks or months as happy as a clam, then something just snaps."

"Well, she has been feeling sort of left out, I think. She'd said something to me; I should have told you. Then, we were pretty late, I guess, and neither of us is exactly dressed for dinner," I said, indicating my filthy jeans.

"Oh, it's usually something niggling," Mark said, pouring us both another drink. "She'll go to her mother's for a few days, then she'll turn up as if nothing had happened." He handed me a drink, not noticing that I was already holding one. "Don't ever let anyone tell you that women are just people, Willie," he said, tossing off the scotch. "They're a breed apart, believe me."

We ate a cold and unsatisfying supper from what we could find in the fridge, had a bottle of wine with it and finished the evening quite drunk. I washed the dishes and joined Mark in front of the fire. He was staring blankly into the flames. It seemed a good moment to bring up what had been troubling me.

"Mark?"

"Mmmm?" He continued to stare into the fire.

"When you were in Belfast . . . when . . . when you were wounded . . . did you recognize the boy you shot? I mean, did you know him before?"

"Yes," he said absently. "He'd been picked up before. He . . ." Mark turned and looked at me for the first time. "That's an odd question," he said. "Why do you ask that?"

I ignored his question. "Did you recognize him before you shot him?" I realized this was important to me.

"Willie . . ."

"Just tell me that, Mark. This may be none of my business, but I want to know. Did you recognize him when he came into the pub?"

Mark stared at me intently before speaking. "I didn't

see him come into the pub, not really. I was aware of the door opening, because it was cold outside, and I felt the draft. The shooting started immediately, and I went over the bar without stopping to look around. I wouldn't be here now if I had looked around."

I held his gaze. "When you came up and started shooting did you recognize him then?"

"I fired toward the door. They were running; their backs were to me; he was already outside when I hit him. The others piled into a car and were gone. They left him dead on the pavement. I didn't see his face until they were bundling me into the ambulance." He turned and looked back into the fire. "They put him in with me. I wanted to see what one of the bastards looked like up close, so I pulled down the blanket. It was this kid . . . I had got hold of him once when a bunch of these young lads were throwing paving stones at my patrol. He cried like a baby, and I sent him home to his mother."

"You never arrested him?"

"No, but I saw him throwing bottles from a rooftop at my troops a couple of weeks after I had sent him home. I'd have arrested him if we'd caught him. He hadn't learned much from his first experience with us, except how not to get caught." Mark turned and looked at me again. "What's this all about, Willie?"

"You're sure that's exactly the way it all happened."

"I asked you what this was all about."

"There's apparently a rumor going around some of the locals that you knew the boy, that you had arrested him a couple of times and, well . . . they're saying that he was tortured in your barracks . . ."

"Oh, Jesus, we never tortured anybody, not my unit, anyway. Mind you, we weren't always gentle with them."

"I get the impression it's thought that you were involved and just waiting for a chance to kill him."

He looked at me incredulously. "Where did you hear about this?"

"Connie picked it up somewhere . . . you know how things travel around here . . . she won't tell me where she heard it. Was it in the papers at the time?"

"Oh, hell yes, in Belfast and in London, too. I suppose it might have made the Dublin and Cork papers, but it couldn't have been much of a story. There was a lot going on in Belfast at the time, something almost every day. It's been nearly two years, anyway. Who'd remember now?"

I shook my head. "Beats me."

He turned back to the fire. It was the first time I had ever seen Mark look worried about anything at all. "Well," he said, "somebody remembers. Somebody surely does."

Fourteen

SHE DROVE TO THE LITTLE COUNTRY CHURCH AND LOOKED carefully about. No other car was in sight; she wondered if he were here yet. Perhaps. She walked quickly into the building, her heels echoing from the stone floor. She stepped into the confessional and sat down. Immediately, the panel slid back.

"Yes, my child?"

"Father, I have sinned."

"What is the nature of your sin, my child?"

"I am too much a patriot."

"All right, we don't have long."

"Bishop?" She could not see him through the screen.

"Yes. Why did you want this meeting?"

"Robinson is the man; there is no doubt."

"What do you propose to do about it?"

"Excommunicate him."

He said nothing.

"He *is* one and the same."

"You may not kill him."

"And why not?" She was angry.

"I am going to answer your question, because you are new enough at this, perhaps, not to understand that you must follow instructions as they are given. First, killing Robinson now would not accomplish any political purpose. Second, we do not wish to bring attention to ourselves in County Cork. Robinson is simply too close to home, at least for the moment. Third, we cannot risk harming the Lee boy in going after Robinson. To kill or even hurt the son of a prominent American politician could cause many difficulties for us in raising funds over there. Does that answer your question?"

She was quiet for a moment. "Yes," she said, at last.

"Good. Never again question an order of your bishop. Do you understand?"

"Yes, but I cannot exercise your authority over the others. They don't know you, and I cannot invoke your name to control them."

"You most certainly may not do that. You will just have to deal with them as best you can. Is there anything else?"

"Yes, it is definitely established that Derek Thrasher is the source of Robinson's funds."

There was a thoughtful pause. "That is very interesting."

"Doesn't that give us a political basis for doing Robinson?"

"Perhaps, but not while he is in County Cork. Plans are in progress to deal with Thrasher, so don't concern yourself about that. If we find ourselves in a position to deal profitably with Robinson outside the diocese, then I may reconsider."

She looked at her watch. "I must get back to the school. I have a class in ten minutes."

"From now on, communicate with me by telephone." He gave her a number and made her repeat it. "It's ex-directory and concealed in my office. Never let it ring more than twice; if I'm in, I'll answer it immediately. Always call from an automatic coin box, never the same one twice. Hang up if anyone answers but me. Understood?"

"Yes."

"Good day, then. Go and sin no more."

Fifteen

I VISITED MY GRANDFATHER, SOMETHING I HAD PUT OFF FOR no good reason, and found a letter from my mother waiting for me. I had written them from Plymouth.

"Your father and I are both pleased that you have found some focus for your year abroad. We think you are very fortunate to have met these obviously charming people who have offered you an opportunity to learn something entirely new and to have a bit of adventure, as well.

"Billy has business in England, so we are coming to London on the fifteenth and will be at the Connaught for three days. We hope you can come to London and spend a day or two with us. We've booked you a room on the off-chance."

My mother does not take chances. A round-trip ticket from Cork to London was enclosed.

I wanted to go but hesitated to ask Mark for time off so soon.

As it turned out, the decision made itself. A couple of days later we arrived at the boatyard for work to find Finbar O'Leary looking annoyed and apologetic, in addition to his usual astonishment.

"They've gone, Captain," he said dourly, as if we knew perfectly well what he was talking about.

"Who's gone, Finbar?" Mark asked, reasonably.

"Not who. What. Those stainless fittings of yours. The special ones."

Mark walked past Finbar into his office. "I saw them here yesterday right behind the door. A small, cardboard box."

"I know the box," Finbar said. "It's gone, and the fittings with it."

"It must be here somewhere. Maybe somebody moved it."

"I've been through the whole place," Finbar said. "Somebody moved it right out."

The fittings were ones that Mark had designed himself and had had fabricated in England. They were essential to the early stages of construction of the yacht, having something to do with the keel area, I wasn't sure just what. We conducted a new search. They were not to be found. Mark did not fret but began to plan.

"How long can we work around this problem before it delays building, Finbar?"

Finbar looked at the upside-down, half-complete mold onto which the yacht's hull would be shaped and scratched his head. "Six working days," he said, with finality. "After that we're stuck without them—I shouldn't think you'd want to improvise something that important."

"Not bloody likely." Mark went into Finbar's office and placed a call to Southampton. Half an hour later he came out and called me aside. "Willie, they can fabricate a new set and put them on the train to London on the seventeenth. If we ship them here, even by air, they could be hung up in customs for days. Will you go over there and bring them back?"

I told Mark of my parents' impending visit.

"Ideal! I'll have them sent directly to the hotel. We'll get you a flight booked, and I'll give you cash to pay the duty."

"They've sent me a ticket. It's all arranged. I hadn't mentioned it to you because I wasn't sure if I'd be needed."

"My lad, on this occasion you'll be needed more in London than here. Something else. I'll get a progress report written up for Derek Thrasher, and you can drop it off at his office."

"Mark . . . would those fittings have any value for a thief?"

He shook his head. "Not unless he was building a sixty-foot yacht."

"Is anything else missing?"

"Nothing. You're obviously thinking the same thing I am."

"Maybe something to do with Belfast?"

"That's pretty farfetched. I doubt it's connected."

"Something personal, then? Are we making any enemies?"

"That would be news to me. Listen, just because that gear would be useless to a thief doesn't mean the thief knows it. I think it's just idle pilferage, maybe one of the apprentices. Let's not attach any great significance to this. Finbar'll let it be known among the lads he's displeased. If we lock up gear that might be lifted, I doubt if we'll have any further problems."

"I hope you're right."

Mark picked up his tool belt and started for the mold. "I hope so, too," he said.

On the morning of the fifteenth I drove to Cork airport. Shortly after I passed through the gates of the estate I noticed a car coming toward me on the road. I would have paid it no attention, except that there appeared to be a woman in the backseat, being driven by a chauffeur, and I had never seen a chauffeur-driven car in Ireland. Then, when my car was briefly abreast of the other I glanced sideways, but there was no one in the backseat. I came around a corner at my usual high speed and found myself almost on top of a cow standing in the road, grazing contentedly. I whipped the wheel to the right, barely missing the animal, ran halfway up a grassy embankment, whipped back to the left and met the road sideways in a spray of gravel before I was able to power out of the skid. In Ireland, if you hit a cow in the road, it is your fault and not that of the farmer who allowed it to stray. For this reason, the grass alongside the roads is referred to as "the long pasture." I drove the rest of the way to the airport trembling, thinking of what might have happened to my tiny car if it had come to rest against a large, bovine obstruction. I imagined myself being removed from the flattened wreckage with a huge can opener. My fear and relief drove the chauffeured car from my mind.

Two hours later I checked into the Connaught Hotel and was surprised to be recognized by the desk clerk. I had forgotten the resemblance to my father. There was a note: they had arrived on an early morning flight and gone straight to bed, not expecting to wake until early afternoon. I was to ring them at three to discuss plans for dinner. I went to my room and unpacked my clothes and the thick envelope that Mark had prepared for Derek Thrasher. I found the card he had given me in Cowes. I asked the hotel operator to ring the number. A silky female voice answered on the first ring, repeating the number.

"Is this Mr. Thrasher's office?" I asked.

"May I have your name, please?" the woman replied, politely but noncommittally.

"My name is Will Lee; I'm trying to reach the office of Derek Thrasher. Do I have the correct number?"

"May I ask the nature of your business, please?"

"I just called to get the address of Mr. Thrasher's office. I want to drop a package by, and he gave me his number but not his address."

"Just one moment, please."

"I don't need to speak to Mr. Thrasher . . ." But she had put me on hold. Almost immediately I heard Derek Thrasher's voice on the line.

"Will! My dear fellow, what brings you to London?"

"Oh, hello, I didn't mean to disturb you. I've come over to meet my parents for a couple of days and to pick up some gear for the yacht, and Mark asked me to drop off a progress report he's prepared."

"Wonderful! Come for lunch. I've just come back from a trip abroad, and I'm having a few people in. You might find some of them interesting. Where are you?"

"We're at the Connaught."

"You're just around the corner." He gave me an address in Berkeley Square. "Half an hour, then?"

"You're sure I won't be intruding . . ."

"Not a bit of it. See you soon." He hung up.

I was hungry and glad for the diversion. I changed and walked down Mount Street into Berkeley Square and found the address. It was a small, elegant building that had surely once been a private house; it certainly did not look like an office building, but all the houses in Berkeley Square had given in to commerce. Before I could open the door, a uniformed commissionaire opened it for me.

"Mr. Lee, is it? Please take the lift to the top floor. Mr. Thrasher is expecting you." He opened the door for me. I pushed the highest of the three, unmarked buttons. Nothing happened. Through a glass panel in the elevator door I saw the commissionaire step to his desk and reach under the top. The elevator began to move. A moment later the door opened, and I stepped directly into a large, sunlit room that was very much out of character with the period façade of the building. A collection of handsome steel and leather furniture was artfully scattered over a thick, wool carpet. The walls were nearly obscured by pictures, large and small. One looked very much like a Picasso; another, like a Van Gogh. Beyond a wall of sliding glass doors opening onto a terrace, Derek Thrasher detached himself from a group of people and strode into the room toward me. He was more formally dressed than when I had seen him in Cowes, wearing a perfectly tailored, three-piece gray suit and a sober necktie.

"Will, how very good to see you!" He shook my hand warmly and drew me into the room. "This is where I get most of my work done. Let me show you around before we join the others." He led me about the room, commenting on this picture and that sculpture. I was jarred to learn that the Picasso and the Van Gogh were not reproductions. Neither was anything else. I began to reassess my notion of how wealthy Thrasher was. I had pictured him as merely a highly paid chief executive of a large company. I had met lots of those, friends and clients of my father in Atlanta, but this man owned an art collection the value of which probably exceeded the total net worth of any three of them. The fathers of some of my college friends were rumored to have fortunes ranging into tens of millions, but when I visited their homes I found they lived sedately, if elegantly, not very differently from the way we lived on our admittedly large farm. I began to see how small a commitment Mark's project was for Derek Thrasher. He did not take it lightly, though. He quickly read through the report I had brought him, nodding and making affirmative noises.

"Good, good, you're ahead of schedule. I like that."

"Excuse me," I said, trying to get my bearings, "is this your home or your office?"

"Both," he replied. "I work on this floor and live in the rest of the house." He indicated a door in the wall opposite the elevator. "That opens into the office building next door; most of my London people occupy that; there are others scattered about Britain and Europe; I keep offices in the Far East, as well. Incidentally, it's not widely known that I live and work in this house; I'd be grateful if you would keep that fact in confidence."

"Of course." He led me onto the terrace and introduced me to the dozen or fifteen people gathered there, going slowly and usually commenting on their work or activities. It often was not necessary, as I knew half of them by sight. There were the male and female leads of a major film about to go into production in London—I had read in the morning paper on the plane that they despised each other and did not even speak off the set. They were holding hands. Two Members of Parliament were leaning against a bar and chatting amiably. One of them was a leader of the left wing of the Labour party; the other had been ousted from a previous Tory cabinet because of his radical, right-wing views. I began to get the feeling that Henry Kissinger could pick up a few pointers from Derek Thrasher.

There was a celebrity fashion photographer who had just published a wildly acclaimed book of photographs of pop singers and with him, a model whose name escaped me, but whose face was everywhere in magazines and newspapers and in gossip columns; there was an Arab called Nicky, wearing an English public-school tie and an accent to match; a couple of stockbroker types; and several other quite beautiful women, one or two as young as I.

Shortly we helped ourselves from a buffet and sat in twos and threes around the large terrace, eating and chatting, while the music of a string quartet wafted in from hidden speakers. I had quickly gravitated toward a striking girl with auburn hair and beautiful, long legs, who introduced herself as Jane. Thrasher moved from group to group and eventually came to us.

"Will, I would be very pleased if you and your parents would join me for dinner this evening. Do you think that would be possible?"

"I don't know. They came in on an early flight and may be too tired." I looked at my watch. "I'm to call them about now. I'll see how they feel."

"Please do. I have a table at nine in the Connaught Grill, so they won't have to stray from home."

He directed me to a telephone, and I rang my parents' room. My mother came on the line, sleepy. "Did I wake you? You asked me to call at three."

"Oh, yes, I'm glad you did. Your father has a business appointment at four, and I want to do some shopping. I suppose we'd better get moving."

"Mother, Derek Thrasher has asked us all to have dinner with him tonight. Do you think you'll feel up to it, or have you made other plans?"

"What?"

"I said, Derek Thrasher . . ."

"Derek Thrasher? Are you joking?"

"No, I'm at his house, now."

"Where on earth did you meet Derek Thrasher?"

"I wrote you about him; he's the one who's sponsoring Mark in the race."

"You never mentioned his name. Hold on . . ." She covered the receiver with her hand, but I could hear her talking excitedly to my father. She came back on. "We'd love to."

Thrasher approached with an inquiring look. I nodded. "Eight-thirty in the bar, if that's all right," he said. I passed the information on to my mother and said I would see them at that time. "Perhaps you'd like your new friend to join us?" Thrasher asked, nodding at Jane.

"Sure. That would be great."

He walked to where she was sitting and spoke briefly to her. She smiled. He turned and gave me a thumbs-up sign. It was after three before the luncheon began to wind down, and I had had a lot of wine. I went back to the Connaught and stretched out on my bed.

The phone jarred me awake at eight. "Will, how are you, boy?" My father sounded very much himself.

"Great, Dad."

"Why don't you meet us in the bar at quarter past, so we'll have time to catch up before Mr. Thrasher joins us?"

"Sure, I'll be down in fifteen minutes."

"Good, your mother is very excited about meeting Thrasher. I must admit I'm a bit curious myself. See you in a few minutes." He hung up.

I quickly shaved and changed from my blazer into my only suit and went downstairs. Both my parents looked wonderful, rested, and delighted to see me. We ordered drinks.

"Listen," I said to them, "what is all this excitement about meeting Derek Thrasher?"

My mother laughed. "Well, it should be very interesting to get a look at such a mysterious figure."

"Mysterious?"

"My word, Will, have you given up reading the papers for the last couple of months?"

"Well, I suppose I just about have. I read one on the plane this morning; first one in quite a while, I guess. They don't deliver to the door of the gamekeeper's cottage at Coolmore Castle, and we don't have a TV, either."

My mother exchanged an amused glance with my father, then turned back to me. "Well, before this summer nobody had ever heard of him—not in the United States, anyway; he was known in business circles over here, but suddenly, he's all over the papers."

My father picked up the conversation. "In early July he surfaced in New York in a takeover bid for Arabco, which is a small oil producer that half a dozen companies were after. He was edged out by one of the big conglomerates, but only just. What blew Wall Street's mind was a rumor that he was in the game with personal funds, which sounded just about impossible. Shortly after the takeover fight ended he bought a major Manhattan skyscraper—again, allegedly with nothing but his own money. Nobody in the business press could figure out how he could have made so much money without being known in the Wall Street community. There were rumors of Arab oil connections, and then, only a couple of days ago, there was a report in the *New York Times* that he had had a meeting with Howard Hughes in the Bahamas."

"I thought *nobody* ever met with Howard Hughes."

"Exactly, that got not only the financial press, but the gossip columns going. There was a big rush to find out everything possible about him, and precious little turned up. There were some very poor old photographs of him from the mid-sixties, enjoying the swinging London night life, at a time when he was known here as simply a real estate speculator, and that was about it. There was a report in the New York papers that *Time* was doing a cover story on him, but couldn't find a photograph for the cover. First time that's ever happened. The story they did was just a rehash of rumors. Apart from not knowing what he looks like, they couldn't even find out how old he is, though the rumor was that he was about forty. Nobody even knows where he lives."

"Well," I said, "I guess he's about forty, and he lives about three hundred yards from where we're sitting right now—just down in Berkeley Square." As I wondered whether telling my parents that secret was betraying Thrasher's confidence, two rather hard-looking men walked into the bar, looked carefully around, then left. I looked at my watch. "As for what he looks like, you should know shortly. It's just eight-thirty."

Thrasher entered the room as if on cue, accompanied by two beautiful women, one, my date, Jane, the other, a woman I had never seen but recognized easily. She was French, the widow of a man named Winston Wheatley, a British cabinet minister who had died about six months previously, when a bomb, said to have been planted in his car by the IRA, went off as he was driving out of the House of Commons car park. She had made an angry statement to the press shortly thereafter and had instantly been transformed by the newspapers into the sort of national heroine that Jacqueline Kennedy had become after the death of her husband. She had gone into seclusion, and I wondered if this was her first appearance in public since being widowed.

I stood and shook Thrasher's outstretched hand. "Mr. Thrasher, these are my parents, Billy and Patricia Lee."

"Governor and Mrs. Lee, I am so very happy to meet you both," he said. "May I present Lady Jane Berkeley and Genevieve Wheatley." As we sat down and ordered our drinks I noticed that every eye in the room was on our table—not on Thrasher, who seemed to be preserving his anonymity very nicely, but on Mrs. Wheatley.

I leaned toward Jane and whispered, "You didn't tell me it was 'Lady' Jane."

"I'm sorry," she laughed, "I thought you knew. My father is the Duke of Kensington. Our family name is Berkeley."

"Oh," I said. The Duke of Kensington was a cousin of the Queen and owned the Berkeley Estate, a substantial chunk of central London. He was said to be the largest property holder in Britain, after the Duke of Westminster with his Grosvenor Estate.

She laughed again. "I think I'm rather glad you didn't know."

Sixteen

WE WERE MET IN THE CONNAUGHT GRILL WITH WHAT I thought might be more than the usual deference and seated at a large, round table in as discreet a corner as could be managed in such a small room. There were place cards; Thrasher was very organized in even small things.

"I've taken the liberty of ordering for all of us," he said, sliding a chair under my mother. "I hope you don't mind." No one minded. He had also ordered champagne with which to begin our meal. I was soon flying, surprising myself with how impressed I was with Jane Berkeley's family credentials. I was unaccustomed to girls of such dazzling station, of such great beauty. I had a brief fantasy of having married into one of England's wealthiest families; of this being my dinner party instead of Thrasher's. Ireland and Connie Lydon seemed very far away. My mother was seated next to Thrasher and was apparently having fantasies of her own; I had never seen her so completely taken with anyone. Thrasher exuded charm without gushing it; he dominated the table effortlessly, attracting everyone to him, even my father, who, as a politician, was a professional skeptic. Genevieve Wheatley, who had been very quiet over her drink in the bar, became expansive, perhaps under the influence of the champagne, and talked quickly in heavily French-accented but syntactically perfect English. She seemed happy to talk about anything, like someone who had not had much conversation for a long time.

The round table brought us all close together, and my recollection is of a pastiche of conversation—some of it between two of us, some directed to everyone by everybody.

My father: "Mrs. Wheatley, I'm very sorry about your husband's death; I was an admirer of his, as was almost everyone."

"Not entirely everyone, Governor, or he would be dining with us tonight." This with a rather sad irony.

"Quite right. I am very happy you could be with us this evening after what I'm sure has been a difficult time."

"Oh, yes, I suppose, but perhaps no more so than that experienced by any widow. My seclusion was quite voluntary; I needed the time to discharge the bitterness. Some people do this by making themselves busy; others by withdrawing and thinking. I discovered that I belong to the latter group."

Derek Thrasher: "Governor, what brings you to London? Business?"

"Yes, an old friend going back to my war years here asked me to handle the purchase of some land in Georgia for him. The seller agreed to close here."

"Then I'm sure you've become acquainted with our rather unsympathetic exchange control regulations. Investment abroad is not easy these days."

"Fortunately, we were able to convince the Bank of England that the movement of capital was in their best interests."

"Were you, indeed? With such persuasiveness at your disposal, perhaps you should be representing me."

My father laughed. "Mr. Thrasher . . ."

"Derek, please."

"And I'm Billy. Derek, if half what I've read about you in the last few weeks is true, then you need no help at all in moving capital, certainly not that of a country lawyer."

Thrasher chuckled. "Country lawyer indeed! Yes, yes. Tell me, Billy, what are your political plans? Have you an eye on Senator Russell's seat? He's getting on a bit, isn't he?"

"Yes, he is, but if anyone can live forever, it's Dick Russell, and no one will take his seat as long as he wants it."

Lady Jane Berkeley: "Will, you seem to be doing exactly what you want to do. I admire that so. I want to see this boat you're building—Christ, I want to sail on it. Will you take me?"

"The boat won't be finished until next spring. Do I have to wait that long to see you in Ireland?"

"I'm leaving for Paris tomorrow. My father has arranged for me to spend a year in a merchant bank there. Why don't you come to Paris instead?"

"I don't know, why don't I?"

My mother: "Derek, did you really meet with Howard Hughes in Nassau?"

He laughed. "Everyone knows that Howard Hughes sees no one, Patricia. Tell me, if you could ask one question about Mr. Hughes and have it answered, what would you want to know?"

"Does he really have a long beard and long nails?"

"That's two questions."

"Long nails, then?"

"Yes. What will you be doing with your time in London?"

"A bit of shopping. We'll see some friends."

"I'd be very pleased if you'd let me send my car and driver for you."

"Oh, we couldn't put you to that bother."

"No bother at all; I'll be away, and your time here will be much more pleasant if you don't have to chase taxicabs in the rain."

"That's very kind of you. I hope we'll be able to repay your kindness in the States one day soon."

Thrasher smiled. "You never know. If I'm within hailing distance of Georgia, I shall certainly take you up on that."

We got through four courses and as many wines, and when we were on coffee, one of the men who had preceded Thrasher into the bar came and whispered something to him. Thrasher nodded, looked at his wristwatch, and said something back. During this brief exchange his smooth good looks took on a quality of weariness and age that surprised me but was quickly gone. When the party had wound down and we stood to go, Thrasher turned to Jane. "I'm sure you and Will are not ready to call it an evening. Why don't you take him to Annabel's?" She looked at me inquiringly.

"Sure," I said.

Thrasher shook hands with my parents and me. "I hope you'll forgive us if we part here. It might be better for all if Genevieve and I leave separately."

"Of course," my father said, clearly puzzled.

Thrasher took me briefly aside. "Will, I'm so very glad to have seen you and to have met your parents. Please tell Mark I'm very pleased with his progress, and I'll let him know where to send his next report and how to receive funds. I may be a bit difficult to reach for a while."

My parents, Jane and I walked into the corridor leading to the hotel lobby, and Derek Thrasher and Genevieve Wheatley walked toward the kitchen door. Jane and I said good night to my parents, and they boarded the elevator. As Jane and I left the Connaught, a bored-looking man holding a camera glanced at us, turned away, then quickly turned back and snapped a picture of us. We made off toward Berkeley Square.

"I see now why Derek left the other way," I said.

"Perhaps we should have, as well," Jane replied rue-fully. "I hope you don't mind having your picture in the papers."

"I've never had cause to give the problem any thought. I'm sure they'll crop me out, anyway. You're the one who must mind."

"Not really," she laughed, taking my arm. "I suppose I'm the family trend- and jet-setter. It's a dirty job, but somebody's got to do it."

We left Mount Street and walked along the west side of Berkeley Square. It was wet but not raining; the square was deserted, but there were a lot of cars parked where we were walking. "What's Annabel's?" I asked.

"This is Annabel's," Jane laughed, suddenly propel-ling me under an awning and down a flight of stairs. We were met inside by a man in a tuxedo who looked at me blankly, then recognized Jane.

"Good evening, Lady Jane," he said, smiling broadly. "It is very nice to have you with us."

"Thank you, Henry, this is Mr. Lee, of whom you'll see more, I'm sure."

"Good evening, sir," the man said smoothly.

Jane signed a book, and we proceeded into a com-fortable bar, filled with soft couches and interesting pic-tures. We got a brandy and settled down to let our huge dinner digest. "Derek likes you very much, you know," Jane said, sipping her drink.

"He's certainly been very nice to me and my parents."

"It's more than that," she said, pulling her knees up onto the sofa and facing me. "What you did in Cowes saved him from a very considerable embarrassment."

"Surely nobody could have seriously blamed him if his boat broke its mooring and scraped a bit of paint off the Royal Yacht."

"Not if he were an ordinary person, no. But he's not, and you must understand his relationship with the press in this country. They're dying to write about him, and there's nothing to write, because he's so clever at avoiding them. They would have leapt upon this opportunity; I can promise you the incident would have made the front page of at least three national newspapers. A combination of Derek Thrasher and Royalty would have been irresistible. Derek wouldn't have liked that. I think he secretly hopes for a knighthood one day, and a highly publicized incident of that sort would not have helped. So, you see, you've been very helpful to him, and he won't forget it."

"I think it's my father he's interested in, not me."

"No, you misunderstand him. Of course, he's aware that your father might become . . . very important in American politics; he's not a fool. But Derek doesn't choose friends for what they can do for him."

"Nonsense, every successful businessman chooses at least some of his friends that way. It's just part of doing business."

"If he were interested in your father for business or political reasons, he would see that someone else made the contact and became friendly with him. Your father would probably never even know of Derek's interest. Most of the business that Derek does is done through intermediaries. He says that his own success is primarily due to his ability to delegate authority. He is an extraordinary judge of people. He will hire someone, always after a thorough check, but often after only the briefest of personal meetings, and give him an absolutely staggering job to do—with complete authority to do it."

"Don't they botch it up now and then?"

"Almost never. It's as if they're in business for themselves. Your friend Mark is a good example, though a very small one by Thrasher standards. Do you think Derek judged him well?"

I nodded. "Absolutely. He will build Derek the best possible boat."

"And in so doing, achieve his own dream of doing this single-handed transatlantic race."

"Winning it, if I know Mark."

"No doubt. And Derek backed him after he'd been turned down by more than a dozen potential sponsors."

I looked at her curiously. "And how do you know so much about Derek's business methods?"

She laughed. "It's typical of Derek not to tell you anything about me. I've been his personal assistant for the past three years." She stood and took my hand. "Come on, let's dance." She towed me into another room, this one dark, lit only by a lamp on each table, and then on to a small dance floor. The music was too loud to talk over, so we gave ourselves to dancing.

Very early in the morning I was awakened, in the most pleasant possible way, by cool lips on my thigh. I lay as still as I could under the circumstances while the lips wandered, then settled in one place. Their work quickly successful, the rest of her took full advantage of me, then we lay, damp and panting in each other's arms while the room grew steadily lighter through cracks in the heavy curtains. I could see more of the room than I had the night before. It was attractively but impersonally decorated. She hadn't spent much time here, she said, as she had led me into the little mews house behind Berkeley Square.

She had led in more ways than one. If I had been somewhat smugly pleased with myself for so quickly and unaccustomedly seducing such a beautiful girl, it now occurred to me that I was, very probably, the seducee. It was certainly an interesting experience. I had had a pang or two about Connie; I had felt curiously unfaithful for someone who had made no commitments, but, in the circumstances . . .

"You have a very muscular body," she said, and I could feel much of it blush. "Englishmen are all so bloody reedy, except for the rugger players, and they're so bloody awful."

I snuck a glance at the clock on the bedside table.

"God, I'm having breakfast with my parents in half an hour," I said and struggled to get my feet on the floor. I still felt weak and light-headed from our lovemaking and its extended climax. I got up and began to locate items of clothing.

She laughed at me and got out of bed. I hadn't seen her naked the night before; we were in bed almost as soon as we were inside. She was slender; her breasts were small but very pretty, and her dark red hair nearly reached them. She found her purse and took a card and a pen from it, scrawling something on the card. "This is the office number in Paris. The number here is the printed one." She handed me the card. "Will you come and see me soon?"

"I'll find a way," I said, taking the card and putting my arms around her.

"I told you an awful lot last night, you know. The champagne, no doubt. I don't think Derek would mind."

"Don't worry. I won't be giving any interviews to *Time*."

I jogged the few hundred yards to the Connaught, startling the hall porter as I dashed into the lift. I had just time to shower, shave, and change, and to reach the dining room looking appropriately freshly scrubbed.

Seventeen

MY FATHER ALREADY HAD A TABLE IN THE HANDSOME dining room with its polished paneling. "Your mother is sleeping late," he said, offering me a menu. "I'm the one with the early appointment. Besides," he grinned, "we all drank a lot of wine last night. I wish I could sleep in. Try the kippers."

The thought of fish for breakfast did not appeal to me, but I took his suggestion. They were delicious. "They're Manx kippers," he said, "from the Isle of Man. No artificial coloring, no preservatives."

I had the feeling we were about to have a talk about something. They didn't come often, these talks; he was away a lot when I was growing up and busy when he was home, and they always made me uncomfortable. "What did you think of Derek Thrasher?" I asked. He seemed to be having trouble getting started.

"Interesting fellow."

"Just interesting? Do you think you might represent him in the States?"

He shook his head. "No."

"I think he might have been serious last night."

"I think so, too, but Mr. Thrasher might turn into very heavy baggage in a political campaign. He understands that. I think it's unlikely he'll approach me further with the idea."

"Is there any indication that he isn't an honest, upright businessman?" I was a little annoyed at the implied criticism of my new, independently found friend.

"Not really, but it's very difficult for any man to do business on the scale that he apparently does without cutting a lot of corners. Men like Thrasher buy politicians as a normal business expense."

"A politician can't be bought unless he's for sale."

"It's not the reality, but the perception. If I represented him, many people would quickly assume he was backing me financially. And if something went wrong for him, if he were only perceived to be dealing illegally or unethically—even in something I had nothing to do with—well, I'd hate to be in the position of proving I was innocent of involvement."

"I see your point. Does that mean that you don't want me to associate with him? Might that rub off on you?"

"It might, but you're old enough to decide who your friends are. He's a very discreet, even secretive person, so you're not likely to get your picture in the paper with him."

"I'm not so sure." I told him about the night before.

"I thought it might be something like that when he left through the kitchen. But you'll notice that he avoided the situation, and in any case, it was probably Mrs. Wheatley the photographer was onto. She was much more likely to be recognized than Thrasher. You and Lady Jane seem to be getting along well together."

I reddened. "I only met her yesterday."

"It seemed to me at dinner that you had made great strides in your relationship," he said drily. "You know who she is?"

I nodded. "I didn't until last night, though."

"Will you be seeing her again?"

"She's off to Paris for a year, leaving today, and that might be a good excuse for a trip to Paris. Her father is apparently getting her ready for the family business, and he has installed her in a bank over there to learn the ropes. She's been working for Derek for the past three years, it turns out. Been very close to him, learned a lot."

"Sounds like a bright young woman, as well as a pretty one. Just how close to Thrasher?"

"Personal assistant." Then I caught his meaning.

"He introduced the two of you?"

Now my ears were turning red. "Yes, at lunch yesterday."

"He arrange the dinner date?"

I didn't answer him.

"You mustn't take my cynicism too seriously."

"Then you shouldn't make it so obvious." I think that was the closest thing to a rebuke I had ever handed to my father.

He paused. "I just want to give you the benefit of some experience in these things."

"What things?"

"Men like Thrasher always want something. Their minds are so constantly engaged in gaining an advantage that I think it becomes impossible for them to have normal friendships the way other people do. They choose their friends, even their acquaintances, from among people they think will be of use to them."

"The way politicians do, you mean?"

He looked down at the tablecloth. "I suppose I had that coming." He paused again. "I catch myself doing that; I try not to do it, but yes, it's one of the liabilities of political life."

This admission caught me off guard. I had always thought of my father as being rather self-righteous, and it came as a surprise to me to find that he might recognize his own faults.

"Listen, Will, you must know by now that there are people who will want to know you because of me. Be careful. Use your common sense."

"I'll try."

"Jane is older than you, isn't she?"

"Maybe. Couple of years, I guess."

"That means the men she's accustomed to seeing are

probably a lot older than you. You should keep that in mind."

"Think I'm getting out of my depth with girls, too?" I would have been annoyed if I hadn't been wondering myself.

"I didn't say that. There's more to it, anyway." He paused and ate some kipper. I waited. "You've grown up an American and a democrat, with a small 'd' as well as a large one. There is a great deal more social mobility in the United States than there is in Britain; people are judged more on their accomplishments."

"It's all family here, then? I can't believe that. Not today."

"Oh, I'm sure a young man from an ordinary background can do very well here if he works hard and all that, but he will find it almost impossible to crack certain social barriers."

"You're talking about Jane's family. The aristocracy."

"Jane's family is more than aristocracy; they are near-royalty, at the very top of the aristocracy."

"And I'm just a country boy."

"You're an intelligent, well-educated, and quite charming country boy. To tell the truth, I was becoming worried that that was all you wanted to be. But since you've been over here something has changed, I'm not quite sure what."

I wasn't sure what, either. I didn't feel particularly changed, except that I felt, perhaps, more independent.

"Your mother was quite pleased with you last night, by the way."

I grinned. "I don't suppose she ever thought her son would introduce her to Derek Thrasher."

"Don't get too puffed up with your social connections, my lad. Remember, you didn't even know who Derek Thrasher was until she told you."

He was right, of course. "So what is it you're warning me about, that a country boy shouldn't aspire to a Lady Jane?"

"Aspire all you like, enjoy it, but don't let it become too important to you. Those people can cut you off at the knees between the soup and the fish. Don't want it too much, and you'll enjoy it more."

It was a good point, but I didn't want to think about it.

"What's happened with your Irish friend, Connie?"

"Oh, come on, Dad, I'm not exactly engaged to her, you know." I didn't want to think about that, either. "So what's your day going to be like?" I was ready for a change in subject.

"I'm not quite through, yet," my father replied, pinning me to my evasion. "I've always believed that we should bring you up as simply as possible, not let politics or too much spending money ruin you on the way up. Your mother is responsible for whatever social graces you left home with; I kept you in jeans and beat-up pickup trucks. I think both our efforts worked well. Now, I think

I'm moving more over to her point of view, because I think maybe you can handle it."

"Well, thanks," I said, not sure of his point.

"How's your money holding out?"

"Pretty well. I didn't travel far before I met Mark and Annie, and I'm getting my room and board and twenty quid a week. I bought the Mini-Cooper, but that's about all."

"I'm going to have an American Express card sent to you. Don't go crazy with it; it will make it possible for you to do the things you really want to do while you're over here." He pulled a Connaught envelope from his pocket and handed it to me. "There's some money and a list of good shops in there. Get yourself some new clothes. You're moving in more sophisticated circles, now."

"Dad, I really appreciate this." I really did, too. All this largesse was clearly not impulsive; my father was not an impulsive man. He had never been exactly stingy either, but he had always made sure I earned something along the way. Like most men of his generation, who had grown up during the Great Depression, he placed great importance on the handling of money. Giving me not just cash, but an open-ended credit card was, I knew, as strong an expression of approval as I had ever received from him. I would have to be careful with it. I knew he would go through the monthly bills to see how I was managing this privilege.

My mother suddenly appeared and sat down with us,

looking great in a caramel-colored suit that went beautifully with her auburn hair. "Morning, you two. Am I in
time for breakfast?"

"Not with us, you're not," my father said, rising and
kissing her. "I've got an appointment."

"Oh, drat."

"That's what you get for being lazy and sleeping late.
Why don't you two do something together?"

"Oh, yes, Will, let's do the Tate Gallery. You've never
seen the Turner collection, and we can have lunch there,
too."

"Sounds good to me."

As we left the Connaught and looked for a taxi, the
dark blue Mercedes drove up and parked. The driver
wasn't Blunt Instrument, but I knew that Derek Thrasher
had been as good as his word.

My mother and I did the Tate and had lunch, then
I spent the remainder of the afternoon shopping for
clothes and was back at the Connaught in time for tea
and a nap before dinner. We dined with my father's old
war buddy and client, Sir Somebodyorother, at the Mira-
belle and got to bed late.

Next morning, as I was packing my new clothes into
a new suitcase, I came across a loose sheet of paper in my
canvas sailing bag, my only other luggage. It was a list of
expenditures thus far on the building of the yacht; I reckoned it had come out of the packet I had given Thrasher.
I stuck it into a Connaught envelope, wrote Thrasher's
name on it, and put it in a pocket. Downstairs, the pack-

age containing the replacement fittings for the boat was waiting for me, right on time. I had a farewell breakfast with my parents, and the doorman got me a cab for the airport.

"Drive around into Berkeley Square," I said to the driver, "I want to drop something off."

"What number, Guv?"

"I'll point it out to you." We drove down into Berkeley Square. "Just up there," I said to the driver, pointing. He double-parked next to a blue van, and I opened the taxi door. The package of fittings was on my lap, and I took it with me; it was my reason for coming to London, after all, and I felt uncomfortable about leaving it in a taxi. I ran up the steps to Thrasher's door and opened it. The elderly commissionaire who had been there at the time of my visit two days before rose to meet me. His desk had been pulled squarely across the hallway.

"Yes, sir, may I help you?" he inquired—cautiously, I thought.

"I just want to leave something for Mr. Thrasher," I said, reaching into my inside pocket for the envelope.

He seemed to flinch and looked relieved when I produced only the envelope. "I'm sorry, sir," he said evenly. "There's no one here by that name."

I heard the heavy, wrought-iron and glass door open behind me. The commissionaire looked over my shoulder and shook his head. "It's all right," he said. I turned to find another man in a business suit standing in the open door. His coat was unbuttoned and his hand was inside, reaching up under his armpit. He was staring at the package in my hand. I turned back to the commissionaire.

"You remember me, I was here for lunch with Mr. Thrasher day before yesterday. My name is Lee."

He shook his head. "I'm sorry, sir, I can't help you."

"Look, I just want to leave this envelope for him. I gave him some other papers that day, and this got left out."

"I think you'd better leave, now, sir. Please." His tone was kindly but insistent. The man behind me pushed the door all the way open and stood holding it, leaving my way clear. I looked back and forth between them. The commissionaire's hand moved to the under edge of the desktop. "Please, sir. I can't help you."

I walked out, down the steps and to my waiting cab. "Heathrow," I said to the driver as I got in. "The terminal for flights to Ireland." As we drove away I looked back and saw the man in the business suit talking with yet another man, nodding in the direction of my departing taxi. I put the envelope back into my pocket, wondering if I had somehow offended Derek Thrasher, or if he just wasn't feeling sociable today.

Eighteen

IT BEGAN TO RAIN WHILE I WAS ON THE WAY TO HEATH-row. By the time I had reached the ticket counter, the weather was lousy outside and flights to Ireland were being delayed. The airline checked me in and accepted my luggage, but as I stood there it was flashed on the departures board that Cork Airport was closed. I could fly to Dublin and change planes, but that wouldn't get me there any sooner. They could give me no estimate of what time the weather might clear, but I decided to wait.

I read the *Times*. I bought a magazine and read it thoroughly. I had lunch and gazed out the steaming, streaked windows at a typically English autumn day, mist and fog. I bought another magazine. As I was turning away from the cashier's stand a man came and thumped down a stack of the *Evening Standard*. The headline stopped me in my tracks.

BERKELEY SQUARE BOMBING!!!

MIRACULOUS ESCAPE FROM IRA ASSASSINS!

Underneath was a large photograph of what had been a car and now was nothing more than a mangled hunk of metal. I snatched up the top copy and dug for a coin, reading all the while.

Death missed its mark in Berkeley Square this morning, but only just. Shortly after ten o'clock a car bomb went off outside the offices of a building company, breaking windows on virtually all of one side of the square and demolishing two other vehicles. Miraculously, a large removals van driving past took the brunt of the explosion, saving the lives of half a dozen pedestrians on the opposite sidewalk. Normally heavy foot traffic in the streets had been kept down by heavy rain, no doubt sparing many other lives. A retired sergeant-major, serving as commissionaire in an adjoining building, was treated briefly at St. George's Hospital for cuts from flying glass but then released. Minor injuries were reported in other buildings, but none required more than first aid. Police immediately sealed off the square, causing massive traffic tie-ups in most of the West End. More than two hours passed before the wreckage was cleared and traffic flow restored to Berkeley Square and adjoining streets.

At 10.18 A.M. a telephone call was received at the offices of the Evening Standard *from an organization calling itself the Irish Freedom Brigade and claiming responsibility for the blast. The caller, who spoke with an Irish accent, said the bombing was in protest against discriminatory hiring*

*practices of Thrasher Ltd., a company specializing in heavy
construction and currently engaged in three large projects
in Ulster. Mr. Derek Thrasher, owner of the company, was
said to be out of the country and unavailable for comment,
but a spokesman said that a threat had been received and
police called shortly before the explosion. Any discrimina-
tion against Catholic workers on the company's sites was
denied. No further comment would be made, the spokesman
said. (More photos inside).*

I flipped open the paper and found pictures of the
demolished moving van and a heavy door of twisted
wrought iron grillwork, its plate glass scattered about the
hallway inside. The desk where I had stood talking to
the commissionaire was overturned. I tried to remember what time I had been in Berkeley Square. About ten
o'clock, it must have been—only minutes before the explosion. I remembered the man at the door, his hand
under his coat and his eyes on the package in my hand.
He must have been a policeman or a security guard. As
well as escaping the explosion, I was probably lucky not
to have been shot.

I returned to my seat and sat down heavily. I felt shaky
and was sweating. I felt that I should do something, but
I didn't know what. I wanted to tell somebody what had
nearly happened to me, but I didn't know whom to tell.
I knew nothing, had seen nothing that would be useful
to the police; I didn't want to frighten my parents with
a story of what had almost happened. There was nothing I could do, nothing I should do. I sat back and tried

to relax, breathed deeply. A woman sitting next to me looked at me.

"Are you all right, young man?"

"Yes, ma'am, I'm fine," I replied, trying to look more normal.

The rest of the day passed as a bad joke about air travel. My plane finally took off at three in the afternoon, circled Cork airport for nearly an hour, waiting for a break in the fog, then was diverted to Shannon. The passengers were herded aboard a bus and driven through a steady downpour to Cork Airport. It was nearly dusk by the time I had retrieved my luggage and found the Mini-Cooper, and I was exhausted. I drove toward Coolmore Castle more slowly than usual, not wanting a high-speed encounter with another cow. I turned into the gates, drove past the castle in the dusk and turned down the single-track road that led to the cottage. I was looking forward to a hot bath and a drink.

As I drove along the rough road, a Volkswagen suddenly appeared from the woods a couple of hundred yards ahead of me, heading in the opposite direction. I was about to pull off the road to let it pass, when it stopped, then suddenly drove off the track into the adjacent pasture and roared, bouncing and rolling, across the field until it reached the road again, some distance behind me. There appeared to be four men in the car. I was too tired to wonder who they were or why they preferred driving across a pasture instead of down the road. They could have easily got past me without leaving the road had they tried. I parked in the clearing where we usually left the cars, got my luggage and walked the last few yards to the cottage.

The lights were out. Mark's van was not there, so he was probably still at the boatyard. As I approached the front door in the failing light I saw that it was ajar and the glass in the upper half of the door had been broken. I set down my bags and approached the door slowly, not sure of what to expect. The men in the car must have been burglars, I thought, though I had never heard of burglary in the neighborhood. I pushed the door open and peered into the semidarkness inside. Total disarray greeted me. Lamps and furniture were overturned, books were scattered about. The picture over the fireplace had been ripped away, and something was painted crudely where it had hung. I moved closer into the room to get a better look at it in the bad light, practically tiptoeing. I heard a loud click and a husky voice said, "Get out of here right now or I'll blow your bloody head off."

I jerked around and saw a dark figure standing in the kitchen door, pointing a large revolver at me. I froze in my tracks.

"Willie?" It was a female voice.

"Annie?" She lowered the pistol and ran toward me.

"Oh, Willie, I'm so glad to see you!" she said, throwing her arms around me, sobbing.

I took the gun from her and eased down the cocked hammer. "What happened?" I asked, holding her tightly. "What's going on?"

"I don't know," she sobbed, then continued, jerkily. "I was just getting out of the tub, when I heard . . . glass breaking . . . I got into my robe and was about to open the bathroom door when . . . I heard a gun go off and . . . voices . . . I locked the door and prayed they wouldn't find me . . . I heard them knocking things about and laughing . . . They sounded drunk . . . When they seemed to be gone I dashed to the bedroom and got some clothes on, then I heard you coming and got Mark's service revolver."

"Gunshots?"

She released her hold on me and turned on the ceiling light. In addition to the general disorder, a shotgun had been fired indiscriminately around the room, making big gouges in the plaster. With the light on I could read what had been sloppily painted over the fireplace.

BRITS OUT!!
PROVOS ORDER!

"Oh, shit," I said. Then I heard the door behind me creak open. I swung around, the pistol in my hand.

Mark stood in the doorway, looking at the room and me incredulously. "Stop pointing that pistol at me, Willie," he said calmly. I lowered the gun and wiped my damp brow. "Well," he said, "is anybody going to tell me what's happened?"

Annie repeated her story, while I searched through the rubble for a bottle that hadn't been broken. The room smelled like a distillery. I found an intact bottle of Jack Daniel's, my personal import, and got some glasses from the kitchen, which remained unscathed. The three of us sat down on the sofa with our neat bourbon. Nobody said anything for a moment. "Jesus, this is awful whiskey," Mark said absently.

Annie suddenly sat up straight. "We've got to call the police! Is the phone still working?"

Mark pulled her back onto the sofa. "We're not calling the police," he said wearily.

"And why not?" she asked. "You're not going to let them get away with this, are you?"

"She's right, Mark. The house has been wrecked and threats have been made."

"Now hang about a minute, both of you; just think about this; what's really happened here?"

"Well . . ." Annie began.

"I'll tell you what's happened. A couple of the local lads have heard rumors about Belfast; they've got a few pints down and played a prank."

"There were four of them, I think," I replied. "I saw them come out of the woods in an old Volkswagen, light green. When they saw me coming they cut across the pasture."

"A light green Volkswagen," Mark said. "You have any idea how many of those there are in the country? In the county? They assemble them in Dublin, you know, and half of them are light green."

"You think we should just go along as if nothing had

happened, then?" Annie asked, clearly amazed at his attitude.

"The Provos are not people we ought to be messing with, Mark," I said.

"What makes you think this was done by the Provisional IRA?"

"They were kind enough to sign their little note," I replied, waving my glass at the paint above the fireplace.

"Now listen to me, both of you. First of all, there is no Provisional IRA in Cork. Some republican organizations, sure, but all they do is drink Guinness and talk about the old days."

"What makes you so sure?" Annie asked.

"I thought something like this might happen; I've done some asking around. Finbar's an old republican, you know. He knows the lay of the land hereabouts."

"You think of this as just a practical joke?" I asked. "Those are gunshots in the walls, there. Suppose one of us had been here, what would have happened then?"

"One of us was here," Annie said tightly.

"If there had so much as been a light on, they'd never have come close," Mark said confidently. "And they used a shotgun, double-barreled, I'll bet."

"It sounded that way," Annie said, "as if they stopped to reload."

"Every Irish farmer has a shotgun. Now, if they'd sprayed the place with automatic weapons, I'd be worried, but this was nothing more than some overpatriotic drunks."

"Even if that's what they are, I still think we should have the police on them," Annie came back.

"Then we'd buy ourselves a pack of trouble," Mark said, his voice rising. "They'd never find out who it was, but it'd be in the papers, and Peter-Patrick Coolmore would want us out of here quick-time. The Belfast thing would get published again, probably hopelessly distorted, and then we might start having problems with local suppliers. Don't you see what could happen to the whole project if we overreact to this?" He was very worked up, now, angry, but not with the people who had done this—with us, who he perceived were about to endanger his project by going to the police.

Neither Annie nor I said anything.

"I agree with you about what the publicity could do to us," I said finally, trying to calm him. "Maybe you're right, maybe we shouldn't go to the police, but what if these guys are the real thing? Don't we have to consider that possibility?"

"Willie," Mark said, shaking his head, a bit calmer, now, "does the Ku Klux Klan still exist in your Georgia?"

"Yeah, they're still around. They still have rallies and burn crosses now and then."

"Do they ever *do* anything, though? Do they still lynch blacks?"

"No, it's all talk, they bluster and hand out leaflets, that's about it."

"Exactly. The IRA in the South of Ireland is just like your Klan—all talk. Oh, up in Galway and Tipperary you hear about some farmer who's been arrested for making bombs out of chemical fertilizer and shipping them to the North, but they don't go out on raids in the Republic."

"That's true, I guess."

"Yes, but what about these threats?" Annie asked, pointing at the message over the mantel.

"Look, the real Provos don't go around overturning lamps and making threats. They snipe and ambush and plant car bombs, and they don't give warning."

"Well, you're right about the car bombs, anyway; have you seen this?" I tossed them the *Evening Standard*. They read it in silence.

"Willie, have you ever told anybody that Thrasher was my sponsor?"

"No, you asked me not to." I reflected a moment. "Well, my folks know. We had dinner with him in London. And I told Connie." I looked at him sheepishly. "I'm sorry about that, Mark. I shouldn't have, but Connie's on our side; she know's that's confidential."

"It's all right, Willie; I don't think Connie would give that away. So there's no way for anybody to connect Thrasher with us or the yacht; one of his companies may be having Provo problems in the North, but the bomb in London and what happened here tonight aren't connected; it's purely coincidence."

"I think you're right about that," I said. "There's just no way that information could have got around. Derek, himself, is too secretive for it to have leaked from him, and we know everybody else who knows about it."

"So what's your plan?" Annie asked. "Business as usual?"

"Absolutely," Mark said, "but with some prudent precautions. You two see what you can do about straightening up here. I'll be right back." He got up and left the cottage. In a moment I heard the dinghy being dragged across the shingle at the river's edge outside our front door and oars splashing.

Annie and I began to right furniture and lamps. By the time Mark got back the place was looking surprisingly normal. Except for the shotgun gouges in the walls, the damage was superficial. I could patch the holes tomorrow. Mark came back into the cottage carrying something heavy wrapped in plastic sheeting. He set the package on the floor and unwrapped it.

"Good Lord, Mark!" Annie exclaimed. "Where did you get all that?"

In Mark's package were a short-barreled, pump shotgun and an American forty-five-caliber automatic. There was another, small gun I didn't recognize. "Call it liberated matériel; this is the sort of stuff we found in weapons caches during searches of houses in the Bogside in Belfast. I hung on to some of it, that's all."

"But where was it hidden?" I asked.

"Aboard *Toscana*. You don't want to know where."

"You mean we brought all that past customs when we sailed into Ireland?" I was aghast. "Do you know what they would have done to us if they'd caught us smuggling weapons into the country?"

"No problem, was there? And now I think we'll all sleep a lot better knowing it's here." He tossed me a shotgun and a box of double-nought shells. "That's an Ithaca riot gun," he said. "American. Loads in the ordinary way but holds twelve shells. You can sweep a street with it." I held the shotgun as if it were a reptile.

"What's that?" I asked, pointing at the smaller weapon, a blunt, ugly instrument that looked like some sort of overgrown, science-fiction pistol.

Mark picked up a thick, black tube and screwed it onto the barrel of the gun. "It's an Ingram machine pistol," he said. "Latest thing. Can't imagine how it got to Belfast." He slammed a long clip into the butt and got to his feet. "Come outside for a minute."

We walked to the front door together. Mark brought the weapon up, cocked it and suddenly fired it into the night. I flinched, expecting a loud roar, but there was only a muffled whumping sound. I could hear the bullets tearing into the brush on the opposite bank of the river.

"Silenced," Mark said. "Fires five hundred rounds of forty-five-caliber ammunition a minute. Serious weapon." He was grinning broadly, and his eyes were bright.

I didn't know whether to be more concerned about our "Provo" visitors or about Mark. It bothered me that, once he had convinced Annie and me not to call the police, he had seemed to enjoy the whole incident. I went to bed that night with the Ithaca riot gun under my bed, loaded, just at hand. I was very tired, but it took me a long time to get to sleep.

Nineteen

A T CORK HARBOUR BOATYARD THE NEXT MORNING, I found that the hull of the yacht had come along nicely during my absence and was ready to accept the new stainless steel fittings I had brought back from London, but nothing else had changed. Finbar still worried over each minute operation; his son, Harry, still did fine work while watching his father's every move; and Donal O'Donnell was cheerful and friendly, while his twin, Denny, hardly spoke.

"Morning, Willie," Donal chirped as we gathered our tools and approached the hull. "How was merrie old London?"

"Not bad"—I grinned back at him—"not bad at all." And I turned to see what Finbar had in mind for me for the day. Then I stopped in my tracks and willed myself not to turn and stare, instead, remembering what I had seen. A few moments later I allowed myself a quick look and confirmed my memory. The O'Donnell who had spoken so pleasantly to me was wearing a half-buttoned work shirt which exposed an untattooed chest; he was Denny, not Donal.

Denny's astonishing good cheer persisted through the morning and at lunch. Donal, who often brought his lunch over and sat with me, kept away, lunching with his twin on the quay of the boatyard. I could see Denny jabbering away as they ate, and Donal looking depressed, even angry. I could think of nothing that would make Denny O'Donnell this happy except trouble for me; he seemed a prime suspect for the events of the previous evening.

When I had finished my sandwich I got up and strolled around to the side of the shed nearest the road, where all the cars were parked. There was no Volks among them. Denny and Donal, I knew, drove a newish Ford Escort. I spent the afternoon's work trying to think of some way I might associate the O'Donnell twins with the ransacking of the cottage. I got nowhere. All I had to go on was the sight of the light green Volkswagen at some distance, containing four men who had been nothing more than shapes in the dusk. I had not seen the number plates.

At the day's end I left Mark conferring with Finbar, as usual, and got into the Mini-Cooper. I had a grocery list to fill for Annie, and I turned in the opposite direction from my usual route, toward the Cork suburb of Douglas and its supermarket. I had been on the road for less than a minute when I glanced into the rearview mirror and did a double take. A light green Volkswagen was driving forty or fifty yards behind me, keeping pace. Another glance revealed four passengers. The Volks seemed suddenly to speed up, closing the distance between us.

I kept looking into the mirror, my heart pounding, trying to get a look at the occupants of the front seats, then I realized that I didn't really want to be that close to them. I accelerated. The car kept pace. There were some miles of country road before the village, fairly deserted road. The car began to close on me again, and I pressed the accelerator further. I was doing seventy by now, with images running through my mind of the car overtaking me and a shotgun protruding from the window; then I saw a sight that would ordinarily have given me a jolt at this speed, but that now looked very inviting indeed. A car marked *Gardai,* Irish for police, was parked alongside the road. I quickly slowed and pulled over a few yards from the two policemen. My impulse was to run to them, pour out my story, and shout something like "Follow that car!" But Mark didn't want the police in this. Instead, I got out a roadmap and pored over it for a few seconds, while the Volks drove past, cutting its speed because of the police. I caught a glimpse of the front-seat passenger, a large man with red hair and a beard. He seemed familiar, but I couldn't place him.

After a moment I pulled back onto the road and continued at a moderate speed until the *Gardai* were out of sight behind me, then jammed the accelerator to the floor. We were on the outskirts of Douglas, now, and I wanted to find out where the Volks and its passengers were heading. Soon, the car appeared ahead of me, slowing for a four-way stop sign. I pulled up behind it but could see little of the passengers through the small rear window. Then something happened that made me feel very foolish. As I stopped, two other cars drove up to the intersection from other directions. Both were light green Volkswagens.

Mark had been right. The country was full of them, and here I was, overreacting to the sight of just one. The odds against three nearly identical cars approaching the intersection at the same time were probably high, but certainly lower than for any other sort of car. The Volks ahead of me turned right toward Cork. I glanced at the number plate, and after a moment I turned left, toward the supermarket. Part of the plate's number stuck in my mind; the letters OOP. The three following numbers I forgot.

I was relieved to see lights in the cottage on my return. The place looked warm and inviting. Mark was not home yet, and Annie gave me a hand with the bags and boxes. We stood in the kitchen, unpacking and stowing my purchases.

"Annie, I'm a little worried about Mark."

"How so?"

"I can't get the picture out of my mind of him standing there last night, firing that machine gun. He looked . . . well, a little crazy. Do you think there's a chance that he might really use that thing on somebody?"

She laughed. "Well, you're right about one thing; Mark is a little crazy. Anybody who'd live the life he has, who'd be doing what he's doing now, would have to be a little crazy. It's one of the things I love about him."

"What about the machine gun, the Ingram?"

"I'm not worried about that because I agree with Mark's assessment of the situation. I think what we have here is the Irish equivalent of a few of your American rednecks, just like the ones you see at the cinema. People like that are cowards. They'd never even have come to the cottage if they'd thought anybody was here. That's why they didn't search the place and find me, cowering in the bathroom. They were in a big hurry to leave their little mark and get out."

"So you don't think we'll have to shoot it out with them."

She laughed again. I loved the way she laughed. "Oh, no. But there's something else you have to remember about Mark. He's had a lot of training in how to deal with violence. Part of an officer's responsibility is to choose the appropriate degree of response to violence. If Mark ever decided to use that machine gun, you can be sure the circumstances would warrant it. He's too proud of his competence to let himself go off half-cocked or to overreact to a situation."

That made sense, and I felt comforted. "Buy you a drink?"

"A small scotch would be lovely."

We took our drinks into the sitting room, and I lit

a fire. We sat on the floor, leaning against the sofa, and gazed into the flames as they grew and spread through the kindling to the oak logs. "Where'd you go?" I asked.

"Oh, out and about. I popped in on Mummy for a bit."

"Pity I didn't know you were in London; you could have met my folks. Still, I must have been among the last people you would have wanted to see. I knew you were feeling down, and I'm afraid I wasn't much help."

She put a hand on my knee and squeezed it. "Oh, no, no, Willie; there was nothing for you to do. It's just . . ." She hesitated for a long time; I had the impression she was deciding whether to tell me the truth. "I was just a bit fed up, stuck out here all the time. I'm not accustomed to having so little to do. The yacht is Mark's project—yours and his. I had nothing of my own, and I was feeling a bit useless and cooped up."

"Useless? You? Don't you believe it. I wouldn't even be here if it weren't for you."

She looked at me, surprised. "Why, Willie, that's the nicest thing you've ever said to me." She reached over to kiss me on the cheek as I turned toward her, and the kiss landed on the corner of my mouth. It was a fuller, wetter kiss than a peck on the cheek might have been. "I'm going to have to watch myself around you."

"You'd better," I said back, smiling at her, "or I'll get you."

"Promises, promises," she said. We both jumped at the sound of a car door slamming outside. "There's

Mark," she said, getting up. "He'll want a drink." She paused. "Willie?"

"Yes?"

"How long has it been since you've seen Connie?"

"A week or so. Not since before London."

She leaned over and scratched the back of my neck with her long nails. "Maybe you'd better give her a call."

Twenty

O N SATURDAY I DROVE TO KINSALE AND HAD LUNCH with my grandfather. He was a bit miffed that my mother and father had not visited him on their trip but mollified that they planned to be in Ireland at Christmas, something I suspected my mother had planned as a surprise, for she had not mentioned it to me.

After lunch I drove to Summercove. I hadn't seen Connie since London. The memory of my night with Jane Berkeley lingered on, her glamor and aggressive sexuality making my relationship with Connie seem rather pale. Connie's car was at the cottage, as was a van. I was annoyed that she had visitors; I wanted her alone. I could hear a lot of girlish giggling through the door as I knocked, and Connie answered with a Guinness in her hand. For a moment I thought I had surprised her with another fellow, but as the door swung open I saw the nun I had met a while back, slouched in a chair, looking very un-nunlike, somehow.

"Ah, Willie, me boy!" Connie cried, planting a large, wet kiss on me. I found myself blushing. I had never kissed a girl in front of a nun before.

"Sister Mary Margaret, how are you?" I asked, disengaging myself from Connie.

"Ah, she's Maeve, still, in my house," Connie giggled, before the nun could answer.

"I'm very well, Willie," she said, laughing at Connie.

I still didn't know what to call her. I had almost never been around a nun at all and hardly thought of them as women. They were simply faces protruding from a lot of black clothing. This face, though, was quite a pretty one, not seeming to miss makeup. The eyebrows were a reddish color, and I assumed that whatever hair she had was, as well. How much hair did nuns really have, anyway? Was it shaved to the scalp, or long and wrapped, as under a Sikh's turban?

"Not letting this one corrupt you, I hope?" I said, nodding at Connie, who was pouring me a glass of wine.

"Ah, she tempts me constantly, she does. One of these days, who knows?"

"Careful, Maeve," Connie said. "He'll have his hand under your skirt in a minute."

"Jesus Christ, Connie!" I was appalled.

"And watch your language in front of a nun!" Connie came back. Both women collapsed in laughter.

I laughed in spite of my embarrassment. "What is going on, here? Are you both pissed?"

This caused further gales of laughter. "Jesus, Mary and Joseph!" the nun was finally able to say. "If Mother Superior were here now, I'd be shipped off to foreign missions tomorrow."

"Ah, you'll have a lot to confess, you will," Connie said, and they burst out laughing again. It was contagious, and I laughed mindlessly with them. Connie came and sat on my lap, wriggling about. "And what's that I feel, sir?" More riotous laughter.

"You well know what it is," I said, hoping to embarrass her into silence, but that only brought on more hysteria.

"So how's Mister Society?" Connie asked archly.

"What?"

"Oh, the darling of the aristocracy," Maeve/Sister Mary Margaret chimed in.

"Okay, you two, what's going on here?" Then I saw the London tabloid on the coffee table. Lady Jane Berkeley looked disdainfully straight ahead, accustomed to this unwanted attention, while I, new to the game, gaped blankly at the camera. I looked quite foolish.

"Oh, that," I said lamely. "A blind date. We had dinner with my parents, in fact."

"Did you, now?" Connie came back.

"We did."

"And who fixed you up so nicely, then? Must have been Mark's friend, Mr. Thrasher, eh?"

I looked quickly at Maeve, who seemed to know everything and be vastly amused by it. "No, she picked me up in a pub," I said, regaining my composure. I wondered how the hell Connie came up with that connection and quickly glanced through the article. The presence of neither Thrasher nor Genevieve Wheatley at the Connaught hadn't escaped the newspaper, though they both had escaped the photographer. There was a picture of Mrs. Wheatley at the time of her husband's death, and one of Derek Thrasher that must have been ten years old. His hair had been cut severely short at the time and he had worn glasses. I would never have recognized him had the photograph not been captioned.

"You'd be better off in a pub than in that company," Maeve said, with a vehemence that surprised me.

"I wouldn't have eaten nearly as well, though." I was trying to think of a way to change the subject. "And I wouldn't have seen my folks."

"Are they well?" Connie asked.

"Oh, yeah," I said, grateful for a way out of the Thrasher corner. "Just great. Mother had already heard about you from Grandfather; she was very curious."

"Holy Mother of God!" the nun exclaimed, looking at the clock on the wall. "I've got to make a move, Mother Superior will have my . . ." She stopped herself, and we filled the space with laughter. She gathered herself together, said her goodbyes, still giggling, and drove away in the van.

"Are you sure that's a nun?" I asked Connie. "She doesn't fit the image at all."

"She's just Maeve when she's with me. By the time

she gets back to the convent she'll be Sister Mary Margaret again, don't worry."

"You shouldn't have told her about Thrasher, Connie. Mark asked me to keep that quiet. I shouldn't even have told you."

"Well, even if I hadn't told her, you're all over the papers with him, now, so it hardly matters. Why is Mr. Thrasher's sponsorship a secret, anyhow?"

"He seems to like to do things quietly at the best of times, and this isn't the best of times. Did you hear about the bomb in Berkeley Square?"

"Oh, yes, that was intended for his company, wasn't it?"

"Yes, and I don't think it would improve our relationship with the locals if there were a connection with Thrasher. Have you told anybody else about him?"

She shook her head. "No, and your secrets are always safe with a nun. Mind you," she said, pulling me toward the sofa, "I'm not sure *you'd* be safe with that particular nun if I weren't about." She pulled me down on top of her. We were soon groping at each other's clothing and made love half dressed. I still had one leg in my trousers when we had finished and lay panting on the floor where we had fallen.

"I think you got all turned on having a nun about the place," Connie teased.

"I'm a Baptist, remember. My fantasies were never about nuns the way yours probably were about priests."

We got dressed, and Connie made coffee.

"What's Maeve's story, anyway? Why did she become a nun?"

"To tell you the truth, I've never really understood it. Had something to do with men, I think. When we were kids the boys were all after her; she's really a great-looking girl. Donal O'Donnell had the most awful thing about her when we were about sixteen, but I think she preferred Denny."

"God, I can't imagine anybody being sweet on Denny. What a complete jerk! Donal's okay, but even he's been acting funny lately, while Denny . . ." I stopped short of telling her about the incident at the cottage.

"Denny just hates Brits, that's all, and you're buddies with a Brit."

"But that's all so stupid, so futile. Jesus, Mark's project is paying Denny's wages for several months."

"All the more reason for Denny to hate him, because he's taking his money. Denny's and Donal's grandfather was a great republican, you know, during the troubles."

"No, I didn't know."

"His problem was, when the troubles were over, he kept settling his differences the way he had during the troubles. They say he burned a couple of fellows out, and eventually he was hanged for killing a man."

"By the government he had fought for?"

"Yes. And I think there's a lot of his grandfather in Denny."

Twenty-one

The phosphorescent glow of the cathode ray tube flitted about the darkened room, changing slightly with the click of each key. Pearce stared into the computer terminal like a surgeon searching for a tiny, hemorrhaging vein to tie off. He shook his head angrily, removed the floppy disk from its drive, and inserted the next disk—a thin wheel of mylar plastic held rigid by a paper envelope.

It had taken weeks to be allowed to stay in the computer room after hours, but finally enough accounting work had piled up so that his offer to toil late had been received with enthusiasm instead of suspicion. Each night for nearly two weeks he had spent an hour rapidly posting figures into the computer's general ledger program and two hours searching the magnetic storage records. He wasn't sure what he was looking for, but he would know it when he saw it.

Now he thought he saw it. Since the labels on the disks were coded and the codebook locked away, he had had to view each one individually to have an idea of its contents. The title of the disk now in the drive made him stop breathing for a moment.

FOREIGN EXCHANGE APPLICATIONS LEDGER, 1968–69

Pearce scrolled quickly through the figures and almost immediately began to see his opportunity. He found the operating system's manual in a desk drawer and referred quickly to its index. Then he went to the supplies cupboard, found a blank disk, inserted it into the number two drive, and carefully following the instructions in the manual, imaged the data from the original disk to the new one. Now he had what he needed. He returned the original to its storage envelope and replaced it in the file drawer.

He inserted the new disk, invoked the systems editor and began to scroll slowly, carefully, through the columns of figures. Every fourth or fifth line, he changed a number, doubling or tripling it. Pearce glanced at his watch. He wouldn't be able to finish this in one evening or two, but he had made a start. He switched on the printer and instructed the computer to make a hard copy of the first ledger. As the machine rapidly spat the eighty-column paper, he flipped through the continuous-form pages, viewing his handiwork. He began to grow excited; it was going to work. A few more evenings of this and he would have a cooked ledger that would be devastating.

When the printout was complete, Pearce put the new disk into its envelope and taped it to the bottom of his center desk drawer, working it a couple of times to be sure the envelope did not foul as the drawer slid in and out. He gathered the printout into its original accordion folds, loosened his belt, tucked the sheaf of papers under his shirt and into his trousers and buckled up again. With his coat and mackintosh on and left unbuttoned there was no noticeable bulge.

Still, on his way out of the building, he approached the security desk with some trepidation. He need not have feared. The guard was by now accustomed to his late hours.

"Still burning the midnight oil, Mr. Pearce?" the man asked.

"Yes, but I think I'll be done in a few days' time. All done."

"Good night, then. Mind how you go; wet out tonight."

"Good night." Pearce walked quickly from the building toward the car park, his heart pounding joyfully. He hoped his mother could feel his happiness, his triumph. After what she had gone through, it would be sweet satisfaction.

Twenty-two

I SLEPT WITH THE LOADED RIOT GUN UNDER MY BED FOR a week. Nothing happened. No more visitors, no threats of any kind. I tucked the shotgun away into my clothing cupboard and left it unloaded, which would not have pleased Mark but made me more comfortable. I continued to see light green Volkswagens at every turn. I even saw the one with the OOP number plate once, parked in front of a cinema in Patrick Street, in Cork. If I hadn't been in a hurry to get Connie Lydon into bed at the time, I might have hung around until the movie let out to see who was the driver.

In spite of my loving Annie from afar, as it were, and lusting for Jane Berkeley from an even greater distance, I was attracted to Connie in a way that endured. She was always fresh and new to me whether we were at a hooley, in the tub together, or sailing *Toscana* in Cork Harbour on a Sunday afternoon. Although I had never done anything as rash as to profess love, she seemed happy and made no demands for declarations, to my relief. Pressed into a corner, I probably would have told her anything she wanted to hear; I was much happier seeing her than not.

We continued to sail, even as the weather turned cooler, then cold, and ever wetter. It rains a lot in Ireland, almost any time of year, but in the late autumn it gets serious. We'd slip the mooring in front of the cottage, motor down past the Royal Cork Yacht Club, and sail idly around the big harbor, tying up at Dirty Murphy's, a pub on the eastern shore, and have a Guinness in front of a turf fire in the smoky lounge bar. Sometimes Connie would cook dinner aboard, and we would make love in the forepeak double berth and not pick up our mooring until nearly midnight, having slipped past the moored yachts at the club on our way upriver.

Work on the yacht continued steadily. By mid-November we were ready to turn the hull, which had been constructed upside-down, and begin work on the interior structure and the decking. The job went surprisingly quickly. We rigged a chain hoist from an overhead support system to one side of the hull, hauled it as far upright as we dared without having it fall on top of us, then braced it, took the chain hoist to eyes set in the wooden keel and, while everybody stood bracing with four-by-fours, let down until the hull was suspended upright from the chains, hanging just over the lead keel, which had been ordered from England. We then lowered the hull gently until the stainless steel keelbolts mated with the holes in the wooden keel and then screwed down the nuts tightly. The hull was left resting on its lead keel, which held it some six feet off the floor, and the keel, in turn, rested on a sturdy little rail car, on which it would roll to the water at launching time. The chain hoist would not be powerful enough to lift the whole boat when it was completed, so the car had to be in place early. The hull was then braced all round with four-by-fours, which were chocked, and, finally, the chain lift was unhooked. The hull stood gleaming with its seven skins of varnish, three more still to come when the entire boat was nearer completion.

"Jesus," Mark said. "She begins to look like a yacht, doesn't she?" It was the first time he had referred to the hull as "she."

"Have you decided on a name, yet, Mark?" I asked. We had once made a list of possibilities, but Mark had ignored it, saying that the proper name would emerge at the proper moment.

Mark grinned. "She's going to cost 150,000 pounds sterling before she's all done. I think I'll call her *Expensive*."

I laughed. "You'll certainly have the sympathy of every boat owner in the world."

The entire crew, except for Denny O'Donnell, stood and looked at her in awe for a moment. She was the largest vessel to have been built at Cork Harbour Boatyard: sixty feet in length, fourteen feet of beam, and eight and a half feet of draft. Denny O'Donnell was already out of the building before anyone else stirred. His twin looked sorrowfully after him. The brothers did not seem to be getting on well lately. Donal was now arriving in his own car, and rumor had it that he had moved out of his lodgings with Denny and found a place of his own. Denny had returned to his usual sour disposition, and Donal, while still friendly, seemed somehow detached.

Mark and I were the last to leave the yard, and it was nearly seven when we arrived home, exhausted. "I thought you two would never show," Annie said. She was wearing a dress, a rare event. "Peter-Patrick and Joan Coolmore have invited us all to dinner at the Royal Cork, and I accepted for us. We're due there at seven-thirty." Mark and I exchanged a glance. We were careful not to rile her these days, after her earlier explosion. Annie continued, "Mark, you have the tub first, and you and I will go ahead. Willie can join us when he's got himself together." We did as we were told.

They had been gone half an hour before I was bathed and dressed, and as I tied my necktie, a sudden memory hit me. Mark had left the building shed first and I had come after him, carrying an armful of wood scraps that we burned in the cottage fireplace. I had not gone back to lock the shed door. The padlock had been left hanging open on the hasp, and I would have to go and lock it before joining the Coolmores at the yacht club. Cursing my carelessness, I raced over the back roads to the boatyard and skidded to a halt in a spray of gravel before the shed door. The wind was getting up a bit and the skies were threatening; a nearly full moon lit the big shed intermittently as clouds scudded past it. The door was wide open, banging against the shed as the wind whipped it back and forth. As I was about to close it I glanced inside the shed and noticed that the light in Finbar's office was on. I must have forgotten that, too, I thought; I stepped inside, secured the banging door, and walked toward the office. On the other side of the chocked-up yacht, a rat ran at the sound of my footsteps, making little scraping noises on the cement floor. Then I heard another, different sound that stopped me in my tracks.

Over the howl of the wind around the tin shed, I heard it again: a creaking of timber under strain. I looked over at the hull, its size seemingly increased by its confines, and thought just for a moment that I saw it move. That was absurd, of course; it was carefully chocked in place. I jerked as I might have if struck by lightning; yet another sound caused this—the sound of a four-by-four piece of timber striking concrete and bouncing. By the time the second four-by-four struck the floor I was moving toward the hull; when the third one fell, I was running. Now the sound was of timber scraping across cement as the huge hull began to lean toward me. All around the hull, four-by-fours were falling as they came loose; the timber nearest me maintained contact with the hull at its center, but the other end of it slid slowly, noisily across the concrete floor.

Stupidly, I flung myself at it as if tackling a running

back head on. Miraculously, it stopped sliding. Pushing hard against the timber with my shoulder I looked about me; the hull was leaning toward me, hovering over me at an angle of about thirty degrees off the vertical; all of the seven other four-by-fours supporting it had fallen and lay scattered about; the only thing keeping the hull from crashing to the concrete floor was the single timber to which I clung. And, I quickly discovered when I moved, all that was holding the timber in place was my weight.

I tried jamming it further into place, but every time I took any weight off it, the timber's end slid further along the floor away from the hull, and the hull leaned even further toward me. It was absurd. A single timber, fortuitously placed at exactly the right spot along the hull's length, was all that kept the hull from falling. If it had been placed a foot differently in either direction, the un-reinforced hull would have spun on its keel and crashed to the concrete floor, ruining weeks, months of work. I saw that if I released the timber now, this would still happen, and moreover, the bloody thing would fall on me.

I looked around for some way of shoring up the hull so that I could move. Another of the four-by-fours was no more than five feet from me. I reached out with a toe in an attempt to drag it toward me. At the shift in my weight, the timber to which I clung slid a bit more, and the whole hull threatened again to fall. That was clearly no good. I tried to think of some way to call for help; the telephone was thirty feet away on Finbar's desk. No good, either. There was no point in shouting, because the shed was a hundred yards from the road. Even a passerby on foot would not hear me, what with the wind putting up such a howl. It slowly became clear to me that I was stuck in this ridiculous position until help arrived or the hull crashed down on top of me, whichever came first.

I lay on top of the timber and wedged a toe under its tip. That allowed me to relax one leg a bit, but I had to push hard with the other leg to keep the pressure on the timber. I looked at my watch. There was no watch. In my rush to dress and get to the Royal Cork I had forgotten to wear it. I tried to figure out what time it was. It had been almost 7:30 when Mark and Annie had left the cottage; I was about half an hour behind them. It took ten or twelve minutes to drive to the yard, and I had been there, what, all of five minutes? They wouldn't even miss me until they had had a couple of drinks and were getting hungry, say about 8:30, then they would call the cottage to see if I had left. When they got no answer they would assume I was on the way and would be there momentarily. When I didn't show, then what?

The leg with which I was pushing was starting to get very tired. By pushing extra hard on the timber, I was able to get my other toe under it and shift the load to my other leg. I had to do this about every five minutes, I reckoned, in order to keep from getting leg cramps. How had this happened? We had chocked all the timbers, hammering them in firmly with a sledge. Of course, if one slipped, then the opposite one might, too, with less pressure on it. But all of them? Could there have been some sort of chain reaction? Or was that really a rat I'd heard when I walked into the shed?

Time passed. The telephone suddenly rang, the extra-loud bell that Finbar had rigged cutting over the howl of the wind. I wished to God that I could answer it. It rang twelve times before it stopped. It had to be Mark, and when he got no reply he'd assume that I hadn't gone to the boatyard. It began to sink in that no help would come before morning, when Finbar or Mark arrived. My legs were getting tired. I was having to switch about every three minutes. I knew I would not be able to hold out for another ten or eleven hours. I craned my neck and looked up at the hull. I knew, too, that I could not let go of the timber and get out of the way fast enough before the hull fell on me. I was stuck, and as well as being tired, I was starting to get scared.

A cramp started to creep into my left leg, which was pushing to keep the pressure on the timber. I made the switch, and almost immediately my right leg began to cramp, too. I was going to have to let go and try to get out of the way; maybe I could dive *under* the hull and get clear near the keel, but if the lead keel hit me, that would be even worse than being struck by the hull, which, without all its interior supports, might at least give a little. Changing back to my left leg, I measured the distance; six or seven feet to get clear, I reckoned. God, I thought, tomorrow morning they're going to find me under the smashed hull, squashed like a bug. Poor Mark, he was going to lose three, four months on rebuilding. I gathered myself for the dive, taking deep breaths; I would go on three. One . . . two . . .

There was a loud, metallic clank from across the shed. Someone had slid back the iron bolt that fastened the door. The door creaked open, and I heard a footstep on the cement floor.

"Mark?" I called out. There was no reply. My leg was cramping badly, trembling with fatigue; I was not sure I could switch to the other leg, now, without losing the timber, everything. Footsteps walked slowly toward me; I couldn't see over my shoulder.

"And what would you be doing, Willie?" a voice asked. I knew the voice.

"For Christ's sake, get some weight on this with me! I'm about to lose it!"

A figure appeared in the corner of my eye. I heard the scrape of another timber on the concrete, heard it bump against the hull. "Hang on," the voice said. He walked a few steps away and came back. I could feel the shock through the hull and down my timber as he pounded the other four-by-four into place with the sledgehammer. "Hang on another minute," he said, then repeated the process on the other side of me. "Okay, relax."

I let go of the timber and sank to my knees, panting. "You all right?" he asked, taking my arm. "Better get out from under there in case it goes." He helped me move a few steps away. My legs were both cramped up, and I could not walk properly. I sat back and looked into his face for the first time, trying to relax.

"Denny?" Now I was worried again.

He shook his head. "Donal."

I heaved a great sigh. "Boy, am I glad to see you."

"What happened? How did you get into that fix?"

I told him. He didn't seem surprised. "What are you doing here?" I asked him.

"What are you both doing here?" The voice made us both jump. Mark stood just inside the door; as he walked toward us I saw the .45 automatic pistol in his hand, dangling at his side.

Donal recovered first. "I was passing and saw Willie's car. I found him holding that up, all by himself," he said, pointing at the hull.

"Jesus," Mark said. "Let's get some more support in there." I tried to get up but couldn't. Mark and Donal quickly picked up the other timbers and jammed them into place. When the hull was secure, Mark put a ladder against it, climbed in, hooked the chain lift to the inside of the hull and took up the slack on the chain. "That'll hold it till morning when the full crew gets in. We'll have to get it vertical again, then rechock it and hammer the chocks to the concrete with spikes." He checked to see that the little railcar on which the hull rested was still safely chocked. "Now, what the hell happened?"

I told my story again while rubbing my legs. "It's damn lucky you came by when you did, Donal. What made you stop?"

Twenty-three

WE AGONIZED OVER THE NEAR-LOSS OF THE HULL (AND of me) for a day or two, but in the end could only put it down as an accident. Mark reckoned that one supporting beam had fallen, setting up a slight rocking motion that dislodged others. We had no evidence whatever that it had been deliberately done and had to accept the timely arrival of Donal O'Donnell as simply fortuitous.

Things continued at the yard in a perfectly normal way. Work progressed; Denny O'Donnell remained surly but useful. He was the yard's electrician and did his work well. Donal remained friendly, if a bit removed. We fitted the engine into the hull before the decks went on, for easier access. Denny began work on the installation of the wiring harness, which Mark had designed. We were tense for a while, half expecting another "accident," but nothing happened, and after a while we relaxed. I did, at least. Mark seemed to be increasingly worried about something. I waited for him to tell me about it, and when he didn't, I finally asked.

"Thrasher told you he would be in touch, is that right?"

"It was the last thing he said to me in London."

"Well, I haven't heard from him, and our next payment to the yard is due on December fifteenth, less than a week to go. I'm going to have to come up with more than thirty thousand pounds."

"He didn't give you all the money at once?"

Mark shook his head. "No, it was to come in installments."

"Why don't you call him, then?"

Mark looked grim. "I tried. The London number he gave me has been disconnected. I called his building firm's offices, but was met with a blank wall. They wouldn't even take a message."

"Well, I've got a couple of thousand pounds in the bank, here—you're welcome to that if you need it."

"Thanks, Willie, but I'm going to have to give Finbar a much bigger check than that."

"Won't Finbar wait a bit?"

"I can't ask him to do that. Finbar borrows to buy materials and pay for labor. If he doesn't get paid, the bank will attach the hull and sell it, since the yard has title to it until the contract price is paid. Then, since he's committed his yard to this project until the spring, he'll have no other work and will have to lay off his crew. He could even lose the boatyard to the bank."

"I may know another way to get in touch with Derek," I said. I went into Finbar's office, dug the card from my wallet and placed the call. It was some minutes before she came on the line. "Jane?"

"Will? How nice to hear from you! Are you coming to Paris?"

"Not right away. How's the world of international banking?"

"Not bad, but the social life is killing me."

"Not a bad way to go."

"And I love every minute of it."

"Listen, Jane, do you know where Derek is? Can you get in touch with him?"

There was a silence for a moment. "What's the problem?"

I explained.

"I'm sorry, Will, but I haven't seen Derek since London: I've talked with him once, briefly, but since the bomb in Berkeley Square he's been keeping a very low profile. There were rumors that they were after him, personally."

"I see. Well, if he should contact you, would you ask him to get in touch with Mark? It's very important."

"Of course, but it's unlikely that I'll hear from him. How are things in Ireland?"

"Damp. As usual. Paris?"

"Very nice, lately. Say, what are you doing New Year's Eve?"

"No plans, yet. My folks are coming to visit my grandfather for Christmas, but they leave before New Year's."

"Why don't you come to Paris?"

"Paris for New Year's?" Mark nodded and mouthed the word, "go." Connie had already asked me to a party, and I had accepted, but I didn't hesitate. "That sounds terrific."

"Wonderful! How long can you stay?"

"Not more than a couple of days. Things are going hot and heavy at the boatyard. Will you book me a hotel room?"

"Nonsense, you'll stay with me. I've got a lovely flat." She gave me the address. "Bring your dinner jacket. We get terribly elegant in Paris."

"Okay." I didn't have a dinner jacket, but I had my new American Express card. We chatted for a moment longer, then hung up. I shook my head. "She doesn't know how to reach him. But if she hears from him, she'll ask him to call."

"Well, that's something, anyway. Not to worry, we've got a few days yet." We headed back to the waiting boat, but he still looked worried.

On Saturday afternoon I went to see Connie and found Sister Mary Margaret there again. I had chatted with her briefly several times, now, and found her intelligent and, as a nun, disconcertingly attractive. I would catch myself trying to figure out what sort of body was hidden beneath the habit, and I think she suspected my thoughts once, because she blushed and left shortly thereafter.

"How goes it with the boat, Will?" Connie asked, when she had got me a drink.

"Very well, indeed, with the boat, but Mark hasn't heard from the sponsor for a while, and there's a payment coming due."

"Where is your Mr. Thrasher these days?" Sister Mary Margaret asked. "The papers say he's dropped out of sight."

I was startled, then remembered that Connie had told her about Thrasher. "I've no idea, and, apparently, neither does anybody else since the bombing in London."

"There's been another one," Connie said, handing me a newspaper. A restaurant in Chelsea had been ripped apart and two people killed.

"I don't understand those creeps," I said heatedly. "What do they have to gain by killing innocent Londoners in a restaurant?"

The nun looked at me sharply. "What makes you so sure they're innocent?"

"You mean they might have been after somebody in particular?"

"No, but they were English."

"And what does that make them guilty of?"

"They allow themselves a government that persecutes people in the North. When a people are fighting for their freedom as Catholics in Ulster are, the war has to be taken to the home of the oppressor. When England understands that the war will be taken to English cities and not just to Belfast and Derry, maybe they'll consider that they've been in Ireland long enough."

I couldn't believe I was hearing this from a nun. "That's the sort of thinking that's behind things like the attack on the Israeli athletes at the Munich Olympics."

"If you like." She was reddening, now.

"Oh, Will," Connie broke in, "you mustn't get Maeve started on the British in the North."

The nun rose. "I've got to get moving, so you needn't worry about a lecture."

Connie walked her to the door. Shortly, I heard the convent van drive away. "Jesus, Connie, does she really believe all that stuff?"

"She's stifled at the convent, Will. She has no one to talk with about this sort of thing, so when she does the marketing she stops by and chats with me, lets off some steam."

"But does she really believe that terrorism is okay?"

Connie wheeled on me. "Now don't you get started on something and somebody you don't understand."

"What's to understand? It sounded to me as though she was clearly taking a stand in favor of the murder of innocent civilians to achieve a political end."

"Isn't that what happens in any war? It's what the Germans and the British did to each other, murdered each other's civilians."

"It's not quite the same thing."

"Well, the civilians were just as dead." She held up a hand to stop me from speaking further. "Now listen,

I'm not going to argue politics with you, Will Lee. If you want a pleasant evening around here, just you stop it right now."

I knew what she meant by a pleasant evening, and I changed the subject very quickly. Later, she turned to me in the dark. "Say, I've got a lovely new dress for New Year's; you'll love it—lots of cleavage."

I winced. "Jesus, Connie, I forgot. You know my folks are coming at Christmastime—well, they're going on to Paris from here and have asked me to come with them. They called today. Do you mind?" I had not even thought about the lie; it just came rolling out.

"Oh. Well, sure, you'd better go, then."

The disappointment in her voice was clear. If I hadn't been such a shit I'd have felt like one.

Twenty-four

I WOKE AT TEN THE NEXT MORNING TO FIND THE BED EMPTY and a note saying she had gone to mass and was spending the day with her parents. I dressed and drove slowly back to the cottage, lured by the thought of the roast beef I knew Annie would be preparing. Mark and Annie had a strong streak of English traditionalism in them, and never was it more apparent than when Annie put a joint of beef or a leg of lamb on the Sunday table. I stopped in Carrigaline and picked up the English Sunday papers, *The Sunday Times* and *The Observer*. We didn't see the papers often, but a nap after lunch and a browse through them seemed a pleasant prospect.

The smell of the cooking beef struck me before I was even inside the cottage. I closed the door. "Hey, that really smells good!"

"Shhh!" Annie cautioned, sticking her head out from the kitchen. "Mark's sleeping in." She pointed to a pad beside the phone. "Your father called last night and asked that you call him back at that number."

She went back to her cooking and I called the international operator and asked for the number, which was to the apartment my parents kept in Atlanta. I waited somewhat nervously for the operator to call back. Neither of my parents used the long-distance telephone with me very often, preferring to write and be written to. I was worried that something might be wrong. The ringing of the phone jolted me.

"Hello, Will?" my father's voice came over the line, scratchy and faint.

"Hello, Dad. I'm afraid we haven't got a very good line. I'm sorry to call so early, but I thought it might be important." It was five hours earlier in Atlanta. "Is something wrong?"

"Not really—we're all fine. But I had a call from a London newspaper yesterday. They knew about our dinner with Derek Thrasher and were calling to find out what I knew about him."

"What did you tell them?"

"I confirmed that we had dinner and that I hadn't met Mr. Thrasher before that time or since; said that he was an acquaintance of yours and Jane's. They wanted to know how to get in touch with you; I said you were traveling in Ireland. I don't know how resourceful they are, but I doubt if they'll find you."

"Why would they be interested in a dinner that took place nearly a month ago?"

"They wouldn't say. I had the impression they had some sort of story and didn't want to leak any details until they'd published. Have you heard anything about him over there?"

"No, but I've just bought the Sunday papers. I'll go through them and call you back if there's anything. How are you and Mother doing?"

"We're just fine. You knew Jimmy Carter won the governor's race?" My father had been a strong supporter of Carl Sanders, Carter's opponent.

"Mom wrote me. I'm sorry about that; I know it'll cause some complications for you."

"Probably. Well, at least we won't have Lester Maddox there anymore. You knew he got elected lieutenant governor this time?" Maddox was a racist clown who had caused great embarrassment for moderate Georgians such as my father.

"Yeah, I guess you won't be rid of him entirely."

"Listen, read the papers and call me back if there's anything worth knowing. Your mother isn't up yet, but she's dying to know any news about Thrasher."

I hung up and sat down with the papers. Mark appeared at the bedroom door, rubbing his eyes. "What's going on? What's all the shouting about?"

"Sorry, Mark. I was talking to my father, and we had a bad line. He says he had a call from a London paper about Derek Thrasher. I'm just looking to see if there's anything in today's papers about him." I had to look no further than the front page of *The Observer*. In the lower right corner I was greeted by the headline:

FINANCIER SOUGHT BY PUBLIC PROSECUTOR

DOCUMENTS MAY MEAN CHARGES AGAINST DEREK THRASHER

Mark snatched the newspaper from me and stared at it.

Annie came in from the kitchen. "Well, let us in on it, Mark."

He read aloud:

The Director of Public Prosecutions has expressed a keen interest in talking with mysterious financial wizard Mr. Derek Thrasher about exchange control violations and irregularities in Thrasher's company reports to the Inland Revenue over the last two years. *The Observer* has learned that an apparently disgruntled former employee of Mr. Thrasher, Mr. Patrick Fitzgerald Pearce, of Streatham, several days ago delivered a set of books from an investment firm principally owned by Mr. Thrasher that are said to be different from the books previously examined by the Bank of England and the Inland Revenue. A spokesman for the Prosecutor would confirm only that information about Mr. Thrasher's business activities had been received, and, as a result, that the Prosecutor wished to meet with

Mr. Thrasher for "discussions" and sought to learn of his whereabouts. The spokesman denied that charges had been brought, though he declined to rule out that possibility in the near future.

Mr. Pearce worked as an accountant for Avondale Enterprises, said to be a company set up to invest profits of other Thrasher businesses in property and holiday resorts on the Continent. A spokesman for Avondale, who declined to be identified, confirmed that Mr. Pearce had been employed for some months by the company and that he had resigned a week ago, saying he wished to return to his native Ireland.

The significance of the documents now in the hands of the Prosecutor lies not so much in the dealings of Avondale, but, *The Observer* has learned, in the personal dealings of Mr. Derek Thrasher himself. It is believed that the documents may shed light on how one of Europe's most reclusive and, it is rumoured, wealthiest businessmen conducts his affairs.

Mr. Thrasher has for some time been seen rarely in public, most recently in mid-November, when he dined at the Connaught Hotel in the company of Mrs. Genevieve Wheatley, widow of Mr. Winston Wheatley MP, Mr. William H. "Billy" Lee, former governor of the State of Georgia, USA, Mrs. Lee and their son, and Lady Jane Berkeley, eldest daughter of the Duke of Kensington. Governor

Lee, reached at his home in Atlanta, said that he had not met Mr. Thrasher before that evening, nor since; that he had been introduced to Mr. Thrasher at the dinner by his son, William H. Lee IV, apparently a friend of Lady Jane. "We found him very pleasant company," Governor Lee said. He denied any business connection with Mr. Thrasher and said the evening was purely social in nature.

Two days following that dinner a car bomb was set off in Berkeley Square, outside a building occupied by a construction firm owned by Mr. Thrasher, and credit for the explosion was later claimed by the Irish Freedom Brigade, a radical offshoot of the Provisional IRA, who said they had a quarrel with the company's hiring practices on several Northern Ireland building sites. It is believed that, because of the explosion and the possibility of threats on his life, Mr. Thrasher has since become even more reclusive. Prior to the explosion he apparently resided in a house adjacent to the office building, according to reports from people who know him, but now none of those people nor anyone else can say with any certainty even what country he now resides in.

The spokesman for the Director of Public Prosecutions said that it may be several days or weeks before a decision is made whether to charge Mr. Thrasher or his employees with violations of the law.

Mark stopped reading and sat down heavily. "Oh shit," he said.

We were hard at work on the boat the next morning when a man in a business suit, carrying a briefcase, turned up at the boatyard. Finbar took the man into his office and talked with him for a moment, then asked Mark to join him. Mark motioned for me to come with him.

"This is Mr. Murray, my bank manager in Cork. Mr. Murray, this is Captain Robinson and Mr. Lee."

"How are you this morning, gentlemen?" Mr. Murray was very cheerful.

"Very well, thank you," Mark replied, with equal cheer.

"Ah, that's a fine-looking craft you've got building, there."

"Thank you very much; Finbar is doing a fine job on her. You're lucky to have such a customer."

"Ah, yes, Finbar's been with us forever." Murray then became a bit more serious. "Ah, Captain Robinson, I wanted just to ask you about something . . ." I knew what was coming. ". . . your next periodic payment on the building of your boat . . . let's see . . ." He put on his glasses and consulted a paper . . . "That's thirty-three thousand, four hundred pounds sterling . . . is due in two days' time, on Wednesday. I believe that's correct?"

Mark nodded affably. "It is indeed."

"Right. Ah, Captain Robinson, do you anticipate any difficulty in meeting that payment on that date?"

Mark appeared surprised. "Why do you ask, Mr. Murray?"

"Well, you see, we provide Finbar with financing for his working capital, and, of course, we're very concerned that his clients are able to meet their obligations."

"I anticipate no difficulty in meeting my obligations, Mr. Murray. My sponsor has been prompt in his payments, and I've no reason to expect him to be any less so on this occasion," Mark replied smoothly.

"Ah, good, your sponsor . . . that would be a Mr. Derek Thrasher, would it?"

Mark wrinkled his brow but maintained his composure. "My sponsor prefers to remain anonymous, Mr. Murray, but may I ask why you think it might be this . . . Mr. Thrasher?" I was glad Murray was looking at Mark and not at me.

"Well, Finbar . . ." Murray turned and looked for confirmation from Finbar, who was looking very embarrassed.

"I've never told Finbar the name of my sponsor, Mr. Murray," Mark said easily, "so anything he may have told you in that regard would merely be speculation on his part."

"Well, now, Captain Robinson, we're all in business together here, so to speak; you may be sure that anything you tell me will remain in the strictest confidence."

"I have nothing to tell you, Mr. Murray. I've already said that my sponsor prefers to remain anonymous, and I must respect his wishes in that regard."

"Well, let me put it this way, then, if I assumed that your sponsor is this Mr. Thrasher, would I be going too far astray?" Murray accompanied this with a wink and a grin.

"I think it would be best for all concerned if you made no assumptions at all, Mr. Murray." Murray's face fell; he was suddenly less cheerful. "And if you should choose to make assumptions along those lines I think it would be in the bank's interests if you kept your assumptions closely to yourself."

Murray was looking decidedly annoyed, now. "Captain Robinson, do you deny that your sponsor is, in fact, Mr. Derek Thrasher?"

"I do not deny it, Mr. Murray, nor do I confirm it."

Murray produced Sunday's *Observer* from his briefcase and handed it to Mark. "Have you seen this, Captain?"

Mark glanced at the newspaper. "I read both *The Observer* and *The Sunday Times* quite thoroughly yesterday."

"Well, now, Captain, unless you will deny it and give me the name of your sponsor and a means of confirming his participation and his intention of continuing his sponsorship, I am going to have to proceed on the basis that your sponsor is, in fact, Mr. Thrasher. As you can see from this report, Mr. Thrasher seems to be in considerable difficulties with the authorities at the moment, and the bank is very concerned that these difficulties may prevent him from continuing his sponsorship."

Mark stood up. "Mr. Murray, you may proceed on any basis you wish. It is my intention to meet my obligations to Finbar; I have no obligation of any sort to you or your bank. My bankers are Coutts & Company of Cadogan Place, London, as they were my father's and my grandfather's. If you feel you need reassurance of my credibility or character you may feel free to contact them for a reference." Mark delivered this quietly, almost kindly.

Murray was turning red, now. "Captain Robinson, I feel I must tell you that if your payment to Finbar is not made by the close of business on the fifteenth, the day after tomorrow, the bank will feel it necessary to take immediate steps to protect its interests. I——"

Mark stuck out his hand. "It has been a pleasure to meet you, Mr. Murray; now I must bid you good day; we have a lot of work to do." He left the office, and I followed him. Finbar remained with the banker.

"Jesus, Mark," I whispered to him as we walked toward the boat, "didn't you come on a little strong with him? It's not going to do us any good to have him mad with you, especially in the circumstances."

Mark stopped and turned to me. "Willie, my father told me a long time ago never to be intimidated by a banker. I'm not about to start now, especially with a little shit like that one. Look at it this way—bankers sell money, customers buy it. Finbar is the customer in this case. If I'd sucked up to that fellow he'd have known immediately that we had no money, and he'd have had his solicitors all over us. As it is, he may back down and wait a bit, even if we're late. There's at least a chance of that. It's a lot of trouble for a bank to foreclose, and Finbar's a good customer. We'll be all right for a few days. In the meantime, let's just keep hoping Derek comes through."

Finbar showed the banker out and joined us. He looked very angry. "I'm sorry about that, Captain," he said to Mark. "He's got no call to come around here like that. I've always paid those people on time. Well, nearly always."

"It's all right, Finbar. Something I'd like to know, though. Where did you hear that my sponsor was Derek Thrasher?"

Finbar looked embarrassed. "Ah, it was just a rumor. I'm sorry I mentioned it to Murray, but I thought it'd put him off a bit if he knew there was somebody big behind your project."

"When did you hear the rumor, Finbar, and where?"

"Oh, a while back. A week or two, I guess. That's when I told Murray. He was all impressed, he was; then he saw that thing in the paper."

"And where did you hear it? Who told you that?"

"Oh, it's not important, Captain."

Mark put his hand on Finbar's shoulder. "Finbar, I must know."

Finbar rubbed the back of his neck angrily. "Well, I'm something of a republican, you know. My father was a fighter during the troubles. I think some of the lads thought if I knew that Thrasher was involved I'd back off the project, what with the Provos being after him and all, but I'd made an agreement, and I'll stick to it. Murray can go fuck himself; I'll——"

"Finbar."

"It was Denny O'Donnell told me," Finbar said, then shoved his hands in his pockets and walked off toward the boat.

Mark stood, frozen, looking at Finbar's back. It was the first time I had ever seen him shaken by anything. This was bad, and it was my fault.

Twenty-five

THAT EVENING I TELEPHONED JANE IN PARIS, BUT SHE had still not heard from Derek Thrasher.

"Have you seen the London papers?" I asked.

"Yes."

"What do you think? Is he in a lot of trouble?"

"I don't think we should talk about this on the telephone. I'll tell you all about it when you come to Paris. I'm looking forward to seeing you New Year's."

I said goodbye and hung up.

"Any luck?" Mark asked.

I shook my head. "She's heard nothing. How did you get in touch with Thrasher in the beginning?"

"I met him at the Royal London Yacht Club Ball during Cowes week, only a few days before we met you. We met at the club the next day for me to show him the plans for the yacht and go over my budget projections. Couldn't have been together for more than half an hour. I suppose he did some checking up on me, during the next couple of days, and the next time I saw him was when you were with us. I haven't seen him since. He didn't give me a mailing address, just the number on the card, the same one he gave you. The one that's now disconnected."

"Well, I suppose his mailing address was the house I visited in London, next door to his office building. Why don't you send him a telegram there? The papers say he isn't there anymore, but he must have some means of having mail and messages forwarded."

Mark jumped up and grabbed the phone. "Bloody good idea! Why didn't I think of that sooner?"

Mark dictated a brief telegram to the cable operator, addressing it to "D.T." at the Berkeley Square address. "Please telephone me soonest. Most urgent. Mark." He instructed the operator to have the telegram delivered to the door first thing Tuesday morning.

"Mark, how could Denny O'Donnell even have gotten a whiff about Derek? It seems impossible." I had a sinking feeling that I knew how, and I was hoping Mark would have another, better idea.

"Only you, Annie, and I know about Thrasher, at least you two are the only people I've told. Thrasher could hardly object to your knowing, since you were both there when the deal was done."

"And I told Connie," I said. And Connie had told at least one other person.

"Well, it's done, now; word's out in all the worst places. The next step is damage control."

"Damage control?"

"A navy expression. When you take a hit on a ship you stop worrying how you got hit. You just do what you can to keep the water out."

"What can we do?"

Mark walked to the sideboard, poured himself a scotch, and knocked back half of it. "I don't know," he said. There was despair in his voice, something I had never expected to hear from him.

I thought there was one small thing I might do. I went to Connie's.

She took the news angrily. "You just don't understand. Maeve is sequestered at the convent. She only gets out to do the shopping, and I'm the only person she sees."

I shook my head. "She's seeing someone else."

"She is *not*. She wouldn't lie to me."

"Let's find out."

"What do you mean?"

"I mean I want you to tell her something else."

"What do you mean?"

"Tell her that Thrasher is out, that he's no longer Mark's sponsor." For all I knew that might be the case.

"Is he?"

"We haven't heard a word from him. We can't get in touch with him. The next payment to the boatyard is due the day after tomorrow, and we don't have it. Tell her that Mark is selling the family farm in Cornwall to get enough to finish the boat." I knew that Mark could not legally sell the farm because of a stipulation in his grandfather's will.

"Is he?"

"It's the only possible way he could finish the boat if Thrasher doesn't come through. Something else. Point out to her that if the boat doesn't get finished, everybody at the boatyard is going to be put out of work for at least four months. Finbar has no work until a fishing boat starts building in April. He can't find another boat to build just on the spur of the moment. The fact is, he would almost certainly go under, and his crew would be out of work permanently. You know what the unemployment rate is around here. They might not work for years."

"Is all this true, or are you asking me to lie to Maeve?"

I stood up and slammed down my drink on the table. "Now you listen to me, godammit. You and you alone are the only possible way we could have gotten into this mess. I told you things in confidence, and you betrayed my confidence. All I'm asking you to do now is to try and help contain some of the damage you've done." I braced myself for the assault I knew might come. Then she sagged, and I knew I had won.

"All right," she said in a small voice.

As I left her cottage I felt like a shit, because I knew that Connie was not the cause of our problems; I was. It was I who had betrayed Mark's confidence when I had told Connie about Thrasher. We had been in bed at the time.

*   *   *

The following day, Tuesday, Annie called Mark at the boatyard. The cable operator had called back: Delivery had been refused of the telegram Mark had sent to Berkeley Square.

That evening I told Mark what I had said to Connie.

"Well," he said, "I suppose it can't do any harm, but I don't really understand what you hope to accomplish."

"Two things," I replied, and they both seemed small to me. "First, if the word does get out, and the right people buy it, Thrasher will be out of the picture for them; they'll believe they can't get at him by sabotaging the project. Second, the crew might not walk off the job right away if they think you're getting the money another way. It could buy us some time, in case Derek does come through."

Mark shrugged. "It might help. At least if they hear the story, we'll know how they got it."

The next day, Wednesday, work went on as usual on the yacht. Finbar said nothing about the payment. Then, at half past four, Murray from the bank turned up with another man. Both were carrying briefcases. Finbar went into the office with them. Through the glass partition we could see him shaking his head and arguing with them. The man with Murray seemed to be trying to get Finbar to accept a folded piece of paper. The telephone rang. Finbar answered it and stuck his head into the shop.

"Captain Robinson, telephone for you."

Mark went to the office. I followed and stood in the door. "Yes? This is Captain Robinson." He listened for a moment. "When?" He listened again. "Thank you very much." He hung up. He started back into the shop, ignoring Murray and the other man, then paused. "Oh, Finbar, I nearly forgot." He walked to where his coat hung on a peg, got his checkbook from a pocket, and dashed off a check. "Here you are," he said, handing it to Finbar. "Thirty-three thousand, four hundred pounds."

Finbar looked as astonished as I did. Mark walked briskly back into the shop with me in tow. I looked back into the office and saw Finbar tuck the paper into Murray's coat pocket. "I'll be having a word with your regional manager about this, Mr. Murray," he said. The two men looked embarrassed.

I caught up with Mark. "Jesus, is that check good?"

Mark grinned. "That call was from Messrs. Coutts & Company in London. Fifty thousand pounds has been lodged to my account." He laughed aloud. "It was delivered in cash by an armored car just at closing time. Blew the manager's mind, I think."

Later, as Mark and I were leaving for the day, Finbar stopped us. "I want you to know that I'd have stood up to the bank as long as I could have. I told Murray I'm going to his boss and complain about the pressure. His boss will have his ass. And the lads are behind you, too. They came to me today and offered to work without wages as long as they could in the hopes of seeing you get the money."

"Even Denny O'Donnell?" Mark asked.

Finbar grinned. "Donal did the talking for them all, but Denny went along."

"Well, thank them for me, will you, Finbar? And thank you too for standing up to Murray."

"Not at all, Captain, I enjoyed it. And, Captain"— Finbar's face took on a sorrowful expression—"I'm sorry you had to sell the farm. I truly am."

Mark patted him on the back. "Not to worry, Finbar. At least we're sure of being able to finish the boat, now."

"Well, Derek came through, and not a moment too soon," I said as we walked toward the car.

"Too bloody right, mate." He clapped me on the shoulder. "You came through, too. I think we'll have a breathing spell, now. They'll want us to finish the boat."

"And we know a bit more than we did, too," I said, thinking of Connie. I would have to go and apologize for yelling at her. She had come through for us. "Still, even though they think Derek's out of the picture, they've still got their version of Belfast to hold against you. They're going to remember that before long."

"Maybe, but now they're thinking their jobs depend on the boat's being finished. We'll have a breathing spell until then."

But what, I wondered, would happen when the yacht was finished?

Twenty-six

CHRISTMAS CAME, AND IT WAS ONE OF THE BEST I CAN remember. My parents arrived, and my grandfather clearly enjoyed having his daughter home. He threw a huge cocktail party and buffet dinner; half the county seemed to be there. I found a fashionably cut dinner jacket at a Cork men's shop just in time to keep from disgracing the family.

My parents were much taken with Mark and Annie, and with Connie. If anything, my mother approved too much of Connie. "There," she said pointedly, when she had my ear at the punch bowl, "is a young woman of substance."

"Come on, now, Patricia, you just want grandchildren with a bit of Irish in them."

"I should be so lucky," she sighed. "Anyway, she's more your style than Lady Jane, I think."

"Ah, now you're worried I'll bring a Brit home." I wasn't so sure just what my style was, anyway.

The party was the first time I had seen Connie since our conversation about the good Sister Mary Margaret. She had been cool on the phone when I invited her, but I think she was curious to meet my parents. She was cool when she arrived, too, and I had to ask her to dance to get a private word with her. "I'm sorry I yelled at you the other day; I was pretty upset."

"I thought you were way out of line, Will Lee, but I did as you asked."

"I know you did."

"I was ashamed . . ." she began, then stopped. "What?"

I pulled her into my grandfather's study and told her what had transpired. She seemed stunned.

"I don't understand what's happening. I don't understand why Maeve would do that to me."

"It's not too hard to figure out. She's made it pretty clear where her sympathies lie."

"But she's not supposed to *have* any sympathies."

"Well, she's human. That's not so hard to understand."

"Not for you, maybe. You're a bloody Protestant. You don't have any real grasp of the discipline of her order."

"I guess not."

"I've got to talk to her."

"Now listen, you can't let her know that we know. That would put us right back where we were before, just waiting for something to happen to the boat . . . or to one of us."

"What is that supposed to mean?"

I told her about the wrecking of the cottage. Her reaction was a shocked silence.

"This can't be happening," she said, finally.

"But it is happening, and it might keep happening. Is that what you want?"

"Of course not."

"Things seem to be stabilized, now; we've got some sort of breathing spell for a while, and you can't do anything to upset that. You must be very careful with Maeve. Do you understand that?"

"Yes," she said resignedly, "I suppose I do."

We opened our presents in front of a roaring fire in my grandfather's library on Christmas Eve. I gave my mother some Waterford crystal, and my father some yards of a Tipperary tweed, enough for a suit. I had found a bottle of a fine Champagne Cognac, vintage 1928, in London for my grandfather. My parents surprised me with a really good suit of foul-weather sailing gear from Captain O. M. Watts' London chandlery and completed the outfit with a pair of top-quality Swedish seaboots and some leather sailing gloves. I was delighted.

But my grandfather rattled me. When all the gifts had been opened, he handed me a buff envelope, sealed with wax. Inside I found a folded sheaf of papers. I spread them out and found a surveyor's map of an area down by Kinsale Harbour. There was a heavy line drawn around a rectangular patch of land. I looked at the other papers and discovered a deed. It was in my name. I looked at my grandfather.

He grinned at me, still clenching his pipe in his teeth. "There's a bit more than four acres there; and a cottage. It's something of a ruin, but it can be fixed up. You seem to like it there, down by the water. You've ridden my hunters there often enough."

"You're an Irish landowner, now," my mother said, "so you be careful what you say about your people from now on, you hear?"

I was too surprised to speak. I knew my grandfather must have meant well, but I thought I felt my family reaching out subtly to take away my newly won freedom. I thanked my grandfather profusely and tried to seem pleased, but somehow the deed in my hand troubled me.

On Christmas morning I saddled two of my grandfather's hunters, and my mother and I rode out toward the harbor to visit my land. We made a full gallop of it, and she beat me by a length, pulling up on a hill overlooking the water. I got out my surveyor's map and looked around for the property lines. It was easy enough to define my new holding. It was bordered on one side by a roadway and a hedgerow, on another by an old stone wall, and on the other two by Kinsale Harbour, near the mouth. I could look down on a sheltered inlet that was part of my property.

"If there's enough water there, it would be perfect for a little dock," I said to my mother, pointing. "I could keep a boat." I consulted the map again. Curved lines representing one, two, and three fathoms followed the outline of the inlet. It seemed ideal. Hangman Cove, it was called. The headland on the eastern side of the harbor entrance was Hangman Point. A large grove of trees ran up from the water, concealing and sheltering the cottage. They had been shaped into a smooth, flowing line by decades of winds.

"It's beautiful," my mother said. "I'm so glad he chose this spot to give you."

We crossed the road and entered a gap in the stone wall where a gate had once been. At the edge of the trees we dismounted and walked the last few yards along the rough, dirt road, leading the horses. The cottage appeared through the trees. The slate roof seemed largely intact, but the insides were a shambles. Generations of sheep and cattle had sheltered in the place, but the walls still stood straight. It could be recovered.

"I used to play down here when I was a girl," my mother said. "An old woman named Nellie lived here; she was the widow of a man who had worked for years for my grandfather, and he gave her the place for her lifetime. She died not long after Billy and I were married. I think she kept going just to see me wed."

I looked at her closely. In spite of all my suspicions, I could see nothing in her that wanted to confine me, and I felt ashamed for my reaction the day before. I looked at all the beauty around me and thought if this was entrapment, I wanted to be trapped.

Twenty-seven

O N THE MORNING AFTER CHRISTMAS I DROVE MY PAR-
ents to the airport, detouring along the way to
show my father my cottage and land. The road led along
the eastern shore of Kinsale Harbour, through Summercove, past Connie's cottage.

"Let's stop and say goodbye to Connie," my mother
suggested.

I didn't want to see Connie at that moment, but we
had time, and I couldn't think of an excuse not to stop,
so I pulled over. Connie was on her school Christmas
holiday and was home. She chatted brightly with both
my parents for a few minutes, and I told her about my
new holding, further along the harbor. "We'll be neighbors, it appears."

She walked us toward the car. "What a nice thing for
your grandfather to do," she said. She didn't seem very en-
thusiastic about the prospect of having me for a neighbor.

"Did you have a good Christmas with your folks?" I asked.

"Sure, fine," she said. She seemed tired, tense. I had never seen Connie tired.

I pulled her aside. "Are you feeling all right?" I asked. "You look a bit off your feed."

"Oh, just a bit nackered from all the Christmas cheer," she said. "Not to worry."

"Dinner tonight?"

"Can't. I'm going to Dublin with my parents to visit some relatives. We're staying until after New Year's."

"Oh."

"Anyhow, you're on your way to Paris, aren't you?"

"Uh, no, I've got to work a few more days on the boat before I join them." She looked at me sharply; then she turned and walked back to her cottage without another word.

I got into the car and headed for Hangman Cove. "Something wrong between you and Connie?" my mother asked.

"Not that I know of."

"She seemed a bit odd to me."

I laughed. "Well, she's a woman," I said, "and Irish."

I showed my father my new bit of Ireland. He approved, and we started for the airport. As we passed Connie's cottage in Summercove I saw the convent van parked outside.

We made our farewells at Cork Airport. It had been

a perfect Christmas for me, for all of us, it seemed, but it would be some time before we saw each other again. "You take care of yourself, now," my father said.

"I'll do that."

"I hope we'll see you in the autumn," my mother said. This was a reference to law school, I knew.

"We'll see," I replied. I hugged her and they were gone.

I drove back through Kinsale, musing on what the new year might bring. If I decided against law school, I thought, I might spend the autumn working on my cottage. Mark's program for the year included a race to the Azores in the new yacht, in July, with Annie and me for crew, then a singlehanded return to Ireland as a qualifying passage for the race the following summer. Perhaps with all that out of the way I could get him to lend a hand with the work.

I stopped at the supermarket in Kinsale to pick up a few things I knew we were short of at the cottage. I did my shopping, and, as I was packing my purchases into the boot of the Mini-Cooper, I heard a woman's voice speak my name. Turning, I was confronted with an unaccustomed sight: an angry nun.

"Just what are you doing, anyway?" she demanded to know.

"What?" I was baffled by this outburst.

"I've never seen Connie so unhappy; she's been that way for two weeks, now. What are you doing to her?"

"I'm not doing anything to her," I said. "If she's unhappy, I don't think it's anything to do with me."

"Lying bastard!" she said, actually stamping her foot.

"Now, wait a minute," I said, astonished and annoyed, "I don't think my relationship with Connie is any of your business."

"Well, I'm making it my business," she came back hotly.

"Look," I said glancing at the shoppers around us, who were beginning to notice our discussion. "I don't think this is the best place to talk about this."

"Oh, there's nothing at all to talk about with you; you suck up to those Brits, then come to Summercove and push Connie around."

"Listen, Sister, I don't much care what your views are about my friends; I don't want to hear them. I'd suggest that you concentrate on your work at the convent, and I'll concentrate on mine at the boatyard. As far as Connie is concerned, if we have any problems, I'm sure we can work them out without your help."

"You're not much of a man, are you?" she taunted.

"And you're not much of a nun," I said, getting into my car and slamming the door. I backed out of the parking place and drove away, leaving her standing in the car park, fists clenched, staring after me. In the rearview mirror I could see her mouthing what I was sure were unnunlike words.

Upset by this scene and annoyed that what she had said to me might be all too true, I drove immediately to Connie's to find out what was going on, but the cottage was locked and her car gone. I drove home angry with Sister Mary Margaret's meddling and annoyed that, with Connie gone, I could do nothing to resolve the situation in which I found myself. It would have to wait until after New Year's.

The next morning, the twenty-seventh, we worked our first day at the boatyard after the Christmas break. The day started routinely enough, then quickly went to hell.

I left Mark and Finbar in the office going over some drawings and walked toward the hull, buckling on my tool belt. I started up a ladder toward the deck of the yacht, but before I had reached the third rung, someone grabbed the tool belt from behind and yanked me roughly off the ladder. I landed hard on my back on the cement floor, wondering what was happening. I had managed to get to one knee and paused there, trying to get some new air into my lungs, when a fist caught me high on the cheekbone and spun me around onto my belly. I still didn't know what was happening. I pushed up with my hands to get to my feet, and someone kicked me in the kidney, hard, rolling me over onto my back.

I looked up to find Denny O'Donnell, with a crazed look about him, standing over me. He was about to kick me again, when his brother caught him by the back of his shirt and yanked him backward. "Stop it, Denny!" Donal yelled at his twin. "Just leave it!"

Denny picked up a crowbar and started toward me. "I'll stop when his brains are on the floor!" he shouted at his brother.

Now I was on my feet, prepared to dodge the crowbar, but Donal stepped between us. Without a word, Denny swung at him. Donal's head snapped back reflexively, but the sharp end of the bar raked across his cheek, bringing blood and knocking him flat. Denny resumed his march toward me, holding the crowbar tightly in both hands. From what I had just seen, I had no doubt what he intended to do with it.

I stepped quickly to one side and grabbed a three-foot scrap of two-by-four lumber. When he swung the bar I managed to get that between the crowbar and my head. Splinters flew, and something got in my eye. Blinking, trying to see, I managed to parry another swing of the crowbar with the two-by-four, while moving backward. Then I tripped and sprawled on my back, losing my grip on the piece of lumber. Denny came in, now, a triumphant look on his face. I raised an arm to protect my head and did not see what happened next. I only knew that the crowbar did not strike me.

I heard a grunt, and when I opened my eyes, Denny was holding his wrist, and the crowbar was clanking to the floor. Mark was standing there, holding a thick strip of mahogany, one discarded from the building of the hull. I got to my feet and cleared my eye. Denny was watching Mark, ready to dodge another blow with the stick. I nearly fainted with relief, and then I realized that Mark was standing back, expecting me to fight Denny. Indeed, so was everybody else.

I had one of those moments when time seems to stand still. A lifetime of backing away from bullies ran through my mind, and I was angry, angry with all of them. Denny was still looking at Mark, and something finally boiled over in me, something that filled me with a sense of abandon. I no longer cared whether I would be hurt; I only wanted to punish the object of my new rage.

I charged at Denny, ramming a forearm into his chest, running right over him as he fell. I gathered myself as he got to a knee, clutching his midsection. There was plenty of time, and it was easy; I bent slightly and hit him with one full, roundhouse punch. As it landed I felt something crunch. Denny sailed backward, and I saw teeth fly; I don't think I had ever felt anything so satisfying.

I weigh a hundred and ninety pounds, and, considering what I had put into the punch, I didn't expect him to get up. Astonishingly, he did, spitting blood and fragments of teeth. I discovered that I wanted to hit him again. I stepped toward him, ready to tear his head off this time, but I was stopped in my tracks by the roar of Finbar O'Leary's voice.

"That's enough!" he shouted, and the surprising authority behind the voice froze everybody where he stood. "There'll be no more of this in my place!"

He was right about that. Denny O'Donnell's eyes

glazed over, and he sagged to his knees, shaking his head, trying to remain conscious. Finbar went to Donal.

"Are you all right, lad?" he asked gently. Donal nodded and held a handkerchief to stem the flow of blood from the deep cut on his cheek.

"I'm not hurt, Finbar."

"Can you drive, do you think?"

Donal nodded. "Sure."

"Then get your brother out of here. You'll need some stitches, and Denny's going to need a dentist. Get over to St. Mary's and get yourself fixed up. Don't come back here today and see that Denny doesn't. Call me in the morning, and we'll talk about this."

Donal nodded and went to help his brother to his feet. I put my hand on his shoulder. "Donal, what's this all about? Has Denny gone crazy?"

He shook off my hand and continued to help Denny. "Just leave it, Willie. I'll take care of him, and you take care of yourself. You'll need to do that, now."

Donal slung his brother's arm around his shoulders and helped him to the shed door. We all stood looking after them. A moment later, we heard a car start and drive away.

"What happened?" I said to nobody in particular.

"I don't know," Mark said. "I looked up and saw him pull you off the ladder. Did you say something to him?"

"Not a word," I replied. "I didn't even know who it was until I was flat on my back."

Mark turned. "You know anything about this, Finbar?"

Finbar shook his head and looked bewildered. "Nos-sir, I don't. I know things have never been too good between the two lads, but I don't know what set Denny off." He looked around at the other workers. "Any of you know what this might have been about?" They all shook their heads and looked as bewildered as Finbar. He turned back to me. "Are you hurt in any way, Will?"

I shook my head. My side was a little sore where Denny had kicked me; I probably had a bruise on my cheek, but that was all. "I'm okay," I said. "No damage."

"You could have him arrested," Finbar said.

"No, I don't want that."

"Then let's get to work," Finbar said, picking up a hammer.

Mark leaned over and whispered in my ear. "I told you you were going to have to fight him," he said, chuckling.

Everyone worked quietly through the day. Driving home that night, Mark asked, "Can you think of any reason why Denny should go after you like that? I think he would have killed you."

I shook my head. "No rational reason. He's always hated me, I think. Something to do with Connie. Maybe it's been building up all this time. What happens, now?"

"Finbar will fire Denny. He says he won't have that sort of thing going on. I suppose Donal will go with him."

"I wonder. Will Finbar be able to find another electrician?"

"He says he knows a fellow working on merchant ships in Cork. He's calling him tonight."

"Mark, I can't see Denny letting this stop here. He's just not the sort."

Mark nodded. "I know he's not. I had a word with Finbar; he's going to hire a guard from a local security service to stay at the yard nights. We've the budget for that."

"Good."

"Willie, don't say anything to Annie about all this. She'd only worry; she'd think this confirms all our worst fears."

"Maybe she'd be right," I said.

Mark stared out into the darkness. "Maybe she would be. What did you do with that shotgun I gave you?"

"It's in the cupboard in my bedroom."

"Best see it's loaded tonight."

Twenty-eight

SHE COULD NOT PRAY.

She knelt and clasped her hands together until the knuckles were white, but still, she could not pray. The wind around the stone building moaned and the echo sang softly down the halls, but there was no other sound. To make a sound would seem almost a sin.

She slipped out of the muslin shift, carefully folded it, and placed it neatly on the bed beside the habit. Naked, shivering in the chill, she took the flat package from the pillowcase where she had concealed it and untied the string. The brown wrapping paper rattled alarmingly as she undid it. There was no underwear, and she wanted to take nothing with her from the convent. She slipped into the jeans. How long since she had worn jeans? The sweater was rough against her bare breasts. There were socks, at least; the canvas shoes would not blister her feet. As she struggled into the nylon parka, she felt an odd weight to one side and unzipped a pocket. The shock of cold metal met her hand. The bastard; this was no place for a pistol. He could have waited to give it to her. She wanted to discard it, but she could not leave a gun in the convent. She shoved it back into the pocket and zipped it again.

Her throat was dry; she poured water from the pitcher on the bedside table. As she set down the empty glass, she saw the rosary there. She picked it up, quickly put it into a pocket, then stopped. Just as she could not leave the pistol, she could not take the rosary. She laid it gently on the habit.

She stepped into the hallway, looked both ways and eased the door shut behind her. The canvas shoes made a tiny, squeaking sound as she ran along the smooth, stone floor, and she slowed to stop the noise. One more door. She slipped into the garden and ran lightly along the rows of dormant plants. No point in bothering with the gate; that would be locked. She found an empty garbage can and upended it. From that she could get an elbow over. Astride the wall, she paused and looked, for a moment, back at the low buildings, awash in moonlight, then threw the other leg over and dropped to the ground. The Volkswagen waited fifty yards down the dirt road, lights out, engine running. The door opened for her as she approached. He laughed and leaned over to kiss her, and she reflexively shoved him away.

"Oh, it's like that, is it still?" he chuckled. "Well, that's over, luv. There's no going back, now."

"Shut up," she said, "and drive the motorcar."

Twenty-nine

THE DAYS AFTER MY FIGHT WITH DENNY O'DONNELL passed uneventfully but not without tension. We expected some sort of retaliation, but none came. Finbar found an electrician who would start in the new year, and we breathed a sigh of relief that a technical matter, at least, had been put to rest. Mark and I both knew, though, that it would be a long time before either of us could put the matter of Denny O'Donnell to rest.

On the last day of December I flew from Cork to Paris at midmorning, took a taxi to Jane Berkeley's apartment building on the Avenue Marceau, deposited my luggage with the concierge as instructed, and set off on foot to absorb the City of Light.

I had had a loose sightseeing plan, but it left me as my shoes struck Paris pavement. I walked down the Champs-Élysées, turned right, crossed the Seine, and continued to walk aimlessly down whatever streets looked interesting. Everything looked interesting. When my stomach growled and my feet ached I lunched in a bistro on dishes I knew only by name. I decided that escargots were nothing more than an excuse to eat garlic butter and that coq au vin was the best chicken I'd ever had—and that French wine tasted differently in France and went down very easily. I resumed my wandering slightly drunk.

Two hours later I stood on the top level of the Eiffel Tower and took in the city of my dreams in one long draught. The day had been clear, cold and still, and now the fading December light struck the rooftops of Paris and turned them golden. From here, M. Haussmann's plan for the city revealed itself as from no other vantage point. I could see all the landmarks I had ignored in my wandering and could nearly pick out Jane's apartment building. Armed with a new intimacy with the city, I walked back to the Avenue Marceau and was told, in childishly slow French, that Jane would be delayed at the office, had instructed that I be given a key to her apartment, and had said, I believe, to make myself at home.

I traveled to the sixth floor of the seven-story building in a richly paneled elevator and let myself into the apartment. I set down my bags and had a look around. It was very different from her London mews house, no less elegantly furnished but full of personal things—photographs, books, porcelain—and I was immediately certain that no piece of furniture, no object, had found its way into these rooms without passing the close, personal scrutiny of Lady Jane Berkeley. There was only one bedroom. That pleased me. I poured myself a brandy from a forest of bottles atop a small grand piano, gulped it down, and flung myself onto the bed. The bone weariness of my miles of walking seeped from me into the soft, silk bedcover, and I had only a moment to reflect that, with my new distance from our troubles in Ireland, a knot inside me had untied itself. I was asleep in seconds.

I woke in nearly total darkness, momentarily disoriented. The luminous hands of my wristwatch said nearly seven, and still no Jane. I switched on a bedside lamp, straggled to my feet, stiff and groggy, undressed, and got into a hot shower. I did not hear the front door open and close. I was unaware of another presence in the apartment until I caught a glimpse of movement outside the pebbled, glass shower door less than a second before it was yanked open. I threw myself back against a tile surface, the memory of a Hitchcock movie racing through my mind. I was Janet Leigh in *Psycho,* and a bewigged Anthony Perkins was slashing at me with a huge knife.

She flung herself at me, laughing, rubbing her naked body against mine, pulling my head down to hers with one hand in my hair, while goosing me in the ribs with the other.

"Jesus," I gasped, "you want me to have a coronary before I've had a chance to improve my French?"

The hand in my ribs traveled to another, better place. "I'm about to teach you all the French you'll ever need to know," she laughed, doing interesting things with the hand.

"It may never work again," I said, looking down, "after that sort of scare. I think you've just rendered me permanently impotent."

"Want to bet?" she asked, still laughing, still continuing her work. I didn't want to bet. I would have lost immediately.

We lay, damp and out of breath, on the bed. I was aglow with my newfound sexual prowess. Apparently, I possessed some animal magnetism for women that had, heretofore, gone unnoticed by them. I could only assume that Jane Berkeley was a keener judge than most; I was unwilling to pursue the reasons for my good fortune beyond that.

"Where have you been?" I asked. "It's nearly nine o'clock."

"Pressures of work and all that," she replied, rearranging herself so that her head rested on my lap. "There was an important meeting to decide on financing a big, new office complex in Lyon."

"What did you decide?"

She laughed. "I didn't decide anything. I'm here to learn, remember? I was lucky to even sit in on a meeting at that level."

"Did you learn anything?"

"Not a thing. I was thinking too much about what *this* would be like."

"You'll never learn international banking that way."

"No, but I'll have a rich fantasy life."

I ran my fingers over her wet hair. "What's on for tonight? How are we spending our New Year's Eve?"

"Oh, there's a party at a friend's that should be interesting. After that we'll improvise." She wriggled her head in my lap.

"I may be all improvised out, you know."

"Nonsense, champagne will bring you back. Champagne is a restorative."

I certainly hoped so.

An hour later we were both dressed to kill; Jane was in something superelegant from Yves St. Laurent, and I was in my dinner jacket from the Cork men's shop. We stepped from her apartment into the hallway and started for the elevator.

"Aren't you going to lock up?" I asked.

She shook her head. "It's a very secure building."

The elevator arrived, and we stepped in. She caught my hand as I reached for the ground-floor button. Instead, she pushed an unmarked button above the seventh, "top-floor" button. The light above the door moved to seven, then went out; the elevator continued to move upward for what seemed to be at least two more floors.

"Doesn't this put us somewhere above the building?" I asked, mystified.

"Not quite," she said as the elevator came to a stop. We stepped into a deeply carpeted, heavily wallpapered vestibule and were immediately greeted by a smartly uniformed butler.

"Good evening, Lady Jane, Mr. Lee," he said smoothly in very British English. Two other men were in the vestibule, large men stuffed into tuxedos; one took our coats, the other merely looked me up and down slowly and carefully, then checked our names off a list.

"Good evening, Brooks," Jane replied. "Are we very late?"

"Oh, no, Lady Jane; very good timing, I should say." He turned and expertly opened a pair of sliding doors. "Lady Jane Berkeley and Mr. William Lee," he announced. A man a few feet away turned and strode toward us, his arms outstretched. It was Nicky, the Arab I had met at Thrasher's place in London.

"Ah, Jane, Happy New Year, and Will, how very nice to see you again; I'm so glad you could come to Paris."

I shook his hand, remarking again to myself how very English he sounded. "Happy New Year, Nicky," I replied. "I'm surprised to see you in Paris; Jane didn't tell me." I was further surprised to glance across the room and see Derek Thrasher coming toward us.

He pecked Jane on the cheek and took my hand in both of his. "Welcome to Paris, Will, and Happy New Year."

As we exchanged greetings I looked at him closely; he had changed, somehow; thinner, I thought, and rather tired-looking. Before we could talk much he turned to greet other people entering the room, and Nicky propelled us toward a knot of people at the center of the room.

The makeup of the group was much the same as had been the case at Thrasher's house in London—film types, politicians, big-business people—only the mix was more international. Genevieve Wheatley was in evidence. Jane guided me among the guests, introducing me to this producer and that cabinet minister; she knew them all. A paper-thin crystal champagne flute was put into my hand and kept full by liveried waiters who glided unobtrusively among the guests. I estimated there were at least three gallons of caviar distributed about the large, ornate salon in heavy, crystal bowls. With the champagne, I began to feel, at once, out of my depth and quite at home. My poor French was not a handicap; people switched easily into English when Jane introduced me in that language. I felt unaccustomedly bright, witty, and, ridiculously, among my peers. Thrasher came and put a hand on my shoulder.

"Jane, may I borrow your gentleman for a few moments?" I thought he had intended to introduce me to someone, but he walked me into a small, mahogany-paneled library, grabbing a bottle of champagne from a waiter along the way. He motioned me to an overstuffed leather library chair. "Now," he said, pouring us both a drink and collapsing wearily onto a sofa, "I want to hear about the boat, all about it."

"You're going to love it," I said. "It's going to be . . .

perfect, I think. Mark is doing a fantastic job on it; you couldn't have chosen a better man."

"At what stage are you now?"

"The hull has been finished and turned; the keel's on; the engine's in; decking is nearly complete; the electrical work begins next week."

"Sounds as if you're ahead of schedule."

"Not really," I replied. "The interior work is going to be very time-consuming. The sort of standard you want on the furniture and electronics installations is going to take a lot of man-hours, and few men will be working on that part. Mark thinks she'll be in the water by early June for sea trials; she'll probably have to go back to the yard for alterations and touching up after that, and she should be ready for the race to the Azores in late July."

"Who's going on that?"

"Just Mark, Annie, and I. Annie and I will fly back, and Mark will sail her back singlehanded to Cork to qualify for the Transatlantic. He really only needs a three-hundred-mile qualifying cruise, but he wants to really give the yacht a tough workout."

"Good, I wish I could come with you to the Azores, but time will just not permit. Believe me, there's nothing I'd like more than a week or ten days at sea with you and Mark and Annie, but the situation ashore is demanding too much attention."

"We read something in the London papers. Is that as big a problem as it sounds?"

He took a long draught of his champagne and laid

his head back on the couch. "It could be. What you've read is absolutely not true, about the exchange control violations, but we're having a hell of a time proving it. I must say I've never been through anything quite like this. I can't even so much as visit England until we've sorted things out." He raised his head and looked at me. "I understand you're having some problems of your own in Cork."

I was surprised he knew anything about it, but at least I was spared the decision of whether to tell him. I poured out the whole story, the trashing of the cottage, the leak about Thrasher's involvement through Connie's nun friend, the equipment disappearances, the attempt to sabotage the yacht, everything right up through my fight with Denny O'Donnell a few days before.

"Do you think this local IRA faction is dangerous?"

"I honestly don't know. Mark thinks not, and thus far he's been proven right, but . . ."

"But what?"

"I think Denny O'Donnell is completely unpredictable. We might never hear of him again, or he might burn down the boatyard. There's apparently a history of that sort of thing in his family, burning people out. Mark's got a security guard from Cork there nights; I hope that'll prevent anything terrible from happening."

"Now, listen, Will, and I want you to pass this on to Mark: I don't want any of you to get hurt on account of something as unimportant as a boat. If at any time you or Mark feels truly threatened, I want you to stop the project. I can always have the boat shipped to England and finished there. Are we clear on that point?"

I nodded. "I'll pass that on to Mark. Mind you, he's not the sort to back down in a confrontation. He'd mount a cannon on the foredeck if necessary."

Thrasher laughed. "I'm sure he would, but I don't want it to come to that. I'll have somebody get in touch with you in Cork about security. That shouldn't have to come out of Mark's budget; I'll see that it's handled quietly."

"Derek, do you think we could do something about establishing better communications with you? We don't want to impose on your time, but there might be occasions when we really need to reach you."

He nodded. "Of course, Will. I'm sorry you've had difficulties in the past." He took a notebook from his pocket, scribbled a number, tore out the page and handed it to me. "Call this number at any hour; it's in New York. You'll hear an electronic beep; leave a message, state your problem as concisely as possible. Be circumspect; don't mention my name. Someone, probably not I, will be in touch as soon as possible. Got that?"

I nodded. The door to the library opened and Nicky appeared, holding a legal-sized manila envelope. "Excuse me, Derek, it's nearly time. We'd better hurry."

"Of course, Nicky." Thrasher stood up. "You must excuse me for a while, Will, I'll catch up to you at the party later."

We walked into the salon, and Thrasher and Nicky went quickly toward the elevator. Apparently, business never stopped for Derek Thrasher; not even on New Year's Eve. I rejoined Jane in time for a sumptuous buffet supper that was being served at the other end of the room.

Thirty

MACADAM IGNORED THE HANGOVER. HE ROSE AT eight, later than he used to, but still managed thirty sit-ups and twenty push-ups. The legs might not be quite what they were, but the biceps were still firm and the belly flat. He looked younger than his fifty-six years. He had cereal for breakfast, read the *Daily Mail,* then dressed in one of his half-dozen three-piece tweed suits. MacAdam fancied himself something of a gentleman and dressed rather like a detective inspector in an Alfred Hitchcock film. It was a trademark.

He made the bed, then stepped into his parlor/office, pulling the curtains that separated it from the bedroom. The large oak desk was neatly arranged, and the leather furniture was dusted; the cleaning lady had been in the day before. He opened the curtains and peered out. He could see South Kensington tube station just down the street. An occasional ring of the cash register could be heard from the wine shop downstairs.

He was open for business promptly at nine, though the morning passed without a ring of the doorbell or the telephone. He checked in with his answering service; not much, some debt collections to do and an anxious husband wondering if his wife had been caught with the boyfriend yet. He would attend to those later in the day. He spent the morning reading a new paperback about making a killing in the stock market. He was conservative with most of what he had tucked away, but now and again he took a flyer. He hadn't done badly.

The letter arrived by messenger precisely at noon. Alfred MacAdam, who had permitted himself to be called "Blackie," but not "Tar," in his days on the force, was unaccustomed to receiving assignments in such a fashion, his clients preferring not to commit their problems to writing. Mind you, this client didn't give away much. There were £120 sterling in twenty-pound notes, an airline ticket, and a brief note, typed, but not signed:

"Sir, with apologies for the brief notice and awkward arrangements, I would like to discuss with you a matter that might require several days of your services. If you can make yourself available under the circumstances please come to the above address at 10.30 p.m. this evening for a meeting of perhaps 30 minutes duration. I enclose an air ticket, 100 pounds to be applied to a mutually agreed-upon fee, and 20 pounds for incidental expenses."

There was an address and flat number. No mention

of what to do with the money and ticket if he should decide not to come. Whoever had sent the note had been pretty confident of his interest. He could simply pocket the money, cash in the ticket and be nearly £200 to the good; still, he was intrigued. Whoever could afford to send £120 to a stranger had more to put behind it.

On the airplane he declined a drink, though, God knew, he could have used it. If this client were as important as he might be, booze on the breath would not be good. Then the stewardess came back with complimentary champagne, and he accepted. What the hell, it was New Year's Eve after all. The client would probably have had a few himself. He had a second glass.

Traffic was light, and he was early. He walked about for a few minutes, found a bar, and had a large whisky. At 10:29 he entered the building, took the lift to the top floor, and found the flat. He rang the bell; there was a delay, and he thought he heard voices before the door was opened by a short, swarthy, rather handsome man in evening clothes. Greek? Arab? Jew?

"Good evening, Mr. MacAdam," the man said blandly. He would have preferred to be called "inspector," though the circumstances of his leaving the force might have cast doubt on his right to that rank. "Please come and sit down." The accent, the intonation were upper-class English. The man did not offer to shake hands, and no drink was forthcoming. MacAdam glanced briefly about. A woman's place, no doubt about it. There were photographs on the piano; he wished he were close enough to see them better. The door to the darkened bedroom was ajar. Somebody in there listening, probably.

The man sat on the sofa and motioned MacAdam to an armchair. "I wish to engage your services for a period of, perhaps, five days."

MacAdam crossed his legs and smoothed the trousers of his tweed suit. "May I ask who brought me to your attention?"

"Suffice it to say that you come well recommended, and that I am aware of the nature of your service with the London police."

"Just what services do you require, Mr. . . . ?"

"I wish to know everything about a certain man. I can tell you his name, his nationality, and his most recent address in Greater London. I wish to know everything else you can find out about him in five days. I must ask you to accept or reject the assignment now, before going any further. If you reject the assignment, you may keep the funds advanced you and return to London. If you accept, I shall give you such information as I have about the man, and you may begin immediately. I shall require a report from you at noon on January fifth. The assignment will pay a hundred pounds a day, plus twenty pounds for expenses. You have been paid for one day; I shall pay you for another before you leave, and the remainder will be sent to you by messenger after you have made your report."

MacAdam shifted in his seat. "I don't ordinarily accept assignments with so little information about the client."

"Then I shan't keep you any longer," the man said, rising.

MacAdam motioned him to sit. "All right, all right," he chuckled, "I'm just a bit curious, that's all. Just one thing; will this require any action on my part that might be other than kosh . . . ah, cricket?"

The man sat again. "You may not construe anything I may say to you as a proposal to break the law, Mr. Mac-Adam; however, I would not presume to tell you how to go about your work."

"Very well, I accept."

"Good." The man handed him a buff envelope. "This contains what I know about the man. His name is Patrick Pearce; he is an Irish national; until recently, he was employed as an auditor for Avondale Enterprises, a registered company, with offices in London. A copy of his employment application is in the envelope, along with a photograph taken on the occasion of his joining the company some months ago. You are not to inquire of Avondale about the man; everything they know is in the envelope."

"Might I not speak to some of his coworkers?"

"He apparently kept much to himself. No one at Avondale is to be contacted."

"Is there anything in particular you'd like to know about Pearce?"

The man looked thoughtful for a moment. "He is

Irish; I'd like to know if he has any . . . political . . . ah, associations; also, if he holds any great grudges—political or personal."

"You'd like me to interview him, then?"

"Not unless you can conduct such a meeting without his being aware that he is being interviewed."

"I see."

"Good." The man got to his feet.

MacAdam rose, as well. "How may I contact you?"

"You may not. I shall contact you at noon on the fifth. Please be in your office at that time."

"Right." MacAdam did not attempt to shake hands again, having once been rebuffed. He had the distinct impression that his client disapproved of him either personally or socially. The man had eyed his tweed suit in a manner that did not indicate admiration; and it came from a fellow who had once worked at one of Savile Row's great tailors. He had kept the fellow out of the nick once, and now he got his clothes done for the cost of the material. MacAdam didn't mind. The money was right. He wondered who the man was, though. Perhaps he might do some checking into that while checking into Pearce. He wondered who might have been in the bedroom listening.

He went back to the bar and had another large whisky. Christ, these Frogs knew how to charge for it. He checked his airline ticket; there was just time to make his plane. The hell with it; one didn't get to Paris every day and get paid for it. He telephoned the airline and rebooked for a flight the next morning, then walked to the Champs-Élysées, almost immediately found an acceptable whore, and spent the night with her in a hotel. On reaching Heathrow the following morning, he barely had cab fare home.

Thirty-one

"YOU'VE BEEN IN TOUCH WITH DEREK ALL ALONG, haven't you?" I tried not to make it sound like an accusation.

She smiled slightly and sipped her beer. "This is a favorite place of mine. Wait'll you taste the *choucroute*."

We were at Brasserie Lipp, in St. Germain des Prés, for lunch, at a prime table. A chauffeured Citroën waited for us at the curb. Paris with Jane was interesting. "Well, we did get the money on time; thanks for that. I just hope he doesn't scare the pants off us again next time."

"Derek is very reliable. He didn't need reminding by me."

"Is that his place upstairs?"

"It's Nicky's."

"It just looked like Derek, somehow."

"They have similar tastes; they've known each other since they were seven. They were at Eton together."

The *choucroute* arrived. I wouldn't have ordered it if I had known it was going to be sauerkraut, but she was right; it was delicious, as were the sausages and ham piled on top. "That's where Nicky got the accent, then. Was he born in England?"

She shook her head, swinging a dangling bit of kraut across her chin. "Nicky was born in a tent in the desert. It was a very nice tent, mind you. Nicky is an actual prince of his country."

"No kidding?"

"No kidding. His grandfather ruled mostly over camels and goats until the oil changed things in the late thirties."

"Is Nicky going to be king someday?"

She shook her head again. "He has thirty-odd brothers. No chance. But he's probably the most important of them, because of his business skills."

"He and Derek do a lot of business together, do they?"

"If it weren't for Nicky, Derek would probably be a successful stockbroker, nothing more. Nicky . . ." She paused and put down her fork. "Almost no one knows this, Will."

I nodded. "Okay, sealed lips." I couldn't wait to pass this on to Mark and Annie, and to my parents.

"Derek's family were well-placed enough to send him to Eton; he went to Oxford on a scholarship. He had no money. His future in business would have been to work for somebody else. But Nicky—once his family un-

derstood how bright he was—had access to virtually unlimited capital. Derek was even brighter, and with Nicky
behind him, there was no stopping him. Just out of Oxford they invested about fifty thousand pounds in some
houses in Islington and Camden Town—just workmen's
houses, really. They fixed them up and resold them at a
handsome profit, then repeated the process, reinvesting
their profits in still more property."

"I'd heard something about winkling old ladies out
of their homes."

"I wouldn't put it that way; they were paid good prices
at a time when there was no market. Derek found cheap
flats for them and they were resettled with a nice little
nest egg. It was a good arrangement for everybody."

I wondered.

"When Nicky's family saw how astonishingly well
they were doing, they made much larger amounts of
capital available, and everybody was happy. Derek grew
very wealthy very quickly, in a lot of different sorts of
ventures, and Nicky was able to stay out of the limelight.
That's important to him. Few people are aware that he
is the financial brain in his family. He lives the part of
the playboy in Europe—and enjoys it immensely, by the
way—and the family's fortune grows. People think of
him as nothing more than Derek's sidekick, like those
characters in your American westerns."

"So Nicky is Walter Brennan to Derek's John
Wayne."

"For purposes of appearances, yes. But each of them

shields the other in important ways. Derek's reputation preserves Nicky's anonymity as a financier, and Nicky can protect Derek by acting for him, seeming to be only a flunky, when Derek is anxious to preserve his privacy."

"Which is the dominant of the two?"

"Neither. Oh, Derek often seems to be in charge, because that suits them both, but they are, in fact, the most perfectly equal partners I have ever known." There was admiration, even sensuality in the way she said that.

I regretted my next question almost before I asked it; it began as a joke, but before it was out of my mouth it was serious. "And which one of them do you fuck?" I asked, stuffing my last bite of *choucroute* into my mouth.

She never missed a beat. "Both," she said evenly, gazing calmly across the table at me. "Sometimes together."

The sauerkraut turned dry in my mouth. I chewed it valiantly, to keep from having to speak.

"I particularly enjoy them together," she said, motioning to a waiter for the bill.

I swallowed hard, chasing the food with some beer. I was shocked to the bone.

"Are you shocked?" she asked.

"Certainly not," I replied.

I felt her hand on my thigh under the table. "Are you excited?"

"Yes," I replied, and I was astonished that it was the truth.

"Let's get out of here," she said, signing the check and pushing the table away. I followed her out of the restaurant and to the car, where the chauffeur was waiting, braced, with the door opened. He handed her a fresh Paris *Herald Tribune.* In the car she handed me the newspaper, then turned, reached down and unzipped my fly. *"Le Louvre,"* she said to the chauffeur.

"Oui, Ma'amselle," he replied, starting the engine.

As her head came down to my lap, I flung up the newspaper to shield us from the chauffeur's eyes in the rearview mirror. A headline at the bottom of the front page said, "INEPT BUT LUCKY GUNMEN ROB CORK BANK AND ARMORED CAR," but my vision blurred before I could read the story.

Thirty-two

I STUMBLED OFF THE PLANE IN CORK, A SHELL OF MY FORmer self, after two almost sleepless days of gorging myself on French food and wine, while myself being gorged on by Jane Berkeley. I had not before, nor have I since known any woman so voracious in all her appetites, and I reached the cottage slaked, sated, drained and shattered. The telephone began ringing as I was unlocking the door. I got it on the fifth ring, not really caring if the caller hung up.

"Hello."

"To whom am I speaking, please?" It was a man's voice, one I did not recognize.

"To whom do you wish to speak?" I replied, annoyed.

"To either a Captain Pemberton-Robinson or a Mr. Lee, please." The voice maintained a businesslike courtesy.

"This is Will Lee." There was something terribly

official-sounding about the man's voice; I wondered if he were a policeman.

"Mr. Lee, my name is Primrose, Major Primrose. I believe you may be expecting my call."

I drew a blank; he guessed that from my silence.

"I've been asked . . . is this a secure line?"

I laughed aloud. "What?"

"May we safely speak on this line?"

"Well, sure, I guess so . . . I . . ."

"This is the number of the cottage, is it not?"

"Yes . . . look, I'm afraid I don't have the slightest idea what you're talking about. Are you suggesting this phone might be tapped, or something?"

"I'm merely being careful, Mr. Lee. I believe you had a discussion with a gentleman in Paris about a potential problem."

The penny finally dropped; this was Derek Thrasher's security man. "Oh, yes, I'm sorry, I just didn't make the connection."

"I've just rung to tell you that all is in place. You may scrub your other arrangements as of this time."

"Ah . . . oh, yes, I'll tell Mark . . . Captain Pemberton-Robinson."

"Let me give you a number to call if you should experience any difficulties or need further assistance from us." I jotted down the number. "Please call any time, day or night; leave a message for me, personally—Major Primrose—or if your problem is . . . of a pressing nature, just tell the man who answers that you have a Code Four situation, and what help you think you may need."

"Code Four."

"Right. Don't telephone us from the place in question unless it's absolutely necessary; that will be difficult to keep secure. The cottage line should be all right, but we'll check it periodically to be certain."

"Yes, fine." All this seemed a little preposterous to me, but it was also curiously comforting. I hung up; it was just noon, Mark would be at the yard and Annie was out someplace. I undressed and collapsed into my bed.

Sometime later I woke, groggy and disoriented. I looked at my watch: nearly four o'clock. I got into the shower and let the hot water run. Dried and dressed I still felt fuzzy around the edges; I picked up Mark's sheepskin coat and walked out into the chilly January late afternoon. Perhaps a walk would clear my head.

I trudged back along the road toward the main house, walking fast to get my circulation going. The tide had turned in the river and was going out fast, now. A cloud passed over the sun, and I noticed for the first time that it was looking like rain. This happened so often in Ireland that I hardly paid attention. I turned and started back for the cottage, hurrying to beat the weather. From a distance I heard the baying of hounds; the hunt was in full cry over the hill to my left. As I half-walked, half-ran toward the cottage the pack crested the hill, and I thought I saw the fox dart into the woods behind the cottage. The hunt was close behind. A hundred yards up the hill horses were clearing one of the many stone walls that criss-crossed the countryside that made Irish hunting so exciting and so dangerous. I could see Lord Coolmore in the lead, riding hell for leather. A few drops of rain fell, now. I hurried on.

As I approached the cottage I could see that two of the hounds had broken from the pack and were worrying something on the foreshore of the river, just in front of the cottage. A sickly odor wrinkled my nose. Things were always washing up with the tide; once there had been a dead dog, another time, a sheep. I would have to push whatever it was back into the water or, so close to the cottage, it would stink up the place for hours until the tide came back in and floated it away. I didn't relish the job, but I jumped down from the stone wall before the cottage and walked along the foreshore, shouting at the dogs, trying to run them off. Foxhounds are not the cute little beagles nonhunting people imagine them to be. They are big, brawny animals, half-wild. I threw a stone toward them. One backed off a few feet, then resumed tearing at the carcass. It was big; a sheep, or maybe even a small cow.

I threw more stones, and this time both dogs reluctantly retreated a few yards and stood, waiting for a chance to get back at their disgusting meal. I avoided looking at the thing and cast about for a stick to move it with. The stench was awful, now. There was an old mop we had used on *Toscana* lying on the wall; I picked it up and started toward the carcass. Once I had it back in the water I didn't think the hounds would swim after it. Approaching the water's edge I finally had to look at it. I stopped, frozen in my tracks. It was not a sheep, not a cow. I was looking at the bloated, discolored corpse of a man, lying facedown on the foreshore, its legs still in the water. The flesh of its back and an arm was torn where the dogs had been at it. Heavy raindrops splashed on its filthy skin.

I turned away and tried not to vomit but failed. When I got control of myself again, I started for the cottage; I had to call someone, but the dogs were still there. I charged them, swinging the mop, chased them until they ran into the woods toward the sound of the pack, receding into the distance. I hoisted myself up the wall, walked weakly into the cottage, found the phone directory, called the local police, and briefly told my story. They would be along shortly. I sat down heavily and put my head between my legs. As it began to clear I was struck suddenly with a thought: who was the man? I stood up quickly. What had happened in my absence?

I walked outside and stood on the wall, forcing myself to look down at the naked corpse a few yards away. The smell seemed to be growing worse. I gagged but held on. It was not a woman, I felt sure of that, even with the awful bloating. Thank God it wasn't Annie, but . . . It was difficult to determine how big or tall the man had been, since the legs were partly obscured by the water. I've got to look at the face, I thought, I've got to go down there and turn it over. But I couldn't do it. Instead, I went back into the cottage and, trembling, dialed the number of Cork Harbour Boatyard.

"Hello?" It was Finbar's voice.

"Finbar, it's Will." I took a deep breath. "Is Mark there?"

"Oh, hello, Willie. No, he didn't come in today. I rang the cottage about ten thirty, but there was no answer. I haven't spoken with him since before the holiday. Where are you?"

"I'm at the cottage."

"He's not there, then?"

"No." I was beginning to think he might be.

"Well, maybe he just needed a day off. He's been putting in a lot of time, y'know."

"Yeah, okay, Finbar, I'll see you later."

"Right, Willie."

I hung up, shaking badly. Panic was creeping up on me, now. What was I doing in this place where people didn't want us, where our work had to be guarded by people like Major Primrose? Why did one of us have to die before I knew that I shouldn't be here? And Christ, where was Annie?

"Willie! Welcome home!"

I jerked around. Annie walked across the room, tossing a duffel onto the sofa, struggling out of her coat before coming across the room to hug me. I held on to her tightly.

"What's wrong?" she asked, taking my head in her hands. She made a face. "And what's that awful smell?"

"Annie . . ." I was having difficulty speaking. "Annie, where's Mark?"

"Right here, old sport." He was standing in the front door, holding two bags of groceries.

I sank into a chair and tried to take some deep breaths while the two of them stood mutely and looked at me. "Just give me a minute," I managed to say. I took some more breaths. I was curiously angry with both of them. "Mark, why didn't you go to the yard today?"

"We decided to drive down to West Cork for New Year's. We spent a couple of nights at Castletownshend."

"Then why the hell didn't you call Finbar?"

"I tried, but the phone down there was on the blink. Anyway, Finbar knows how to run a boatyard without me. What's going on, Willie? What's wrong?"

"There's a goddamned corpse out there on the fore-shore, that's what's wrong, and I thought it was you!"

Mark turned and left the cottage, and Annie started after him. "Hold it, Annie! Please don't go out there. Really, you don't want to." She stopped.

Mark stuck his head inside the door. "The police are here; you'd better come and talk with them."

I walked from the cottage to find two policemen on the foreshore, kneeling over the corpse. They were wearing yellow rain gear; it was coming down hard, now. One of them, the sergeant in charge at the little Carrigaline station, got up and came over to me.

"Mr. Lee?"

"Yes, I'm Will Lee. I called you." I told him my story.

"I don't think it was there when I left the cottage; I would have smelled it. It must have washed up while I was out walking."

The sergeant nodded. "I'd say you're right. They don't smell much when they're still in the water, but once they're out, they go bad very quickly. He's been in the water for a few days, I'd say."

"Do you think he was dumped around here?" Mark asked.

"Maybe, but he could have been put in the water in Carrigaline, or almost anyplace in Cork Harbour. The tides do some odd things, and the current in the river here is pretty stiff at times."

"About two knots at full ebb or flow," Mark said.

The sergeant turned and looked at his men, who were rolling the corpse into a plastic bag for loading onto a stretcher. "I'd like you both to come and have a look at him; I know he's not a pretty sight, but he won't get any prettier, and I'd like to know if you recognize him."

We followed the sergeant down to the foreshore; a policeman was just zipping the bag shut. He partly unzipped it again for our benefit. Mark and I looked at the face.

"I don't know him," Mark said. "At least, I don't think so. It's pretty hard to imagine what he looked like without the swelling."

"And you, sir?" the sergeant asked of me.

I started to say, no, I didn't recognize the man, but then my eyes drifted downward from the face and stopped. "Just a minute," I said. I found a tin can on the wet foreshore, got some water, and splashed a little on the corpse. Some mud and weed washed away.

"Jesus Christ," Mark said quietly.

We were looking at a heart-shaped tattoo on the corpse's chest; the initials "M. M." were clearly visible. "His name is Donal O'Donnell," I said to the policeman.

"One of the twins? From Kinsale?"

"Yes. The tattoo is the only way I could tell them apart."

"Do you know where he lives?"

I shook my head. "I think he and his brother used to share a flat somewhere, but I heard he had moved into his own place; I don't know where, though."

"We'll find out, then we should be able to get a fingerprint identification, as well. I'll need you to sign a statement of identification in a day or two."

"Any idea how he died?" Mark asked.

"Well, this is unofficial, but he was shot in the back of the head."

"A proper execution, then."

The sergeant nodded. "Looks that way. What's more, he was kneecapped."

We were all a bit subdued at dinner.

"Donal, he was the nice one, wasn't he?" Annie asked.

I nodded. "I liked him. He wasn't like Denny at all. I always thought that identical twins were supposed to be more alike than anybody. They could hardly have been more different. To think that Denny could . . ." I left the remark hanging.

"I'm thinking the same way you are," Mark said quietly. "Without any sort of evidence, I believe implicitly that Denny killed his brother. I think he was perfectly capable of it."

We ate silently for a while.

"What does this mean in terms of the boat?" Annie asked.

"Not much, I suppose," Mark replied. "If anything, it means we'll have to worry less about Denny. If he did it he's surely on the run. He won't have time for us. He won't stay around Cork, where he's known, either."

"It's ironic that just when Derek has arranged all this security, we're less likely to need it," I said. I had told Mark about Major Primrose, and he had canceled the local guard.

"I'm quite happy to have it, anyway," Mark said. We were silent again.

"Well, I've told you about Paris," I said, finally. "What's the news here?"

"Not much," Annie replied. "Oh, there was a bank robbery in Cork; it was quite funny, really. The robbers seemed rather awkward, apparently, then by coincidence, an armored car rolled up to the bank to make a delivery, and they got three or four times as much as they might have a few minutes earlier. They just blundered their way through and walked off with a fortune."

"They haven't caught them?"

"No; they found the car they'd used—stolen from a local fisherman—remember that big fellow with the red beard on the fishing boat when we ran over his salmon nets last autumn? Shook his fist at us? His car, it was—a Volkswagen."

I remembered. I also remembered the Volkswagen that had followed me when I left the boatyard, and the familiar-looking, red-bearded man in it, and the number plate, OOP. All these things, the bank, the car, the fisherman, the murder of Donal O'Donnell, seemed to be rubbing together. There was one more link in the chain, but I didn't know about that yet. I would soon.

Thirty-three

I T WAS NEARLY TEN O'CLOCK WHEN I ARRIVED AT THE COT-
tage, but I knew she wouldn't be asleep yet.

"Oh, it's you," she said, without enthusiasm, when
she opened the door.

"Do you mind if I come in?" I asked, when she didn't
automatically show me in. "I want to talk with you."

"I don't much want to talk to you," she said sullenly.
She still didn't ask me in.

"What's going on, Connie?" I asked.

"Not very much that I'd care to discuss with you. Why
don't you go back to Paris and do your talking there?"

So that was it. She'd somehow found out that I hadn't
spent New Year's with my parents. I certainly didn't want
to discuss *that* with her. "Donal O'Donnell is dead," I
said. That did it; she let me in. Oddly, she didn't look
terribly surprised.

"How?" she asked. She didn't offer me a drink.

"I found his body washed up at Drake's Pool this afternoon. It had been in the water several days."

"How?" she asked again.

"He was shot in the back of the head." I stopped, uncertain whether to go on. Her face would not let me stop. "And kneecapped."

"Oh, God," she said softly, sinking down onto the couch. "I can't believe he did that."

"Denny?"

She nodded. "And I certainly don't believe Maeve could have been a party to it."

I sat down beside her. "Maeve? Why Maeve? Why would she be mixed up in Donal's death?"

"I hope she's not," Connie sighed, "but she left the convent on New Year's Eve; just walked out in the middle of the night. I think she's with Denny. But I don't think she could have had anything to do with killing Donal, I won't believe that."

I was baffled by all of this. "I don't understand; why would Maeve be with Denny O'Donnell?"

"She's been seeing him for a long time; she finally told me about it after your fight with Denny at the boatyard."

"Well, I had sort of a fight with her, too." Now I was beginning to understand why Denny had attacked me.

She nodded. "I know. That was my fault, I guess. I'd been telling her about my troubles with you."

"Jesus, what troubles?"

"You son of a bitch," she shot back, "you were supposed to be with me on New Year's Eve; and then, supposed to be with your parents. All along it was that aristocratic bitch in heat from London, wasn't it? Lady Jane." She spat out the name.

"All right," I said, backed into a corner. "All right, I lied about that. It was just. . . ."

"Just a better offer."

I squirmed under her gaze. I couldn't think of any way to reply to that. "What about Maeve?" I asked, grateful for a new subject to hide behind. "Where is she? What will she do now?"

Connie turned and looked into the dying turf fire. "I don't know where she is," she said sadly, "but I think I may know what she's doing; I have a feeling she's doing banks."

"Banks?" I was baffled again for just a moment. "You mean that thing in Cork? Jesus, what makes you think that?"

"Oh, in some circles it's the time-honored method of raising money."

This was all coming too thick and fast for me. "Now, wait a minute, let me get this straight: You think that Maeve and Denny O'Donnell killed his brother—his identical twin, for Christ's sake—then stuck up a bank and went off to join the IRA?"

"I do *not* believe Maeve had anything to do with killing Donal."

"But the rest? Is that what you think?"

"Something like that."

"Well, I'll tell you what I think." I was annoyed at all this outrageous fantasizing and happy to have something to be annoyed about to keep from discussing how I had spent New Year's. "I think that's the craziest thing I ever heard. I think *you're* crazy. I think that none of this makes any sense at all . . . except . . ." I faltered as I began to think about it.

"Except," she ticked off her points on her fingers, "that Donal is dead, ritually murdered; Maeve is gone from the convent without a trace; the bank has been robbed——"

I broke in. "I haven't heard anything about one of the robbers being a woman."

"Maeve is a big girl, five nine or ten—taller than Denny—and in a stocking mask, if she didn't speak, she could pass for a man. The shorter of the two robbers did all the talking."

"Where are you getting all this information? I haven't heard any of this."

"You forget that my father was manager of that bank before he retired. He's had all the gossip."

"But why would Maeve do all this?" I felt I was beginning to lose this argument on points.

"Well, you've heard a bit of her politics, haven't you? Maeve is a very angry person; she's very political; and she's always been very activist in everything she's done. Lately, she's been spouting a real load of rubbish about what brave people the Baader-Meinhof gang are, and how nothing's ever going to change without——"

"Baader-Meinhof? Those crazy people in Germany?"

She nodded. "Them, and the Red Brigade in Italy, those are sort of her heroes, those and the Irish Freedom Brigade . . ."

"Jesus, isn't that the outfit that claimed credit for bombing Derek Thrasher's office in London?"

"Now you're getting the picture," she said.

I was very much afraid that I was. "Well, shouldn't you tell the police about all this?"

"Oh, no," she said firmly, "this is just all my crazy notion, remember? I don't have any real evidence of all this."

"But Donal is dead. Surely . . ."

"And I can't bring him back. Maeve is still my friend, and I know she couldn't have had anything to do with that. If you're so hot about this, why don't *you* go to the police?"

That shut me up. I just wanted to be as far from all this as possible.

"I thought not," she said, after my silence. "Anyway, you're out of it, now. Maeve and Denny are gone, and they won't be back here. Now you can build your boat in peace."

I hoped to God she was right.

Thirty-four

"S UNSHINE TRAVEL." THE VOICE ON THE PHONE WAS pleasant, eager to help.

"I wish to arrange a special holiday in a warm and sunny place."

There was only a tiny pause. "What sort of holiday did you have in mind?"

"I have one or two ideas, but I'd like the advice of your managing director."

"Who recommended our agency?" The voice was cooler, harder now.

"My bishop."

"How many in your party?"

"Two. A priest and a nun."

"Are you interested in a retreat?"

"I'm more interested in something educational."

"That could be very expensive."

"The parish coffers will bear any expense nicely."

"Your name?"

She paused and thought for a moment. "Sister Concepta."

"Please hold." He covered the phone with his hand and held a muffled conversation. "Where are you now?"

"In a call box in Grafton Street, across from Switzer's."

"Are you alone?"

"The priest is with me."

"Get rid of him. Buy a newspaper, stand in front of Switzer's for fifteen minutes, reading the paper. Then walk to the southwest corner of St. Stephen's Green. There's a call box there. Wait for a call."

"Right." She hung up the phone and turned. "Take this stuff," she said, thrusting her packages upon him, "and go back to the hotel. Wait for me there."

"Oh, no," he replied. "I'm coming with you."

"They insisted I come alone," she said tightly, grateful that they had. "It's the way it has to be."

"Not a chance," he said. "You're not going anywhere without me."

"Listen," she said impatiently, "this is our only chance, the only contact we've got; everything depends on it. They want me alone; we'll do it their way. Otherwise we're done. Do you understand?"

He wavered, then gave in. "All right. Call me in an hour to let me know you're okay."

"I'll call you when I can. We'll both have to wait; this is their game, now, but if you haven't heard from me by six o'clock tonight, consider that you're on your own. Take the money and go."

"Jesus, go where?"

"England would be best. Try for another contact there."

He looked at her for a moment, then nodded and walked away, rearranging the bulky packages. She walked across the street, bought an *Irish Times,* walked to Switzer's, stopped and, glancing at her watch, began to read the newspaper. There were two stories to interest her, both on the front page. The first made her smile; the second made her grind her teeth. Fifteen minutes later she started up Grafton Street toward the Green.

She walked quickly through the park, thinking, even in January, that it must be the most intensely gardened piece of ground on earth. She was certain that she was being followed. At the southwest corner she stood next to the call box. Ten minutes later it rang. She picked up the phone. "Yes?"

"Look down the street toward the Shelburne Hotel. There's a green van. Do you see it?"

The van was there. "Yes."

"Get into the van; the back door." The caller hung up.

She walked quickly to the van and opened the rear door. She was grabbed by two hooded men, yanked quickly inside and pushed roughly to the floor. "Be quiet and lie still," a muffled voice said. She arranged herself as comfortably as possible on the metal floor. One man kept his foot on her back. The van drove for nearly half an hour, as best she could tell, making many turns. Finally it stopped, doors slammed, and she heard the rattle of a garage door. The van moved a few feet forward and she heard the door rattle again. She emerged from the van in a dark place that smelled of oil and grease. The two men marched her quickly through a door, down a hallway, and into another room. A man of about fifty, gray-haired, heavyset, sat facing her in a straight chair. She recognized Michael Pearce immediately from his photographs. So this was the wild revolutionary, the one the Provos had found too hot to handle. The only light filtered through drawn drapes.

"What, no hood?" she said.

"It doesn't matter if you see my face," the man said. There was a touch of the North in his accent. "Unless you have the right answers, this place is your last stop." He nodded to one of the men, who removed his hood and began searching her. His hands lingered on her thighs and at her buttocks and crotch; she stood very still. He felt her breasts, then pinched her nipples, hard, and stood back.

"She's clean," he chuckled.

She caught him, roundhouse, full in the mouth with the back of her hand, staggering him. He pushed off the wall toward her, swearing and spitting blood. The gray-haired man simply held up a hand, and he stopped.

"Who are you?" he asked her.

"You don't need to know my name," she said. "All you need to know is that the bishop sent me here."

"Who's the bishop?"

"Call him and ask him. You've got the number."

He rose and left the room, leaving her with the two guards, one of whom was dabbing at his lips with a handkerchief.

"Bitch," he said. "I'll have you for that."

"You've had all you're going to," she replied. "Touch me again, and I'll put your eyes out."

The man came back and sat down. "So you want to join the Brigade, do you?"

"Not a bit of it," she said. "Not yet, anyway. All we want is transport to a training camp and an education."

"What sort of education?"

"Arms, explosives, the lot. Whatever's going."

"You expect us to pay for your training?"

"We'll pay ourselves. You'll get twenty-five thousand pounds when we're on our way. We'll make another, similar contribution to the camp."

He laughed. "So you're those two. I read your notices; pretty funny, they were. Amateurs."

"Effective amateurs, I'd say. We won't be amateurs for long."

"Where is it you want to go?"

"I hear Libya's nice this time of year."

"One of you is hot. That's going to make it more difficult."

"What we're paying should cover it. We want proper passports. I believe you can do that."

He nodded. "You're well informed. All right, we'll run you out of here in about a week. You'll fly to Lourdes on a charter flight; we'll get you to Rome from there and then to the camp. Where are you staying?"

"You don't need to know."

"All right, be in the lobby of the Burlington Hotel tomorrow at three with passport photos of you and your mate. One of the lads will pick them up and tell you the day of your departure. You'll have the passports and the name of a contact the day before you leave. We'll want the money tomorrow."

"You'll have the money when we're in Lourdes safely. I'll telephone you the location."

"Don't you trust your brothers?"

"Of course, it's just that you'll be so much more concerned with the quality of the passports and our well-being if you've something to gain by our safe arrival in Lourdes."

"Half tomorrow, the rest on your arrival."

"I'll give your man five thousand tomorrow with the passport photographs, the rest you'll get as I've said."

"Half tomorrow, the rest later; take it or leave it. Who else can you go to?"

"*You* take it or leave it. The bishop would be very unhappy to learn that you'd passed up twenty-five thousand for the cause because of stupid bargaining."

The man looked annoyed. "All right, done, but you'd

better understand you won't be out of our reach in Lourdes if we don't hear from you." He nodded to the two men. "All right, lads, take her back to the Green."

"And you'd better understand that we're going to be very nervous about anyone following us while we're in Dublin. Such a person could get himself shot."

The man rose. "Miss, I couldn't care less where you go in Dublin. Just have the five thousand ready tomorrow at three. If you have any problems, you know the number, but watch yourself. If you lead the *Gardai* to any of our people I'll see you done. They don't cure death in Lourdes." He left the room.

When she returned to the hotel he was pacing the lobby. "Okay? Is it okay?"

"Not here," she said. "Upstairs."

She was grimly quiet in the elevator. As soon as the door to the room was closed, she threw the newspaper at him. "You stupid bastard," she hissed at him. "Nobody would've cared that you're gone; nobody would've cared that I've gone; nobody would care if they knew we'd gone together; they've no idea who did the bank, and we've enough money to blow up the world, but you . . . you killed your own brother, and now they're looking for you!"

His eyes were wide. "What the hell are you talking about?"

She picked up the newspaper and shoved it at him. "That's what I'm talking about."

He looked at the paper, his jaw slack, his eyes glazed, then he sank down onto a bed.

"Why did you do it?" she demanded, her voice tight. "He would never have done anything to hurt us. Never."

Denny looked up at her, surprised. "Do it? Do Donal? Me? You must be mad."

She stared at him blankly. "You didn't kill him?"

He met her gaze. "I never even touched him. I wouldn't, Maeve."

She looked at him and knew he was telling the truth. Her mind was working quickly, now, and it could come to only one conclusion. She sat down next to him on the bed and put her hand on the back of his neck. He was beginning to cry softly. "It's Mark Robinson, then," she said. "From what the paper said, it was someone who knew what he was doing. Robinson'd know. Nobody else could have had a thing against Donal. Nobody."

The two of them were quiet for a long time, but for Denny's sobbing. Finally, he composed himself and took a deep breath. "Maeve," he sighed, "when we finish the training, I'm going to do Captain Robinson."

She nodded. "I'll help you," she said.

Thirty-five

MY FIRST DAY BACK AT THE YARD THERE WAS TALK OF Donal O'Donnell, and of Denny. Mark made a point of telling Finbar, within earshot of the other workers, everything we knew. Everybody had liked Donal, and while shocked, everyone seemed willing to think that Denny O'Donnell had killed his twin brother. The police had implied that to the newspapers, announcing the details of Donal's death and that they wished to interview Denny in that connection. Finbar said he would give time off for the funeral, and Mark willingly agreed.

The depression I felt over the break in my relationship with Connie was lifted by the sight of the boat. The laid teak decking was now completed, and somehow, for the first time, the whole thing looked like a yacht instead of a building project. I now felt what Mark must have been feeling all along; the boat, the whole project, was beginning to live for me. I could stand on the new decks and imagine that she was surrounded by salt water instead of a tin shed. If there had been a moment when I had wanted to abandon the project and leave Mark to carry on alone, it was gone in that instant.

Mark joined me. "She's going to be something, isn't she?"

"She sure is. We'll launch in June, then?"

"I reckon."

At the end of our workday I took Annie's shopping list and started toward the supermarket in Douglas, as I often did. I was the last to leave the yard. No more than a couple of hundred yards from the gate I saw a man standing next to his car; the bonnet was up, and he was waving for me to stop. I pulled in behind him. As I got out and started toward him, another car pulled in behind mine. It was a green Volkswagen. I turned to see who else had stopped to help, and I was grabbed by two men and hustled off the road into some tall reeds at the river's edge. The third man, the one in the stalled car, joined us. He was carrying a lug wrench.

"Is it him?" the third man asked.

"It is," said another man. I recognized the red-bearded fisherman whose nets we had once run over in *Toscana*, Red something, he was called. I looked quickly about me. We were now completely hidden from the road, and it was nearly dark. I yanked one arm free and took a wild swing at Red, but I missed. The other two quickly pinned my arms. Red took the lug wrench from the other man and stood before me. "You'll answer for Donal O'Donnell," he said.

For some reason, the fight with Denny O'Donnell ran through my mind. Now, as then, I knew there was no way out of this unless I made it myself, and my chances didn't seem good. I kicked at him and connected. My foot caught him in the pit of his stomach and sent him backward onto the ground. I struggled wildly to free myself from the other two, but they held on doggedly. Red was getting to his feet. I managed to come down hard on the instep of one of the other two, but although he yelled in pain, he still held on. Red was coming at me with the lug wrench.

Suddenly, we were bathed in an intensely bright light. "Stand where you are!" a deep voice shouted, and there was a click of metal like a gun being cocked. I could see nothing but the circle of light, and neither could the others. *"Gardai!"* The voice shouted. "Don't move." Everybody froze. "What's happening here?" the voice asked.

"Ah, just a bit of personal business," Red said nervously.

"Personal, is it?" the voice asked. "With a bit of steel in your hand?"

"We was just fixing the motorcar," Red replied.

"You, in the middle," the voice said to me. "Step away from there."

I quickly jumped a couple of steps away but was still in the beam of light.

"It appears to me that you meant to harm this lad," the voice said.

"Ah, no, 'twas nothing like that, now," Red said back. "Just a bit of personal bother."

"Well, I know you," the voice said to Red, "and if there's any more bother with this lad I'll be paying you a visit, do you hear me?"

Red nodded. "We'll be going, if it's all right."

"Move, then."

They moved, and quickly. Both cars were driven off in record time. The light came closer to me, then flicked off, leaving me blinded. "You all right, Mr. Lee?" The accent suddenly changed from Irish to English. I was confused.

"Yeah, I guess so, but if you're a policeman I think you should arrest those fellows; I'll bring charges."

"I'm not a policeman; my name is Primrose, Major Primrose. We spoke on the phone."

Derek Thrasher's security man. I sagged with relief. "Jesus, I'm glad to see you."

"I'd stopped to check on my man opposite the yard, there." He pointed up the hill. "Come on, let's get you back to your car."

We walked through the reeds back onto the road. "What are you going to do about this?" I asked. "Should I report it to the police?"

"No," he said. "I shouldn't think so. Our mutual acquaintance would rather avoid that. Anyway, those blokes think I *am* the police and that I know them. They'll back off, I think. Do you know them?"

"Just the one with the beard. His name is Red something. He's an illegal salmon fisherman."

"Ah, good, I'll have a word with a friend of mine in the *Gardai*, perhaps have his boat looked at. He won't be back around; I know the sort."

"If you say so."

"Don't worry about it further," he said, opening my car door for me. "You're in good hands."

It certainly seemed that way. I thanked him and drove off toward Douglas, trembling as the adrenaline died away. I was lucky not to be lying in those reeds with a broken head.

I drove through the gates of Coolmore Castle and headed toward the cottage. As I passed the castle I saw Lord Coolmore getting out of his Mercedes. He waved me down.

"I read about Donal O'Donnell," he said, leaning against my car. "I'd rather not read about things that happen on my land in the newspaper. I'd rather be told." In the dark I couldn't see his face well, but he didn't sound happy.

"I'm sorry no one told you, Peter Patrick," I replied, "but we were a bit too shocked to think of telling you, I suppose."

He nodded. "I know the papers are saying Denny O'Donnell did it, but I shouldn't be surprised if some of the local lads think Mark had something to do with it, seeing the body was found near the cottage."

"I'm afraid some of them do think that," I said. I told

him about what had happened to me an hour before. "A . . . uh, policeman arrived at the right moment."

He nodded. "Good. The redheaded fellow sounds like Red O'Mahoney. I know a fellow who knows him. I'll have a word. You shouldn't be bothered by that lot again."

"I hope not."

"Will, if anything else like this happens—if anything else *at all* happens—I think it would be best if you came to me first, do you take my point?"

"All right."

"Mention that to Mark, too, would you? I haven't seen him for a bit. I think I can be of assistance in seeing that you have no more local bother through the completion of the boat, but remember, if anything else should happen, *see me first.*"

We said good night, and I drove on. I wondered if he really meant that, should we find another dead body on the foreshore, we should come to him first.

Thirty-six

BLACKIE MACADAM SPENT THE AFTERNOON OF NEW Year's Day in a sauna club in Kensington, sweating out his Parisian excesses. He would have to be dry for a few days in order to make his deadline of the fifth; there was a weekend in between and that shortened his working time. Late in the afternoon, on nothing more than a hunch, he called an acquaintance, a librarian at the *Times*.

"What can I do for you, Blackie?"

"I want to know if a bloke has been in the papers during the last month or so."

"Public figure?"

"Hardly. Name's Pearce." He spelled it. "Patrick Fitzgerald Pearce."

"How much of a search am I doing, Blackie?"

"Twenty quids' worth if you can do it quick."

"I don't know; fellow's a nobody, after all; could take time."

"Don't stretch it, mate, I know bloody well what you've got in your head; you're not going to be poring over the stacks until midnight."

"Know anything at all about him?"

"There might be something to do with a company called Avondale Enterprises."

"Avondale, eh? Give me your number."

Blackie hung up and gave in to the ministrations of a tiny Japanese girl, who walked up and down his back for twenty minutes, pressing on the low ceiling for leverage. He tried not to think about booze, not even hair of the dog. The girl had hardly finished when there was a call for him.

"Got it, Inspector."

"I'm listening."

"Pearce was an accountant with Avondale; he made *The Observer* a short time back when he turned over a set of books to the public prosecutor which dropped Avondale right in it for exchange control violations."

This was interesting to MacAdam, but not very. He had a feeling there was more to it; thirty years of snooping told him there was something sexier here. "Come on, mate, there's more to it than that; let's have it."

There was a chuckle. "Too bloody right there's more. Avondale is Derek Thrasher's."

"Boy wonder Thrasher?"

"The very same. Thrasher's in it for possible criminal charges on moving lots and lots of twenty-pound notes across the Channel. They might already have charged him, but he's gone to ground; nobody's seen him since or has the foggiest where he is."

Now the light went on. He knew where Thrasher had been less than twenty-four hours before: in the bedroom of a Paris flat, listening to Blackie MacAdam talk with the Greek/Arab/Jew. Something else occurred to him. "Didn't the Provos park a car bomb outside Thrasher's offices a while back?"

"Right, and Pearce is Irish, but there doesn't seem to be a connection."

"Anything else?"

"A statement out of the prosecutor's office, but nothing more about Pearce. I doubt if he's ever had his name in the papers before; certainly not since."

"Your twenty will be in Monday's post." MacAdam hung up. Oh, yes, very sexy. He had a feeling there would be more than 500 quid in this for him before he was done. He eased himself into a hot tub and let the Japanese girl scrub his back. The booze seemed less important now.

On Saturday MacAdam drove down to Streatham, a grim South London suburb, and found the house where Pearce lived, not far from Streatham Common. He wanted a look at the man, and he didn't have to wait long. Pearce came out of the house looking sleepy (not an early riser; it was past two) and walked a block and a half to a pub, the Bramble. MacAdam followed him, collecting a newspaper along the way. At the bar Pearce ordered a pint of Guinness and a sandwich and read his own paper. MacAdam made himself comfortable at a table and ordered a sandwich. Pearce chatted with the barman, stole an occasional glance at MacAdam, and nursed his pint until closing time at three, either too cheap to buy another or, for an Irishman, amazingly uninterested in drink.

"Time, gentlemen," the publican called and shooed his customers toward the door. MacAdam didn't move. The publican looked at him, then locked the door and walked over to the table. "Something I can do for you, sir?"

"I expect you know who I am," MacAdam said, folding his newspaper carefully.

"I expect," the publican replied. He had seen more than one policeman in his time.

"Sit down," MacAdam said, "and tell me about the geezer who just left."

The man sat down. "Which geezer?"

MacAdam sighed wearily. "Come along, now, don't annoy me."

"Oh, you mean the bloke at the bar. Pearce, his name is; Pat Pearce."

"Is it, now?" MacAdam began rolling the newspaper into a tight tube. "Tell me *all* about him."

The publican shrugged. "Not much to tell; comes in, has his pint, goes home; talks about the football." He was making an effort to be affable, but he was nervous.

In one motion, MacAdam swung the thick roll of newsprint across the publican's face, backhanded, then rose and followed as his chair spun sideways and spilled him onto the floor. The blow hadn't hurt him much, but the newspaper had made a hell of a noise inside the man's head, and his ears would be ringing. Mac-Adam seized him by the back of his belt, got him up and walked him quickly on his toes toward the back room. He found two chairs, sat the man in one, and pulled the other up until they were sitting knee to knee, facing each other.

"This is a dirty little place you run, here," MacAdam said, conversationally. "Why, I saw an illegal bookie taking bets in here not ten minutes ago, and if I was a betting man I'd wager with him that a proper analysis of the contents of the bottles behind your bar would reveal a shocking percentage of tap water. Now, a man of a more rigid frame of mind would close you down blindingly fast, but you're fortunate, because I'm a quite reasonable chap, unless I'm annoyed. Don't annoy me. Tell me *all* about your mate, Pat Pearce."

"He lives just around the corner there . . . used to live with his mum, but she died a year or so ago . . . he's a bookkeeper, or something like that, until recently had a job with a firm in the West End . . . he quit, I think . . . but he's not short of a few bob . . . his mum left him a bit, you see . . . she sold her house in Islington a few years back and never bought another . . . moved out here and took a flat . . . he's always been quite upset about that, says the fellow who bought the house did her wrong, didn't pay her what it was worth, then he tarted it up a bit and sold it for triple or better to some advertising bloke or solicitor . . . goes on about that all the time, he does. . . ." The man paused, panting.

"Who are his friends?"

"Doesn't seem to have any . . . he's always in here alone . . . a loner type, if you ask me . . . funny for an Irishman, they're usually great ones for a chat with the boys, but not Pat Pearce."

"Come now, you're not going to tell me that he isn't pals with some of that Irish rubbish you get in this place."

"Well, to tell the truth, they don't seem to want much to do with him . . . he's a bit eccentriclike, you see. . . . I think that worries them . . . they don't think of him as reliable, if you know what I mean. . . ."

"You mean he's IRA, and he frightens the boys—is that it?"

"No, no, just the opposite. I don't think they'd have him . . . he's too strange . . . he told me he's got a brother, though, what's in with those lads, somebody pretty big . . . he told me that when he'd had a bit much, after he quit his job . . . he never talked about it but that once."

MacAdam stared quietly at the man, thinking. "What was his mother's name?"

"Ah, Bridey, that was it, Bridey."

"And what street was her house in, in Islington?"

"I don't know, honest, chief, he never said, honest, he didn't . . ."

"What else?"

"Jesus, that's all I know about him, honest to God . . . I'd tell you if I knew any more."

MacAdam rose, removed a small notebook from his coat pocket and began jotting down the number of the coin telephone on the wall. "Oh, yes you do, you know something else. You're just a bit flustered trying to think so hard at the moment, and you can't think of it. So I'm going to give you until opening time tomorrow to think about it, and then I'm going to ring you up and ask you, and you're going to remember what it was and tell me. Right?"

"Oh, yeah, right, sir. I'll do me best."

"Your best had better be good enough, son, or I'll come back here and break up this place with your limp body, do you understand me?"

"Yes, sir, I understand."

"And I hardly need mention what I might do if you should let drop to Pearce that I've inquired about him. Now, unlock that door and let me out of this pesthole."

Pearce ducked away from the window as the big man and Tim, the publican, came out of the back room. He stepped into the doorway of the news agent's next door while Tim let the man out of the pub. As soon as the man was around the corner Pearce rapped sharply on the pub door, and shortly, the publican opened it but kept the chain on.

"It was about me, wasn't it, Tim?"

"Oh, Jesus, Pat, I didn't tell him nothing—honest I didn't."

Pearce knew from the fear in the publican's voice that he had told the man as much as he knew.

"Who was he, Tim?" Pearce shoved his foot in the door to keep the publican from slamming it.

"A copper, Pat."

"What's his name?"

"He didn't tell me."

Pearce was surprised. "Did he show you his warrant card?"

Tim shook his head. "He didn't have to. I can spot 'em a mile off."

"He didn't show you a card or tell you his name. Did he actually tell you he was a policeman?"

"No, but I know 'em, I reckon he is, no doubt."

Pearce had doubts. He allowed the publican to close the door, then quickly walked to the corner in time to see the big man getting into a BMW—from the number plates, only two years old. That was no copper's car. He reached his own car at a trot, and pulled out as the BMW turned the corner. He followed at a block's distance as the car drove into central London and parked near South Kensington tube station. The man used a resident's parking sticker, so he lived nearby. Pearce parked and followed the man at a distance until he turned into a doorway next to a wine merchant's. Pearce could see movement upstairs a moment later. He crossed the street and walked quickly to the doorway, looking for a nameplate on the bell. A business card was stuck into a holder. "John MacAdam, Confidential Investigations, Scotland Yard experience."

Thrasher had a goon on him.

At noon the following day MacAdam rang the Bramble in Streatham. "This is the gentleman you spoke with yesterday," he said to the publican. "Tell me."

"Oh, hello, sir." The voice was bright and eager to please. "I did remember something. The outfit that bought the old lady's house in Islington was T&M Properties. Pat mentioned it a couple of times a while back."

"What else?"

"Oh, and I remembered the name of the street in Islington; it was Sebbon Street."

"You've done nicely, lad," MacAdam said. He hung up.

On Monday, an hour with the corporate records at Companies House told him the rest. The T in T&M Properties was Derek Thrasher; the M was Muldah. Sounded Arabic, could be the bloke in Paris. MacAdam chuckled to himself. Simple when you knew how. He would blow their tiny minds with all this when they phoned the next day for their report. But he wanted more out of this, and he thought he might know how to get it. From a call box he rang an old mate in Special Branch at the Yard.

"Hello, Wilf, it's MacAdam."

"Bloody Tarmac, how are you, mate?"

"Getting by. Actually a bit better than that these days.

Listen, I'm doing something private, and what I'm working on might be to do with what you're working on. Thought we might trade a bit of knowledge."

"You'll want my knowledge first, if I know you."

"Too right. Besides, I've only a hunch at the moment."

"What do you need?"

"I want to know about a mick named Patrick Fitzgerald Pearce. Seems to have a fairly straight background in accountancy, but word is he has a brother who's high with the rebels."

"I think I know the one. I'll run him on the computer now, if you've got a moment."

"I've got a moment." MacAdam fed more coins to the telephone. He heard the clicking of typing and the rapid spitting of an electronic printer.

"Here we are, Blackie. The brother's Michael Pearce, forty-nine. Thought to have been involved in a dozen assassinations and army ambushes. For certain, though, in sixty-nine he bombed a police station in Derry, killed eight coppers, and brought the wrath of God down on the local Provos, for which they didn't thank him. He's been something of an outcast since, thought to be uncontrollable. He's gathered about him a dozen of them like himself and called them the Irish Freedom Brigade."

"They the ones who did the Berkeley Square thing last autumn?"

"Right. They were after Thrasher, the financier, for

a bit, but he was too hard to track down. That seems to be the way it was, anyway. They'd try again if they had the chance."

"What about Patrick?"

"He's forty-one, the baby brother and mammy's boy. He was thought to have been in on the police station but had an alibi. Settled in England with his mother, who lived in London, worked as a domestic. Last address, Sebbon Street, Islington."

"No activity since?"

"Not that we know about. We thought he kept in touch with Michael, and we kept somebody on him for a while, but with no results, and we didn't have the manpower to keep on him. It's a nasty family, though, going back to the twenties, so if you've anything to do with any of them, watch yourself. Now what've you got for me?"

"Nothing just yet, but I might be able to give you Patrick on something pretty good in a few days."

"I knew it. You've bled me dry, and I've nothing to show for it."

"Patience, Wilf, I'll be able to give you something before long, a new address for Patrick, at least, and maybe some charges. Thanks, now." He hung up and heaved a satisfied sigh. Now he had something that might get him a hell of a lot more business out of Thrasher and his people. He could milk this for weeks at a hundred a day. The pubs were just opening, and there was one across the street. He could afford to relax a bit, now.

*   *   *

On Tuesday morning Pearce waited in a café across from MacAdam's flat. When the man left, he would follow him until he got his chance. When it was nearly noon, Pearce had become nervous; perhaps MacAdam had already left. He crossed the street, let himself in through the unlocked downstairs door and climbed the stairs, keeping near the wall. If MacAdam were out, then he might get a look at the flat if the lock weren't too much. As he reached the top of the stairs he heard a telephone ring on the other side of the single door. Now, at least, he would know if the man was home.

MacAdam was on hair of the dog all morning, but he held it in check, knowing that he had to report. At precisely noon, the telephone rang.

"MacAdam here."

"Mr. MacAdam, this is the gentleman with whom you spoke in Paris last week. May I have your report, please?"

"Of course, sir. I believe I have the information you want. Pearce is the son of one Bridey Pearce, an Irish domestic who owned a small house in Sebbon Street, Islington. Some years ago, the house was purchased from the woman by T&M Properties, with which I believe you might be familiar. Pearce believed that his mother had been cheated in the transaction and has borne a grudge against the proprietors of T&M since that time. It seems likely that Pearce became employed at Avondale in the normal way of things, and afterward, discovered that Avondale and T&M shared an ownership. Since holding a grudge is one of the principal talents of the Irish, he decided to do what he could to cause the owners discomfort. You would be a better judge than I as to how successful he was."

"Indeed. Were you able to ascertain whether he has any political affiliations?"

"There are indications that he may have, sir, but I hope you can appreciate that such matters require a much more complex sort of investigation than the more rudimentary one I have just completed. If you wish to engage me further, I should be glad to take on the assignment, which I imagine could run to some weeks."

"I will let you know about that, Mr. MacAdam."

"Oh, sir, I should mention that if that investigation should bear fruit I might very possibly be in a position to have Pearce arrested on rather serious charges, and in such a manner as to in no way reflect your interest in the matter."

"I see. The remainder of your fee will be delivered within the hour, Mr. MacAdam. Thank you for your assistance."

"Not at all, Mr. Muldah, please let me know if I can be of further help to you and Mr. Thrasher."

There was a pause at the other end of the line. "Good-bye, Mr. MacAdam."

MacAdam put the phone down laughing and reached for a bottle. "That should put the hook into the bastards," he said aloud, nearly shouting. "They'll want Pearce put away; I'll hear from them before the day is out, I'll wager." He laughed again and knocked back a large whisky.

Outside, his ear to the door, Pearce was trembling and sweating heavily. He could wait no longer, not a minute. He knocked on the door.

"Who's there?" MacAdam shouted without getting up.

"Express post for Mr. MacAdam," Pearce called out. "Someone'll have to sign." He braced himself. He could hear MacAdam lumbering toward the door, hear him curse as he apparently knocked over a bottle.

MacAdam yanked open the door, and before he had time to focus on who was standing there, Pearce came up hard with both hands, driving the knife upward and in. MacAdam reflexively grabbed Pearce's wrists, pushing down, going up onto his toes. Pearce walked him backward, still shoving upward as hard as he could, until MacAdam struck the desk and fell back. Pearce was quickly on top of him, gouging in and out an inch or two, but never letting the blade leave the man's chest. MacAdam, wide-eyed, fought on, but more and more feebly, until finally he went limp. Pearce twisted the blade and yanked out the knife, then plunged it in again—once, twice, and a third time, making sure there was nothing but mince left of the heart. When finally he pulled back there was a lot of blood. At least it had been quiet. He kicked the door shut.

He went to the kitchen and cleaned himself up. His mackintosh was ruined; he took it off and cleaned out the pockets, stuffing the contents into his jacket pockets. He went to MacAdam's sleeping area and found a pair of clean socks in a drawer. He drew them onto his hands, then went carefully through the flat, taking what cash and valuables would fit into his pockets, making a burglary of it. When he had tossed the place adequately, he dragged MacAdam's body to the kitchen, threw the bloody mackintosh over it, and found a can of paraffin, used for a portable heater. He doused the body thoroughly, then the desk and whatever else would burn quickly. He found a packet of cigarettes and a book of matches. He lit a cigarette and folded the matchbook closed over it, then placed it in a pool of the paraffin. The glow of the ash wouldn't ignite the kerosene, but when the cigarette burned down enough the matchbook would go, and there would be a fine blaze. He forced himself to stand for a moment and think, just to keep from doing anything stupid. As an afterthought he blew out the pilot light on the cooker and turned all the jets on. Satisfied, he put the latch on and closed the door behind him.

At the bottom of the stairs he took a good look up and down before stepping out into the street and walking unhurriedly toward South Ken tube station. He was in

Piccadilly before the explosion went and by the time the fire engines arrived in South Kensington he had knocked over and smashed an expensive bottle of port at Fortnum & Mason, an incident the staff would remember well. He treated himself to a new mack at Burberry's before catching the bus for Streatham.

Thirty-seven

I WOKE ON A SUNDAY MORNING IN LATE MAY WITH SUCH a heightened feeling of well-being that I should have known I could not sustain it through the day. For months, through the winter and now into spring, we had enjoyed a peace so thorough that we could hardly believe it. Nothing whatever had been heard from Denny O'Donnell and Maeve, although Denny was, presumably, still being sought for Donal's murder, and once Major Primrose and Lord Coolmore had intervened on our behalf, we had gone unmolested by their local friends. The yacht was on schedule and due for launching in a couple of weeks, and she was living up to all our expectations. We would have time to try her extensively at sea before the race to the Azores, as we had planned.

Things had not gone as well in the interim for Derek Thrasher, though. Although charges had not been brought against him and he was, thus, not actually a fugitive from justice, the circumstances of his problems with the Public Prosecutor made it advantageous for him to stay out of Britain, and he had. I had spent another Rabelaisian weekend in Paris at Easter, and Jane had told me that his enforced absence had caused a number of harassing lawsuits to be filed against him by business competitors, and since he could not be present to answer them, he was faring badly.

Mark and Annie had had another couple of spats, and Annie had pulled her by now accustomed disappearing act for a week or so on each occasion, but all had been made up. Only my relationship with Concepta Lydon did not go well—in fact, was not going at all. She had declined to see me since New Year's, and when we did meet accidentally she was cool and uncommunicative. She was polite, not even admitting annoyance with me, but she would not enter into a discussion of anything personal. Since I was congenitally a negotiator, this attitude drove me mad. On this Sunday morning Mark and Annie were out for a day sail in *Toscana*, and I had slept very late. Now, as I showered and shaved, the thought of the situation with Connie began to dissipate my feeling of well-being, and by the time I was dressed it was completely gone. I wanted a showdown, to thrash this business out once and for all. My visits to Jane Berkeley were fun but curiously unsatisfying; they did not displace my yearning to be with Connie. I missed her.

Determined to adopt a direct assault, I drove to Kinsale, intending to beard the lioness in her den, but as I passed the Spaniard, I saw her car parked out front. The pub was filled with Sunday brunchers, most of whom had just fled mass and were now making a joyful noise unto the pint. I saw Connie sitting, alone, at a small table across the room; I headed for her. She did not look up until I had nearly reached her, and then someone else reached her a tiny moment sooner. He was tall and slender and had a shock of carrot-red hair; he sat down next to her, and then I noticed that there were two drinks on the table. I stopped short but too near to change my direction. "Hello, Connie," I said, as bravely as I could. I had a terrible, hollow sensation.

"Hello, Will." There was a slight, polite smile; nothing more. "Have you met Terry? Terry, this is Will Lee."

"How are you?" I stuck out my hand.

"Very well, thanks." He took it.

I knew immediately that he not only knew who I was but a great deal more about Connie Lydon and me. I had a flash of them curled up before the fireplace in her cottage on long, winter nights, Connie telling him about the American who had treated her so shabbily. I knew, of course, that she must have been seeing other people, but now, confronted with the fact, I was shocked. I felt as though I had just gotten a Dear John letter.

"Are you all right these days?" I asked feebly.

"Very well, thank you." She paused and took a sip of her drink. "How's the boat?"

"It's going well. We launch in a couple of weeks."

"Good." She didn't seem to want to say anything further.

"Nice to have seen you," I said and turned away. I walked to the bar, found a stool and ordered a pint. I wanted to flee the pub, but I could hardly walk in, say a few words to her and walk directly out. I was trapped there, and I had to make the best of it. I wasn't doing it very well. I held on to the cool pint with both hands, afraid they would tremble if I removed them. I stared fixedly ahead, but I could still see her reflection in the mirror behind the bar. They chatted amiably. I shrank inside, and the cool lager didn't seem to help. I felt mildly nauseated. I put my hand to my face and it came away cold and wet. I drank more of the lager. This was my first experience with serious jealousy. I seemed unable to form a coherent thought; my mind was one damp, squishy, emotional sponge; I wrestled to squeeze some rationality from it.

I finally was able to ask myself a question. Why was I so upset? No reasonable answer. This was a girl I had spent some time with—well, all right, a *lot* of time with—who now preferred to spend her time with someone else. This wasn't the first time that had happened, wouldn't be the last. Not a big deal. A bigger deal than I had thought, though, else why were my hands too slippery to hold on to the pint? Was I jealous? Sure. Why? I evaded the question.

Shortly, thank God, they got up and left, passing just

behind me, laughing about something. About me? Not only jealous, paranoid. I waited until I heard her car drive away, then paid for my drink and left. I drove back to the cottage numb, stricken. By the time I reached home I was overwhelmingly sleepy, my mind seeming to cry out for unconsciousness. I flopped on the living room sofa and slept.

I was awakened by a familiar noise, a bumping sound, and I did not identify it until I heard Mark curse and Annie laugh. Their voices were ghostly, coming from a distance, and I tried to shake off my grogginess and figure out what was happening. Then I heard the quiet chug of *Toscana*'s engine, and I knew they were back. The noise was the fiberglass dinghy bumping against the hull of the boat as they picked up the mooring in front of the cottage; it always annoyed Mark to have anything colliding with the shiny topsides of the little yacht. Their voices floated toward me over the water.

They were just dragging the dinghy up on the fore- shore when the telephone rang. I struggled to my feet and picked it up.

"Is that you, Will?"

The voice was distant and crackly. English accent. Female. "Jane? Is that you?" I was surprised to hear from her; we didn't telephone much.

"Yes. Will, there's a problem with the boat."

I shook my head, still groggy. "No, there's no problem here; everything is going great; we're launching in a couple of weeks."

"No, you don't understand. There's a new problem, something we've just found out about."

"Hang on," I said. Mark and Annie were just coming up from the river. "Mark, pick up the extension, will you? It's Jane; she says there's a problem."

I heard the click as he picked up the phone on his desk. "How are you, Jane? This is Mark Robinson."

I realized with some surprise that they'd never met. "Okay, what's the problem?"

"D.T. is in the midst of a legal battle over a building project in Dublin. I won't go into detail, because it doesn't matter what the circumstances are; all that matters is they're going to try to take the boat."

"Take the boat? How can they do that?"

"They've somehow identified it as an asset of D's, and I've just learned that a solicitor is flying from London to Cork tomorrow morning to meet with a Cork solicitor who is going to file to attach the boat. It's just harassment, really. This whole business is nothing to do with the boat."

Mark spoke up. "Well, can they do it? Can't we fight it some way? Get a solicitor of our own?"

"Of course, but I'm told the likelihood is that they'll ask that the boat be impounded by the court pending settlement of the suit, and that could take months. And no work could be done on it in the meantime."

"So what should we do?" Mark asked. "Is there anything at all we can do?"

"The only thing you can do is to get the boat out of Ireland before court convenes tomorrow morning; preferably to the Channel Islands. There's apparently a very good yard in Jersey. The process could be stalled long enough there to let you finish the boat."

I covered the receiver and called out to Mark. "Jesus, would she be seaworthy enough for that?"

"Not a hope," he called back. His voice came on the line again. "Jane, what are our chances of hanging on to the boat long enough to finish her if we appear in court tomorrow and try to make our case?"

"The best advice I can get is that you'd win in the long run and lose now; but if you can't get the boat out of the country, I guess there's no other choice."

All three of us were silent for a moment. Finally, Mark spoke. "Jane, we're going to have to hang up now and see what we can do. We'll call you tomorrow and let you know; are you in Paris?"

"Mark, it would be better if I didn't know anything. If I know, they might make a case that D. knows. Do you understand?"

"I understand," Mark replied.

"All I can do is wish you luck, then."

We hung up, and I heard Mark dialing in the other room. I joined him. He waited impatiently for the phone to ring, then hung up. "No answer."

"Who are you calling?"

"Finbar."

"Try the yacht club."

Mark hurriedly dialed the Royal Cork. Finbar was found.

"Listen, Finbar, I can't explain right now, but I need to meet you at the boatyard. Can you go over there right now? Good. Is Harry with you? Good, bring him, too. No, none of the other lads, just Harry. Will and I will meet you there as soon as possible." He hung up and began flipping quickly through his address book while I watched dumbly. He dialed another number. I went and picked up the other phone.

"Is that Mr. Mulcahy?"

"Yes."

"This is Mark Robinson, sir; we've met at the yacht club a couple of times."

"Yes, Captain Robinson, what can I do for you?"

Mark quickly explained what was to happen the following morning.

"Does this Mr. Thrasher, in fact, own the boat?"

"That won't be relevant if you will be able to do as I ask tomorrow morning in court."

"What is that, Captain Robinson?"

"I would like you to simply appear representing me and say that you have been given to understand that the yacht has left the Republic of Ireland."

There was a pause at the other end of the line. "Has the yacht, in fact, left the country?"

"It is my intention to move her tonight."

"I understood you would not be ready to launch until next month. Does the yacht even have a mast in her?"

"She has an engine, Mr. Mulcahy."

"I won't presume to advise you on seamanship, Captain Robinson, but you must understand my position as a solicitor and an officer of the court. If I tell a judge that the yacht has left the country, then I must be able to tell him that truthfully, to my best knowledge."

"I understand that, Mr. Mulcahy; I promise you that the yacht will leave the country tonight, and that you will be able to tell the court that, in good conscience. If, for any reason, she does not leave the country, I will telephone you before ten o'clock tomorrow morning. You may . . . in fact, I suggest that you visit Cork Harbour Boatyard tomorrow morning and see for yourself that the yacht has gone."

"I think that would be a good idea, Captain Robinson. All right, I will follow your instructions."

"Thank you, sir. And if you can convince the judge that the yacht has gone, can you stop the opposition attaching it?"

"The judge will not likely grant an attachment of property he has reason to believe is not in his jurisdiction."

They hung up, and Mark came into the living room, tossing my foul-weather gear at me. "You'll be needing this, Willie. The wind's getting up out there."

I could hear rain starting to spatter down. "Mark," I said, struggling into my parka, "you said a few minutes ago that the boat wasn't seaworthy, and now you're talking about taking her to the Channel Islands, with the wind getting up?"

"We can't get her to the Channel Islands, Willie," he said, grinning at me and heading for the door, "but we can get her out of the country, and then we can make her disappear."

I followed him at a trot, wondering what the hell I was getting into, now.

Thirty-eight

FINBAR AND HIS SON, HARRY, WERE WAITING FOR US WHEN we arrived at the yard.

"Evening, Captain, Willie." Finbar didn't bother to ask what we were all doing there on a Sunday evening; he figured he would be told.

"Evening, Finbar, Harry," Mark said. "Thank you for coming on such short notice. We have to launch the boat tonight."

Finbar chewed on his pipe stem for a moment, apparently trying to figure out whether Mark was joking. "I don't suppose you're joking," he said, finally.

"I'm afraid not. It's probably better if you don't know all the details, but tomorrow morning we're going to have a legal problem on our hands if the boat is still here. We have to get her in the water; that's all of it."

"We'll have a bit of work to do first, I expect," Finbar

said, scratching his head, "and we'll need the other lads; I'd better call them."

"I'm sorry, Finbar, but it would be better if they knew nothing at all about this."

Finbar took the pipe out of his mouth and gazed at Mark, wide-eyed. "You mean for just four of us to get a sixty-foot boat out of that shed and into the water?"

Mark nodded. "I've been thinking about that, and I've figured out a way we can do it, but first, we've got to be sure she's watertight and then get all her gear aboard and get the mast lashed to the decks."

Finbar shrugged. "Well, I'd say we'd better get at it. High tide's at one-thirty a.m., and if we don't have her launched by half-tide, at four-thirty, there won't be enough water in the creek; she'll be high and dry until nearly noon tomorrow. Harry, ring your mother and tell her not to wait up for us."

We were shortly aboard the yacht and at work. "First thing, let's get the through-hull fittings sorted out," Mark said. "She may take something of a bashing to-night. Harry, you hook up the spray machine and get another coat of antifouling paint on her bottom." The yacht had had her first coat on the Friday before, and her waterline was still masked for painting.

Harry went to get the air compressor, and I got at the hull fittings. I attached the seacocks for the engine and toilet to the holes through the hull that had been prepared for them. The engine needed raw, salt water for cooling, and the two toilets, of course, would have to flush overboard when they were installed. Mark went to work taping and labeling all the loose wiring in the boat—and there was a lot of it—to avoid confusion when the instruments and other electrical gear were installed later. We were to have begun that job the following day. Soon, I heard the air compressor start up, and we all donned masks to protect us from the poisonous anti-fouling paint that Harry was applying to the bottom to keep marine life from growing there. Then I ran into a problem.

"Mark, I can't find the other seacock, the one for the galley sink drain." We searched in vain for the fitting, and then Mark stopped us.

"We can't waste any more time on this. Just plug the hole for now, and let's get on with it."

I found a conical, softwood plug, squirted some sealant on it and hammered it tightly into the hole under the sink with a wooden mallet. That would hold it until we could find the proper fitting. All holes sealed, we began to load gear. Locked in the storeroom were all the new interior fittings and instruments that were to have been installed during the two weeks prior to launching. There was an enormous amount of stuff—electronic instruments, radios, pots and pans, three anchors, several large spools of various-sized rope, the ship's toilets, cushions, tools, spare parts for the engine, the galley stove, gas bottles, a diesel generator, a cabin heater, the saloon dining table, the yacht's sails, neatly folded and bagged—all the gear that a new boat needs, and all made bulkier because much of it was still boxed. It was after two in the morning before all of it was aboard, and practically the whole interior volume of the boat was filled with the jumble of gear, only an area around the chart table left clear for maneuvering below. Heavy rain hammered on the tin roof of the shed, causing us to have to shout to be heard. We were now in a race with the tide, which was falling rapidly.

We got the boom lashed to the deck, and then came the mast. This was like an eighty-foot, aluminum tree that had to be got off the floor of the shed, up on deck and securely lashed. It was managed with the chain hoist more easily than I had imagined it would be, but the process was time-consuming, and it was a quarter past four in the morning before it was safely aboard. Now all we had to do was launch a sixty-foot, heavily laden yacht with only four pairs of hands. We had fifteen minutes. I didn't see how we could do it, but Mark was at it quickly.

While I ripped the masking from the waterline, he and Harry cleated lines to strong points on deck and tossed the ends to the ground, where Finbar and I took hold. The boat's keel already rested on a little car, and there were eighty yards of rails sloping down to the water's edge, with only four of us to hold the big yacht in check. Mark and Harry lashed a huge block and tackle to a rafter of the shed, threaded one end of an enormous coil of rope through it, and made it fast to the yacht. This was his idea, and if it worked it would enable the two of them to let the yacht down to the water slowly, while Finbar and I, on opposite sides, helped keep the yacht upright in its cradle. I was terrified that it might topple on us; I had already had one experience with that hull looming over me, and I didn't want another. We were ready. It was four-thirty. Half-tide. Now or never. It flashed through my mind that the whole project, all the work we had done, rested on what happened now. If we couldn't handle the launch, and the yacht toppled, it was all over. And if we got her launched, and there wasn't enough water in the creek, then Mulcahy the solicitor would arrive in a few hours to find her high and dry on the creekbed and he would have no position in court.

Mark and Harry climbed quickly down, Finbar and I rolled back the doors of the shed, and we all took hold of our lines. Harry stepped over to the car with a sledge-hammer and knocked the chocks from under the car wheels. The yacht began to move; Finbar and I moved with it. It rolled slowly down the track for ten yards or so, Mark and Harry straining to pay out the line slowly through the block and tackle. Finbar and I held tightly to our lines, giving what puny support we could to the boat's balance. We were about even with the shed doors, and the boat was halfway outside, when I heard a sharp snap. I looked up to see a strand of rope near the block waving in the breeze.

"Oh, shit!" Harry yelled. "The bloody line's going!"

Even as he spoke, another strand went, and immediately after that, the third. The boat quickly began to move faster.

"Quick, Harry," Mark yelled, "let's get some chocks under those wheels!"

"No! No!" Finbar shouted. "She'll pitchpole if she stops short! Leggo, Willie! Leggo!"

I leggo. She was out of our hands, now. Disaster was seconds away. The big yacht trundled down the track, picking up speed, rocking from side to side. On each of the rocking motions, she went a bit further. Thirty yards; forty. In a moment she would either be shattered, on her side in the boatyard, or in the water, it was a toss-up which. Her speed increased, and so did the rocking. I reckoned she must have been doing twenty miles an hour by then, and suddenly, I knew she wasn't going to make it. She rocked crazily to the left and didn't rock back; she began to go. But as she leaned over, the car hit the water and the boat continued forward, even as she fell.

There was an ear-splitting smack as her topsides met the surface. For a moment, the water poured into the cockpit, and then, to everyone's perfect astonishment, she was back upright and afloat. The four of us stood, transfixed, in the rain.

Finbar was the first to speak. "Jesus Christ," he said. "I've built over a hundred boats in my time, but I've never launched one like *that*."

Then Mark shot past me, running flat out, and I saw why. The yacht was quickly drifting past the stone quay and downstream with the tide. We were losing her again. Mark planted one last step on the quay and leapt into space. His leap was long enough, but there had been no time to aim. He landed in a heap in the cockpit, and I heard him yell in pain.

"Let's go, lads!" Finbar shouted. "She'll either be gone downstream or aground in a minute." We ran for Finbar's dinghy, got the outboard started, and went after the drifting yacht. She seemed to be staying in midstream, but as we drew alongside and I leapt on board, she stopped suddenly. "She's aground," Finbar yelled. "Harry, grab a line and we'll tow. Get the engine started, Willie."

Mark was lying in the bottom of the cockpit, clutching his left knee, the one that, two years before, had taken the shotgun blast. I didn't have time to think about that. I dove below and opened the cooling-water seacock. "Start her, Mark!" I stared at the engine and prayed; it had never been started before. I heard Mark fumbling with the controls and saw the cable that controlled the accelerator move; the engine began to turn over. "Hold it!" I shouted. "Use the glowplug!" Diesel engines have to be warmed electrically before being started cold. It takes about thirty seconds. It seemed like an hour, while the tide ran out under us. "Now!" I yelled, glancing at my watch. The accelerator cable moved again and the engine turned, then caught. I started up the companionway ladder; Mark was already at the wheel, giving the engine full power.

The yacht stood still while the water behind her churned, in the nautical equivalent of spinning her wheels. Finbar's outboard whined. The yacht broke free.

"We're off!" Mark screamed, as the boat surged forward.

"Good luck!" Finbar shouted, as we passed him and Harry.

Mark waved. "I'll be in touch!"

I collapsed on a cockpit seat. "Okay, now what?" I asked.

"Now we get her out of the country," he replied, steering carefully down the middle of the creek, the first glow of predawn lighting our way.

I turned and looked below at the jumble of boxes and gear, now scrambled even more by the violent launching, then lay back and took deep breaths. Rain pelted my face, and the wind swayed even the biggest trees along the shoreline. "Swell," I said.

Thirty-nine

AN HOUR LATER, WITH THE SUN COMING UP, WE WERE PASSING ROCHE'S POINT LIGHT, AT THE ENTRANCE TO CORK HARBOUR. THE WIND HAD COME UP EVEN MORE WITH THE DAWN, AND WE WERE MOTORING DEAD INTO A FORTY-KNOT SOUTHEASTERLY. SEAS WERE BREAKING OVER THE BAR AT THE HARBOR ENTRANCE AND MARK BORE AWAY TO TAKE THEM AT AN ANGLE. ONCE PAST THE BAR, HE STILL HAD TO BEAR AWAY TO KEEP FROM MOTORING INTO THE SEAWAY THAT HAD BEEN WHIPPED UP BY THE INCREASING WIND.

I had been half-dozing in the cockpit during our trip down the harbor, but now the motion had me awake. "Okay," I shouted over the wind, "what's the plan? Where the hell are we going?"

Mark laughed. "We're going just far enough out to sea to keep from making a liar out of Mulcahy—that's to the three-mile limit—and then we're going to come back and hide the boat in Cork Harbour."

"Hide it? Where? It's a pretty busy place, you know. Aren't you worried about somebody spotting her?"

"No, not where I have in mind. You want to take the helm for a while?"

I relieved Mark and he sat down heavily in the cockpit, rubbing his knee.

"Are you okay?"

"Sure, I just landed wrong when I jumped. The bad one took all the weight. It'll be okay in a day or two."

I had my hands too full with the yacht to worry about Mark's knee. There is a certain rhythm to a sailboat, even going to windward in heavy weather, because the wind against the sails keeps her pressed. Not so under power with no sails. The boat pitches and rolls, and the lack of a rhythm to anticipate makes it very tiring just to be aboard, let alone to steer. For two hours I tacked back and forth, making distance to the south, motoring for the imaginary line that bordered Irish waters, the crossing of which would satisfy Mark's sense of the proper thing to do with regard to Mulcahy. I would have said the hell with it and hidden the boat immediately, but not Mark. He had promised the man to get it out of the country. The size of the seas and the direction of the wind caused us to make slow progress; three miles was coming hard.

Mark spelled me and said, "We'll give it another hour just to be sure, then turn and run for Cork. Take a look below; I think there may be some chocolate bars in the chart table."

I worked my way to the main hatch and started down the companionway ladder into the dark cabin. I stepped off the last rung and found myself in water up to the knee. "Jesus, Mark," I shouted out the hatch. "We're taking serious water down here; you better cut the engine and start pumping while I see if I can find where it's coming in."

I heard the engine die to an idle and felt the change in the boat's motion as she came beam on to the seas; she rolled a bit, but was a lot more comfortable. I knew I had installed the seacocks properly, so there was only one place where that much water could have come in: the through-hull fitting for the galley sink drain, where I had hammered in a softwood plug. It should have held, but in her wild launching the yacht had struck the water hard on that side, and that must have loosened it. The plug must have been completely out by this time. I tried to get into the locker under the sink and discovered that, incredibly, a small wooden crate had jammed itself into the opening. It wouldn't budge when I tried to pull it free, and I began to feel about for something to pry or smash it with.

Mark stuck his head through the hatch. "Hey, there's no handle for the pump up here. It must be below somewhere; see if you can find it or a substitute, will you?"

Wonderful. Here I was in the pitch-dark cabin of a rolling yacht, on my hands and knees in eighteen inches of water, and he wanted me to find a pump handle among the tangle of gear and boxes. I waded forward and began feeling my way through what was there. There was a steel toolbox somewhere in the vicinity of the chart table; I had put it there myself, but if it was still there, it was underwater and had probably spilled its contents into the bilges. After ten minutes of groping, while water continued to pour into the boat, I found it. I got it onto the chart table seat, yanked it open, and found a large screwdriver and a mallet. Using both tools, I tore at the box wedged in the galley locker until it splintered and came free. I handed up the screwdriver to Mark.

"This is close as you're going to get to a pump handle; I hope it works." I dove back below and began feeling for the through-hull fitting. It was easy to find, as a stream of water was gushing through it. Finding the plug was not as easy. I went to the chart table and, thank God, found a flashlight and, in the tool box, another plug and some sealant that would work underwater. Five extremely awkward minutes later I had the new plug pounded into place, and water stopped coming into the yacht. Using the flashlight I was able to find a bucket. There is an old saying that there is no better pump than a frightened man with a bucket, and, believe me, it is true. In an hour's time the cabin was, if not dry, then only damp. I climbed wearily into the cockpit.

"Now listen," I said, or rather, panted. "I say we've made three miles out, have you got that?"

He nodded, resignedly. "And if we're ever questioned as to why we returned to Cork Harbour, we can say we were driven back by severe weather and difficult conditions."

"No fucking joke," I said. "Now, let's point north and see how fast the tub will run before the wind under power."

We made Roche's Point in less than an hour and crept into the harbor in heavy fog. It could hardly have suited our purpose better. Mark at the helm, we followed the shoreline east, away from the boatyard, and came to East Ferry and the waterside pub, Dirty Murphy's, keeping on the other side of the channel to avoid notice.

"Along here someplace will be good," Mark said a few minutes later. "There are some deep pools back in the trees along this shore."

He was right. In another couple of minutes he turned into a narrow cleft between the trees that opened into a neat little pool, not much longer than the yacht, and nearly round. I swam ashore with lines, and we tied up to trees, holding the yacht neatly in the center of the pool. Mark measured the depth with a makeshift leadline and announced that there would still be ample water, even at low tide. Then we went below, made room for ourselves among the boxes and gear and slept, unwilling to think about what we would do next.

Forty

THE RINGING OF THE TELEPHONE STARTLED HIM. IT WAS the second line, the ex-directory one he had had such a devil of a time getting, and it rang only when there was diocese business. He breathed deeply, then picked it up.

"Yes."

"Is the bishop available?"

"Who is calling, please?"

"Sister Concepta."

He was jolted for a moment. He hadn't been ready for this call, and he would have to handle it carefully. "This is the bishop."

Her voice was warm, eager. "We're back. We're in—"

"Don't," he said quickly. He had been ready for that. "It's not necessary for me to know. Are you on an automatic exchange?"

"What?"

"Did you dial directly?"

"Of course," she snorted. "Do you think I'm daft?"

"Just remember that it's very important that you not go through an operator when ringing this number. Have you completed your education?"

"Oh, yes."

"Were you pleased with it?"

"Quite. We studied a bit of everything. I think you might say we earned an honors degree."

"Good. I'm sure you'll put your education to good use. Are you ready for a posting?"

"Nearly. We'd both like to make a trip to the diocese to right a great wrong."

"Are you speaking of the priest's brother?"

"Yes. The priest is anxious to conduct the sinner's funeral personally, and I am looking forward to assisting him. We were thinking of a burial at sea."

"The sinner you're referring to is the nautical chap— is that what you think?"

"Absolutely."

Good, that was a relief. "I'm afraid you're a bit late. I've just learned that he left the country last night—sailed away, in fact, to avoid a legal problem."

"Bound for where?"

"I haven't been able to determine that."

"Do you think he might come back?"

"I don't know, I might have further information later. But listen to me very carefully, now; you and the priest are not to return to this diocese unless I explicitly authorize it, on pain of excommunication. Do you understand that?"

"Excommunication? Are you serious?"

"I am quite serious, I assure you. The order you have chosen requires the strictest obedience, far stricter than the one you left. You must take your instructions from me and from those I delegate, is that quite clear?"

There was a moment's sullen silence. "Yes, it's quite clear," she said, finally. "What are your instructions?"

"I want you to contact the Dublin parish; the number you used before is still good. Take your instructions from the monsignor."

"But . . ."

"He understands that you and the priest are to work independently, but you must coordinate your tasks with him. You are still well-financed, I believe?"

"Fairly well. If we undertook any major new charitable work we would have to look for new funds, though."

"Clear that with the monsignor, as well. I trust you can now handle fund-raising with somewhat more élan than in the past."

She laughed. "I believe so."

"Good, best not to rely on luck in these matters. Go now, and do good works. I'll keep track of you through the monsignor, so don't call me here unless it's absolutely necessary, and then only with the proper precautions."

"I understand."

"Good luck, then." He hung up and heaved a great sigh of relief. It wouldn't do to have those two blundering into his diocese, going after Mark Robinson. He would have to keep close tabs on them. He turned back to the farm accounts he had been working on.

Forty-one

WHEN I WOKE, LATE IN THE AFTERNOON, IT TOOK ME several seconds to realize where I was, and only an instant to regret it. I had been sleeping in an awkward position on a sailbag, so my back was killing me, and I had a full-blown, very heavy head cold. The atmosphere was cold and damp. Mark was sitting at the chart table, scribbling something on a pad by flashlight.

"Morning," he said, cheerfully, "or rather, afternoon. It's past five. Get any rest?"

"Not much," I grumbled, sitting up. "Nobody's arrested us yet?"

"Certainly not," he laughed. "We haven't broken any laws. All we've done is launch a new yacht a couple of weeks ahead of schedule."

I looked around at the shambles of gear around us. "Nothing here is ahead of schedule," I said. "Not anymore. And if we try and take her back to the yard, we'll be right back where we started. If whoever's suing Derek knew about the boat before, you can bet your ass they'll know about her if we take her back."

"We're not taking her back," Mark said.

"Well, we're sure as hell not taking her to the Channel Islands, either, if experience tells us anything." I blew my nose loudly into a sodden handkerchief. The rest of me was still pretty damp, too.

"No," he agreed. "We'll finish her here."

I stared at him sadly; he had finally gone right out of his head. "Sure," I said. "Why not?"

He kept writing on the pad. "Willie, will you do me a favor? Dig out the new rubber dinghy, row over to Dirty Murphy's and ring Annie, will you?" He ripped off a sheet from the pad and handed it to me. "Ask her to get as much of this stuff together as she can and bring it over here tonight aboard *Toscana*. I reckon there's no more than one dinghy load here; she should be able to get it all aboard all right. Tell her to tow the dinghy and outboard when she comes, okay?"

I took the list and shoved it into my pocket. "Sure, Mark." I thought it better to humor him. I rummaged about until I found the dinghy, neatly folded into its canvas bag. It was, of course, under everything else. Everything on the boat seemed to be under everything else. I humped it into the cockpit and unpacked it. Mark made no move to help me; he just kept writing; he seemed to be making more lists. I inflated the dinghy with the foot pump, pausing frequently to rest. The head cold seemed to have robbed me of all my energy. Finally, the dinghy was firm, and I got it into the water and started for the pub. It was still foggy, though not as bad as before. I rowed slowly, trying to think.

I wanted out; it was as simple as that. I found it hard to believe that only the morning before, I had greeted the day feeling just great. In less than thirty-six hours everything seemed to have gone to hell. The shock of realizing how much I wanted Connie again lingered painfully with me, like a spear in the chest, and the more than three unthreatening, productive months we had spent on the boat seemed to have evaporated into nothing. We were stuck, now. We hadn't the resources—power, tools, help—to finish the boat where she was; we couldn't take her back to the yard, and we couldn't get her to Jersey in the shape she was in. It was nearly June. I could spend the summer traveling, spend some time in Paris with Jane, who, at least, offered physical consolation, even if she never seemed to think about anything else; then, in the fall, I could return to law school. Law school was beginning to look pretty good.

I tied up in front of the pub and, on my way to the phone, got hold of a large brandy. I needed it. I dialed the cottage, and Annie answered on the first ring.

"Yes?" Her voice was anxious.

"Your faithful and slightly bruised servant," I said. Slightly drunk, too; the brandy was making its way quickly to the important places, uninhibited by anything in my stomach.

"Willie, where are you?"

"I'm at Dirty Murphy's. Mark and the boat are nearby."

"Thank God. I talked to Finbar, and he said you were actually taking her out of the country."

"Oh, we did, we did. Right past the three-mile limit and back again."

She giggled. "That's just like Mark; devious to the end."

"He's made up a list of stuff; he'd like you to bring it over here aboard *Toscana*." I read her the list; food, clothes, booze, flashlights, a couple of lanterns, some tools and a shotgun, my riot shotgun, which lived in my cupboard. "And he says to tow the dinghy and outboard over. Can you manage?"

"Of course. Exactly where are you?"

"Two or three hundred yards past the pub, in a little inlet on the opposite side of the channel; you can hardly see it. We'll flash a torch for you. Make up bow and stern lines and lead them back to the cockpit. You can toss to me and we'll tie you up alongside the big boat."

"Right. It'll be about . . . two hours, I should say."

"See you then." I went back to the bar and ordered another brandy and some sandwiches; I took a bottle of brandy, too. Mark was still scribbling when I got back to the boat. I didn't ask what, just gave him a sandwich and a pull from the brandy bottle. We were both quite drunk by the time Annie arrived in *Toscana*. At Mark's insistence, we tied the smaller yacht across the stern of the larger one. That way, anyone passing would see only the smaller one, if he didn't look too closely. *Toscana* was a welcome haven—warm, dry and inviting. Annie made us some hot soup, while we stumbled about, laughing drunkenly over nothing, getting out of our wet clothes and into sleeping bags.

"Oh, Mark!" Annie suddenly wailed, shock in her voice. Mark was struggling out of his jeans. I followed her line of vision to his knee. It was horribly discolored and badly swollen.

"Not to worry," he mumbled, reaching for a sleeping bag. "Not to worry. Be fine in a day or two." He was asleep almost immediately.

I told Annie about the launching and Mark's leap for the boat; then I fell asleep, myself.

I woke the next morning to the smell of cooking breakfast. Mark, incredibly for him, was still asleep. It was nearly ten o'clock. Annie didn't even say good morning.

"Listen to me, Willie. We've got to get Mark to a doctor this morning."

"Well, yeah, his leg doesn't look too good, does it?" I was thoroughly hungover.

"It could be a lot worse than it looks, even. He nearly lost it before, you know."

I looked at the sleeping figure. "I've never seen him sleep late before. I didn't know he could."

"He can't, ordinarily. He's hurt, and his body is reacting accordingly. Here's your breakfast. As soon as you eat, will you row over to Dirty Murphy's and phone for a taxi? I'll get Mark up, and we'll be along shortly."

"How are you going to get him to leave the boat?"

"Don't worry, I'll get him over there; you just get the taxi. Tell them it's to go to Bon Secour Hospital in Cork."

I did as she said. Half an hour later they turned up at the pub in the other dinghy, Mark looking angry as hell. We all got into the taxi and started for Cork. Mark produced his lists.

"Here's the way we handle it, Willie. First, we get all that gear sorted out. The sails and other unnecessaries can go aboard *Toscana*; that'll give us room to work."

I glanced at Annie. Her eyes told me to go along.

"Next, we get the generator running. That shouldn't be too tough."

"Mark, neither of us is an electrician."

"We don't have to be. The boat's whole wiring loom is in place, and everything is marked with tape. All we have to do is hook up. And once we get the generator going we'll have power for tools. We'll siphon diesel from *Toscana* to keep it going. It's all going to take longer than we'd scheduled, of course; there's a hell of a lot to be done, but we can do absolutely everything there is left to do right where she is, except get the mast in; we'll need a crane for that. Look, I've got a whole work plan outlined, with everything in the order it's to be done." He shoved his lists at me. I pretended to look at them. He talked all the way to the hospital.

* * *

Annie and I sat in the doctor's office and listened. The doctor, short, plump, and extremely Irish, clipped an X-ray film to a lightbox and switched it on.

"D'you want me to point at things and all that, or do you just want me to tell you?" he asked, in a musical Cork accent.

"Just tell me," Annie replied.

"He needs surgery, I'm afraid, and fairly quickly. Won't help to delay. Trouble is, there's nobody in Cork I'd want to do it; that knee's a mess, for a fact. There's one or two in Dublin and lots, I expect, in London. Who did the original surgery?"

"A Major Browning, at the Royal Naval Hospital in Plymouth."

"Then that's where I'd take him back," the doctor said, emphatically. "This was a gunshot wound before, and they know about those things in the military. I expect he still has his service medical benefit, doesn't he?"

Annie nodded.

"Well, he's going to need at least one operation, maybe more, and it'd be expensive in a civilian hospital, I can tell you. There's a daily, direct flight from Cork to Plymouth. Shall I see if I can get you on today's plane? He's a strong fellow; he could manage with a wheelchair at both ends of the flight."

"Please, doctor, if you would," Annie said quietly. "I'd better go and tell him."

I waited in the hallway, expecting to hear an explosion of protest; there was none. The doctor went into the room, and shortly, the three of them emerged, Mark in a wheelchair.

"The plane leaves in an hour and a half, Willie. You ride with me to the airport in a cab while Annie picks up some things at the cottage."

As an orderly helped Mark into the cab I turned to the doctor. "Assuming the surgery goes well, and the recovery, how long before he'll be all right again?"

The doctor shook his head. "I could only give you a guess," he said, "but I don't think he'll ever be all right in the sense that he was before this accident. I'd say he'd be as good as he's going to be in, maybe, a year—that's with a good recovery. He'd be walking with a brace by then. He might not ever again walk without one."

I thanked him and got into the taxi with Mark. He started going over the list again, and then, maybe sensing that I wasn't with him, stopped. "Willie, I know this looks bad, but we can still do this; really, we can."

I looked at him. "It doesn't look too good, Mark. Maybe with Finbar's and Harry's help I can get the boat in good enough shape to motor to England or the Channel Islands, but we're not going to make the Azores race, and remember, you've got to do a qualifying cruise before December thirty-first if the committee is going to accept you for the Transatlantic. Don't you think it might be better to pass on the seventy-two race and aim for seventy-six? I'm sure Derek would let you have the boat."

He took hold of my arm, and if I had never seen a zealot before, I knew I was looking at one now. "Listen to me, Willie. I know myself very well, and what's more, I know you. If you'll get some help from Finbar and get started, you can have this boat sailing in six weeks, and she'll make the starting line for the Azores race on July seventeenth. And I don't care what that doctor told you back there, I'll be aboard, I promise you. You and Annie and I will have the sail of our lives. We can do it. You can do it."

I looked back at him, and just for a moment, I believed him. "Okay, Mark," I said, my throat tightening. "We'll do it."

By the time their plane had left for Plymouth, I was no longer sure. I was all alone, now, and not noted for finishing things.

Forty-two

I TOOK A TAXI FROM THE AIRPORT AND PICKED UP MARK'S van, which we had left at the boatyard. I didn't go inside to speak to Finbar or Harry; it seemed best to keep them out of it for a while, at least, until I knew what I was going to do. What Mark had proposed was impossible. Even if I got the boat into some sort of shape, he was clearly going to be out of commission for a long time to come.

At the cottage I sat, numbly, for a long time. Late in the afternoon I found my notebook and dialed a New York number. There was a beep after the first ring. "This is Will Lee," I said. "I would appreciate it if . . . somebody would contact me as soon as possible." I gave the number and hung up. Then it occurred to me that there was another call I should make. I left a message, and within minutes the call was returned.

"This is Major Primrose, Mr. Lee; how can I help you?"

"Major, the boat is no longer at the yard, so there's nothing for you to guard anymore."

"I'm aware of your launching. My man says it was very exciting."

"Too exciting."

"Where is the boat, now?"

I told him.

"I'll have a man nearby in an hour's time."

"I think maybe that's a good idea. There's a lot of expensive gear on board, and it wouldn't be difficult to break in."

I spent the rest of the afternoon and evening trying not to think about the boat at all, and instead, kept trying to think of a way out. I couldn't just bug off to Paris, leaving things as they were, but there had to be some orderly way to wrap things up and then go. I was trying to figure a way out, when the phone rang at about eight o'clock.

"Willie?"

"Hello, Annie. How's Mark?"

"Annoyed, but resigned. He's over at the naval hospital with his leg packed in ice; he goes to surgery at eight in the morning. Somehow, he managed to make them give him a room with a phone; he hasn't been off it since. He's arranged for you to be able to write checks on the London account for whatever you need for the boat and yourself. He'd like you to send them a specimen of your signature. Got a pencil? I'll give you the address."

I wrote down the bank's address, all the while trying

to think of a way to begin to tell Annie how impossible the situation was, but she stopped me in my tracks.

"Willie, I don't know what I'd do without you. Mark will do so much better knowing that you're still working on the boat. I told you how depressed he was when he had the original surgery. I honestly don't think I could go through that again. But now he's still got the boat to look forward to, and best of all, he's got you."

I had been prepared to put myself up for the Shit of the Year award by backing out, and now I knew I couldn't do it, not while Annie still needed me around. "Well, I don't think his plan is realistic; I don't see how I can possibly get the boat in shape in time to make the Azores race; and I don't see how Mark can possibly be in any sort of shape to do the qualifying cruise before the end of the year. Those two items apart, we're in perfectly wonderful shape; that is, if somebody's lawyers don't descend from the sky and take the boat away." I thought of mentioning that the IRA might come and bomb it, too, but thought better of it.

She laughed, and I knew I would have to go on trying to keep her laughing. It was such a wonderful sound. "Well, I'm going to turn in, now," she said, yawning. "I'm at the Mayflower Post Hotel, if you need to reach me." She gave me the number and Mark's number at the hospital. "It'll probably be day after tomorrow before you can talk to him. As soon as he's safely out of post-op I'll start looking for a flat hereabouts. You take care of yourself, now. I'll talk with you in a day or two."

I hung up, and the phone rang almost immediately.

"Will? This is Nicky. We got your message. What's doing?"

"Oh, hi, thanks for getting back to me." I told him about the premature launching of the boat and Mark's accident.

"Well, that's bad news," he said, "but it sounds as if you've made the right decisions."

"Look, Nicky, we're going to have a hell of a time getting the boat finished if I can't take her back to the yard. What are the chances of this legal situation getting resolved soon?"

"Not good, I'm afraid. Unfortunately, it's tied to a whole string of other difficulties; it can't be favorably resolved until a number of other things happen first. You certainly aren't going to be able to go back to the yard with the boat this summer, not without its being attached, and to tell you the truth, I think Derek would rather you scuttled her than let that happen."

Scuttling her was beginning to seem an attractive option. "Well, maybe motoring her to Jersey might be the best plan, once I've got her sorted out a bit."

"From what you've told me, I think leaving the boat right where it is is the best, possibly the only alternative. You've got Primrose watching over you, and at least some of the resources you need. The yard in Jersey is very good, but we've no guarantee that she won't be found there, and then we'd be right back to square one. Have you got enough money?"

"I think so, for the moment, anyway. I can write checks on Mark's London account."

"Good. We'll make the final deposit of our agreement in that account immediately, so you can go ahead and pay Cork Harbour Boatyard what you owe them to date. Does anybody in Cork know that the boat has not actually left the country?"

I thought for a minute. "No, nobody, not even Finbar at the yard. Mark purposely didn't tell him."

"Good, my advice would be to keep it that way. Both the boat and Mark are safely out of circulation. Is there somewhere you could stay—someplace out of the way?"

"Well, I guess the logical thing for me to do would be to live aboard *Toscana*. She's tied up next to the boat, and she's quite comfortable."

"That sounds a good idea. Now, Will, if you need anything, you let us hear from you, all right? Just call the New York number. Derek is very grateful for the way you're handling this, and we'll do anything we can to help."

"Okay, Nicky, thanks. If you should have trouble reaching me and can't, call Mark or Annie at the Royal Naval Hospital in Plymouth."

I had a sudden urge to get out of the cottage before I had to explain anything to anyone. I sat down and wrote to Mark's bank, then to Lord Coolmore, enclosing a check for the remainder of our lease on the cottage, through September. I said we wouldn't actually be moving out until then but wouldn't be around much. I certainly couldn't move all of Mark's and Annie's things out, and it seemed better to leave everything in the cottage but what I needed. I began getting my things together and loading them into the van. There wasn't all that much, really. I went into Mark's and Annie's bedroom and had a quick look around. I found some sailing gear of theirs and loaded that, too.

On my last trip, I looked into their wardrobe and found the Ingram machine pistol and the .45 automatic. Those shouldn't be left lying about; I put them into the van, as well, hiding them under everything else.

Then I telephoned Finbar.

"Where are you, Willie? Where's the boat?"

"It's better if you don't know, Finbar, believe me."

He estimated the amount owing on the boat, and I included instructions for payment in the envelope I was sending to the London bank. That way, the check would come from England.

I had one last look about, collected some bottles of wine, some books and other odds and ends, locked the cottage and got into the van. At the main road, I put the note to Coolmore in his mailbox and in Carrigaline, I posted the letter to the bank. It was after midnight, now, and I drove slowly and carefully through the deserted streets of Cork, nervous about the possibility of being stopped by the police; I would have one hell of a time explaining what I was doing with a machine gun in the van. Then I turned east. The boat was moored on Great Island, on the other side of the harbor. I drove slowly

across the bridge and through Cobh, formerly Queens-
town, where passenger ships had once called regularly,
even the *Titanic*, on her one and only voyage. The village
was still a marine center, and I passed a couple of shops
where I would be able to find things I might need for
the boat.

I could see from my map that a road ran close to
where the boat and *Toscana* lay. I found a dirt lane leading through a field toward the water and, after closing the
farmer's gate carefully behind me, drove into the trees.
As I neared the boat, the headlights of a vehicle came on,
startling me, but they went off immediately, and a figure
waved from a Range Rover. Primrose's man. I was able
to park within ten yards of the water, then I had to swim
out for the rubber dinghy. Transferring the gear from the
van to the boat took some time, then I rowed across
the East Ferry Channel to Dirty Murphy's and retrieved
the hard dinghy and outboard that we had left there that
morning, feeling terribly furtive. It was after four in the
morning before I was able to climb into a sleeping bag
aboard *Toscana* and, with a groan, start to fall asleep.

I had effectively disappeared. I was alone, now, with
what I had to do.

Forty-three

I T WAS NEARLY NOON BEFORE I COULD DRAG MYSELF FROM the sleeping bag and force myself to face the mess at hand. I ate a makeshift breakfast while gazing absently through a port at the day outside. It was raining steadily. Trust the Irish summer to produce what the Irish call "a fine, soft day." Just the sort of day to stay in bed with my cold.

Finally, I stepped from *Toscana* aboard the big boat and hurriedly unlocked the hatch, hunching my shoulders against the rain. The reality in the dim, green light below was even worse than my memory of it. "Chaos" would have been too polite a word. Thousands in electronic gear was jumbled together with thousands in other, more mundane equipment. It took me twenty minutes of shifting before I could even get a floorboard up to check the bilges. She was still taking water. I checked the soft-wood plug under the galley sink and gave it a couple of whacks with the mallet for good measure. It was leaking, but not fast enough to account for all the water she had taken. I laboriously pumped the bilges, thinking all the while that somewhere in the jumble of gear there was an electric bilge pump that could make my life a great deal easier. It would be first on my list of installations.

That done, I decided that neatness would help; just putting the boat in reasonable order would make my task seem easier and give me cause for optimism. Besides, sorting and cleaning didn't require much thinking. I wasn't ready for thinking yet. I would have liked to put everything on deck and start from there, but the rain prevented me. Instead, I had to rummage for things that could safely get wet, shove those on deck, and leave the rest below. It was slow going. By the end of the day I had separated much of the gear, but had stowed or connected nothing. My cold sapped my strength and slowed me down.

That evening I went into Cobh, found a telephone, and called Annie in Plymouth.

"He was in surgery for six hours," she said. "They did a lot of very delicate work, and the doctor says that all we can do now is wait for the healing. The leg will be in plaster for about three weeks, and they won't know until it comes off whether the surgery has been as successful as they hope. If everything is all right at that time, then Mark can begin physiotherapy to regain use of the leg."

"It doesn't sound as if there's a prayer of his doing the Azores race, does it?"

"No," she said, "not for an ordinary person, but then, Mark's not ordinary. He was still pretty groggy when I left him, but he was talking about the race. I know this sounds mad given the circumstances, but he just might make it. I think Mark must have the greatest recuperative powers of any human being who ever lived, Jesus Christ only barely excepted. But he has to have something to aim for, something to keep him going. That's why what you're doing with the boat is so important. Call him tomorrow, if you can. It'll boost his spirits."

For three days it rained steadily, inhibiting what I already considered an impossible task. I talked with Mark twice, and he was full of helpful ideas and suggestions, but I told him that my circumstances made it difficult for me to call every day. I wanted to have progress to report when I talked with him. On the fourth day it stopped raining, and I made better progress. At the end of the week my cold had improved, and I had everything sorted and had made a list of the location of every piece of equipment and where it was to be installed.

The next morning the cold that I had thought was healing had degenerated into something awful. I took to my bunk, and it got worse. Everything went wrong; I couldn't keep anything down or, for that matter, up. I grew very weak and was obviously running a high temperature. I drifted in and out of sleep, too sick to fix myself much to eat or even to think about going into Cobh for a doctor. Even when I began to come out of it some days later, I was so weak that I couldn't sit up. It was another couple of days before I could move about without fear of falling, and by the time I felt like thinking about work again, ten full days had been lost to whatever bug I had had. I checked the calendar; I had just about four weeks before I would have to sail away from Ireland in order to be in Plymouth in time to provision the boat and make her ready for the race. And nothing had been installed yet.

Now that I was recovering, I was starving, too, and I had eaten absolutely everything aboard. I gathered up my dirty laundry and sweat-soaked sleeping bag, staggered to the van with the bundle and drove into Cobh. I found a fish-and-chips place and gorged myself, then left the laundry in a coin-operated washing machine and went grocery shopping. My packages in the van, I went back to the laundry and got everything into the dryer. Then I nearly fainted. I sat down heavily on a bench, alone in the place, sweat pouring off me. I reckoned I had made my outing a bit too soon. Shortly, I found a bucket and threw up the fish and chips. Dizzy and light-headed, I began to hallucinate, thinking I could hear the sound of children singing. Then the door opened and a moment later a voice said, "Mother of God, Will, what's wrong?"

I didn't answer; it was clear to me that this was a part of my hallucination, along with the singing children.

"Is this a friend of yours?" another voice asked with obvious distaste.

"Yes, Sister. You go on with the girls. I'll join you in a minute."

I put down my bucket and sat back. The sound of the dryer going round seemed calibrated to the spinning of my head. I was almost certain Connie Lydon was standing in front of me.

"Are you ill?" she seemed to ask.

Then the spinning stopped, and I saw that she really was there. "Hello," I said. "What are you doing here?"

"We've brought the girls over on their end-of-term outing," she said. "I asked if you're ill."

"I've been ill," I said. "I thought I was over it."

"Are you all right, now?"

I nodded. "Oh, yeah, I just need to rest for a minute." Then I thought, What am I saying? If I'm all right, she'll go away. I leaned against the wall and groaned slightly. She took my arm and led me back to the bench.

"You look awful," she said.

She was right, of course. I hadn't shaved in ten days; my hair was matted and hadn't been cut for weeks, and my filthy clothes hung on me. My belt was two notches tighter than usual. I stole a glance at my reflection in the soap machine; there were dark circles under my eyes. Perfect. I wiped my sweaty forehead with my sleeve. "I'll be okay," I said, as unconvincingly as possible. "I just need to get back to bed."

"What are you doing in Cobh?"

"I'm . . . uh, staying over here, temporarily. Really, I'll be okay, I'll just get my laundry in the van and get going."

"You stay right here," she said. "I'll be back in a minute."

She left the shop. I ran to the window and saw her having a discussion with a nun next to a schoolbus full of little girls. The nun nodded and got aboard the bus; it pulled away. Connie started back to the shop. I ran for my bench.

A few minutes later, I was directing her down the dirt lane toward where the two yachts were moored. "Stop here for a minute," I said. She stopped the van. "I'm going to have to have your promise not to tell *anyone* what's down here. If you don't think you can keep quiet about this, I'll drive you back to town right now. I'm feeling a bit better." I wiped my forehead again for effect. She gave me a disgusted look and continued to drive. From her expression, I thought my plan was working.

Then she saw the two yachts and stopped again with a gasp. "What is going on here? I heard that you and Mark had left the country with the boat."

"Mark has left the country," I said. "He's in a military hospital in England. And you're the only one who knows that the boat and I are still in Ireland. I hope I can trust you, Connie."

I woke late that night and looked about me. *Toscana* was spotlessly clean again. The food and my clean clothes were neatly stowed. Connie Lydon slept softly on the settee berth opposite mine. And I felt really good for the first time in a long time. I fell asleep again easily.

Forty-four

PATRICK PEARCE STOOD IN THE CALL BOX FOR NEARLY half an hour before the phone rang. It was raining lightly outside, and no queue had formed for the box. He had stood all that time with his hand holding down the cradle and the receiver to his ear, pretending to talk. When it finally rang, he released it so quickly there was only a tiny tinkle. He had not spoken with his brother since his mother's death.

"Pat, how are you?"

"I'm grand, Michael. God, it's good to hear your voice." He was nearly trembling with excitement.

"Pat, do you think you'd still like to do a bit of work?"

His heart leapt. "Oh, Jesus, yes. You just tell me what."

"How about a spot of lunch then, old boy?" His upper-class English accent was very good.

Pat laughed. "Are you sure it's all right?"

"Ah, sure it is. It's all in how you do it. Can you meet me in Central London in an hour?"

"Sure. Where?"

"A pub called the Grenadier. It's in Wilton Row, just off Wilton Crescent; a dead-end mews right behind St. George's Hospital, at Hyde Park Corner."

"Right."

The Grenadier was among the most fashionable of the West End's pubs, full of businessmen, debutantes and affluent American tourists. Trust Michael, it wasn't the sort of place the police might keep a watch, like the Irish pubs in South London. Pat laughed aloud when he saw his brother ambling down the mews. He was wearing striped trousers and a bowler hat and carrying an expensive briefcase and a furled umbrella. They got some sandwiches and a pint and sat on a bench in the mews. It had stopped raining, and the June sunshine was warm. Pat noticed immediately that the bench commanded a full view of the approach to the pub, and that there was a walkway leading toward Hyde Park Corner. The mews was not a dead end for a man on foot. Michael would not let himself be boxed in.

"You look bloody marvelous, even in that getup," Pat said.

"Just a bit of camouflage," Michael chuckled, keeping his posh accent. "One can't go about looking like a policeman's idea of a terrorist, y'know." He took a sip of his pint and a bite of his sandwich. "You know, your little number with Thrasher's books did a lot better than our gelignite. We've had many a good laugh about that. How much did he actually run out of the country?"

"Not a penny, that I know of," Pat said smugly. Michael's eyebrows went up. "I cooked the whole thing."

"How?"

"It was easy, once I got a grasp of their computer procedures. I used their own programs against them, just changed a lot of entries to establish a pattern."

Michael looked at his brother with new respect. "That's bloody marvelous, it really is. It's given Thrasher fits; can't even come into the country, from what I hear. I'm surprised there haven't been any repercussions. Or have there?"

"I haven't been able to find any very good work since. The Avondale thing has got about in accounting circles, so I'm done for in the City or the West End. I've been making ends meet by doing freelance bookkeeping for some small businesses down Streatham, mostly."

"Is that it? Thrasher hasn't retaliated in any other way?"

Pat took a deep breath. "There was something else, but I handled it."

"Tell me." Michael was all business now.

"Thrasher put a goon on me. Ex-copper called MacAdam."

Michael's eyes widened. "Pat, did *you* do Blackie MacAdam?"

Pat looked at his brother evenly, his pride welling. "I did."

Michael stiffened and began searching faces in the little crowd outside the pub. "Pat, has anybody been on you? I need to know that now."

"Relax, Michael. They came to see me once, very politely. Didn't even ask me in for a chat. I think somebody on the force may have known he was looking at me, but there was absolutely nothing to connect us. I looked 'em in the eye and told 'em I'd never heard of MacAdam, didn't have a clue."

"And you think they bought it?"

"I promise you, Michael, there hasn't been so much as a hint of interest since, and that was in January. If they'd had anybody on me since, he'd have been bored to death, I can tell you, following me about to job interviews and to the pub and the like. A week after the bastard went the papers had it all wrapped as a fire to cover a burglary/murder. It was a hot blaze; took out the wine merchant downstairs and the building next door. I arranged a gas explosion. Couldn't have been anything left but cinders."

Michael relaxed a bit. "That'll go down well with the lads. MacAdam was a real bother when he was on the force; hated the Irish. Pity we couldn't have taken credit somehow."

"Well, he won't bother another Irishman again."

Michael took one more careful look about, then took

a new tack. "Pat, there's something you can do for us, something bespoke for you."

"Just tell me."

"We've a couple of new people we think are going to be very useful. They're green, just out of training, really, but they've got guts, and they're . . . well, one of 'em's smart. My bishop wants 'em controlled at a distance, and I reckon you're ideal. Oh, it's known you're my brother, but nobody's made us together for years, and they've never successfully connected you with anything. Are you game?"

"You know I am. How d'you want me to handle it?"

"Well, it's delicate. First, I want you to transmit orders to them; second, I want you to keep tabs on them, as closely as you can."

"You worried about them? Too green?"

"I'm worried, all right, but not because they're green. They're dangerous. They've insisted on an independence that worries me, and the bishop has gone along with it, I don't quite know why. I think there may be some personal connection there that I don't know about. Certainly they're from his diocese, and I think he must have recruited them. There's something going on there."

"All right. How do we manage communications?"

Michael tapped the briefcase that lay on the bench between them. "There's a nice bit of money in here. I want you to set up a business of some sort, but I don't want you so busy that you can't get away when you need to."

"I could open an accountant's office, do the same sort

of thing I'm doing now. It only takes a couple of days a week."

"That's ideal. Don't hire any help, though. Get a phone and a second, ex-directory number. Put an answering machine on it, one of those with a remote device. Check it twice a day, no matter where you are. Before we part today, I'll give you some phone numbers for contact purposes. They'll have the same numbers, if for any reason they can't communicate with you."

"Are we never to meet face to face?"

"On the contrary. I want them used to seeing you from time to time. If they give us too much bother, they'll be excommunicated, and you'll perform the ceremony, so I don't want them uncomfortable about meeting with you."

"I understand. What do they look like, and where will I meet them?"

"Set your meetings for places like this. Keep it upmarket. Dress well. As for what they look like, they're sitting on the bench across the mews, just opposite."

Pat turned and looked, being careful to keep it casual. A young couple, trendily dressed in the best Kings Road style, sat sipping their drinks. The man was thickly built, clean-shaven, his hair carefully cut. The young woman was tall, robust, with fairly short and beautifully styled auburn hair. "The girl's a stunner," he said quite involuntarily.

"In more ways than one," Michael replied wryly. "She's the smart one; very clever. He's right under her thumb. Remember this, Pat, it's important: if she's taken out of the picture in any way—killed, even detained—do him immediately. He can't be left to run loose on his own. Got that?"

Pat nodded. "I'm going to need a weapon."

"That's in the briefcase, too. Nice little nine-millimeter automatic and two boxes of cartridges. I expect you still carry a knife. If you get the order to excommunicate, do it without hesitation. I know it might be tough with somebody as beautiful as that, but do it."

"I understand. If you say it's to be done, it'll be done."

They talked a few minutes more about communications; Michael gave him some phone numbers to memorize. "They'll be known to you as priest and nun. You'll be the curate. They've already got their first assignment. I'm sending them down to the west country. There's a concentration of training for Her Majesty's forces down there. I want a little havoc wrought at the Royal Marine establishment in Poole and at Plymouth, too. After that they'll communicate with you. As soon as I've left, go over there and make their acquaintance briefly. Set up your own contact schedule, and leave a message for me at one of the Dublin numbers if you need me, and I'll call you back. We'll stick with automatic call boxes, they're safest." He stood up and shook hands, leaving the briefcase on the bench.

"Goodbye Michael. You're doing fine work; I hear about it all the time; I'm proud."

"Take care, Pat. It's been good seeing you. I don't expect we'll manage it again for a while to come. Take care."

Michael turned and walked up the footpath toward Hyde Park Corner, his bowler cocked at a jaunty angle, his umbrella resting on his shoulder in a mock military manner. Pat Pearce picked up the briefcase and walked across the mews toward the young couple, who turned to meet him.

Forty-five

CONNIE'S PRESENCE TRANSFORMED MY ATTITUDE TOWARD what needed to be done on the boat. Abruptly, my dire pessimism was changed to a wild optimism. A clearing of the weather and a long, sunny spell helped, too. Connie had completed her school year, now, and had time on her hands. Although she refused to sleep aboard *Toscana* again, she came nearly every day and offered the best possible sort of support. She handed me tools, made notes on our progress, shopped for food and prepared it, lent muscle when mine alone wasn't enough, and applauded, encouraged, and even admired my work.

We began by locating the electric bilge pump (it was in the bilges) and connecting it. It ran off the ship's twelve-volt batteries and kept the boat dry, in spite of steady leaking, which I still could not locate. I got the diesel generator hooked up and going, and that gave us power for tools and bright working lights. I installed the two toilets, fitted the heater and attached dozens of small pieces of gear. Connie sanded and varnished the interior, applying coat upon coat until it began to gleam. I noticed that the power cord on the sander was fraying badly and made a mental note to replace it, something I would, to my everlasting regret, forget to do. I drilled holes in the stern and bolted on a prefabricated steel bracket, then mounted the large, Hasler windvane self-steering gear, leading the control lines to the helm, using *Toscana*'s similar but smaller installation as a guide.

With less than two weeks to go before the boat's absolute last departure day, I began to install the electronic gear, and here I ran into problems. When Mark had taped all the electrical wiring he had marked every piece of the glossy, plastic tape with a felt-tipped pen. While nobody was looking, the damp atmosphere inside the yacht eroded the markings until they finally vanished. That meant I had to work my way through the whole of the wiring loom, identifying each wire as I connected it, which brought on the kind of frustration that always comes when one person begins a job and another finishes it.

Connie arrived every morning about nine and left about six in the evening. Although it was an hour's drive each way, she adamantly refused to stay overnight and lightly brushed aside my tentative attempts to get physical, until I was afraid to try for fear of outright rejection. The other guy, I knew, was hanging in the background, and while she was spending every day with me, she was spending every evening—maybe every night—with him.

It drove me crazy. It didn't seem to bother her in the least. That drove me crazy, too.

As soon after my illness as I could I called Mark. Annie answered the phone.

"Willie! Where have you been? We've been worried sick! Are you all right?"

I explained my illness and recovery. "How's Mark?"

"Coming along quite nicely. He's down the hall having the plaster off his leg just now. I'm glad you caught me here, because we're moving into a flat on the base tonight." She gave me the address and phone number. "If the knee has healed properly from the surgery I'll be working with him twice a day on physiotherapy. I've been taking a short training course at the hospital while he's been recovering."

"No idea yet how effective the surgery was?"

"The X-rays look very good, the doctor says. Now we have to see how he responds to the therapy. How's it going at your end?"

I told her about Connie's presence on the scene. "I feel a lot better about it with some help at hand. I'm reckoning to be in Plymouth with this bloody boat no later than the fourteenth of July. There'll be some work to do still, I'm sure, but if you can get the provisioning organized in advance, that'll help a lot. Do you think Mark's going to make it?"

"With luck, yes."

"And without luck? If he isn't able to make it, will he be able to accept it?"

"You don't understand. Not doing the race is just not a possibility in Mark's mind. He'll do it lying down, strapped on deck, if necessary, then return singlehanded for his qualifying cruise."

We continued to talk a couple of times a week, and Mark improved steadily. He took quickly to the therapy, and a couple of weeks later, a leg brace fitted, was walking awkwardly with a crutch. Apparently, Annie had been right about his recuperative powers.

By the end of the first full week in July Connie and I were nearing completion of our multitude of tasks on the boat. The electronic gear was mostly hooked up—God knew if it would work when it had to—and all the essential equipment was installed and working. Connie's varnishing job was sensational; the ship was looking shipshape.

But two essential jobs remained, and I wasn't sure how I was going to do either of them. We might motor to England in the condition the boat was now in, but we couldn't sail unless we got the mast into her. Depending on the engine entirely would be dangerous. It would be foolhardy to take a sailboat that distance unless she could sail. And we were still without the seacock being connected under the galley sink. I had found the fitting buried in the jumble of gear, but the boat would have to be removed from the water to install it. I could hardly do it while a stream of water poured from the bare hole in the hull. Both these jobs, the mast and the seacock, demanded that the boat be taken to a yard, but if I did that I risked some lawyer slapping a lien on her.

After a great deal of worrying, I thought I might have a way to do the seacock without swamping the boat. I had once watched in a marina while a man tipped a boat nearly to the horizontal by making the halyards fast to the dock and then winching until she heeled sufficiently to lift a through-hull fitting above the water. We couldn't do that with this boat, because she didn't have a mast in her. She had something else, though. She had a keel.

I got a spool of heavy, plaited, nylon anchor warp on deck, took an end ashore, and ran it through the heaviest block I had and made that fast to a stout oak. I made a loop in the end, tied a slipknot in it, and took it into the water. At the waterline of the boat I took a series of deep breaths, packing air into my lungs, then dove. It only took me a couple of dives before I was able to get the loop around the keel at its bottom and pull the slipknot tight so that the line wouldn't ride up the keel and cost me leverage. Then I got back aboard, led the other end of the line through a pair of strategically placed blocks and around one of the main winches, and, with Connie tailing, began to grind. It was slow work, with the winch in its lowest gear, but the boat began to heel. The warps taken ashore from her other side kept her from drifting sideways. Slowly, but surely, the keel swung up, and the through-hull fitting peeked above the waterline, high and dry. In another hour I had the seacock installed, the line freed from the keel and the boat floating upright in her shady berth. I felt like a bloody hero.

On the tenth of July I telephoned Mark. "How're you doing?"

"Listen, all I need is you here with that boat. How are *you* doing."

"She's finished, Mark. Done. All except the mast."

"The seacock?"

I told him how I had managed it.

"Bloody marvelous. I'd never have thought of that."

"There's still the mast, though. There's no possible way to do it where she lies, now."

"Right. You're going to have to go to the yard. You'd better call Finbar."

"That way we risk losing the boat again."

"Not necessarily." I could hear him grinning. "Now listen."

We spent the rest of the day provisioning the boat for the trip to England and generally tidying up. We packed most of the sails away, leaving at hand only the main and headsails we'd be most likely to need. Early Sunday morning I telephoned Finbar.

"Willie! Are you back?"

"In a manner of speaking," I replied. "Listen, Finbar, I need you and Harry to help me tonight."

"Of course."

"High water's just after one tomorrow morning. I want to bring *Toscana* up the creek and have you haul her at about ten, when the tide's risen enough for her to get up there. You've storage space for her there, haven't you?"

"Yes, sure."

"Good, Mark will want to leave her there for the rest of the season and through the winter. Oh, and there'll be another job to do. I want to get the mast into the boat."

"Which boat?"

"*The* boat, Finbar."

"Jesus, I thought she was in England!"

"That's what everybody thinks, and they have to go on thinking that until the mast is in her. Now don't ask any more questions, okay?"

"Sure, sure, I'll see you tonight, and don't worry, not a word to anybody!" He sounded positively gleeful.

By late in the afternoon we had finished; everything that could be done had been done. The big boat was, but for her mast, ready for sea and provisioned for the sail to England. What light gear and charts we needed from *Toscana* were aboard. The remainder of the smaller boat's gear we had packed in boxes for storage ashore, along with her neatly folded sails. I was surprised at what an organizer I had become in Mark's absence; I was even more surprised that we were so ready and, what was more, had a few hours to spare.

I shoved a cassette into the boat's newly installed tape player; it was *Wave*, an album of guitar and strings by the Brazilian Antonio Carlos Jobim, something we had listened to often during sails aboard *Toscana*. I grabbed a bottle of wine and joined Connie, who was stretched on deck in a dapple of late afternoon sunshine that came through a gap in our canopy of trees.

"That's nice," she said, cocking an ear to the music and taking a glass of wine. "I remember that from last summer, when we cruised down to Castletownshend."

"Hold it," I said. "Don't drink yet." I walked to the rail and tipped a bit of wine into the water. This was the first bottle opened aboard the new boat, and I didn't want to get off to a bad start.

"I remember that, too," she laughed. " 'Give Poseidon his, and maybe he won't want you.' "

"What else do you remember about that cruise?" I asked.

She laughed again. "I remember somebody shouting at us late one night when we were anchored in Castletownshend. We were rocking the boat, I believe."

I sat down beside her and bent to kiss her on the neck. "Why don't we rock the boat again? Christen the new one?"

She shrugged away. "Don't. I can't do that."

"Oh, Connie, are you still so angry with me?" I had apologized for New Year's more than once, but she always changed the subject.

"No, I'm not angry anymore."

"Is it the other guy, the one I saw you with at the Spaniard?"

She smiled slightly. "Terry? Well, he is quite a fellow."

That stung badly. "I thought . . . I know I wasn't honest with you before, but I thought we had something that could ride that out."

She was silent, but a tear rolled down a cheek.

"Connie, there's this . . . this bond between us." If I had ever doubted this, it had become clear to me during our weeks together working on the boat.

"I know," she said.

"Well, what are we going to do about it?"

"I don't know." She got to her feet. "What time do you want to start up the harbor?"

"We ought to start getting the boats out of here a bit after eight, I guess."

She stepped across the deck and started down the plank to shore. "I'll be back then," she said over her shoulder. I thought she was still crying.

A moment later I heard the van start and drive away. Well, I thought, I still had the sail to England with her. Maybe, alone together at sea, we could start to talk to each other. I dumped the rest of the wine overboard. "Here," I said to Poseidon, "have the lot."

Forty-six

CONNIE RETURNED ON TIME, DRIED-EYED, BUT QUIET. I thought she had probably gone back to her place to pack for the passage to Plymouth, but she came aboard emptyhanded.

"Where's your gear?" I asked.

"Gear?" She looked surprised.

"Won't you need some things for the trip to England?"

"I'm not going to England."

Now it was my turn to look surprised. "But . . ."

"You never said anything to me about going to England with you."

"Well . . . I just assumed . . ."

"Never assume," she said, then looked about her. "All right, how do you want to do this?"

"Wait a minute, Connie," I protested. "This is one hell of a big boat, you know." I spread my arms to indicate her size.

"You built her for singlehanding, didn't you?"

"Well, yeah, but . . ."

"Then singlehand her." She tossed me *Toscana*'s bow line. "Hold her bows in while I reverse the engine. That'll point her stern into the channel." She hopped aboard the smaller yacht, taking the stern line with her, then started the engine and put it into reverse. *Toscana* began to back into the channel. "I'll wait while you untie," she shouted back. "Then you lead the way."

I came to life, started the engine, and began bringing the big yacht's lines aboard. Soon she was in the channel, and I put her in forward and started into the main harbor. *Toscana* tagged at our heels all the way up. There was still plenty of light, and I could see Connie, expressionless, standing at the helm, steering. We passed a couple of yachts from the Royal Cork, and people came on deck to look at the big boat and wave. Now the news was out, but before anybody could do anything about it, we'd be gone, she and I.

We reached the mouth of the creek just before ten, with the last of the light. I waved Connie ahead and yelled for her to go alongside the quay. Finbar and Harry were waiting and took her lines. I circled in the mouth of the creek while they loosened *Toscana*'s backstay, slipped straps under her, and plucked her from the water with the yard's ancient crane. Finbar set her expertly on a waiting cradle. She looked a bit forlorn out of the water, with her dirty bottom. I had had some of my best sailing aboard her, and I wouldn't see her again. I would miss her.

The smaller yacht out of the way, I came slowly along-side, unused to docking such a large boat and feeling my way to be sure there was enough water under her keel. Finbar and Harry had to have a look below before proceeding.

"Jesus, Will, she's in good nick; you've done a fine bit of work on her," Finbar said.

I warmed to the praise. "Thank Connie for the var-nishing," I said. "And God only knows if everything will work." I already knew the log was working; I had tried that out on the trip up.

The four of us fell to, unlashing the mast from the decks and attaching the upper ends of the rigging, pre-fabricated in Cowes, to the mast. That done, Finbar manned the crane, hooking up to a bridle we fashioned near the upper spreaders. He slowly lifted the top of the mast from the decks while Harry and I kept the lower end from doing damage. After considerable maneuver-ing we got the lower end properly positioned above the opening in the big yacht's decks and Finbar ever so gen-tly lowered the mast, while Harry and I worked below, settling the mast into its step on the keel and relaying hand signals to Finbar through Connie. In half an hour we had the mast in place. Finbar and Harry attached the stays and shrouds, while I made the electrical connections for the mast lights and wind indicator at the masthead. When I had screwed the last junction box shut, I walked to the chart table, took a deep breath, and turned on the Brookes & Gatehouse wind instruments. The needle quickly showed five to six knots of wind. I exhaled in a rush.

I switched everything on, just to see the dials register. Everything registered. At least I had found the right wires. I turned to the main switchboard and flipped on the masthead light, then peeped fearfully up the hatch. On. Triumph.

On deck, the rigging was in place. We tightened everything, then bent on the mainsail. "Finbar," I said, "I've got to leave for England tonight. Do you think you and Harry could come down into the harbor with me and do some tuning?" Translated, this meant, I'm not at all sure I can sail this bloody thing. Help me learn how.

"Wouldn't miss the chance." Finbar grinned. "I don't suppose we'll get another."

With the yard's workboat in tow we motored down into the main harbor and cut the engine. A full moon was rising and helped us find blocks and winch handles and sheets. Somehow, my newly organized mind had forgotten to get the running rigging, the ropes that controlled the sails, in place. After half an hour of scrambling we got the main up, then the genoa staysail and the yankee. The boat was cutter rigged, and each of the headsails was set on an aluminum stay that could be turned with a reel and a winch, furling the sails like window blinds from the cockpit, an ideal single-handed rig. The yacht began to sail for the first time.

In ten knots of wind she swept across the smooth waters of the harbor, Connie at the helm, while Finbar,

Harry, and I scrambled about the decks, tensioning the rigging to its ideal state and making adjustments. We tacked back and forth, went upwind and downwind, checking everything we could think of. Finally, we all went back to the cockpit. I put in a couple of tacks, singlehanded, to get the drill right, then we all settled back and I latched in the self-steering. The silence and the moon and the breeze and the flat water were glorious. So was the boat.

Finbar glanced at the big windvane, steering us steadily toward Crosshaven, something about which he had had his doubts. "Bloody thing works, don't it?" We all laughed with him, then his face took on an expression I had never seen on it before. He looked up and down the mast, at the sails and over the side at the yacht's clean way through the water. "We did it right, didn't we?"

At the mouth of the Owenboy River, just down from Crosshaven, we hove to, and Finbar, Harry and, last, Connie climbed into the workboat. I held her hand as she stepped down, and when she was in the boat I didn't let go. I mustered every ounce of feeling I had in me and said, "Come with me."

She gripped my hand tightly and looked up at me. "I can't," she said. There were tears streaming down her face.

Finbar started the boat's engine. "Can't or won't?" I shouted over its rumble.

She pulled her hand free, sat down in the boat, and looked up at me, saying nothing. The boat began to move away from me toward Crosshaven and the Royal Cork, Finbar and Harry waving and shouting luck.

I watched, frozen in place, until its stern light mingled with the village lights of Crosshaven, then I wore the big yacht around onto the starboard tack and, catching the freshening southwesterly, sailed for Roche's Point, the Atlantic Ocean, and England.

Forty-seven

MAEVE MOVED HER CART BRISKLY THROUGH THE SUPER-market, choosing items quickly and without much thought. Neither of them was picky about food, which was just as well, since she couldn't have done much in the way of cooking in the caravan where they were living. It had turned out to be ideal; they moved the good-sized trailer every two or three days from one caravan park to another, mingling with the horde of holidaymakers that streamed into the West Country at this time of year. In these parks, and in their year-old Ford Cortina, they were indistinguishable from a hundred other middle-class tourists, down to Devon and Cornwall for a bit of July sun. The caravan made an ideal cache for weapons and explosives, too, in the compartments under the floor that Denny, with his boatbuilding skills, had built. He had also rigged the trailer so that they could blow it at a moment's notice, should it become necessary.

Maeve stopped short in the laundry detergent section, riveted by something she had heard from the other side. "Oh, Mark would love that!" a woman's voice had exclaimed. On that and little more than instinct, Maeve wheeled the cart quickly around and into canned fruits and vegetables. Two women, one short, slender, with dark hair, the other a tall, sun-bleached blonde, were pushing two heavily laden carts toward the checkout counter. Maeve forgot her own half-completed shopping and followed them. She had never seen Annie Robinson before, but she had a hunch.

They rattled on about this and that as their groceries were checked through. Maeve tried to sneak a look at the tall woman's checkbook, but could not read the imprinted name, just the bank, Coutts & Company, London. Maeve watched impatiently as they wheeled out their two carts and loaded the contents into the rear of a Vauxhall estate wagon, while her own purchases were being totaled. She managed to get to her own car before they pulled out of the shopping center car park, then followed while they made two other quick stops, at a launderette and a dry cleaner's, where they picked up clothes, then continued behind them as they drove through Plymouth. Soon, past a block's length of chain link fence, they turned into a gate and were waved through by an armed Royal Marine. Maeve made a U-turn, stopped outside the gate and rolled down her window.

"Excuse me, Corporal," she called out to the guard,

smiling and taking care to sound as English as possible. "Was that Mrs. Pemberton-Robinson in the estate car just now? I thought I recognized her."

The guard leaned out of his box. "The blond lady? I believe so. I know the other lady was Mrs. Fortescue, Major Fortescue's wife. He commands the marine detachment here."

Maeve beamed at him. "Oh, thank you so much. I must give her a call." She waved to him and drove away, looking for a call box. She dialed the number and there was an electronic beep at the other end. "This is Sister Concepta," she said, glancing at her watch. "I have a question about my Inland Revenue forms. It's now two p.m. Please ring me on line three in half an hour, or on line one an hour after that. Thank you." She hung up and drove back to the shopping center, parking near a call box in the car park. If it didn't ring at 2:30, she'd drive to Plymouth Station and wait at another call box at 3:30.

At 2:28 she went to the box. A couple of minutes later the phone rang.

"Hello."

"May I speak to Sister Concepta, please?"

"Who may I say is calling?"

"This is the curate."

"Is your phone secure?"

"Of course," he snorted. "Now what's up, girl?"

"I want permission to perform an excommunication."

"Who?"

"Ex–Royal Marine captain. Mark Pemberton-Robinson. Ex-Belfast. The monsignor will know of him."

"What about the Poole matter? How's that coming?"

"It's coming. We want to do this first."

"I'll check. Be on line one at six o'clock. Maybe I can get through this afternoon."

"If the monsignor's cool on this, tell him to check with the bishop. I won't take no on this unless the bishop says not."

"Don't push your luck, girl."

"Line one at six." She hung up.

There was no call at six. She rang and set up another call for the following morning at ten. Denny was excited when she told him. "I say we do him no matter what the bishop says," he enthused.

"Let's wait and see," she answered. "We still need them; best to keep them happy, if possible."

At 10:00 the next morning the phone rang.

"The excommunication is approved, but only after Poole is completed."

She swore under her breath. She could be patient, though, and there was still research to do. She'd do them back to back. Poole on Friday morning, she thought, and Robinson as soon as possible thereafter. "Understood," she said into the phone.

She got into the car, drove back to the naval base, and parked along the chain link fence, where she could see the vehicles entering and leaving. It was nearly noon before the Vauxhall wagon drove out and headed toward the shopping center again. She started the car and pulled into the traffic, following several cars back, as she had been trained. The two women again. More shopping? Jesus, they ate a lot, these British.

Forty-eight

A S I SAILED THE BIG YACHT OUT OF CORK HARBOUR, AN appalling thought struck me. I had to think back over a few years on boats to confirm it, but soon I was sure. This was the first time in my life I had ever sailed singlehanded. The thought was very nearly paralyzing. I stood at the helm and steered the boat for nearly an hour thinking about this. I hadn't even set a course, I just sailed, going roughly southeast. It gave me something to do, didn't require any decisions.

Finally, the need to navigate moved me. I set the self-steering, waited a couple of minutes to make sure it still worked, then went below and occupied myself with chart and logbook, setting down my departure time and log reading and plotting a course for Wolf Rock, which lies between Land's End, the southwestern tip of England, and the Scilly Isles, which lie about thirty miles off Land's End. This gave me a nice gap to aim at. That done, I started to restow gear that had begun to fall about with the heeling of the boat, making frequent trips to the hatch for a look about. The last thing I needed was a collision at sea.

When everything seemed in order below, I went and played with the sails a bit to get the maximum out of her, then settled down in the cockpit. The boat tore along close reaching at about ten knots, dead on course, steering herself. I felt like a passenger. All sorts of things can go wrong at sea, but once in a while, everything goes right, and this seemed to be one of those times. Gradually, my nervousness gave way to a kind of confidence, although I didn't know how long that would last if something went wrong. What I was enjoying here was the fruit of years of thinking and planning by Mark, a fine boatbuilding job by Finbar and his yard, unlimited supplies of money from Derek Thrasher, and finally, and very satisfying it was, weeks of rather good work by none other than myself. For the first time in my life, I was able to look at something important and think, If not for me, this wouldn't be happening. I was, at last, important to something besides myself.

There was another thing still picking at me inside, though; it was Connie, or rather, her absence. I had so anticipated her being with me on this trip that I was having difficulty adjusting. She had been with me every day for weeks, and I constantly caught myself about to speak to her, only to remember that she wasn't there. Look at the moon, I wanted to say, or, There's Orion coming up now. She left a big hole.

I stayed awake in the cockpit all night, going below only to make coffee and a snack. At dawn we were still tearing along on course, and there were no ships in sight, so I went below and got some sleep. In the early afternoon I tried out the radio direction finding equipment and got a pretty good position fix. I was coming up fast on Land's End, now, and there is a marine radio station there. Time to try still more equipment. I got on the VHF radio and, through Land's End Radio, placed a call to Mark in Plymouth.

"Where are you?"

"About twenty-five miles off Land's End."

"Good news. Somebody named Nicky called. Derek's legal problem with the boat is solved. She's no longer a fugitive."

"Well, that's a relief."

"How's she sailing?"

"Going like a train. My average is nearly ten knots from Roche's Point."

"Fantastic. Let's see, that should put you in Plymouth, if the wind holds, about . . . daybreak, I should say."

"I guess so, if the wind holds. What do I do when I get there?"

"Look on your chart of the harbor . . . inside the breakwater, go on up the river, past the Mayflower Marina on your right; you'll see Spedding's boatyard on your left a bit further up. Giant letters on one of the sheds; can't miss it."

"Listen, Mark, I'm kind of nervous about docking this great huge thing."

"Don't worry, we'll be on hand to take your lines. Once you're inside the breakwater, just stop and take everything down and get your lines ready. That's the whole thing about sailing singlehanded—do everything in advance. Then just motor on up. I'll be the guy on the quay waving a crutch."

"How's that going, anyway?"

"Nothing to worry about. I'm managing."

"How's Annie?"

"Fantastic. She and Roz Fortescue are doing the provisioning. Roz and her husband Andrew are old friends. He's commander of the Royal Marines in Plymouth, and she and Annie were at school together. They've been great about lending their car and helping out in general. We've got a ton of food here already. Annie and Roz are buying not only for the trip out, but all the staples for the trip back, too. Lots of cheap, fresh food in the Azores, but the other stuff is a lot cheaper here. What's the boat going to need when you get here? I want to be ready."

"Well, I think she ought to be hauled. She's taking water somewhere I haven't been able to locate, and we ought to look at that if for no other reason than to make sure it's something that won't get any worse. Her bottom's bound to be foul, too, and you'll want that clean for the race. If there's somebody from Brookes & Gatehouse in Plymouth maybe he ought to have a look at the way I've connected things. The instruments all seem to be working, but I'd feel better if a pro had a look. Are you going to have the compass swung?"

"I'll do that myself, with your help. Have you noticed any inaccuracy?"

"I'll let you know after I've made my landfall. Listen, we'd better sign off. Anything else?"

"Nope. Call the boatyard on Channel Sixteen from the breakwater. I'll get customs arranged for you."

"Great. Over and out." I hung the microphone back in its bracket. Customs. Jesus, I hadn't thought about that. And I had three extremely illegal weapons aboard. I'd have to think of something.

Land's End turned up when and where it was supposed to, so there didn't seem to be anything wrong with either the compass or the RDF equipment. At dusk, I was looking back at Wolf Rock light when it came on. We were off the wind now and going slower. I resisted a not-very-great urge to set a spinnaker. I'd wait for Mark on that one. The wind dropped as the night wore on and by dawn we were still twenty miles short of Plymouth and sailing slowly.

I had to do something about the weapons. My first impulse was simply to toss them overboard, but that would make Mark mad as hell, and anyway, I was sure he'd only replace them. Besides, I had gotten used to the idea of having them around, and, in the circumstances to which we had become accustomed, they didn't seem a bad idea. Still, I didn't want customs to find them, and I sure as hell wasn't going to declare them. After a lot of thought I remembered something. I dug into a locker and found a three-foot-long, heavy-duty plastic bag with a zipper closure. Some parts for the self-steering had come in it, and it had looked too useful to throw away. The .45 automatic, the Ingram machine pistol and its clips, and the short-barreled riot shotgun all just squeezed in. I zipped it shut, reinforced the closure with plastic tape and dropped it into the bilges. Nice fit. The lot lay on top of the automatic bilge pump, nearly four feet down in the keel sump. I switched the pump off. It was nine o'clock in the morning before we were at the breakwater. I checked the bilges; nearly full. For good measure I poured in some engine oil, too. It would be a bitch to clean out, but it left a nice, opaque film on top of the bilge water. I called the yard on the VHF, and Mark came on immediately. When I motored up the river half an hour later I could see him standing on the quay, waving, as he had promised, a crutch.

Annie was first on the boat, giving me a big hug and a wet kiss. Then Mark stumped aboard, his leg in a steel brace, the aluminum crutch helping him with his balance. Andrew and Roz Fortescue were pleasant, humorous salt-of-the-earth people. Mark had H. M. Customs standing by and they brought their launch alongside and tied up to the yacht. I began to sweat. Mark looked at me curiously but said nothing. They went through the whole yacht, but not very thoroughly. At one point, one of them lifted a floorboard and looked into the oily bilges.

"Taking some water, eh?" he asked.

I nodded. "We're going to haul her and have that looked at. Probably the stern tube."

He agreed. "That's what it usually is." Once they were assured we weren't permanently importing the yacht and had no declarable goods aboard, they gave us our clearance and left. I breathed a heavy sigh of relief.

"Okay," Mark grinned. "Where did you hide them?" I told him, and he laughed aloud.

While everybody else had a cup of coffee, Mark and I went over the boat thoroughly. Finally, we joined the others. "I told you you could do it," he said to me. "And you did it as well as anybody could've and better than most. Now, let's go over what we have to do."

We talked for an hour, making lists of work against time available. The boat would be hauled, her bottom cleaned, leaks sealed, electronics inspected, and everything possible, in the time available, put right. This was Tuesday. She'd have three days ashore, then, on Friday morning, she'd be put back into the water, her compasses swung, then she'd be turned over to Annie and Roz for provisioning. Andrew Fortescue had laid on a navy lorry to bring everything over from Plymouth.

Mark pointed at a little ferry plying the river. "That's the quickest way to town," he said. "In order to drive over here, you have to cross the Tamar Bridge and go down a maze of country lanes. The ferry takes five minutes."

I looked around us. For the first time in what seemed forever, we had everything we needed at our disposal: a good yard, skilled help, and willing hands from the Fortescues and Plymouth's Royal Marines. Our four days of preparation time, short as it was, seemed an absolute luxury. I plugged Antonio Carlos Jobim into the tape player and poured myself another cup of coffee. His song "Wave" washed over us.

"Oh, that's lovely," Annie said, putting her feet on the saloon table and stretching. "So long since I've heard it." Then her face took on a look of discovery. "That's it," she said. "That's her name!"

"Whose name?" Mark asked, looking up from his lists.

"The boat's name, dummy. Don't you think it's time she had one?"

And so, three days later, Annie stood on a scaffolding, a bottle of champagne clutched in her hands, tied with a red ribbon and held at the ready. "I christen thee *Wave*!" she sang over the heads of assembled friends and yard workers. "May God bless her and all who sail in her!" She swung the bottle, froth sprayed everyone, and the big yacht slid back into the water, at last properly finished, properly launched, and properly named.

Wave. I liked it.

Forty-nine

MAEVE FOLLOWED THE WOMEN TWICE MORE, AND their pattern was the same. Each afternoon they ran small, domestic errands, then went to the supermarket. The quantities of food puzzled Maeve, until she picked up a *Times* and read a report of the race to the Azores, starting at noon on Saturday. Late in each day Annie Robinson and her friend drove down to the banks of the Tamar and took the little foot ferry across to Cremyl, the tiny settlement on the other bank. At dusk, they would return on the ferry with Mark Robinson in tow, him wearing a leg brace and using a crutch. On Thursday afternoon she followed the two women aboard the ferry.

Although she and Annie Robinson had never met face to face, being only a few feet away from her made Maeve a bit nervous. She shook off this irrationality, though, and forced herself to relax. After the five-minute crossing the two women walked briskly toward the boatyard, Spedding's. Maeve bought some crisps and a soft drink at a nearby shop, then followed.

So they had got their bloody boat built, after all. She looked at it, perched on its cradle in the yard, a workman lettering something on the hull near the bows. She couldn't make out the name. She walked closer, then sat on a rock, drank her Coke, and looked about. She could see Mark Robinson, his wife and the Fortescue woman, sitting high in the cockpit of the boat, talking. She grew angry at the sight of him. She would have dearly loved to blow the boat with them all on it, but there were problems. She had checked out this place, Cremyl, on a road map, and getting in here in a car, not to mention out, would be bloody awful. To get back to Plymouth, only a few hundred yards away, one would have to drive miles of country roads on a route that would be all too easy to block. That left only the ferry as a means of escape if something went wrong. She and Denny would be bottled up here; it would have to be somewhere else, and finally, after weighing all the alternatives, she knew where it would be. Denny would love it; it would be just his sort of thing. But they had to do Poole first to keep the bishop and the monsignor happy.

Maeve rose and tossed her Coke can into a wastebasket, dusted off her jeans, turned, and ran head on, forcefully, into Will Lee. She was shocked speechless; she had had no idea he was in Plymouth.

"I'm very sorry," he said, laughing, putting his hand

on her elbow. "I didn't know you were going to turn this way. Are you all right?"

"Yes . . . yes, I'm quite all right, thank you. My fault, really." She fought the urge to bolt, to kick him in the kneecap and run. At least she had the presence of mind to keep her accent English. She told herself that he had never set eyes on her out of a habit, that he couldn't possibly recognize her.

He smiled engagingly at her. He seemed taller, leaner than she remembered. It was easy to see why Connie had been so attracted to him. "I've seen you around here, haven't I?" he asked, frightening her. "Do you live here?"

"Ah, no . . . that is, my parents live in Plymouth; I'm just down for a visit." My God, she thought, he's coming on to me. I've got to get out of here.

"I'm working on a boat for the race down here. Would you like to come and have a look at her?"

"Well, I . . ." She looked over his shoulder; the ferry was about to depart. "Oh, thank you, but I really must catch the ferry. Perhaps another time. Do excuse me." She stepped past him and ran down the path.

"Hey, what's your name?" he called after her.

She kept running, making the ferry in the nick of time. Once aboard and under way she looked back. He was waving to her. She forced a smile and waved back. God, that had been close, but he hadn't known her, she was sure of it. She wiped sweat from her brow. She was wet under the arms and in the crotch, too.

*   *   *

That night she told Denny the idea, and he laughed aloud. While she checked street maps of Poole and Plymouth for escape routes, he made the two bombs. The Poole one was bigger; it would need to be. The one for Plymouth had only to do the car.

Early Friday morning they drove to Poole in the Cortina and parked in a shopping center car park on the outskirts of the city. They took a bus into town, and after walking about for only a few minutes, quickly stole a newish Rover, Denny hotwiring the ignition, while Maeve kept a lookout. Denny quickly picked the boot lock, tossed in the large canvas sailing duffel and found a hole to run his wires through, forward into the passenger compartment. As Maeve drove away, Denny sat in the back and attached the wires to a battery and a kitchen timer, tucking them out of sight under the passenger seat. A block from the Royal Marine base she stopped the car, and he got out.

"Just reach down, turn the timer all the way, then leave it."

"Right," she said. "I'll meet you at the car as soon as I can." He walked off toward a bus stop, while she applied bright red lipstick, tied a scarf about her head, put on dark glasses and opened the top two buttons of her blouse. She drove to the base and stopped at the front gate.

"Good morning, Sergeant," she said to the guard, who was a corporal, in her broadest, upper-class drawl. "I wonder if you could direct me to the office of the public information officer? I want to see about using the tennis courts for a charity tournament."

"That would be in the main administration building, ma'am," he said, leaning down to the car and never taking his eyes from her cleavage. "May I have your name, please?"

"Mrs. Wells-Simpson," she replied and waited while he scrawled it on a clipboard, still looking down her blouse.

"Thank you, ma'am," he said, saluting her smartly. "Pass through."

She drove to the administration building, which also housed the office of the base commander, and glanced at her watch. She had a bus schedule to keep, and she wanted to time it right. She parked in a guest space, reached down and turned the kitchen timer all the way clockwise, and got out of the car, locking it behind her. She walked rapidly down the road for two hundred yards to the bus stop. Ten of her sixty minutes passed before the bus came. She got off at the first stop outside the base, walked three blocks, and took another bus. Forty minutes after setting the timer, she was at the car, where Denny was waiting. By the time the bomb went off they were well on their way to Plymouth.

They drove back to the caravan park and spent the afternoon listening to news of the explosion on the BBC, and making the trailer ready to move. Late in the afternoon Denny got into some dirty coveralls with the name of a garage on the back and put a five-gallon gasoline can and his tool kit into the trunk of the car, then they checked out of the caravan park and drove into Plymouth.

They parked several blocks from the ferry and walked there by separate routes. Maeve arrived first and saw the Fortescue Vauxhall wagon already in the car park. She stood on the street, frequently glancing at her watch as if she were waiting for someone. Denny approached from the opposite direction, carrying the petrol can and toolbox. Maeve had another quick look about, then nodded at the Vauxhall. While she kept watch, he unscrewed the tank cap and emptied the gasoline into the car. That done, he opened the boot and set his toolbox in the rear, then lifted the floor panel which covered the spare wheel. After a quick glance at her he worked for, perhaps, two minutes, then closed the back of the car, taking his tool kit but leaving the petrol can inside. He wiped the door handle carefully with an oily rag, then left, walking quickly up the street.

Good, Maeve thought. Anybody passing would think he had simply been called from a garage to put petrol into an empty tank. When she was sure that no one had followed him, she walked away in the opposite direction. They met at the car, stowed the tool kit, dumped the coveralls into a waste bin, and drove away, out of Plymouth toward the Tamar bridge and Cornwall, a holiday couple down from London with their caravan.

"Is it all right?" she asked. "You didn't do the ignition."

"Didn't have to," he chuckled. "I did a pendulum switch instead. The pendulum hangs vertically between two contacts. The car is parked on a bit of an angle. They'll get in, and as soon as they drive onto level ground, the pendulum will swing and make contact." He grinned broadly. "Big bang, petrol tank and all. They'll barbecue."

"Good," she said. She didn't think Will Lee would come to the car with them; he never had; must be sleeping on the boat. It would annoy the bishop if an American politician's son got blown away. Fortescue's wife was a bonus—wife of the commander of the Plymouth Royal Marine detachment. She smiled to herself; couldn't be bad. It was getting dark, now. They'd be back on the ferry soon, and she and Denny could stop thinking about Mark Robinson and get on with it.

Fifty

THE FIVE OF US, MARK AND ANNIE, ANDREW AND ROZ Fortescue, and I sat in *Wave*'s cockpit with drinks and relished the early evening. The big yacht was now as Mark had dreamed of her—complete and provisioned for her first blue-water passage. Every detail of the boat was in perfect order, though that condition does not last long on any yacht. Every instrument worked, and the leak in the stern tube had been put right. We had been talking about the car bomb at the Poole Royal Marine installation that morning, in which a number of marines and civilian workers had been killed and most of the main administration building destroyed. Mark and Andrew had both lost acquaintances in that attack and Andrew would be attending funeral services on Monday. The Irish Freedom Brigade, which I well remembered from the Berkeley Square explosion, had telephoned a newspaper and claimed responsibility.

Mark set his braced leg on the opposite cockpit seat and changed the subject. "You know, there's something about this time that I really like, when everything has been done that can be done, when a yacht is ready for anything, and when there's nothing to do but have a drink and enjoy the anticipation." He laughed. "In fact, this is almost the only time it's ever happened; usually before a race there's nothing but chaos, and things are still being screwed down and bolted on while you're jockeying for position on the starting line." He raised his glass. "I give you a toast to those who made it possible—us!"

We drank to that. God knew the Fortescues deserved inclusion. Roz's help with provisioning and Andrew's contribution of Royal Marine manpower had made the four days slip by smoothly and without panic. I glanced across the river and saw the ferry depart the opposite shore.

"Last ferry in five minutes," Roz said. "Willie, why don't you come back to the base and have a hot bath and a last night ashore? We'll all go down to the Barbican and have a good dinner. We might even find you a girl."

"Sounds good to me," I said. I had been living on this boat and on *Toscana* for weeks, now. It would be nice to sleep in a bed again, and the only girl I had even spoken to in Plymouth had been the one I'd nearly knocked down near the boatyard. Something about her had been terribly familiar, but I had been unable to think of what it was. Probably I had just seen her somewhere in Plymouth.

"We'd better get a move on," Annie said and began collecting glasses and tidying the cockpit. We checked the boat's lines to see that they would allow for the rise and fall of the tide, then stepped ashore. Watching Mark make the maneuver, I was amazed at how agile he was with the crutch and brace. It was as if he'd been using them since childhood. We walked slowly toward the ferry dock, chatting among ourselves. The Fortescues' car waited on the other side for us.

We bought our tickets, went aboard, and sat down. Then Mark stood up again. "I don't want to leave her," he said.

"What?" Roz puzzled.

"We've had so many problems along the way, I just don't want to leave her alone tonight. I don't want anything else to go wrong."

"Neither do I," I said and stood up, too.

"Annie," Mark said, "why don't you go on back with Andrew and Roz? Willie and I will sleep aboard tonight and see you in the morning."

"All right," Annie replied, "if you're really worried about the boat."

"I know there's no real reason to worry," Mark said. "But I would."

"I've got a better idea," Annie came back. "Why don't we all stay aboard tonight? Roz and I can cook—we've certainly enough food aboard—and God knows there's plenty of room, too."

Andrew and Roz looked at each other. "Okay?" Andrew asked her.

"Okay," Roz replied.

We left the ferry as the helmsman revved his engine for the departure. I felt immediately better, just as Mark obviously did. We hadn't come all this way to have something happen to the boat at the last minute, just because we weren't around. Later, I would wonder if maybe we hadn't felt something else besides concern for the boat.

Annie and Roz whipped up a spaghetti dinner; that and much wine were consumed with gusto. We got to bed early, Mark and Annie aft in the owner's cabin; Andrew and Roz forward in the larger of the two guest cabins, and I in the smaller one. We fell asleep to the sound of the river lapping against *Wave*'s hull.

We were up early and had a hot breakfast. Remembering my seasickness after Cowes aboard *Toscana*, I took it easy.

Mark looked at me across the saloon table. "Nervous?" he asked.

I nodded. "Lots of butterflies."

"Me, too. It's always this way; a combination of fear and excitement, I guess."

"Fear? You? But you've done a lot of this sort of thing."

"Sure, but the fear is always there. Will I ram somebody at the starting line? Will I be run down by a merchant ship? Will I come back from this one? Once you're out there it goes away—at least, most of it does. But fear's a good thing. Sharpens the senses, makes you more aware."

If that were the case I would be very sharp this morning. Andrew and Roz prepared to leave.

"Why don't you come out with us?" Mark asked them. "We'll have a couple of hours of thrashing about, getting used to her before the gun. You can grab a ride back with one of the spectator boats."

"Fantastic," Andrew said. "We'd love to have a sail."

And so we all remained aboard for a while longer. At half past nine we cast off from the quay at Spedding's boatyard and stowed our fenders and mooring warps. We wouldn't be needing them for another ten days or so. We motored down the river and, out in the harbor, just in front of the Royal Western Yacht Club, the sponsoring organization, we set sail, to waves and cheers from the crowd on the terrace. For an hour and a half, we sailed about the harbor, while Mark got the feel of his new boat. He planted himself in the cockpit, the braced leg jammed into a corner, and tacked the boat again and again, without help from us, then practiced reefing the roller headsails.

"She's a dream." He grinned. "I'll get some practice reefing the main a bit later."

"No rush," I said. "There'll be three of us aboard, remember?" I knew he wouldn't be happy until he felt he could do everything aboard.

At quarter to noon, the fifteen-minute gun went off on the Royal Navy ship that served as committee boat. "All ashore that's going ashore," Andrew called below to Roz. He whistled and waved at one of the Royal Marine runabouts that had been keeping the spectator fleet away from the starting line. They came alongside. "Will you take us off, Sergeant? We'll need a lift to the Cremyl ferryport on the Plymouth side after the start."

"Right, sir!" the man called back and held his big rubber assault boat steady against the rail while Andrew and Roz climbed aboard.

"Good luck!" they both cried as the runabout moved away. "See you in a few weeks!"

We waved them off and turned to our work. The twenty-odd entrants in the race, of which *Wave* was the biggest, reached up and down the starting line, trying for position, while a hundred or more spectator craft ran about, jockeying for a better view. The ten-minute gun went, then the five-minute. With Mark braced at the helm, me grinding the self-tailing winches and Annie keeping time with a stopwatch, we positioned ourselves at the starboard end of the line.

"Thirty seconds!" Annie called out.

We put in our final tack and started for the line, which was very close, now.

"Fifteen seconds!"

We picked up speed.

"Five, four, three, two, one . . ." The starting cannon aboard the nearby ship went, loud in our ears. Perhaps half a second later *Wave*'s bows sliced across the starting line.

"Beautiful!" I screamed.

"Bloody good luck!" Mark screamed back.

Since we had never practiced, it must have been, but that didn't make it feel any less good. We tore out into the English Channel, neck and neck with a large trimaran. The big multihulls, four or five of them in the race, were going to be our competition. In the right conditions, they could beat us. A mile or so out, Andrew and Roz appeared briefly in the Royal Marine boat, waved, then turned back for Plymouth.

Mark kept us on the starboard tack, making for the Eddystone Light, some ten miles offshore, which was the first mark of the race. The next mark was the finish line, off Horta, on the island of Faial, in the Azores, some twelve hundred miles down the North Atlantic Ocean. We made the Eddystone in a bit more than an hour, having averaged nearly nine knots in the fresh breeze. As we tacked around the tall lighthouse, a faint boom hit our ears.

"I hope the Royal Navy's not having gunnery practice out here today," Mark laughed, looking around for the source of the noise. Then he pointed in the direction of Plymouth. A column of black smoke was rising from the town.

"Jesus," I said. "What's that?"

"Looks like it could be one of those oil tanks down by the river."

Then one of my jib sheets came adrift, leaving the sail flapping, and we forgot about everything else while we retrimmed for the next long tack down the English Channel.

Fifty-one

WE WERE NOT OUT OF THE ENGLISH CHANNEL YET when I discovered that Mark and I had entirely different views of what we were doing. I had been looking forward to a cruise to the Azores; Mark had been looking forward to a race.

We were hard on the wind down the Channel, and Mark liked it that way. "This is what we need if we're going to beat the multihulls," he said, grinning. "They don't like sailing close to the wind in a chop. First of all, they aren't all that close-winded, and second, while we go through the waves, they go over them, up and down, up and down. I promise you, there are blokes on trimarans all around us puking their guts out right now."

I had avoided that fate by eating and drinking carefully the evening before and at breakfast, but there was no getting away from Mark's racing frame of mind. All the way down the Channel, we were tuning everything, making minute adjustments in sail trim, increasing or decreasing tension in the rigging to make sure the mast was standing up absolutely straight on both tacks, watching wind and waterspeed instruments to be sure she was sailing equally fast on either tack. Mark wanted a position fix every hour, so we were constantly taking bearings on landmarks when close to shore, and on the RDF equipment when we weren't. Annie kept us in food and drink and spelled us at the helm when we were both working. Mark wouldn't allow the use of the self-steering.

"We've got to make every tenth of a knot we can while conditions favor us," he said. "If the wind frees, the bigger multihulls will be past us like a shot. The self-steering steers a nice, average course, but it won't take us as consistently close to the wind as a good helmsman."

By the following evening, we were off the continental shelf, out of the green water near land and into water that was a blue I had never seen, a color that comes to the sea only when the bottom drops away to a depth that might as well be bottomless, and the water reflects a blue sky. With our escape from the heavily trafficked shipping lanes of the Channel, the need for a constant lookout decreased, and we were finally able to begin to catch up on the sleep we had lost nearer land. I was becoming a better helmsman out of sheer practice, but I was also discovering that the self-steering gear had a big advantage—it never got tired. We settled into a routine of using it on night watches and steering for long periods during the day. Even then, we would occasionally latch it in so that we could all sit down and enjoy a meal together.

I don't think I had ever eaten better. Annie had splurged on the best of everything, the tenderest cuts of meat, the most expensive cheeses, and first-rate wines. We wanted for nothing.

The headwinds held, too. The prevailing wind for that part of the ocean was southwesterly, and we were sailing southwest. Mark exulted in it; Annie and I grew tired of living at fifteen degrees of heel. I wondered how she managed to keep up her standard of cooking while leaning against a safety strap on one tack, or pushing herself off the cooker on the other.

We had at least some sun on most days, but the occasional squall called for shortening sail. I practiced taking sun sights with the sextant, and Mark taught me the drill for reducing a sight to a position line, using the nautical almanac and the marine sight reduction tables.

Mark was having difficulty standing steadily on deck in order to reef the mainsail, something he would have to do alone on his singlehanded passage back. Finally, three or four days out, he asked Annie to toss a package to him from the chart table, then he sat down, struggled out of his baggy shorts, and started to unbuckle the waist strap that held the leg brace in place.

Annie was horrified. "Mark, you know you can't do that," she cried. "It's too early to go putting all your weight on the knee."

"Look, Mark, I know it's tough, but it'll get better. You've still got a couple of weeks before starting back."

Mark held up a hand to quiet us and began unwrapping the package. "I got a fellow in the brace shop to make this up for me. Designed it myself." He pulled out an odd-looking thing made of leather and steel and padding.

"And did the doctor approve your design?" Annie asked.

"I forgot to show it to him," Mark said, buckling the thing on. He tried standing, played with the straps and buckles for a minute or two, then stood and put his weight on the weak leg. "Not bad," he grinned. "Not bad at all. Maybe I should have shown it to the doctor; he might have liked it."

He showed us how it worked. Instead of running the length of the leg, like the brace, it ran from the lower thigh to the upper calf, with a hinge at the knee. He could lock it in a straight position, or at a ninety-degree angle for kneeling, or at two stops in between. He showed us how quickly he could change the angles. The front side was thickly padded with foam rubber and covered in leather, so that kneeling on deck wouldn't damage the knee. I was impressed. I looked at Annie; so was she.

"So? What do you think?" Mark asked.

"Well, maybe if you're really careful," Annie said, hesitantly.

"Looks good to me, Mark, but for God's sake, move slowly, will you?"

"What you're both forgetting," he said, "is that I am the last person who wants to injure this knee again."

After that, nothing more was said about it. Mark got about the decks much faster and, it seemed to me, more safely. Annie and I relaxed.

Annie came on at four in the morning to relieve me; I got her a cushion, and sat her down next to me; I wasn't ready to turn in yet. We were less than a day from our landfall, the weather had warmed a lot, and the sky was cloudless and moonless. I had never seen so many stars. She took my hand and held it in both of hers.

"How are you, Willie?"

"Very well, thank you." I was, too. I was tanned and healthy and relaxed, and, most of all, I had begun to put some emotional distance between myself and Connie. That hadn't come easily. "How about yourself?" I asked.

She lay her head against my bare shoulder. "Oh, so much better, so much better. I think if I'd had to spend another day in Plymouth I'd have gone mad. I don't care if I never see another doctor or hospital or whirlpool bath or brace again."

"I guess your days have been full of nothing else the last couple of months." She was still working with Mark twice a day, exercising the leg.

"I'd never have made a nurse," she sighed. "I'm having a hard enough time with wife."

I didn't know quite what to say to that.

"When we're back, and the boat's laid up for the winter, and Mark's leg is as good as I can help him get it, I'm going to have to get away. I need some time for myself." She looked up at me. "I'm a selfish person, did you know that?"

"No," I said, honestly. "I didn't know that."

"It's true. More than most people, I mean. When I have to be unselfish for a long time I get resentful and petty. You've seen it happen."

I remembered what she was like just before the occasions when she had packed up and left for a week and ten days at a time. "I guess I just didn't know why it happened," I said. "I know that Mark got pretty demanding at times, and I'm sure I didn't help much."

"You helped more than you know. If I hadn't had you around to talk to I might not have made it through the Irish experience."

"I'm glad if I helped," I said, "even though I didn't know I was helping at the time."

"Next time I'll let you know when you're helping," she said and put her head on my shoulder again.

We sailed on into the dark and fabulous night.

Late in the afternoon of our ninth day at sea I came on deck. Mark was at the helm. He looked over my shoulder, and his expression changed. "Have a look at that," he said, grinning.

I turned and saw nothing at first. Then I saw a greenish-gray lump on the horizon. "Land?"

"The island of Graciosa, situated in the Azores archipelago, a group of islands lying eight hundred miles off the coast of Portugal."

"Annie!" I shouted below. "Land ho!"

Annie scrambled into the cockpit and looked out at our landfall. "And on the nose! Well done, Mark!"

"He's done pretty well, too," Mark said, nodding off to port.

I looked and saw what was unmistakably a sail. "Who is it?"

"The big yellow tri, *Three Cheers*, I expect. And we're being freed by the wind right now. So is she."

I took the helm, and Mark went through his tuning routine yet again, getting every ounce of speed from *Wave*. At nightfall the lighthouse on Graciosa began blinking its signal, and the navigating lights of the trimaran showed that she was overtaking us. Suddenly I found myself as heated as Mark about our race.

By morning, the tri was slightly ahead, but we were in the channel between Graciosa and St. Jorge, a neighboring island, and hard on the wind again. Additionally, there was a good-sized sea running in one direction, and a chop on top of that from another. The trimaran was being buffeted a lot, now, and *Wave* was in her element. We began to overtake *Three Cheers*.

We weren't overtaking her very fast, though. The island of Faial, our destination, was looming before us, now, high and green, and we were running out of time. We redoubled our efforts, concentrating madly on sailing the big yacht to windward. *Three Cheers* sailed across our bows, not much more than a boat length ahead of us. Mark took the helm, and I kept a wary eye on our competition. We put in our last tack.

Wave and *Three Cheers* were widely separated, now, she on the starboard tack, we on port, on different sides of the channel, sailing for the same point, an imaginary line between a red marker in the water and the mast of the committee boat, perhaps a mile ahead. We slipped through the chop, making nine, sometimes nine and a half knots, going for all we were worth. The big trimaran was bearing down fast, too. The trouble was, she was on the starboard tack, and we were on port. Under the racing rules, she had the right of way.

If we tacked onto starboard at the last minute, the time lost tacking would cost us the race. "I'm damned if I'm tacking!" Mark shouted. "If I lose this race it'll be on a protest! I'm crossing that line first!"

The two yachts plunged on toward the line and each other. I was transfixed, now, unable to take my eyes from the other boat, trying to judge who was ahead. Finally, I could take it no more. "Mark, I don't think we can make it past her. Come on, let's do a super-fast tack."

"Forget it!" he shouted. "I'm going for it!"

And go for it he did. *Wave* roared across the trimaran's bows with not ten feet to spare. We were over the line, finished. We had won by less than ten seconds after a race of more than 1200 miles. If I had ever doubted the necessity of getting everything out of a racing boat at every moment, I never doubted it again.

Fifty-two

WE PICKED UP A MOORING IN HORTA HARBOR AND, immediately, were under a happy siege of well-wishers, most talking rapidly in Portuguese, and all bearing gifts of wine, fruit, brandy and such. Customs hardly bothered, which suited me, because the illegal weapons were still in the bilges, which we kept half-full for the purpose of hiding them.

The commodore of the Club Nautico, a sort of yacht/fishing/swimming organization, made a welcoming speech on deck, and a Commander Foster, of the Royal Western Yacht Club and chairman of the race committee, was aboard, too, with a welcoming bottle of champagne. After an hour or so, the crowd drifted away, and Commander Foster asked if he might have a word with us below.

"I'm afraid I have some rather bad news, which I know will mar your victory, and I'm sorry it can't wait any longer."

We all sat down. I wondered what new bad news we could now have.

"An hour or so after the start of the race, Andrew and Roz Fortescue were killed in a car bomb explosion in Plymouth."

He was quiet for a moment, but none of us broke the silence. Blank disbelief was all he got from us.

"I'll give you what details I have," he said, "but I'm afraid there's not much. The Royal Marine installation at Poole received a car bomb on the day before the start of the race; perhaps you heard about that before leaving."

"Yes," Mark said.

"It's assumed that the same group came to Plymouth and did the job on Andrew's car. It's supposed that, because of Poole, the terrorists would meet difficulties with getting onto the base in Plymouth—quite true of course; security was immediately increased after word of Poole—and, since bombing the base was too difficult, they went after a symbol, the commander of the Royal Marine detachment. Andrew's car was parked overnight at the Cremyl ferry on the Plymouth side—did he and Roz stay aboard with you that night?"

"Yes," Mark said.

"My God," Annie broke in, "perhaps if we'd gone back to the base with them on Friday night it never would have happened."

"Perhaps," the commander replied, "but it's just as possible that the bomb could have been planted on Friday, and in that case you would have certainly been killed, as well. What's more, the car park was deserted at the time of the explosion; if you'd come off the ferry and gotten into the car, there would have been other passengers all about, and many more people would certainly have been killed. As it was, most of the shops on the street had their windows blown out, and there were twenty-odd people hurt with flying glass and debris."

"They were aboard *Wave* with us until the fifteen-minute gun," Annie said.

"Yes, and I understand they got a lift back to the ferryport with one of the marine crash boats. They happened to arrive at a time when the ferry was across the river; that was fortunate, I think."

We were all silent again.

"I'm afraid that's everything I know," the commander said. "The funeral was on Tuesday, just a week ago, so there's nothing much to be done. A detective in the Plymouth police has asked that you telephone him as soon as possible. Since you were the last to spend any time with them, he'd like to ask you some questions." He handed Mark a piece of paper. "Andrew's parents' number is there, too. I thought you might like to ring them."

"Yes, thank you, Commander," Mark replied.

"If you'll excuse me, I should stop off on *Three Cheers* on my way back to the club. I'm very sorry to have to bring you such bad news, but I thought you should know without delay."

Mark thanked him, and he left. It was another hour

before we could stir ourselves to move about and go ashore.

Annie and I sat at a table in Peter's Sport Café on the Horta waterfront. Mark was talking on the telephone there and, shortly, joined us.

"Nothing new from what the commander told us," he said. "Except that the same group that did Poole rang up and took credit."

Annie's eyes were red from weeping. "I still can't believe it," she said. "Mark, do you think this might have had anything to do with us?"

"No, I discussed that with the detective. I told him we'd had a brush with the bastards, but his attitude was, and I think he's right, if they'd wanted us they'd have gone after the boat, not Andrew's car. He thinks there's no doubt they wanted Andrew because he was C.O. in Plymouth, and Roz was just unlucky enough to be with him. I talked with Andrew's parents. They're crushed, of course, but seem to be bearing up."

We spent the remainder of the day ashore, getting our land legs and shopping for fresh food. We had a subdued dinner and were back on the boat and turned in by ten o'clock.

Mark planned a week in Horta before sailing back. He would sail directly to Cork, now that the legal problems were solved, and leave the boat with Finbar for the winter. He wrote to Finbar and gave him an ETA. Annie and I would stay on in Horta for a holiday, then fly back in time to meet him. Through the commodore of the club, we found a little flat for our stay and were able to hire a car.

There was a lot to do during that week, and we were all grateful to have our minds occupied. We had had alternator problems and spent a lot of time on that and other minor repairs to the yacht and her sails, working our way through Mark's inevitable lists. As other, slower competitors arrived, the social life picked up markedly. The Azoreans had planned a series of parties and were marvelous hosts. Our spirits improved as the week wore on.

At the end of our week, predictably on schedule, Mark sailed. We took the last load of fresh stores out to the boat, and I deflated and packed away the rubber dinghy. We had breakfast in the cockpit, enjoying the Azorean sunshine. "Well," Mark said, "I'm off."

"Nothing else I can do?" I asked.

"Not a thing. You've been great, Willie. Once in Cork we'll get her laid up and her gear stowed, then the job's over. You'll come for the start of the Transatlantic next June won't you?"

"Sure I will. Wouldn't miss it. Listen, are you feeling really in control with the leg, now?"

"Absolutely, old chum. Not to worry."

"Mark, can I extract a promise from you?" I asked.

"Depends. What did you have in mind?"

"Don't set a spinnaker on the way home. I've watched

you move around the foredeck, and I don't think the leg's ready for that. Oh, you'd get it up and down all right in light weather, but if you got a wrap or something it would be a real problem."

Mark looked at me, but said nothing.

"Come on, Mark, promise him," Annie chimed in. "He's never tried to tell you what to do on the boat; you owe him this much."

"Save it for next spring," I said. "The leg will be much stronger by then, and you'll still have time to practice. This is no race home; just cruise and enjoy yourself."

"All right," he said, finally. "No spinnakers on the way home. I'm cruising." He hesitated. "I promise."

We stood and shook hands. Mark and Annie embraced perfunctorily. I helped get the main up, then stood by to slip the mooring while Mark started the engine. The club tender took Annie and me off, and we chugged along beside *Wave* out past the breakwater for a last goodbye.

"And be careful reefing the main," I shouted across to him as he broke out the headsails and started to sail the boat. "Take your time."

"Yes, sir!" he shouted back, giving me a large, mock salute.

Then he was gone, *Wave* reaching across toward Pico, the next island, before rounding the headland and sailing off toward Ireland. Annie and I were left, waving, in the club boat. Finally, the coxswain turned back toward Horta, and we began our holiday.

Fifty-three

WHEN MARK HAD GONE, A CHANGE CAME OVER ANNIE that astonished and delighted me. I knew that she had been tightly wound for a long time, but I don't think I understood how tightly until I saw her unwind. We partied with the other competitors until they, too, began to sail away, hurrying back to jobs and families in England. In a few days we were alone, and then a transformation that had already begun to take place was completed.

Always affectionate with me, sometimes to my consternation and guilt, Annie now became loving. It was evident to me in every moment we spent together, and we were never apart. We became a couple, a state of being I had never really experienced. We ate, drank and walked together, drinking in the lushness of our surroundings, enjoying the green beauty of the island and the charm and friendliness of the people of Horta. We sat in the little park in the town square and watched the black swans glide to and fro in the ponds; we took the ferry to Pico and climbed the 7,000-foot volcano, marveling at the view; we drove to the west side of the island, to the area called Costa Brava, climbed down the high cliffs, and swam in the sea, naked and alone. And then, on a hot and sunny afternoon, we found our way to the crater at the top of Faial.

As the little car chugged up the steep roads, clouds enveloped us, and I had to turn on the windshield wipers to deal with the clinging moisture. At the top of the road we parked and came to the tunnel that had been dug through the side of the old, extinct volcano; we ran through it, laughingly dodging the water dripping from the stone ceiling. We emerged into the large crater, now partly filled, with tropical plant life growing at its bottom. Annie began to climb; I followed, and as we neared the top sunlight began to dapple the grassy slope. We found an indentation in the green crater wall, like a huge palm cupped to receive us. The coolness of the clouds gone, Annie quickly stripped off her clothes and lay on her back in the sun, making little noises as the cool grass touched her body. In a moment, I was lying beside her, making my own noises as I got used to the wetness.

Annie turned and put her head on my shoulder; I felt her breasts against me. "Oh, Willie," she said, "I can't remember a time when I felt so absolutely carefree. You've made me so happy this week."

I couldn't say anything. She had seemed so perfectly,

naturally happy that it never occurred to me that I might have had anything to do with it. I put my arm around her and hugged. She turned until her leg was over mine, then reached up and turned my head toward hers. Annie had kissed me many times before, but never quite this way. It was sweet, tender and oddly consuming for so light a touch. Then her tongue found mine and, while still gentle, the kiss grew into an embrace that no part of us avoided. Soon, she pulled me on top of her. Our bodies effortlessly found each other. And for a single hour that afternoon, in that surpassingly beautiful place, with that perfect girl, I knew what it was to be one with another human being.

That night, back in the flat, we made love again, then lay, sweating, in each other's arms. In a few hours we had a plane to catch, and it seemed to me we had to sort some things out.

"Listen, Annie . . ."

"Mmmm?"

"The land outside Kinsale."

"Mmmm?"

"You remember, my Christmas present from my grandfather?"

"Oh, yes, I remember."

"There's a cottage, too. It's not really habitable, but I could get it together in a couple of months, if I hired some help."

"Sounds nice." She sounded very sleepy.

"I think it could be. I've still got some money in the bank in Cork, too. It's not a lot, but it's some sort of start for us."

She sat up, abruptly. "Willie . . . you're not . . . what are you saying, exactly?"

"Look, I know I don't have a career, exactly, but my grandfather's place is big, and . . . well, it's there, and I'm sure he'd be delighted if I wanted to join him."

"Willie . . ."

"There's our place in Georgia, too. I'm an only child, and someday that's going to be mine. It wouldn't be a bad—"

"Willie, stop."

I stopped.

"Willie, you know I love you dearly, and we've finally done something we've both wanted to do since that day in Cowes, but . . ."

"But what?" I thought I knew what was coming, and I didn't like it.

She turned and hugged her knees. "This has been marvelous for me, this time with you; I've loved it, I really have . . ."

I was right, she was going to tell me we couldn't go on this way. In fact, she told me a great deal more.

"If it hadn't been for you, and for Derek, of course . . ."

"Derek?" Now I sat up. "What do you mean?"

She looked at me. There was just enough light in the room for me to tell that she was surprised.

"But surely, you knew. That day in the car . . . you saw me."

I groped for her meaning for just a moment, and then it flashed before me: a car passing on the Carrigaline road, a chauffeur-driven car—a woman in the backseat who, when I looked a second time, wasn't there—and then the cow had stepped into the road, throwing me into a spin, and in my fear and excitement I had forgotten.

She read my face quickly. "You didn't know. Oh, my God, I thought you did, I thought you were being kind, not making me explain."

"Tell me. Tell me all of it."

She turned back and rested her forehead on her knees. "Oh, Jesus, it started in London before I even met you, before Mark met Derek. It was when Mark was still in hospital the first time. I was going mad in Plymouth, and I went up to London to see my mother for a few days. I met Derek in Harrods Food Halls, of all places, buying smoked salmon. We had lunch; we had dinner, we . . ."

"I see," I said dully.

"It was just something I needed at that moment in time. Mark was hardly speaking; I was married to a man who seemed to be headed for a mental hospital."

Now I was beginning to see it all. "So you introduced Derek to Mark."

"It seemed ideal . . . it *was* ideal. Derek wanted a boat; Mark was going insane because nobody would sponsor the boat he wanted to build. I told Derek what Mark wanted to do, and it suited him very well. He came to

Cowes, and I got Mark to the Royal London Ball, and, well, it worked out beautifully."

"And then, whenever you got fed up in Cork, you hopped over to England and Derek."

"No, he took a place in Ireland. He came whenever I could get away, even after all the trouble in England. He could get in from France to a private landing strip. I just thought when you saw the chauffeur you knew immediately. I'm sorry to burden you with all this, now."

I felt hollow inside, but my mouth still worked. "Let me sum this up: you couldn't handle it when Mark was hurt, so you went to London and started screwing Derek Thrasher. Then, you kept screwing him to buy Mark his boat, or was it the other way around—you got Mark to take the sponsorship so you could keep screwing Derek? Jesus, my summer job was nothing more than the fruit of a little casual prostitution . . ."

"Willie . . ."

"That's what it was, wasn't it? One way or the other, you were buying something and paying for it with a little fucking. And me, I was just kept around, like a steak in the freezer, until you wanted to fuck somebody again . . ."

She slapped me, hard, then leapt from the bed, winding the sheet around her. "Willie, I don't need this from you . . ."

I pursued her across the room. "Just what the hell *do* you need from me, then?"

"A little understanding might help," she said, backing away from me. I think she was afraid I was going to hit her.

I was afraid I was going to hit her, too. I turned away and started pulling on clothes. "Oh, I think I understand," I muttered. Then, still stuffing in my shirttail, I grabbed a jacket and slammed out of the flat.

It was nearly dawn. I stalked down the narrow, cobbled street, my deck shoes slapping against the stones, echoing down the hill. I reached the waterfront and headed for the Estalagem, the ruined fort on the harbor. Having gone as far as I could go without getting wet, I sat on the wall overlooking the sea and wept, grateful for the privacy of the time of day. I had wanted to give her everything, and she had wanted nothing from me but a roll in the hay. My righteousness made my pain sharper and my weeping longer. I let myself forget that I had been trying to take my best friend's wife. I was a wronged man.

I sat there until midmorning, then went back to the flat. Annie was gone, but her bags were there, packed. I packed my own. Our plane was to leave in little more than an hour. She came back at the last possible moment, and I threw our stuff into the car without a word. The rent-a-car man drove us to the airport and took the car away. The flight to London and the change for Cork passed in hostile silence on both sides. We both tried to sleep on the plane. I couldn't.

Fifty-four

"BOTH THE BISHOP AND THE MONSIGNOR WERE VERY pleased with your work in the West Country," Pearce said. "Why haven't you been in touch? It's been almost three weeks."

"It seemed a good idea to lie low for a bit," Maeve replied. "And we weren't so happy with the Plymouth results."

"Considering who you got, I don't think you should be worried about who you missed. He's not that important, anyway."

Maeve looked at the newspaper in her hand again and ground her teeth. "I wanted to let you know it'll be a week or ten days before we'll be ready for further instructions. We've some personal business to attend to."

"Personal business? You must be joking. The monsignor wouldn't like it."

"Fuck the monsignor," she said. "I'll call you when

we're ready again." She hung up the phone and read the brief article on the sports page again.

Former Royal Marine Captain Mark Pemberton-Robinson, accompanied by his wife and one other crew in his new, 60-foot yacht, *Wave*, has won the Azores Race in just under ten days, finishing only seconds ahead of the 49-foot trimaran *Three Cheers*. Captain Pemberton-Robinson, who built the yacht for the 1972 Singlehanded Transatlantic Race, is returning singlehanded from the Azores to Ireland, where the yacht was built, thereby greatly exceeding the required 200-mile qualifying cruise for the Transatlantic. "I want to see she has a real workout," he was quoted as saying. *Wave* departed Horta, on the island of Faial, on August 3, and her skipper expects the sail to Ireland to take only eight or nine days, since the return passage should be downwind.

She drove back to the caravan park. "We're taking a little Irish holiday," she said to Denny, tossing him the paper.

He read it quickly, smiling. "So we'll get another go at him, then."

"At him and the boat, too, with what I've got in mind." She briefly explained her plan.

"Red will be all for it, I know he will, but how are we going to get weapons over? The ferryports are crawling with Special Branch types."

"We can manage with what's available locally," she said. "We'll take the Swansea-Cork ferry as foot passengers, do the job, and take it right back. Call Red and tell him to meet us the day after tomorrow. That should put us there a day or so ahead of time. And tell him to keep his mouth shut; you know how he talks."

Fifty-five

WE MISSED OUR CONNECTION IN LONDON, SPENT AN uncomfortable night at Heathrow, and got a noon plane for Cork the following day, still talking only when absolutely necessary. As we came out of customs at Cork Airport, I was surprised to see Connie. She rushed up.

"Come on," she said urgently. "My car's outside."

She hustled us to the car park. "What's going on, Connie?" I asked, puzzled.

"I'm to get you down to the Royal Cork. Finbar's waiting for you there."

I was exhausted and annoyed. "*What* is going on?"

"I heard on the grapevine that Red O'Mahoney and some friends of his are planning to intercept Mark before he sails into the harbor," she said. "I called Finbar, and he told me you were expected. I've met the last three planes. Finbar's got a boat waiting at the club. He reckons we should try to head off Mark and divert him to England."

"Swell," I said and tried to nap on the short drive to the club.

Finbar was, indeed, waiting for us with a boat—a very nice, old prewar, wooden cabin cruiser of about thirty-five feet that I knew belonged to a Cork dentist. Finbar had done a lot of work on it.

"Is Mark's ETA the same?" Finbar asked as we came aboard.

"Yes. Today or tomorrow, he thought, depending on weather," Annie replied.

"Well, Connie's put some grub aboard. I reckon our best bet is to go out a few miles and try to raise him on the VHF."

Once out of the river and into the harbor, Finbar put the throttles down, and we moved along at about fifteen knots. "Sweet, isn't she?" Finbar said proudly.

We went out about six or seven miles and began patrolling up and down a five-mile line at five knots. There wasn't much sea, and we were comfortable enough, with Connie and Annie making coffee and sandwiches. We called *Wave* repeatedly, but got no response. Darkness came, and we continued.

"Finbar," I said, about midnight, "maybe we should go in a bit closer to the harbor entrance. This far out, if he doesn't have the VHF on, he might get past us. Closer in, we'll be nearer the neck of the bottle."

Finbar nodded and turned toward Roche's Point Light, flashing in the distance. "We'll be nearer Red O'Mahoney, too, but I reckon he won't be expecting us, and anyway, we can outrun his trawler. He couldn't get more than eight knots out of her."

We resumed our patrolling closer in, calling *Wave* every ten minutes on channel 16 of the VHF. At nearly three in the morning, five minutes after I had tried calling, the radio came alive.

"Cork Harbour Radio, Cork Harbour Radio, Cork Harbour Radio, this is the yacht *Wave*—do you read me?"

I grabbed the microphone. "*Wave, Wave,* listen to me; switch to channel M, channel M." Channel M in the British Isles is reserved for marina and yacht club use. I knew a fishing boat wouldn't have the crystal in its VHF.

"Switching to channel M," Mark's voice came back.

"Mark, this is Will, do you read me?"

"Willie?" Mark came back, surprised. "Where are you?"

"I'm with Finbar on a cabin cruiser about two miles south-southwest of Roche's Point Light. Annie and Connie are with us. Where are you?"

"I estimate three, maybe three and a half miles south of the light. Wait a minute, I'll fire a white flare."

"No, No!" I shouted into the radio, but I was too late.

Finbar pointed across the water. "There! There he is!" He put the throttles down and turned toward the bright white light.

A couple of minutes later the flare died, and Mark came on the radio again.

"Do you see me?"

I pressed the talk button. "Listen to me, Mark. Red O'Mahoney and his crowd are out here on a trawler somewhere looking for you. We saw you, and we're coming, but Red may have seen you, too. Do you read that?"

"I read you. I'll heave to so you can come alongside."

Shortly, we saw a flashlight on *Wave*'s mainsail. "Douse the light, Mark!" I shouted into the radio. The flashlight went out. In another minute or two, we were alongside *Wave*. Mark already had fenders out to receive us. Annie tossed her gear to Mark and prepared to hop aboard the yacht, while Finbar cut his engines. As soon as he did, I heard another engine. "Down there!" I pointed off into the darkness. "I hear a boat!"

"Finbar, you keep Connie aboard and stand well off," Mark said quietly.

"But I want to help," Finbar came back.

"We'll call you on channel M if we need help, now just start your engines, turn off your nav lights, and keep well off unless I call you." Finbar did as he was told. Mark motioned Annie below, then followed and tossed up the Ithaca riot gun to me. "It's loaded," he said. "Twelve shells." He came on deck with the Ingram machine pistol, slapping a clip into it and tossing two more onto a cockpit seat. "Let's get sailing," he said.

We quickly pointed the yacht southeast and got her going, but the wind was light, and she was only making four or five knots. The other boat's engine grew steadily louder. I stood, looking over the water, trying to locate it. "Listen, Mark, let's don't start shooting, okay? That might be some perfectly ordinary fisherman, you know." On the other hand, I knew, it might *not* be a fisherman, in which case *they* might start shooting.

"I'm not out to kill anybody, Willie, but I'm going to defend if I have to. You can put down the shotgun and go below if you want."

"Well," I said, my voice not very steady, "if they start shooting, I'll shoot back." I was feeling very weak in the bowels. The other boat was very near, now, and she wasn't wearing navigation lights, or we'd have seen her sooner than we did.

"Good man," Mark said.

His statement was suddenly punctuated by a roar and a flash from about thirty yards away. Simultaneously, there was a loud crack, and a large hole appeared in the mainsail, about two feet above my head.

"Shotgun!" Mark shouted, pulling me down into the cockpit. "Pump a couple over their heads, Willie! I don't want to use the Ingram unless we have to!"

I took a deep breath, popped up from the cockpit and, blindly, but high, fired two quick shots. I ducked, then peeped over the cockpit coaming to see what was happening. The trawler was closer and broadside on to us, now, running a parallel course. I wished the wind would come up so we'd have more of a chance to outrun her. Then I saw a flame on her foredeck.

"Jesus!" shouted Mark. "Molotov cocktail!"

The flame arched high into the air toward us, and I

reflexively did the only thing I'd ever really done with a shotgun. It was easier than shooting skeet, really, it seemed to come so slowly. I led it just a bit and fired. The bottle burst like a Roman candle, showering down burning gasoline, which hissed when it hit the water, short of *Wave*. I saw another flame on the foredeck and pumped the shotgun, ready to fire again, but Mark was ahead of me. He had unscrewed the silencer on the Ingram and was firing noisily at the trawler. I was relieved to see splashes along her waterline as the big .45 caliber bullets pounded into her hull. There was shouting from aboard her, and the flame fell to the foredeck. There was a splash of fire, and the whole forward end of the trawler seemed to burst into flames.

"Look at that!" Mark shouted gleefully. "I couldn't have hit anybody, they must have just dropped the bloody cocktail!"

We watched, transfixed, as the trawler suddenly fell away from us, flaming like a giant torch in the night. Just for a moment, I thought I saw the outline of a woman against the flames, but then it was gone.

"I think she's listing a bit," Mark said as the trawler motored away from us. "The Ingram must have done some damage at the waterline."

Annie stuck her head up from below. "Is it all right up here, now? Is anybody hurt?"

"We've got a nice hole in the mainsail, but that seems to be it," Mark replied, looking around. "Well done, Willie, that was a nice shot!"

"Excuse me, I have to go below," I said, and scrambled down the companionway ladder. Five minutes later, with a better grip on myself, I came back into the cockpit as Mark was heaving to. Finbar stood just off in the cruiser, shouting.

"Bloody marvelous, Mark!" he yelled, as he came alongside. "They've got their tails between their legs, now!" The trawler was now only a speck of flame in the distance.

"Willie, we'll head for England, I think," Mark said. "Want to come along?"

"I think I'll go back with Finbar," I replied, taking deep breaths. "But thanks for a lovely evening."

"I don't think there'll be any more trouble with that lot," Mark said, looking off toward the disappearing trawler, then turning to me. "Willie, I can't thank you enough for coming out here and helping. You've saved my bacon again. She'd be on fire if it weren't for you." He stuck out his hand. "Better go quickly. The wind's coming up, now. We'll be out of here like a shot."

I grabbed his hand and held it for a minute. "Well, anyway, you're in good shape, now. The boat's wonderful, the leg's on the mend, and you're qualified for the Transatlantic."

"We'll see you in the spring, then."

I avoided answering; instead, I clambered aboard the cruiser and shoved us off. I didn't say goodbye to Annie. As Finbar pulled away from *Wave* and turned toward Cork, I saw Mark wear the boat around and start her sailing, then wave from the cockpit. Annie was nowhere in sight. I stumbled down into the cruiser's saloon, ignoring an outstretched coffee cup from Connie, and threw myself onto a settee. I was asleep before we had gone another hundred yards.

Later, Finbar dropped me at the cottage. I said only a perfunctory goodbye to Connie. I didn't want to think about women for a long time.

Finally, after dialing lots of digits and wading through two operators and a secretary, I heard his voice on the line, unchanged, dry, skeptical.

"Yessss?"

"Dean Henry? This is Will Lee. How are you, sir?"

"I'm very well, thank you. To what do I owe the honor?"

"Sir, I'd like to come back to law school this fall."

There was a short silence. "I assume you've done some thinking about this."

"Yes, sir, I have; a lot of it. I know it's what I want to do, now, and I know I can do it well."

"Well . . . registration begins on the twenty-fifth of this month, you know. I suppose you can find your way here from wherever on earth you are?"

"Yes, sir!" I said. "I'll be there with bells on!"

"A nontinkling presence will do nicely, Mr. Lee. Until registration day, then."

I hung up, vastly relieved. Still bone-tired from the exploits of the previous wee hours, I stepped among the packed boxes of Mark's and Annie's things, gathered my remaining belongings, put the recharged battery back into my car, locked the cottage, and drove away. I left the key in Lord Coolmore's mailbox, with a note saying that a removals company would pick up the Robinsons' possessions, then drove to my grandfather's. I had a glass of sherry with him, then said my goodbye and left my car with him to be sold. His groom drove me to Shannon airport to catch the Aer Lingus flight to New York, where I would change for Atlanta, there to be met by my parents. I would have some time with them before school started.

As the jet lifted over the green fields of County Limerick and turned toward the Atlantic, I thought about the callow youth who had landed here fifteen months before and what had happened to him since. In the washroom I splashed water on my face and looked into the mirror. The fellow who looked back at me was leaner, older, and quite definitely sadder than his predecessor. I wondered if he were wiser, too. More confident of himself he was, surely; more self-possessed, with a better opinion of himself and what he was made of. But wiser? It would take some time to figure that one out.

I settled back into my seat with a groan and, gratefully, closed a chapter of my life in which women betrayed me and people shot at me. I didn't know it then, but the place was well-marked; the book waited to be reopened.

Fifty-six

I TOLD MY PARENTS EVERYTHING, EXCEPT ABOUT OUR IRA problems and my personal difficulties, and then I lost myself in mindless drudgery on the home farm. I replaced fenceposts, strung wire, sowed winter pasture, and helped paint a barn. I used work the way some people use sleep; instead of sleeping on it I toiled on it. I was angry at Mark for getting me shot at, angry with Connie for holding me at bay, angry with Annie for using me as a diversion. As I labored at my tasks, the barbs of my anger grew duller. There was still pain, but it was not as sharp.

I presented myself at the University of Georgia Law School on time and, with no fences to mend nor barns to paint, I plunged into the study of the law as if I were a terminally ill man who had been told that in those lectures and books lay a cure for my ailment and, if that failed, the key to the hereafter. I began the term as a student, and by Thanksgiving, I was becoming a scholar.

Dean Henry began to nod at me when we passed in the hallways.

Mark wrote to me; the letter was postmarked St. Tropez. He and Annie had taken a job as paid skipper and cook on a ninety-foot ketch belonging to a friend of Derek Thrasher, wandering the Mediterranean. The owner was rarely aboard, and they had it mostly to themselves. *Wave* was safely laid up in a quiet little yard in Falmouth, in case friends of Red O'Mahoney still had any interest. With continuing therapeutic exercise, Mark's leg was coming along nicely; the steel brace had been replaced by an elastic bandage. They would return to England in mid-May to get the yacht launched and ready for the Transatlantic, the first week in June. He wanted me there as soon as I had graduated. I didn't write back to him.

Derek Thrasher also wrote to me, saying he had seen the completed yacht and thanking me for my work. The letter was postmarked Paris, but there was no return address.

North Georgia had a particularly beautiful autumn that year, I kept hearing, but I hardly noticed. I had a single room in the law dorm, and it might as well have been a cell. I seemed to divide all my time between that room and the law library. I had bought a used Chevrolet, but it sat in the dorm parking lot while I walked the short distance to and from school. When I was ready to leave for home for the Thanksgiving holiday, I discovered the battery was dead, had been, probably, for some time. My old classmates had graduated, and I resisted new friendships. I got a very short haircut, mostly because everybody else was wearing his fashionably long. Everybody thought I was very strange, except Dean Henry, whose ideal young man was one who had a short haircut and spent all his time in the law library.

To say that I was unhappy would have been inaccurate. I was simply numb. My anger had shrunk into something cold and hard inside me; all other emotion I seemed to be able to channel into the law. If my parents were hurt because I didn't visit home except for the major holidays, my first-term grades convinced them that I was using my time well. My father was spending a lot of time laying the groundwork for a run for the U.S. Senate in 1972. Senator Richard Russell had died in office, and Governor Jimmy Carter, whose opponent my father had supported, had appointed a man named Gambrell to fill the unexpired term. Even at Christmas, there was a constant stream of people at the farm, and we didn't have much time to talk.

My mother tried. We went riding together during my Christmas vacation.

"Will," she said as we walked the horses along a creek bank, "I'm awfully pleased about your academic record so far, but you're not yourself, somehow."

I laughed ruefully. "That isn't like me, is it? Good grades."

"You know that's not what I meant. You've always had that capacity, and I'm glad you've suddenly decided to use it. Did something happen during your time in Ireland that you haven't talked about?" We rode along silently. "A girl? Is it Connie?"

"Something like that," I said. It seemed an easy way out of explaining.

"Well," she said, "I think I'm bright enough to know that I can't be of much help with that sort of problem, but if you want to talk about it sometime, I'll do the best I can."

I smiled at her. "I know you would, Ma, but don't worry. I'll work it out for myself."

I didn't even try to work it out. When I finally began to think about it, I did so in spite of trying not to. There was a spring day, April, first green abounding on the lovely, old campus, a lot of rain interspersed with brief periods of dazzling sunshine. I was nearly overwhelmed with a strange emotion; there was a rush of Ireland—the green, the damp, the soggy odor of the earth—just for a few moments. I walked faster toward the library, and it went away.

A day or two later, I got a letter from, of all people, Jane Berkeley. It was a surprise, because all our long-distance communication had always been by telephone, and that, brief and to the point. In Paris, our communication had been verbally telegraphic and physically expansive. Her letter was brief but illuminating. Derek Thrasher's problems with the Public Prosecutor had been resolved with the discovery of a backup computer disk in Avondale's files, which confirmed the accuracy of the company's original reports. The books given to the prosecutor by the accountant, Pearce, had thus been exposed as forgeries, and the man was being sought by the police in that connection. There was some sort of IRA involvement, too, through a brother, and they would want to ask him about the Berkeley Square bombing when they found him.

Derek, although cleared, had remained reclusive, growing even more so, if that were possible. She rarely heard from him, except through Nicky.

Then came her little bombshell. "I'm being married in June," she wrote. "He's French, from a wine and banking family; works in well with my plans and those of my family. You didn't meet him, but he was at the New Year's party, and at Brasserie Lipp the next day. We'd had a spat at that time. You were unwittingly helpful then and at Easter, too. Drove him mad. Can't thank you enough. Don't worry, I'm sure we'll still see each other from time to time. Ring me for lunch when you're in Paris. I won't be able to resist."

That stung. I had merely been a pawn in her game. And even though she wasn't yet married, she was already suggesting that we could go on fucking whenever I was in town.

The pin of that prick to my ego lodged someplace inside me and brought on the old anger, hot and swelling. For someone who had not felt anything for months, it was nearly unbearable. I missed two days of classes, while I tried to figure out what was going on inside me.

My anger, I discovered, was rooted in guilt, and that was particularly hard to deal with. My guilt about Connie was straightforward; I had used her badly, and she knew it. With Annie, it was harder to fathom, because I still believed *she* had wronged *me*. Why should *I* feel guilty? And yet I did.

I resumed classes but continued to pick at my emotional scabs. A week later, a letter arrived, postmarked Monte Carlo.

My dear Willie,

We are coming to the end of our glorious Mediterranean season and are turning our eyes toward England again, I, somewhat reluctantly. Mark has enjoyed himself down here, of course, but his heart is with *Wave,* and he won't be content until he has her in the water and sailing again.

This paid holiday of ours has been the answer to a prayer. We've had the time and the peace to get to know each other again, and we both seem to like what we've found.

I hope that enough time has passed that you feel we can be friends again. I hope you will come to Plymouth for the start of the race. Mark will have all the help he needs, of course, from all his service chums, but in a very important way *Wave* is as much yours as his, and for Mark, there will be a large gap in his effort if you are not here to share it. For myself, I miss you very much, and I want us all to be together again. I hope Connie will come, too. I've written to ask her. We're planning a cruise of Cape Cod and Maine after the race. I hope you can both join us. It would be like old times.

Please let us hear from you. Write care of the Royal Western.

With love,
Annie

I read the letter again and again, plumbing its meaning. I still wasn't sure why I felt guilty about Annie, but I was sure she had forgiven me.

With Connie, it seemed to me that I should begin from the beginning, to forget what was past and try to build again from scratch. I wrote her a chatty letter about school and springtime in Georgia, taking care to make no emotional statements or references. Three weeks later, I got an equally chatty letter in return, enclosing a snapshot of my bit of land and the ruined cottage near Kinsale. She thought I would like to remember the way it was in the spring, she said. The letter closed with "Love."

It was the middle of May, now, and I quickly wrote her again, more warmly. "You have a stake in *Wave*, just as I do," I said. "Without your help I would never have finished the work on her. I wouldn't want to watch her sail from Plymouth without you there to see it, too. Please come."

It took a week for a letter to reach Ireland, and a week for a reply. For the last week before graduation I was at the mailbox the minute class was over. The race was to start on Saturday, June 10. Graduation was on Monday, the fifth. I got a plane for New York the next morning and from there, a plane to London on Tuesday night.

There had been no reply from Connie.

Fifty-seven

MAEVE SAT IN THE JUNE SUNSHINE IN THE GARDEN OF A country pub west of London, reading the London *Evening Standard*:

DUBLIN POLICE IN MAJOR COUP AGAINST PROVOS

Dublin police last night shot and killed six members of a Provisional IRA splinter group styling itself the "Irish Freedom Brigade," in a raid on a South Dublin house. The leader of the group, Michael Pearce, was thought to have taken his own life as police closed in.

The piece ran on, with a fairly accurate summary of the group's activities over the past two years, not excluding her and Denny's exploits. She had become quite used to news stories about the "Red Nun." The English tab-

loids had had a field day when she had finally been identified. They had run photographs of her in habit and had
even dug up her school pictures. Fortunately, there had
been no recent likenesses available. They had identified
Denny, too, but had not been able to come up with a
photograph. The police artists' impressions had not been
accurate enough to hurt. She handed the newspaper back
to Denny. "Just as well," she said. "We're lucky to have
them off our backs. Now we can join up with our com-
rades in Europe."

Denny shook his head. "I don't know, Maeve. We're
low on just about everything in the way of matériel, except
what's in the caravan in Plymouth. Money, too. We're
going to have to do another bank, soon, and they're
getting tougher." He looked terrible, she thought. He
almost certainly had an ulcer; he had been living on
stomach remedies for weeks. "I wouldn't want to try
getting through a ferryport or an airport just at the moment, either," he said. Their last job had been only two
days before, in Liverpool, and the country was very hot,
now. "Besides, we've still got Robinson to do." Denny
was still smarting from the fiasco with Red O'Mahoney.
They had made port in Oysterhaven, but the boat had
sunk at dockside. Red had been badly burned.

"I know," she said. "We'll do that, no matter what.
Maybe the curate will have something for us. Maybe that's
why he wanted this meeting." They had not often seen
the curate since their meeting at the London pub; most
of their dealings had been over the telephone network.

At that moment he entered the garden from the pub. He walked straight over and sat down heavily at their table. Maeve thought he looked a bit drunk; his entrance had certainly been incautious.

"So?" she said.

"You've read the papers?" he said.

"Of course."

"We're done, then. There's no one even to contact."

Maeve tensed. "You've no other network on this side?"

He shook his head. "None. Michael was my only contact."

It was the only time he'd ever referred to Michael Pearce as anything but the monsignor. "Michael Pearce was your brother, wasn't he?" He had hinted as much when he assigned the curate as their contact.

Pearce nodded. "Yes. He was a brave man, Michael. Didn't let the bastards take him alive."

"So what resources do you have, now?" she asked quietly.

He looked at her, surprised. "None. Oh, I've a bit of money in a London savings bank, but I can't touch it, now, not with them after me."

"Why would they be after you?" Maeve asked, starting to worry.

"Oh, nothing about the cause, at least I don't think so. Another thing entirely. Some books I cooked."

Maeve exchanged glances with Denny, and they both

began looking about the pub as casually as possible. "I think we'd better leave here. How did you come?"

"Train to the station and a taxi."

They got up and moved without hurrying to the car. They put Patrick Pearce into the front seat next to Maeve, who drove. She turned down the first lane they came to and drove toward a grove of trees.

"Where are we going?" Pearce asked, suddenly taking note of his surroundings.

"We've got some gear buried down in the trees, there," Maeve said smoothly. She met Denny's eyes in the rearview mirror. He nodded. They couldn't have anything further to do with this fool, who could easily have brought the police down on them with this stupid meeting.

She parked in the trees. "This way," she said, striking out along a footpath. Pearce nodded, but he looked very tense, she thought. Oh, well, in a few minutes he would be relaxed. Pearce followed her, with Denny bringing up the rear. A dozen yards along the path she heard a grunt, followed quickly by a gargling sound. She turned, relieved that it was over. Then she threw herself sideways into some brush, clawing at her handbag. Denny was standing in the path, both hands to his throat, trying to stem a pulsing stream of blood. Pearce was coming toward her with a knife.

She had her hand in the pocketbook, but the gun was catching on the lining. She shot him twice in the face, right through the bag. He fell down beside her in the brush, rolled halfway over, and died. She leapt to her feet and ran for Denny. He was on his knees, now, in a muddy puddle of his own blood. He was trying to say something, but the wind was not getting past the bubbling slash in his throat. He was mouthing something. She knew what it was. His lips were repeatedly forming one word: "Robinson."

"Yes, yes," she said, then dodged out of his way as he fell forward on his face. She couldn't be covered with his blood. She stepped carefully around the puddle on the way to the car.

In the village she quickly found the station and a phone box. She dialed a Cork number; it answered and the beeps started; she fed the machine all the ten-pence pieces she had, and the beeping stopped.

"Yes?"

"This is Sister Concepta."

"You don't sound well."

"The priest and the curate have just given each other the last rites."

There was a silence. "Don't give me any details, now," he said. "You know about the Dublin parish."

"Yes."

"There won't be any more postings from there, nor from here. I'm shutting down the diocese."

"I understand."

"What are your plans?"

"I expect I'll apply to an order on the continent when I'm finished here."

"Finished?"

"You'll recall that one major sinner remains that we have not ministered to."

He was silent again. "I remember," he said, finally. "You know where he is, of course."

"It was all over Sunday's *Observer*."

"I think we'd better perform this particular ritual together," he said.

She brightened. "I could certainly use assistance."

"Do you have the matériel?"

"Yes, the caravan and a car are stored at a garage in the city in question."

"Good. Can you be there by six tomorrow evening?"

"No problem."

"I'll get the afternoon plane. I'll meet you at the main station at six. The event doesn't begin until Saturday. That'll give us thirty-six hours to plan."

"That should be plenty."

"Until we meet, then."

"Yes." She hung up and leaned against the wall, relieved. She wouldn't be alone in this after all. She would have the support of the leader who had brought her into this. A train pulled into the station, pointing west. She ran for the ticket kiosk.

Fifty-eight

MY PLANE LANDED EARLY WEDNESDAY MORNING AT Heathrow, beginning a day the terrible clarity of which I have often wished I could simply erase from my mind. It began well, certainly. Connie was waiting when I came out of customs.

"Hi," she said breezily and allowed herself to be kissed on the cheek and briefly hugged. It was clear I still had a great deal of lost ground to make up.

"How did you know which plane?" I asked.

"I've been in Plymouth helping Annie provision *Wave*. They got your wire at the yacht club."

"Why didn't you let me know you were coming to Plymouth?"

"I wrote. Must have missed you at the other end."

We got my luggage into the car and were quickly on the M4, headed West.

"How are Mark and Annie?"

"Never better, I'd say. Mark limps, but you'd hardly notice."

"How's everything going with the boat? I wish I could have been here sooner to help, but graduation was . . . day before yesterday, I guess it was. I couldn't cheat the folks out of that."

"Oh, it's gone very smoothly. They're putting the boat next to the inner quay at Spedding's today, to dry her out and clean her bottom. So—how was law school?"

"First in my class."

"My word!"

"Well, first my senior year, anyway. But even after averaging that with my first two years, I made the top ten percent, which is what the best law firms want."

"Got a job yet?"

"I've got an offer from Blackburn, Hedger, Acree, Abney and Susman, in Atlanta. That's the firm my father worked for briefly before World War II. He's still pretty close to them."

"That's a mouthful. Family connections got you that, huh?"

"Of course not. You're chauffeuring a highly sought-after young attorney. I've had a couple of other nice offers, too, one of them in New York, but I'm more inclined to stay in Atlanta. Dad's running for the Senate this fall, and he wants me to help. So what's new with you?"

"I'm assistant principal of the school now."

"Moving into management?"

"You might say that."

"I read about Maeve and Denny in *Time*."

She nodded. "Everybody in Cork is stunned by the whole business. We've had no end of reporters coming around the school, asking what she was like as a girl. The mother superior finally posted a notice at the door, barring them. Maeve and Denny have made us famous," she said wryly.

"They haven't been caught yet, then?"

"No; they've had a couple of close shaves, I think, but they've been either very clever or very lucky; probably both."

"Would you have ever thought it could come to this with Maeve?"

"To tell you the truth, I'm not that surprised. She was always a zealot about whatever she did, and I was relieved when she took the veil. I thought she'd pour everything into that."

"Were there any repercussions after our little sea battle?"

"Not really. Red O'Mahoney spent a couple of weeks in the hospital with burns, and he lost the boat, of course. He tried to get Finbar to rebuild it after it was raised, but he was told to get stuffed."

"Couldn't happen to a nicer fellow," I said. "What time do you reckon we'll be in Plymouth?"

"Oh, late in the afternoon, what with the new motorway mostly finished."

Plymouth couldn't come quickly enough for me. I wanted to see Annie, to put things right with us again.

I had been rehearsing an apology all the way across the Atlantic. Connie and I chatted on through the morning, then stopped for lunch at a motorway café. After that, I let the jet lag take me, while Connie drove on.

I woke on the outskirts of Plymouth, groggy, and with a sudden feeling of unease. Something I had dreamed? I looked about me. The skies were still sunny, I was with a girl I had missed terribly and on the way to see Mark, Annie, and the boat; still I was uncomfortable. I have never before nor since been prescient, but as we drove into Plymouth I was weighed down by a pervasive sense that something was wrong. By the time we reached the Cremyl ferry my unease had turned into an unreasoning fear. As we parked the car I saw a blackened brick wall that must have been where Andrew and Roz Fortescue had been consumed in the ball of fire when their car exploded, and that didn't help.

As the ferry reached the center of the Tamar River, the inner quay at Speddings opened up, and I was relieved to see *Wave* leaning against the quay wall, high and dry, the tip of her keel just being lapped by the water. I could see Annie, in the yellow sweater and jeans I remembered from the first time I had laid eyes on her at Cowes, standing under the boat with a bucket in one hand and a brush in the other. Mark was on a ladder at the stern, apparently scrubbing the propeller.

Still, by the time the ferry had docked, my anxiety had almost reached the stage of panic. Connie and I were first ashore, hurrying across the hundred and fifty yards to Speddings. As we approached the quay, I dropped my gear and ran over to the edge of the wall. What happened then always comes back to me in slow motion. *Wave*'s decks were some six feet below. An electrical cable ran from a quayside power point down to the boat, ending in an electric sander lying on deck near the opposite rail. I couldn't see either Annie or Mark from where I stood. In too much of a hurry to use the ladder at the stern, I jumped for the deck, and as I did so, the heel of one of my street shoes caught momentarily on the rough stone surface. I landed on my feet, but off balance, and reeled across the boat, coming to rest against the lifelines opposite, knocking the sander over the edge of the deck.

I could see Annie standing below, her jeans rolled up, in water to her knees. She looked up and saw me, and her face opened in her broadest, most welcoming style.

"Willie!" she cried. She saw the falling power sander at the same time and stepped neatly out of its path as it struck the water.

Then I heard Mark scream. "No!" he cried out at the top of his lungs. But he was too late. Reflexively, Annie stooped and grabbed the sander. There was a blue flash and a loud crackling noise; Annie's back arched and an arm was flung out as she fell back into the water, still holding onto the sander with her other hand. The crackling noise continued.

Mark was splashing toward her at a dead run from the yacht's stern, forty feet away. "The cord!" he screamed up at me. "The cord!"

I grabbed the cable at my feet and yanked; the plug came out of the power point, and the crackling noise stopped. The whole thing couldn't have lasted more than two seconds. I looked back over the rail; Mark had picked up Annie and was struggling through the knee-deep water toward the slip, just around the bows of the boat. I ran for the ladder, hoisted myself up onto the quay, and ran to meet him. Connie, who had seen him from the quay, was well ahead of me. By the time I got to them Mark had laid Annie out on the grass next to the slip and was listening at her chest. Then he sat back, struck her, hard, in the chest with his fist, then began pushing on her breastbone with both hands, one on top of the other. He did that for a moment, then stopped, tilted her chin back, held her nose and blew into her mouth.

"I'll do that—you do the massage," Connie volunteered, catching his rhythm.

"You!" Mark shouted to one of the yard workers who had just run up. "Stop the ferry. We've got to get her to the other side! You!" he said to another. "Get me something rigid to use for a stretcher! Willie! Call the Royal Naval hospital, and tell them to get an ambulance and a respirator to the ferryport on the Plymouth side, now!"

I ran for the phone. It took an eternity to find the number, four rings for it to answer, and only seconds for me to relay what had happened and give the instructions. When I got back to the slip, Annie was being shifted onto an old door somebody had found. Three or four of us carried it to the ferry while Mark and Connie continued to work on Annie. The ferry ride seemed to take an hour, and the ten-minute wait while the ambulance screamed toward us through Plymouth's rush-hour traffic seemed longer still. Two paramedics piled out, one carrying what looked like a large black briefcase.

"We'll take over, now, sir," one of them said to Mark, brushing Connie aside and placing a rubber cup attached to a hose from the case over Annie's nose and mouth. Mark refused to move, simply kept up his massage, as Annie was transferred from the door to a stretcher and put inside the ambulance. As the doors closed, I could still see him working on her, while one of the paramedics operated the respirator and the other closely watched Mark's work.

"Keys!" I said to Connie. She gave them to me; we piled into the car and quickly fell in behind the ambulance, keeping as close to it as possible during the wild drive. At the hospital, Annie was hustled into the emergency room, and a doctor pried Mark away from her.

"Severe electrical shock," Mark said to him. "We started CPR no more than thirty seconds after." Then he stepped back and let the doctor do his work. A nurse with a clipboard hustled Connie and me out into the corridor and began taking information: name, age, nature of injury. . . . She finished and went back into the emergency room.

"So clumsy," I said, half to myself. Then I remembered that sander; I had used it after we hid the boat at

East Ferry. The power cord had been frayed; it had been on my list to repair.

"She's going to be all right," Connie said quietly. "I know she will. We all did everything that could be done, and now she's in a hospital. She'll be all right."

I think she was trying to convince herself as much as me, but I believed her. Annie might be in the hospital for a day or two, but she'd be all right.

Mark came out of the emergency room and leaned against the opposite wall, facing us. "She's dead," he said softly. "No heartbeat, no brain activity, nothing. She's gone."

Fifty-nine

WE SAT IN *WAVE*'S SALOON, OUR HALF-EATEN DINNER before us. We were on a mooring at Spedding's, now, to get away from the press and the curious who had descended on Cremyl after word about Annie had got around. I had been exhausted when I had arrived in Plymouth, and now I was barely able to remain conscious.

"Willie," Mark said, "there's something I want to say to you, and then I don't ever want the subject brought up again."

I looked at him dumbly. Mark seemed in much better shape than either Connie or me. Within an hour after Annie had been pronounced dead, he had called Annie's mother, called an undertaker, rung the vicar at the village church near his farm in Cornwall and arranged a service, called Royal Marine headquarters to ask for pallbearers from among his and Annie's friends, and called the Royal Western to post notice of the funeral and to withdraw from the race. He would receive visitors on the boat after the funeral. "What happened to Annie was an accident," he said. "You are not to blame. You took reasonable care when you jumped onto the boat. I am the one who left the sander there on deck. If I had not left it there, this would not have happened."

"I knew about the frayed power cord on the sander. I should have replaced it at the time."

"You did a fine job in Cork under difficult circumstances. You could not have been expected to think of absolutely everything. I have some very strong feelings about fate. I think that some things are meant to happen. I don't think Annie's death is without meaning. I don't know what the meaning is, but I believe it has meaning. But remember this, you are not to blame. Apart from Annie you have been my closest friend. We will remain friends, and close ones, I hope. Now, let's say no more about this. Let's get some sleep, and tomorrow we'll do the things that must be done. In the morning I'd like to talk with you about something else, when we're all a bit less tired."

Connie finished clearing the table, and we each took a cabin and went to bed.

We ate better at breakfast. Mark's brisk attitude, as he ran through a list of things to be done on the boat, seemed to buoy us a bit. If he could carry on, so could we.

"That's it," he said, making a check against the last of the items on his list. "Those things and she'll be ready."

"Ready for what?" I asked. He had already taken himself out of the race, quite understandably. He couldn't just lose his wife on a Wednesday, bury her on Friday, and sail off into the sunset on Saturday. Besides, there'd have to be an inquest.

"I want you to do the race," he said.

For a moment I didn't get his meaning. Then I did. "What?"

"You know this boat every bit as well as I do. You helped build her. You've sailed on her in all sorts of conditions. I want her to do the race she was built for; I can't do it myself, and you're the only person who can in the circumstances."

"But I haven't qualified with the committee," I protested. "Entries closed months ago; they'll never accept me at this late date."

Mark shook his head. "When you sailed the boat from Cork to Plymouth singlehanded, you completed the two-hundred-mile qualifying cruise. When I made my final application to the committee after the Azores passage, I listed you as alternate skipper, just in case. You were accepted at that time. I didn't tell you, because I didn't think it would ever come up."

I could only stare at him.

"You do see this is the only way, don't you?"

I didn't feel strong enough to resist him. When I tried to picture myself in the race, it seemed a better alternative than moping around onshore. "All right," I said. "I'll do it if you're absolutely sure that's what you want."

Even as I said it, I was overwhelmed with the idea. I had never even contemplated doing such a thing.

"Good." He grinned. "I told the committee yesterday that you would."

I gripped the cold, brass handle of Annie's coffin and, with five Royal Marines, lifted it and walked down the stone aisle of the tiny village church. For a day and a half I had kept going, ticking off the items on Mark's list of things to do. Now the list was complete, I was where I least wanted to be, and everything was catching up with me.

Mark had been extraordinary, especially at the funeral. He had greeted each of the two hundred or so people who came—race competitors, marines, and other friends—putting them at their ease, thanking them for their sympathy and offering his. From the moment of Annie's death, Mark had seemed to accept that she was gone—unlike everyone else, especially Connie and me, who still couldn't believe it. I had been barely coherent and, at this moment, could hardly get one foot before another. We marched in step out of the church and down a path to the open grave, where we rested the coffin on planks across the hole in the ground and waited for the final words. As the vicar intoned them, we removed the planks and lowered the coffin with ropes. The obligatory handful of earth was thrown into the grave, then everyone began moving away. Annie's mother was led away, sobbing, by her brother, to be driven back to London. She had been inconsolable.

Mark and I were left at the graveside, with her for one last moment. Our thoughts must have been similar. In this damp earth we were leaving one of those people who had had that rare talent of seeming the best possible person—a lovely young woman, not yet thirty, who in the brief time we had shared with her had imprinted herself indelibly upon our lives. Before I could burst into tears, I glanced up and saw Connie waiting down by the car and realized that there, with her, was where I belonged at this moment, not here. Mark belonged here. I left him and joined Connie.

At the marina, the crowd took up an entire pontoon. Mark was the perfect host, showing friends about the boat, seeing that everybody had a drink, putting everyone at ease, talking about Annie, avoiding no one's eyes. It was like a party at which Annie had not yet arrived. I was glad that everyone, including even me, with Mark's example, seemed to be bearing his grief well.

I was standing near the edge of the crowd, away from the boat, talking with Connie, when I looked up and saw a tall, bearded, rather seedy man in a rumpled, corduroy suit standing on the dock where it met the floating pontoon. He beckoned to me. I excused myself and walked slowly toward him. I was in no mood for a newspaper reporter or curiosity seeker.

As I approached, he extended his hand and said, "Hello, Will."

I had already taken his hand before I finally recognized him. "Hello, Derek," I said.

"I'm glad to see you; you're looking well."

"It's good to see you, Derek, I . . ." I was at a loss for words.

"Forgive my appearance. I was . . . some distance from here when the news about Annie finally reached me. I . . ." He seemed to be having as much difficulty talking to me as I to him. "Do you think you could ask Mark to come and speak with me for a moment? I'd rather not go down to the boat, if you don't mind."

"Of course," I replied and went to look for Mark. When we came back, Derek offered a few awkward words of sympathy, then took an envelope from his coat.

"I'd like you to have this—please don't open it just at the moment. It's just . . . something I . . ." He foundered in embarrassment. "Ah, Mark, I really must be going. I didn't want to intrude on such an occasion."

"Nonsense, Derek," Mark replied. "You're very welcome here. Come and have a drink."

"I . . . hope you'll forgive me if I don't. Mark, ah, do you have a pound note about you?"

Surprised, Mark dug into a pocket and came up with the money.

Derek shook hands with us. "Goodbye to both of you, then. I suppose we shan't see each other again . . . for a time. Thank you both." Then he was gone, striding up the dock and up the stairs to the car park, where we could see a man waiting with the Mercedes door open. The car drove away in a cloud of dust.

"That was very odd," Mark said, opening the envelope Derek had given him. Then his eyes widened. I looked over his shoulder at the paper in his hand.

"I, Derek Thrasher," it read, "do hereby sell to Mark Pemberton-Robinson for one pound sterling and other valuable considerations . . ."

"Jesus," Mark said. "He's given me *Wave*."

I was seized with a sudden conviction, one that I was later to look upon with regret. "Mark," I said, "you have to do this race. It's your boat, now, and . . . well, I think Annie would be extremely annoyed if you dropped out because of something to do with her. She was part of this project, too, you know, and she wouldn't like to be the cause of aborting it." She had been more a part of it than even Mark suspected, I thought, remembering how she had brought Derek Thrasher into it. Mark would never know about that.

Mark looked at the letter and the registration papers in his hand. "You're right," he said. He looked back at me. "Did you meet my solicitor, John Aslett?" He pointed at a large man with ginger hair in a blue suit, standing among the crowd down on the pontoon. "Could you ask him to come up here, please? We're going to have to leave for a bit. Could you let the others know?"

I went and sent the solicitor to Mark, then watched them as they hurried toward the marina office.

Sixty

MARK WAS GONE FOR THE BETTER PART OF TWO HOURS.
"You'd better hurry," I said to him when he
came back. "The skipper's briefing is at five o'clock at the
yacht club. Where have you been, anyway?"

"Pulling some strings, at least John Aslett has. The
inquest is tomorrow morning at eight o'clock."

"That's fast."

"John's a good man."

We squeezed into the back of the Royal Western's
dining room and listened carefully for an hour as the
skippers of the forty competing yachts heard a long-
range weather forecast, a discussion of the location of the
Gulf Stream, which was an important factor in the race,
and instructions on finishing and docking at Newport,
Rhode Island, the race's termination point. Afterward,
we met Connie in the bar for a drink. She thrust a newspaper at us.

"Denny O'Donnell's turned up dead," she said. "He actually had his own Irish driving license in his pocket."

"He was always a bit thick," Mark said. "What about the girl, Maeve?"

"Still on the loose, according to this," I said, reading quickly. "Denny was found with some other bloke."

"Poor Maeve," Connie said sadly. "Now she's out there alone someplace. I wonder what'll become of her?"

"Probably the same thing that became of Denny," Mark replied.

The solicitor, John Aslett, appeared in the bar. "All done," he said. "I didn't know you were coming here so I left it on the boat."

"New will," Mark said to me. "Seemed a good idea. John, why don't you have a drink and then come back to the boat and witness it."

"Jolly good," Aslett replied. "A large, pink gin, please."

"I've got some laundry to do back at the marina," I said, getting up. "Why don't I go ahead now? You and Connie finish your drinks and come in John's car."

"Fine," Mark said. "We'll only be a few minutes."

I parked the car in the marina car park and started toward the pontoons. It had clouded over and was beginning to drizzle. As I started down the ramp two people simultaneously started up it from the pontoon; I recognized them both, but was surprised to see them together.

"Hello, Peter-Patrick," I said. "What a nice surprise."

"Oh, hello, Mark," Lord Coolmore said, looking surprised, himself. "Uh, this is my, uh, niece, Mary."

I stuck out my hand. "We've met, at least, sort of. Last year over at Cremyl, at the boatyard."

"Yes, I remember," she said. She seemed nervous. So did Lord Coolmore, for that matter.

"I was just down to the boat to pay a call on Mark," he said. "I read about Annie in the papers. Terrible business, that."

"Yes, well, Mark'll be along in a few minutes. Would you like to come back to the boat for a drink?"

"I'd love to, old fellow, but we have to catch a train for London in just a few minutes. Give Mark my best, will you, and tell him I'm awfully sorry."

"Of course," I said. "He'll be sorry to have missed you." I turned to the girl, who was just putting up the hood on her navy blue parka against the increasing rain. "Nice to have met—" I stopped in mid-sentence. She was drawing the string of her hood tightly under her chin and tying it. I stared at her. The shoulder-length auburn hair that had wreathed her head had disappeared under the hood, and now all I saw was a face, a face with no makeup, surrounded by dark cloth. "Oh, shit," I said involuntarily.

I felt something hard in my ribs. "All right, now, my lad," Coolmore said. "That's the barrel of a pistol. Just come along quietly, now."

I looked quickly about me. The car park was deserted. I could see the night watchman in the marina tower above me.

"No, no," Coolmore said. "You'll just get him hurt. Just move along a step ahead of me, there."

He pointed me toward the main gate. We walked quickly along, not speaking, through the gate, turning left, toward the water. There was a small boatyard down there, but it would be closed by now. Jesus, I thought, they're going to take me down there and shoot me. I thought of running, then thought better of it. Maeve would surely be armed, as well. "Look, Peter-Patrick, what's this all about?" Talking seemed better than nothing, somehow.

"All in good time, my boy," he said in his upper-class drawl. "All in good time."

They marched me a couple of hundred yards down the road, to where it curved to the right. The little boatyard came into view. No lights. Deserted. A car and trailer were parked in front of the main shed. Coolmore opened the trailer door and motioned me in. The two of them followed, Maeve switching on a light.

"Now what?" Maeve asked, pulling her parka hood back.

"Now," Coolmore drawled, flopping in a chair next to the door and motioning me to a sofa, opposite, "we put an end to all this."

"Is that a good idea?" she asked. "You yourself have told me how awkward that would be, considering who his father is. Anyway, Robinson is one thing, he's got that coming for Donal, but this dumb kid may be the only innocent in this whole thing."

"Donal?" I asked, astonished. "You think Mark Robinson killed Donal O'Donnell?"

"Too bloody right, I do," she snapped back at me. "And he'll pay for it."

"But that's crazy! Mark and Annie weren't even in Cork when Donal was killed. I know, I found the body!"

She looked at me a long time without speaking.

"I'm telling you the truth!" I nearly shouted at her. "He couldn't possibly have done it!" That wasn't necessarily true, since we didn't know exactly when Donal had been murdered, but it seemed like a good thing to say at the time. Then Coolmore saved me any further protestations.

"He's quite right, you know."

Maeve turned and looked at him. "Is he?" she asked.

Coolmore nodded. "I shot Donal O'Donnell myself. He became a terrible nuisance. When he learned that you and Denny were going to do the bank, he came to me and threatened to go to the *Gardai* unless I stopped you. He could have identified me, you see." He wagged the pistol in my direction. "So, for that matter, can he, now that he's seen me with you." Then he turned the pistol toward her. "So, for that matter, can you."

The silence was breathtaking. Maeve casually walked over to the kitchen area, turned and leaned against the stove. An egg timer was on the counter near her hand. She seemed to be waiting for him to continue. He did.

"I told you I was closing down the diocese," he said. "I've already closed down the Dublin parish, and now I've got to finish up here, don't you see?"

"*You* closed down Dublin?"

"They were getting out of hand. A phone call did it, a mention of the address. I knew Michael Pearce and that lot would never let themselves be taken alive. You were getting out of hand, too, you and Denny, not following your instructions, disappearing for weeks at a time. Patrick Pearce was to have killed you both."

"You sent him," she said. "You wanted me dead, too."

He nodded. "You and Denny could identify me. Pat Pearce couldn't."

"Shit," Maeve said and twisted the knob on the egg timer to what looked like sixty seconds. It began to tick. I looked more closely at the timer and saw a wire running from it, along the wall of the trailer kitchen, past the sink and down the edge of the counter, where it disappeared under a floorboard.

Coolmore saw it, too, and started to speak. Maeve dove across the space that separated them. He was bringing the pistol around and it went off as she collided with him. There was a roar and a slapping sound near my ear, and a hole appeared in the trailer wall next to my head.

Coolmore was a tall man, but thin and close to sixty.

Maeve was young, a big girl and strong as an ox. They wrestled about on the floor as I watched, mesmerized. "Run, you stupid bastard!" she yelled at me. Coolmore had somehow dropped the gun and was trying to get to the timer. She clawed at his back, pulling him away from it. I ran.

I didn't bother with the flimsy door handle. I hit the door, running, and it came right away from its hinges. Outside, I stumbled, fell, got up again, and sprinted across the pavement. I had just reached the bend in the road, perhaps a hundred yards from the trailer, when it blew. God, how it blew. I was knocked flat on my face, blasted with dirt, and showered with chunks of burning debris. I got up and ran a few more steps, then turned and looked back.

The trailer simply did not exist anymore. There was a fairly large chunk of the car left, but it must have been twenty-five yards from where it had been and was on fire. The main boatyard shed was a ruin of tangled timber and corrugated sheet metal, and half a dozen boats that had been sitting on cradles outside it were lying at crazy angles in the yard.

Boats. Boat. *Wave.* I started running again. As I reached the main gate of the marina, I saw John Aslett coming up the ramp, tucking an envelope into his pocket.

"Will!" he cried. "What the hell happened down there?"

"Where's Mark?" I shouted at him.

"On the boat. I just left him and Connie."

"Call the fire department and the police, John!" I yelled, brushing past him and running down the ramp. As I turned down our pontoon I nearly knocked Connie into the water. "Get out of here, Connie, run!" I shouted. "Go with John!"

I ran down the pontoon toward *Wave*. I could see that the main hatch was open. Nobody was on deck. I screeched to a halt. "Mark?" I called out.

"Yes?" he answered from below. "Willie? Come aboard."

I climbed on deck, went to the hatch, and looked below. Mark was sitting on the cabin sole, a small sailing duffel lying open between his legs; he was holding a flashlight in his teeth, pointing it at some wires and an object in his hand. He removed the flashlight with two free fingers.

"Come down here and hold this torch for me, will you, mate?"

I crept down the ladder and gingerly took the flashlight from his fingers.

"Bloody interesting, this," he said, obviously fascinated. "Rigged to a digital alarm clock, set for noon tomorrow. Right at the start of the race. About thirty pounds of plastique here." I saw several bricks of what looked like modeling clay. "There'd be a bigger bang than the starting cannon, for certain. Found it in the flare locker. I went in there for a box of ballpoint pens I'd stowed away. Had to sign my will."

"Look, Mark, don't you think I'd better call the police or the bomb squad or something?"

"Oh, the police by all means," he said. "Never mind the bomb squad. I've pulled the plug on this one." Then I saw the wirecutters on the floor and, in the light from the torch, saw that two of the half dozen wires in his hand had been snipped.

"How'd you know which two?" I asked, appalled.

"Oh, the Royal Marines teach you that sort of thing," he said, smiling. "I told you. Just like boy's fiction, it was." Then he noticed my tattered clothes and blackened face. "Jesus, mate," he said. "What happened to you?"

Sixty-one

ON SATURDAY MORNING, THE DAY OF THE RACE, ALL HELL broke loose. The institution of British journalism, having got wind from a Plymouth police officer that an unfrocked, terrorist nun and an Irish peer had died in an explosion while wrestling in a holiday caravan, whipped up a conflagration of reportage the likes of which must never before have been visited upon Plymouth. At first, the newspapers had had to depend on their bemused yachting correspondents, the only reporters on hand; and the BBC, on a West Country camera team more accustomed to filming stories on the dairy industry, but by midnight the car park at the marina hosted a maelstrom of journalistic fervor. Innocent yachtsmen, caught doing their laundry late, found themselves backed against washateria walls, bracketed by spotlights, with microphones threatening their dental work. Sleepy sailors, conscious of the problem of water pollution and trying to make it to the shoreside heads, were pursued into the stalls by men and women with tape recorders, notebooks, and cameras.

Fortunately, the Plymouth police had posted men at the pontoon ramp to keep reporters away from the boats, so we remained aboard *Wave*, unmolested, during our interrogation by Special Branch. After that, when an enterprising journalist had stripped off, swum out to the boat, and had to be repelled with a boathook, we cast off and took the boat back to Cremyl, where we spent the night on a mooring at Spedding's.

We had a brandy and let ourselves wind down.

Mark sipped his cognac and put his feet on the saloon table. "Exciting evening, wot?"

"A little too exciting," I replied.

"Do you suppose there's any more danger from these people?" Connie asked.

"Who's left?" Mark pointed out.

"They seem to have self-destructed," I said.

"All terrorists do, eventually," Mark said. "They're like some species of fish who, when they're prevented from finding another species to eat, feed on themselves."

On that comforting note, we turned in. The following morning, an enterprising John Aslett, who had spent a busy evening on the phone, brought the inquest to us. Half a dozen local officials were brought out to *Wave* in a yard boat, arranged themselves about the saloon, and asked their questions. We were done in twenty minutes. Ten minutes after that, we were under way, headed down the river toward the harbor. It seemed a good idea to put some water between us and the horde of reporters still ashore.

For more than two hours we lazily tacked back and forth across the big harbor, sipping Bloody Marys and sunning ourselves. The only jarring note was the blank space in the air where Annie should have been. I kept expecting her to pop up through the main hatch, asking if anyone wanted a refill. We talked about the happy times in Ireland—the cruise to Castletownshend, the afternoons in Cork Harbour, the oysters and Guinness at Dirty Murphy's, Drake's Pool under a full moon. We agreed to meet in Newport; the cruise of Cape Cod and Maine was still on. And after that?

"The world," Mark said. "Why not the world? I've got the boat for it, God bless Derek Thrasher. Always wanted to do a circumnavigation. Why don't you two join me?"

I looked at Connie. "I think I may finally have to go and earn a living."

"I've still got a job, you know," Connie said to him.

"Well, I'll be out there somewhere; we'll keep in touch. Come and do some of the shorter legs on your holidays."

"Great!" Connie and I said simultaneously.

By 10:30 the harbor was filling with boats, and by 11:30, the forty competitors and hundreds of spectator boats were thrashing about in the vicinity of the starting line. Connie and I got our gear packed and into the cockpit. The fifteen-minute gun went. John Aslett appeared alongside in a runabout. We tossed our duffels down to him. Connie gave Mark a long hug and got into the boat. Mark took my hand.

"Jesus, Willie," he said, and his eyes filled with tears. So did mine. We embraced. I got into John Aslett's boat.

We lay off the committee boat and watched Mark maneuver up and down the crowded starting line. With his usual keen timing he put *Wave* about with forty seconds to go and headed for the line. His start was so perfect that we wondered later if someone on the committee boat had simply decided to fire the gun when *Wave*'s bows touched the line. She was immediately in the lead. John put the throttle down and we ran alongside *Wave* for a moment.

"Win it, Mark!" I shouted over the few yards separating us. "Win it for Annie!"

"I'll do my damnedest, Willie!" he shouted back.

"Be careful reefing the main!"

"Never fear!"

"How do you feel?" I called out, not wanting to break the contact.

He grinned broadly. "Like your fellow Georgian!" he shouted. " 'Free at last! Free at last! Great God Almighty, I'm free at last!' "

Then he was gone.

Sixty-two

John Aslett took us back to the marina. "I expect you two would like to disappear for a few days," he said as we tied up his boat.

I looked at Connie; she nodded. "We certainly would," I said.

"I've a cottage at Helford. Do you know the village?"

"Yes." Mark, Annie and I had stopped there on *Toscana* on our cruise from Cowes to Cork.

He handed me a key and a hand-drawn map. "It's just down from the pub, on the point. Best pick up some groceries in Helston on your way. The police may want to talk with you further. I'll try to confine it to the phone, if I can. They haven't given your name to the press; you've been described as a 'foreign visitor.'"

We thanked him, took our gear to the car, and drove west, out of Plymouth.

*   *   *

Helford is a jewel of a village on the Helford River, one of England's great cruising grounds, which cuts into the Lizard, the last promontory in the English Channel before the Atlantic. It has a dozen houses, a tiny church, a pub, and one of the best restaurants in England. We spent a glorious week there in John Aslett's comfortable "cottage," which turned out to be quite a large house. We rented a little motorboat and explored Frenchman's Creek, setting of the Daphne du Maurier novel, and the other little tidal streams of the estuary; we had wonderful pub lunches on the terrace of the Shipwright's Arms and wonderful dinners at The Riverside; we lay in the grass on the hill above the river and watched the dinghy races of the local club; we drove around the countryside and visited the wonderful church at St. Just in Roseland; and finally, after too long a time, we made love and slept in each other's arms.

The next morning I had finally found the courage to ask her. "What happened with you and the other guy? The one I met at the Spaniard?"

She giggled. "Terry? He's my brother, the priest; I told you about him long ago. He's gone back to India."

"Your *brother*? And you let me think . . ."

She rolled over, clutching herself with laughter while I sputtered. Soon we were both laughing uncontrollably.

The police telephoned once for some further information. The press didn't know where we were. We listened to the BBC and heard a report that Mark, two days into the race, seemed to be among the leaders. I had no doubt that he would remain there. After six days of this bliss we drove back to Plymouth and gave John Aslett his house key.

"Any more news of the race?" I asked.

"I was at the club this morning. They're marking positions on a chart there as they get reports. Nothing on Mark since the second day. That's not unusual, though. He has no long-range radio, and it's a big ocean."

We said our goodbyes and drove east out of Plymouth toward London and Heathrow, where Connie would fly to Cork and I to New York and Atlanta. I had a bar examination to prepare for. At Exeter, we turned on the car radio for the noon BBC news, hoping for further word of Mark. There was word.

"Position reports on yachts in the Singlehanded Transatlantic Race have been patchy, at best, as the fleet scatters into the North Atlantic, each competitor following his own idea of the best route," the announcer said. "Just a few minutes ago, though, word came that one yacht has been sighted by the Plymouth Coast Guard station, sailing back toward Plymouth. The yacht is *Wave*, a sixty-foot custom design, sailed by former Royal Marine captain Mark Pemberton-Robinson, whose wife was killed in a tragic accident in Plymouth three days before the race. There has been no report yet of his reason for returning, and Coast Guard spotters said the yacht showed no sign of damage. We'll try to have further information on the six o'clock news."

I stopped the car. "Why?"

"They said there was no sign of damage."

"Even if there had been damage, Mark would have repaired it and sailed on." I turned the car around and headed back toward Plymouth.

We arrived at the Royal Western Yacht Club an hour later, in time to join the crowd on the terrace and watch *Wave* sail past Plymouth Breakwater into the harbor. Members of the yachting press stopped questioning me when they discovered that I had no more idea than they of what was happening.

"We've tried to raise him on the VHF," a committee member said, "but he's not replying. He must not be switched on."

We watched as the yacht came toward the club, then, before we could get a good look at Mark at the helm, turned and continued up the Tamar toward the marina.

"Come on," I said to Connie. "Let's get over there."

We drove to the marina as quickly as possible, followed by carloads of committee members and journalists, but traffic was heavy. By the time we arrived at the pontoon ramp, we could see *Wave* neatly tied up on an outer float. We ran down the ramp and out toward the yacht.

"Hello, down there!" I called out, hoisting myself over the lifelines and into the cockpit, with Connie right behind me.

"Hello!" a voice called back. And then a man appeared in the hatch. I didn't know him. "Hello," he said. "My name is Martindale. Are you a friend of Mark Pemberton-Robinson?"

"Yes," I said.

He looked at me sadly. "I'm sorry," he said.

I sat at the saloon table with Martindale, surrounded by committee members, looking at *Wave*'s logbook and trying to grasp what had happened. Mark's last entry said, "Wind getting up, time to reef the main. Must be careful for Willie."

"I'm sorry you had to find out this way," Martindale said. "Our high-frequency radio was down on the ship, and there was simply no other way to get in touch. Then, when I was closer to Plymouth, it seemed a better idea to break the news in person rather than using the VHF."

Connie got up and began to rummage through the galley lockers. Seeming not to find what she wanted, she turned to me. "Give me the car keys," she said.

I gave them to her and turned back to Martindale. "Did you conduct a search?"

He shook his head. "The last log entry was about thirty hours before we found the boat. She was under windvane self-steering and could have changed course radically during that time. We wouldn't have known where to begin."

The chairman of the race committee asked Martindale to repeat everything, so that they could have it absolutely straight for the press. After half an hour a statement was given to the reporters, and they ran for telephones. Then

Connie appeared with John Aslett, both of them laden with sacks of groceries.

"What on earth are you doing?" I asked, wearily.

"Tell him," Connie said to John.

The solicitor set down the bags and reached into his pocket. "Read this when you have time; it's a copy of Mark's will. He's bequeathed *Wave* to you."

I stared at him, speechless.

"I knew about it," Connie said. "John and I witnessed the will."

"He's instructed that *Toscana* and the farm be sold and the proceeds divided between the Royal Lifeboat Association and the Royal Naval Sail Training Association. But *Wave* is yours, free and clear. I'm Mark's executor; I'm dispersing this part of his estate now."

"John," I said, "when you and Mark were preparing the will, did he seem . . . do you think . . ."

"No," the solicitor said. "Annie had been his principal beneficiary, and with her gone, he had to do another will, that's all. I've known Mark a long time, and I don't think he's the sort to do away with himself."

"Neither do I," I said. "It seems clear to me that he lost his balance while reefing and went overboard. With the boat on self-steering, she'd have sailed right away from him. Perhaps the leg wasn't as good as he wanted us to believe."

Connie began unpacking and stowing groceries. "John," she said, "will you get a hose and top up the boat's water tanks, please?"

Then my mind caught up with Connie's. I owned this boat. I had qualified to sail in this race. I turned to the committee chairman, who had stood next to me, listening to this exchange. "Sir, can I still be an official entry in this race as Mark's alternate?"

He glanced around at the other committee members, getting nods. "I don't see why not," he said. "You're a bit over six days behind the others, but you've a fast boat."

I looked around the boat. Connie had finished her reprovisioning. I could hear water running into the tanks. "Well, then, if you gentlemen will excuse me."

They clambered ashore. I took the moment to put my arms around Connie Lydon. "Will you meet me in Newport?"

She wouldn't look at me. "I don't know, Will, I have a lot of thinking to do."

"What's to think about?" I asked. "We've put it back together, haven't we?"

"Yes," she said, "I suppose we have. Now I have to figure out just what 'it' is. Can you understand that?"

I wanted a more romantic departure than that, but I restrained myself. Connie didn't respond well to pushing. "Yes," I said. "I can understand that. I hope you'll be there. Cape Cod and Maine still sounds like a great cruise, doesn't it?"

She nodded and buried her head in my chest. I held on to her for a moment, then she broke free and climbed into the cockpit. "How's the water coming, John?"

"All topped up," I heard him shout as I climbed into the cockpit.

"Then stand by that bow line," she ordered. "I'll get the stern."

I started the engine. "All right," I called out, "cast her off." John tossed his line aboard and pushed the boat's bows away from the dock. Connie kept the stern line snubbed while the yacht pointed toward the Tamar. Finally, she stood, held on to the end of the line for just a moment, looking at me, then tossed the line aboard. I pointed *Wave* downstream, toward Plymouth Harbour, the English Channel, and the North Atlantic Ocean.

Sixty-three

I TOOK THE RHUMB LINE FROM WOLF ROCK TO NEWPORT, heading due west, as Mark had planned, ignoring the conventional wisdom of the shorter, great circle route, and the fond hopes of the longer, southern route, where skippers prayed for more favorable winds. I sailed fast. Every nuance of *Wave* was familiar to me, I thought, but she taught me some new things about herself. We had a total of nine days of heavy weather, but usually from the right direction, and only one day of flat calm.

There were books aboard, and a radio to listen to, but I hardly bothered with either. I had a lot to think about, and I relished having the time to do it. I learned the value of solitude. I relived many small chunks of my life, and one large one—the one that began when I met Mark and Annie, the one that would end in Newport. I wept at certain times, with certain thoughts. It was easier to do with no one there to see me; easier to laugh, too;

easier to think about the future in terms of what the past had taught me. In the future, I would make better judgments about what was important. I would let those I loved know it, before it was too late.

I would like to tell you that we won the race, *Wave* and I, but we did not. Six days was too great a head start to overcome. We did, however, with a great deal of luck and, perhaps, just a bit of skill on my part, cross the finish line at Brenton Reef Light some twenty days, twelve hours, and fifteen minutes after we began. That was exactly one hour less than the time of the winner, and a new record for the race.

We headed into Newport, surrounded by a small, noisy flotilla of other yachts and boats, toward a berth where I hoped someone waited.

The years have passed, and all this has remained fresh with me. I think of Mark often. I cannot bear to think of Annie.

A Technical Note

For those writers who might be interested, this book was written on a PolyMorphic 8813 microcomputer using a word processing program. After the finished manuscript had been manually copy edited, the spelling was corrected yet again using a program written by Frank Stearns Associates of Vancouver, Washington, then all the necessary changes were made in the computer. Using file transmission software prepared by Bob Bybee of Polyletter, the final manuscript was then transmitted over telephone lines to the Source Telecomputing Corporation, which sent it on IBM-compatible magnetic tape to ComCom, which then set the book in type directly from the tape. This procedure both saved time over the usual method of retyping the manuscript into the typesetting machine, and prevented a new generation of typographical errors.

This is, to my knowledge, the first time a novel has been

transmitted electronically from its author's computer to a typesetting computer. There were many technical snags to overcome, and I must here give my heartfelt thanks to my friend, Mark Sutherland, who so generously gave his time and expertise to solve these problems. It was worth the trouble, and I believe that in the future, books will be routinely transmitted in this manner.

Author's Note

I AM HAPPY TO HEAR FROM READERS, BUT YOU SHOULD know that if you write to me in care of my publisher, three to six months will pass before I receive your letter, and when it finally arrives it will be one among many, and I will not be able to reply.

However, if you have access to the Internet, you may visit my website at www.stuartwoods.com, where there is a button for sending me e-mail. So far, I have been able to reply to all my e-mail, and I will continue to try to do so.

If you send me an e-mail and do not receive a reply, it is probably because you are among an alarming number of people who have entered their e-mail address incorrectly in their mail software. I have many of my replies returned as undeliverable.

Remember: e-mail, reply; snail mail, no reply.

When you e-mail, please do not send attachments,

as I never open these. They can take twenty minutes to download, and they often contain viruses.

Please do not place me on your mailing lists for funny stories, prayers, political causes, charitable fund-raising, petitions, or sentimental claptrap. I get enough of that from people I already know. Generally speaking, when I get e-mail addressed to a large number of people, I immediately delete it without reading it.

Please do not send me your ideas for a book, as I have a policy of writing only what I myself invent. If you send me story ideas, I will immediately delete them without reading them. If you have a good idea for a book, write it yourself, but I will not be able to advise you on how to get it published. Buy a copy of *Writer's Market* at any bookstore; that will tell you how.

Anyone with a request concerning events or appearances may e-mail it to me or send it to: Publicity Department, Penguin Group (USA) LLC, 375 Hudson Street, New York, NY 10014.

Those ambitious folk who wish to buy film, dramatic, or television rights to my books should contact Matthew Snyder, Creative Artists Agency, 9830 Wilshire Boulevard, Beverly Hills, CA 98212-1825.

Those who wish to make offers for rights of a literary nature should contact Anne Sibbald, Janklow & Nesbit, 445 Park Avenue, New York, NY 10022. (Note: This is not an invitation for you to send her your manuscript or to solicit her to be your agent.)

If you want to know if I will be signing books in your

city, please visit my website, www.stuartwoods.com, where the tour schedule will be published a month or so in advance. If you wish me to do a book signing in your locality, ask your favorite bookseller to contact his Penguin representative or the Penguin publicity department with the request.

If you find typographical or editorial errors in my book and feel an irresistible urge to tell someone, please write to Sara Minnich at Penguin's address above. Do not e-mail your discoveries to me, as I will already have learned about them from others.

A list of my published works appears in the front of this book and on my website. All the novels are still in print in paperback and can be found at or ordered from any bookstore. If you wish to obtain hardcover copies of earlier novels or of the two nonfiction books, a good used-book store or one of the online bookstores can help you find them. Otherwise, you will have to go to a great many garage sales.

TURN THE PAGE FOR AN EXCERPT

CIA analyst Kate Rule goes head-to-head with a brilliant KGB operative who's the architect of a secret plot to invade Sweden. Rule must dodge one death trap after another, while a Russian nuclear submarine threatens the Swedish government.

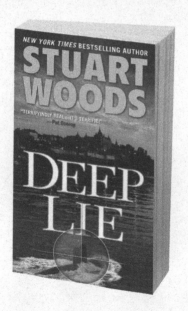

1

Oskar Oskarsson squinted into the brightly lit mist and looked for a bird. Somewhere above his boat was sunshine, but down on the water, where he was, there was fog. It was like being inside a fluorescent tube, surrounded by gases radiating light. He sighted a petrel off to starboard and from its presence estimated there were, perhaps, five hundred meters of visibility, no more. For Oskarsson, for what he was doing at this moment, conditions were perfect.

He throttled back to 1000 rpm, turned, and nodded at Ebbe. The boy smiled faintly, released the brake on the main winch, and began feeding out the trawl, a long sock of steel mesh that would drag the bottom, twenty meters down. Oskarsson watched with satisfaction as his grandson performed the work; not expertly, just yet, but competently. The boy was wearing only jeans and a T-shirt. These youngsters never felt the chill. Oskarsson marveled at the beauty of the boy's body, the well-muscled, perfectly proportioned physique. All young

Swedish men looked like that when he was a boy, he thought, the result of hard work and hard play. Now they were skinny hippies and fat accountants. Ebbe was the exception, not the rule. The boy skied in winter, hiked in summer and rowed for his school. If he was no academic, he performed physical tasks with joy and little apparent effort.

The boy's father, Oskarsson's son, ran a discotheque in Stockholm. A discotheque—imagine! Oskarsson had visited his son, once, and had been taken there. God in heaven, what a place! The noise—they called it music, these days; the flashing lights; the heat; the smells! It was no way for a grown man to make his living. Ebbe would not do such work; he had told his grandfather that. He knew he was not bright enough for university, and he did not mind. He would come to his grandfather when he was finished with school—only another year—and, together, they would fish. They would make money, too. The light trawler was easily handled by two good men—no crew to split the catch with. The boy would have a good life with his grandfather, and in a few years, when he knew all the places, he could take a partner, and Oskarsson would retire and take a share for the gift of the boat. The boat was good, and Oskarsson was glad he had spent so much of his profits on maintenance. If the boy took care of it, it would last him for many more years. Ebbe's father would be furious when the boy came to his grandfather to fish. All the money he had made at the discotheque, and his son a common fisherman! Oskarsson smiled at the thought of it.

When the trawl was fully played out, Oskarsson

waved the boy to the wheelhouse and unfolded the chart. "Here." He pointed with a thick, gnarled finger. His were a fisherman's hands, permanently swollen from years of cold-water work, fingers scarred, twisted from badly healed broken bones, the daily hazard of working bare-handed with unforgiving tools and powerful machinery. "Here we will fill the trawl to bursting."

The boy's brow furrowed, and he pointed. "But what about this, Grandfather?" he asked, running a finger along a ragged magenta line. "This says we are in a restricted area. Why restricted? Can we get into trouble?"

"It's the naval base at Karlskrona," the old man replied, pointing off into the fog. "They don't want the Russian trawlers sneaking in here and taking pictures of them." He jabbed his thumb into his own chest. "But I'm not Russian, and neither are you, eh?" He winked at the boy. "And the navy won't miss the fish."

The boy laughed. "If you say so, it's all right with me."

"The fish know it's restricted, too, you see. They think nobody will catch them here, but on foggy mornings like this, you and I can pop in early, trawl for a couple of hours, and be away before the mist burns off."

"Don't they have radar? The fog doesn't affect that, does it?"

"Sure, sure, they have radar, but I've taken down our reflector, and a wooden boat like ours doesn't show up so well, I think. At least, they've never caught me. I think if they see us on the radar when it's foggy, they don't pay much attention, because the Russian boats would only come when it's fine, so they can take their pictures. And even if they do catch me, they'll just say, 'Go and fish someplace else, old fellow.' It's not a big thing."

Oskarsson wasn't worried about getting caught. He knew these waters better than any navigator in the Swedish navy. He had been born on the island of Utlangen, not far away, and he had fished here under sail in the old days. He could dart among the islands and away from a patrol boat. He would maintain a proprietary interest in these waters, no matter how many sailor boys the Swedish navy sent here in their fast boats.

They motored along slowly for a quarter of an hour, towing the trawl and chatting companionably. Then there was a loud creaking noise and the boat suddenly stopped short, throwing them both against the bulkhead. Oskarsson quickly cut the throttle and put the engine out of gear.

"What's happening, Grandfather?" the boy asked.

The old man did not reply immediately but put the engine into gear again, and eased the throttle forward. They moved for a few seconds; then the trawl cable went bar tight and the boat stopped again. "We're hooked onto some obstruction," Oskarsson finally replied. He consulted the chart. "There's no wreck charted anywhere near here. I hope the sailor boys haven't sunk something for target practice and left it here. Get the trip cable onto the auxiliary winch, and let's see if we can free the trawl that way."

Ebbe went aft and wound the light cable onto the auxiliary power winch. Oskarsson put the engine into gear again and gave the boat some throttle. "Now," he called out, "now give it some winch. The boy threw the switch and tailed the cable as it began to wind onto the winch. It was tripping, Oskarsson thought, it's going to trip, and we'll be free. Then the trip cable went bar tight, too, and the boat stopped again. "Off! Cut the power," he shouted. The boy threw the switch, and the winch stopped. "Cleat it there; I'm going to try something else."

Oskarsson put the engine into gear and the helm hard to port. "We'll make a circle and reverse the trawl," he called to the boy. "That way it should come off whatever it's snagged on." He hoped so. To replace it would cost thousands of kroner, and even though his insurance would pay most of it, it wouldn't pay for the time lost while the steel sock was being made. You didn't buy a trawl off the shelf.

He swung the boat wide to prevent motoring over the cable, then edged to port, in toward the obstruction, to get some slack. He held his course for a moment; then the boat started to swing to starboard. This baffled Oskarsson for a moment, since he now had the helm hard to port; then he realized that, although the boat's bow had swung to starboard, it was not traveling in that direction. The boat, astonishingly, was running *sideways*. Whatever he was hooked onto was *moving*.

Oskarsson let go the helm and started aft, but the wheel spun sharply to starboard, and the resulting lurch of the boat threw him heavily to the deck. He struggled to his feet, holding a bruised shoulder and shouted to the boy. "Quick, we've got to let go the trawl!" The boat swung back in the opposite direction, then settled. They were now being towed backward.

"What is it, Grandfather?" the boy called, holding tightly to the auxiliary winch. "What's happening?"

"Let go the trip cable!" the old man shouted, struggling back toward the boat's controls. The boy quickly did as he was told, uncleating the cable and unwinding it free of the winch. Still the boat moved backward, and with increasing speed. Horrified, Oskarsson threw the engine into reverse and opened the throttle wide. He had to get some slack in the trawl cable. The boy immediately saw what he was trying to do and moved to the main winch. There were still a few meters of the main trawl cable wound around it. Oskarsson tried to steer the boat in reverse and watched as Ebbe struggled with the brake. If he could release it, they would have slack to unhook the cable, and they would be free.

There was too much load on the winch, though, and the brake would not budge. Oskarsson felt pride as the boy, without hesitating for orders, grabbed an ax from the bulkhead and swung it toward the brake handle. A single blow freed it, and the winch drum spun wildly. The boat dug in its broad stern and nearly stopped, throwing them both to the deck. Oskarsson flung himself toward the cable's cleat, knowing he only had seconds to free it before the slack was snatched up again. He got hold of it and was trying to get some purchase with a foot when the cable was snatched taut again. Oskarsson screamed as the cable crushed his hand against the winch drum. Within seconds of heart-stopping pain, the sawing effect of the cable's strands took away his fingers.

Oskarsson fell back onto the deck and looked incredulously at his hand, which now had only a thumb and was gushing blood. He forgot about what was happening to his boat and dived for his "string bag," a canvas hold-all fixed to the bulkhead that held remnants of line. He quickly came up with a piece of light nylon rope, wound it around his wrist and, one end in his teeth, pulled it tight and knotted it, all the while wondering at the fact that it didn't hurt anymore, that a strange warmth was flooding into his mangled hand.

Now he turned his attention to the boat again. Even at full throttle in reverse, it was still being towed backward, he reckoned at eight or nine knots, increasing every moment. Water was flooding over the stern, and in its wash, Ebbe was struggling to his feet, looking stunned from his fall. Oskarsson looked about him helplessly. Nothing in a long life at sea had prepared him for a situation like this, an absolutely, ridiculously implausible situation. He was up to his knees in water, now, and the boat had to be doing an incredible fifteen knots, stern first.

"What is it? What is it?" the boy was calling to him over the roar of rushing water.

He did not know. He only knew that it couldn't last much longer. Then, as if in response to his thought, there was a sound of unbearable straining of timber and metal, and the two forward bolts which held the bottom plate of the main winch to the deck came loose from their moorings.

"Ebbe!" he screamed. "Get out of the way! The winch is going!"

"What?" the boy yelled back. He was still stunned. "What?"

There was a final, explosive tearing, and the whole part of the deck to which the winch was bolted came away. The winch, still cleated to the trawl cable by which they were being towed, flew over the stern, striking the boy full in the face as it went.

Then all was suddenly, impossibly quiet. The boat came immediately to a stop and bobbed in the light sea. A trail of bubbles disappeared astern with the trawl and the winch. The engine, by now flooded, had come to a stop. Oskarsson stood in water to his thighs. He waded quickly aft, to where Ebbe's body floated, spilling red and gray matter into the water around it. Oskarsson gathered the boy in his arms and sat down on a gunwale, now only inches above the water. The boat's inbuilt buoyancy was keeping it afloat, although the decks were awash. Most of the boy's head was gone, and Oskarsson hugged the limp corpse to him, sobbing.

From somewhere out in the fog he could hear a boat's engine closing fast on him, but he didn't care. Now there would be no days with his grandson, telling him, showing him where the fish were and how to catch them. Now there was only old age and loneliness, stretching toward death. He wanted it now. He plucked at the knot at his wrist until it came loose, and the blood flowed from his finger stumps again.

The patrol boat came out of the fog, now, and slowed. A loud, metallic voice came at him from across the water. "You are in a restricted area; you must leave at once. Please follow me. You are in a restricted area . . ." The boat came alongside his swamped craft, and the voice stopped. The tanned face of a young naval lieutenant came from behind the loud-hailer and looked at him from a few yards away. The face turned white.

Oskarsson looked up at the pale boy in the ensign's uniform. "Go fuck yourself, sailor boy," he said.

STUART WOODS

"Addictive . . . Pick it up at your peril.
You can get hooked."
—*Lincoln Journal Star*